The
Ghost Children

Other novels by Eve Bunting
Face at the Edge of the World
Someone Is Hiding On Alcatraz Island

The
Ghost Children

EVE BUNTING

Clarion Books
New York

Clarion Books
a Houghton Mifflin Company imprint
52 Vanderbilt Avenue, New York, NY 10017
Copyright © 1989 by Eve Bunting

Library of Congress Cataloging-in-Publication Data
Bunting, Eve, 1928-
    The ghost children / Eve Bunting.
        p.   cm
    Summary: Matt's investigtion of vandalism of life-sized dolls belong-
ing to the strange but well-meaning aunt with whom he and his sister
live takes him to the art world of Los Angeles.
    ISBN 0-89919-843-0
    [1. Mystery and detective stories.]   I. Title.
PZ7.B91527Ghf 1989
[Fic]—dc19   88-20356
                                                              AC

P   10   9   8   7   6   5   4   3   2   1

To Margaret Mary Jensen

We've been friends for a long time.

Before...

Arabella, Bethlehem, Cleo, Derek, Edwin, Fern and George stood silently in the dark.

Once Harriette would have been with them, but Harriette was dead and poor Isadora had died before she had lived.

Swaying gently in the night air, Arabella, Bethlehem, Cleo, Derek, Edwin, Fern and George smiled their painted smiles and watched the road through their sightless eyes.

The
Ghost Children

1

AUNT GERDA wasn't there to meet us when we got off the airport bus at the hotel.

"Where is she, Matt?" Abby asked, clutching her teddy bear, trying to peer through the dark and the rain. "And you and Mrs. Valdoni told me it didn't *rain* in California."

She gave a forlorn hiccup and I put my arm around her and said quickly, "Don't cry. Aunt Gerda will come any minute. It's O.K., Abby." I could feel her sharp little shoulder bones through her wet T-shirt and I edged her under the overhang of the hotel where the airport bus had let us off.

"You go inside the lobby, Abby. I'll wait here."

Abby cringed against me. "I don't want to go any-where. I want to stay with you." I heard the edge of panic in her voice and I squeezed her shoulder again. It must be hard to be five years old, to have no mom, to be in a strange place with only your not-very-big thirteen-year-old brother to keep the scaries away. I was having a problem keeping the scaries away myself. Where WAS Aunt Gerda?

"Well, try to find your jacket and put it on, Ab," I said. "No sense getting pneumonia."

She couldn't open the knot in the strings on her duffel bag so I gave her Mom's portfolio to hold and did it for her. Her red jacket was on the very bottom. I tried to shake out the wrinkles. "Do you think Aunt Gerda's forgotten we're coming, Matt?" Her eyes were big and scared.

"No way!" I pulled the hood over her straight black hair. "She'll be here any minute."

A gray Cadillac drove in and stopped and the bell-man came pushing through the hotel doors to help the driver with his luggage.

"Don't you kids want to come out of the rain?" the bellman asked.

"We're waiting for our aunt to pick us up."

He nodded. "Well, if she doesn't get here real soon, why don't you come on inside."

"O.K. Thanks." I wiped a smear of wet off the precious portfolio. What if it wasn't waterproof any-more? What if inside it Abby's future and mine were washing away? I pulled a sweatshirt from my bag and wrapped it around the worn plastic. My Seattle Mari-ners cap tumbled out and I jammed it on my head.

"What time is it, Matt?" Abby asked.

"Ten-thirty."

"Is it ten-thirty back home, too?"

"Yes."

A taxi slid in under the hotel overhang behind the Cadillac and sat with its lights on. I could see the driver behind the beat of the windshield wipers. If Aunt Gerda didn't come in the next half-hour I'd ask him to take us to Sierra Maria Canyon, wherever that was. "My aunt owns the little market there. How much to take us?" I'd ask. There was $138 left after paying Mom's last expenses and our airline tickets from there to here. $138. All we had in the whole world, except for the paintings.

A truck was driving in, a pickup, blue and battered and spattered with mud. The driver rolled down the window. "Are you Matt O'Meara?"

"Yes."

"And I'm Abby," my little sister piped up.

"I thought you had to be." The driver was opening the door, jumping down, a tall man wearing a wide cowboy hat and jeans tucked into leather boots. "I'm Slim Ericson. Your aunt asked me to pick you up."

He was grabbing our duffels and smiling down at Abby. "Hi, sweetie! How are you?"

"Fine." Abby took a step toward him, but I held onto her arm.

Mr. Ericson tossed our bags inside the truck. "Sorry I'm late, but when it rains here the drivers go crazy. There was a pile up on Sierra Maria Boulevard that you wouldn't believe and . . ." He stopped. "Aren't you coming? Do you like standing in the rain?"

"No. Ah . . ." I held Abby's arm tightly. All sorts of

thoughts were rushing around in my head. You don't just get into a truck with a strange man even if he does say he knows your aunt. You especially don't let your little sister get into a truck with a strange man. So what if he did have our names?

The man was looking at me, puzzled, and then he pushed back his hat and smiled. I saw the gleam of a gold front tooth. "I get it. You're just being a bit cautious, making sure I am who I say I am. That's good. I've got two kids of my own and I hope they'd be that smart. Well, let's see now. I guess showing you a license wouldn't do any good. How about if I tell you what I know about you? Your Aunt Gerda lives up in the canyon. She's really your great aunt, your mother's aunt." His voice softened. "Your dad died four years ago and when your mom passed on . . ."

"Went to heaven to be with Daddy," Ab corrected, and Mr. Ericson murmured, "That's right, sweetie. When she went to heaven too, your Aunt Gerda said you were to come here."

Abby was nodding with that attentive look she gets when someone's reading to her or telling her a bedtime story.

"Aunt Gerda's the only family we've got," she said. "Mom told us."

"So I hear." Mr. Ericson touched Abby's cheek with a stubby finger. "Your mom was an artist, a painter . . ."

It was my turn to interrupt. "A *great* painter," I said and Mr. Ericson nodded. "Your Aunt Gerda has one of her pictures hanging right there in her living room,

· 4 ·

one of a house and the ocean, kind of misty."

I pushed Abby forward. "It's O.K. to get in now. Thanks for coming for us, Mr. Ericson."

"My pleasure. Gerda didn't want to leave the children."

"Children?" What was he talking about? What children?

Abby was sliding into the truck, bumping herself across the wide front seat but I paused, part in, part out.

"I don't understand," I said. "Aunt Gerda doesn't *have* children. Does she babysit, or what?"

"She hasn't told you about them?"

"No."

Rain ran off the brim of his wide hat in a steady stream.

"Well, the children aren't alive. They're . . ."

From inside the truck came a scared little voice. "You mean there are dead children at Aunt Gerda's? You mean, dead . . . like Mom?"

"No, no sweetie," Mr. Ericson said. "Nothing like that. Wrong choice of words. I mean they're not real, that's all. Gerda imagines they are . . ." I sensed him fumbling for words. "It would be better if she tells you about them herself. It's too hard to explain. Climb in, Matt. You're getting soaked."

I got in, slammed the door behind me, and in a few seconds we were whizzing through city streets, rain rushing down the gutters on either side, cars meeting us in a dazzle of headlights.

Mr. Ericson nodded down at the portfolio. "Do you

· 5 ·

have your mom's drawings in there?"

"Some of them," I said. "We left most of them with our neighbor in Seattle."

"Mrs. Valdoni," Abby said. "She's our friend. Matt says, if it's awful here maybe we can . . ."

"Sh, Ab. you aren't supposed to blab about that, remember? It would hurt Aunt Gerda, and besides. . ."

Abby nodded and put her thumb in her mouth. No use finishing that "besides." Mrs. Valdoni had only a two-bedroom apartment for Mr. Valdoni and her and their five kids.

I peered at the shining street ahead and thought about our Aunt Gerda, the one we knew about but had never met. What was this about imaginary children? People who live alone get weird sometimes. I understood that. And it had been three years since Uncle Joseph had died. But in her letters Aunt Gerda sounded fine. "Your mother was very dear to us. When your neighbor called, I knew your home from now on should be here with me."

She'd sounded nice. Mrs. Valdoni had thought so, too. And there'd been her letters when Mom was alive. Mom had read them to us, all of them filled with love and caring. Aunt Gerda had sent money sometimes, when things were hardest for us. Mom had told us stories about how wonderful she and Uncle Joseph had been when Mom was young, when she'd gone to spend vacations with them. It would be all right. Mom would never have told Mrs. Valdoni to get in touch with Aunt Gerda for us if it wasn't all right. Mom had loved us so much. I blinked and swallowed.

· 6 ·

Ab had fallen asleep with her head on my chest, just the way she'd done on the plane. I moved a little to make her more comfortable. "Take care of your baby sister, Matt," Mom had said, just before she died.

"I will, Mom. I will."

We were driving through a small village with one narrow street now, then we turned left on a dirt road, gravel sputtering from under our wheels.

"This is the start of the canyon," Mr. Ericson said. "Home to artists, rock hounds, nature lovers. And old-timers." He pointed. "That there's the Greeley house." The headlights picked up a small cabin. "Clay Greeley's about your age, but he hasn't too many friends."

I'd had friends in Seattle. John Estevez and Blinky Irvine and Knock Knock Silverstein. We called him "Knock Knock" because he was all the time asking goofy knock knock jokes. Knock Knock said he'd write if he heard a good new one. They'd all said they'd miss me.

Mr. Ericson glanced at me sideways. "Mostly the canyon kids are scared of Clay Greeley. Not my Kristin, though. My Kristin's not afraid of anything."

I didn't answer, but I was thinking, What's so great about that? What does his Kristin have to be afraid of? She has a nice dad, and probably a nice mom, and a home, and enough to eat, and no worries. She didn't have to leave her friends and come to a strange, new place. I wouldn't be afraid of anything either if I were Kristin.

Three figures were walking on the road in front of us

and Mr. Ericson slowed. Boys, I thought, all of them wearing slick rain ponchos, each of them carrying a heavy-looking white plastic grocery sack.

They glanced back as Mr. Ericson sounded the horn and moved to walk in single file.

"That's Clay Greeley now," Mr. Ericson said, passing carefully. "And Castor and Pollux, the twins. They're just about his only buddies. People around here call them the heavenly twins because of their names, but don't be fooled. There's nothing heavenly about either of them. I wonder where they're heading and what they're up to on a night like this? Nothing good, whatever it is."

Teddy had slipped off Ab's lap and I bent to pick him up without disturbing her.

"You must be tired too, Matt," Mr. Ericson said gently. "Hang in there. It won't be much longer."

I closed my eyes for a couple of minutes, then opened them again as I felt the truck slow and stop.

"Here's your new home," Mr. Ericson said and I sat, holding Teddy, my arm still around Ab, staring at the house that was going to be our home.

It was faded white, square and wooden, and it tilted drunkenly to one side. Every window had a light in it, as if to welcome us. A spotlight at the front shone on slick metal signs stuck in the front grass. "DRINK COCA-COLA." "MORTON'S SALT." Pieces of soggy cardboard dripped from the trees. "HOMEMADE SANDWICHES SERVED HERE." "WE HAVE POP ON ICE, BUT WHERE IN HECK IS MOM?"

"Abby." I shook her shoulder gently. "Wake up, Ab. We're here."

When I opened the door, cool air wafted in. The rain was over but I heard it rustling in the trees, heard the noisy chorus of crickets, that stopped, then started again. I eased my wet jeans from my knees, took Mom's portfolio and jumped down. Abby held on to my shoulder and climbed out beside me, clutching Teddy. My legs were weak and shaky. This was it then. The end of the line.

A bare, yellow bulb shone down on the porch, lighting up two rattan rockers, and a table with a book propped under one leg. The patch of grass beyond the path lay in darkness, out of reach of the spotlight, but I sensed something there, some things. What was that whispering, breathing sound? I peered into the shadows, my skin prickling. There were figures there, swaying slightly. There were lumpy, shapeless bodies.

Instinctively I stepped back, tripping over Abby.

"Who are those people?" she asked, her voice too high, filled with fear.

"I don't know." I turned, to shield her, to edge her back toward the truck.

"It's all right." Mr. Ericson stood on the path behind us, holding our two bags. "No need to be scared. Those are the children."

2

THAT TALL, broad woman opening the front door now must be Aunt Gerda. I turned, feeling the drag of Abby's little hands on the back of my jacket.

"Loosen up, Ab," I muttered. "You're strangling me."

"We're here, Gerda," Slim Ericson called. "Half-drowned, but otherwise safe and sound."

I couldn't see Aunt Gerda's face, only the gray shine of her hair and her large bulky outline that almost filled the doorway. I could see the way she held out her arms in welcome and hear the warmth in her voice as she called:

"Matthew! Abigail! You poor dears. You must be worn out. And me not there to tell you how glad I am that you've come."

Mr. Ericson was trying to urge us forward, but Abby had her feet stubbornly planted and wouldn't move. Fear rose from her like steam. I turned my head sideways, just a little. The light from the open door fell in a white block across the grass, picking up one of the figures as if in a spotlight.

It was a doll. Just a girl doll, life-sized, with a smooth, brightly painted face. She wore an old-fashioned pink dress with a wet droopy frill round the bottom, white stockings, black shoes. I could see other dolls, too, a shadowy group of them, all huddled together on the grass.

The girl doll turned toward the porch and as if on a signal the others turned too. My skin prickled. They could MOVE? And then I saw that each one stood on a big wooden thing, like a turntable. Criminy! That had been scary for a minute all right.

"They're just dolls," I whispered to Abby. "Nothing to worry about."

Aunt Gerda was coming down the steps now, putting an arm around each of us.

"I'm so happy to have you. Thank you for bringing them, Slim. What would I have done without you? You'll come in, too, for a few minutes?"

"Thanks, Gerda, but I have to be off," Mr. Ericson said. "I'll just put these bags inside."

He was behind us as we went up the steps and onto the porch.

"Do the children look all right?" Aunt Gerda asked Mr. Ericson, and for a minute I thought she was talking about Ab and me. But she wasn't. I saw that she was peering past us into the darkness, to the grass beyond the house lights where the dolls stood.

"They look just fine to me, Gerda," Mr. Ericson said gently.

"I don't like them to be out in the rain like this," Aunt Gerda said. "It worries me. I really should have tried to get them all in before it started."

"It won't do them any harm, Gerda. You fuss about them too much." Mr. Ericson set our duffels by the bottom of a flight of stairs that ran up from the living room.

"Well, now," Aunt Gerda said. "Let me look at you two! Abigail, you are so pretty. You're just like your mother when she was your age . . . those lovely dark eyes, that hair . . . and Matthew!" She smiled down at me. I could tell she'd had big dark eyes once herself, but they had faded to a pale, pale brown. There was nothing faded about her smile. "Your mother wrote so much about you, Matthew. You were her Rock of Gibraltar, she said. Her strong, wise, capable son."

She knelt in front of us and Abby hung back at first, then swayed forward to hug her, to snuggle tight against her neck. Aunt Gerda smoothed Abby's hair and said, "There, there. Everything's going to be all right, my dear." And suddenly I believed her. We were wanted, we were welcome. It *was* going to be all right.

Over Aunt Gerda's shoulder I saw Slim Ericson wave to me and mouth "so long" as he let himself out of the front door, and then a slight movement somewhere else in the room made me look in that direction. One of the big dolls stood in the middle of the room. He had silvery hair, spun like candy floss, and he seemed to be getting fitted for a new jacket. His pants were black and white checked. He wore a white T-shirt with a mended tear across the front and half of a black blazer and he was looking straight at me and smiling. That smile turned my bones to mush. How could he be so real looking? How could the skin on his face be so smooth and fleshy? Of course it wasn't skin. But what was it?

I shivered and Aunt Gerda turned to look where I was looking.

"Oh, Matthew, Abigail, this is Derek. Derek stands closest to the road and somebody threw paint on him. It got all over his front, but I found him some new pants and pretty soon he's going to have a new jacket, too, aren't you, Derek?"

"Is he a doll?" Abby asked, standing and taking an unsure step toward him. For some reason I wanted to reach out and jerk her back.

Aunt Gerda lowered her voice. "Don't ever let him hear you ask that, Abigail. He's very sensitive about what we call him."

Abby was smiling and nodding now and I could tell she thought this was a neat game, the kind of "let's pretend" she really liked.

"Hello, Derek," she said.

"I wouldn't be surprised if Derek got that paint on himself on purpose," Aunt Gerda whispered. "He never did like the nice green jacket and pants he had before. Derek is our picky one."

Now Abby was giggling. "Picky Derek!"

"Abby!" I hadn't meant to say her name so sharply. "Why don't you grab your bag and Aunt Gerda can show us where we're going to sleep. Abby's real tired," I told Aunt Gerda.

"Of course. What am I thinking of? There'll be lots of time for you to get acquainted with Derek and the others. I'll show you your room. Here, Matthew. Let me carry something for you."

I let her take Mom's portfolio and I picked up the two bags and followed her and Abby up stairs that were steep and narrow, each step sloping to the right. It was like being on board a tilting ship. I wondered if there'd been an earthquake since the house was built or if it had just gotten tired of standing straight. It had to be really old. I glanced back over my shoulder into the room below and for the first time I saw that it was part shop, part living room, part kitchen. For the first time, too, I saw what kept Derek upright. He wasn't on a turntable after all.

A long wooden pole went under his clothes in back and came up behind his neck. Its end was fitted into the center hole of the round wooden platform he stood on. The platform was big as an automobile tire but shaped like a spool of thread. From here, it looked as if Derek had three legs, his own two in the black checked pants and a third in between. The pole, loose in its setting, moved easily and he moved with it.

In front of me Abby was chattering to Aunt Gerda. "Do you have any girl dolls?"

"Indeed. We have three girls. Three girls and four

boys. Your uncle made them all for me and named them alphabetically. We have Arabella. She's our eldest. We have Bethlehem, Cleo, Derek, whom you've met. Then we have Edwin, Fern, and George. Quite a little family. We did have another girl, Harriette, but we lost her."

"Can I play with Arabella and George and . . . and the rest of them?" Ab asked.

"They're looking forward to it," Aunt Gerda said. "I've told them all about you."

"Maybe we could have a tea party and my teddy could come?" Abby suggested. Mrs. Valdoni and Abby and Teddy had had lots of tea parties in Seattle. I hadn't minded those. But I didn't like the thought of this one.

"They love tea parties," Aunt Gerda said and I felt cold and clammy. There was something not right about the way Aunt Gerda talked about these dolls. "They're not real, but Gerda imagines they are," Mr. Ericson had said. Oh, brother! What *was* this? Was she crazy? I'd have to try explaining to Ab that she shouldn't start thinking about the dolls the way Aunt Gerda did, as if they were alive. But I'd have to be careful not to scare her. Real careful.

Aunt Gerda threw open a door. "Here we are."

The light was already on inside the room and I saw a single bed with a white tufted spread, a scarred dresser that had rows of little drawers and a spotted mirror, and a big plump chair. A folding cot with a faded blue cover had been placed right next to the bed. On the floor was a rug made up of blue, white, and red circles that went round and round in an endless braid. On the wall was a painting my mom had done, the one Slim Ericson had told us about.

I stood, looking up at it, and Aunt Gerda put the portfolio on the bed and came to stand beside me.

"I had that in the living room downstairs where I could see it all the time. But I thought you should have it up here, to bring her close to you."

My throat had gone dry, my eyes stung. Clear as clear could be, I remembered my mother standing in front of her easel, her head cocked, the old shirt she wore covered with streaks of paint. I saw her face when she turned to me, eyes shining.

"What do you think, Matt? Did I get it? Is that the way the sun looks on the water? Oh, how I wish I was better at this! It's all here, behind my eyes. But does it come out right? Is that the way you see it?"

I clenched my fists around the strings of the two duffels. Mom! Mom!

"My mama did that," Abby said, looking up at the painting, nodding her head. "My mama was a terrific artist, Matt says."

"Yes, she was." Aunt Gerda's voice was soft. "This was her room when she was a little girl and stayed with us. I have another bedroom, Abigail, and that can be yours if you want it. But for now I thought you might like to be here with Matthew. You and I can start fixing up the other room. We can put new wallpaper on and you can help me make curtains."

Abby moved closer to me. "Can I just stay with Matt all the time?"

"If that's what you want, my dear. Now the bathroom's right next door. If you're too tired to take a bath tonight, leave it till morning. Come down when you're ready. You must be hungry after your trip."

"Thanks," I said. "Are you hungry, Ab?"

Ab nodded.

"I am, too," I told Aunt Gerda. "But getting clean first might be a good idea."

"I've left out towels," Aunt Gerda said.

As soon as she left I went in the bathroom and ran water into the big, claw-footed tub.

"And don't just sit in it and play," I told Ab. "Wash!"

While she was gone I took my sweatshirt from around the portfolio and spread the paintings on the bed. They were all dry. The one of Abby and me, Ab in her little shorts and striped T-shirt gathering pebbles on the beach, me with my kite; the one of the ferry on its way to Orcas, the blue green of the water flecked with foam; the self-portrait of Mom. She'd been pretty sick when she did that and you could see her bones through her skin. I looked at it for a long time before I put it back. How could we bear to part with a single one? Because we had to, that's how.

When Ab came back I took my bath, wallowing in the water, trying to let the worries go. Too soon to worry anyway. And silly. I should just be glad we had somewhere to go, someone to take us.

Ab was already in her yellow nightgown when I came out of the bathroom. She was sitting cross-legged in the middle of the bed, Teddy with his head on the pillow.

"I see you've taken the bed, brat," I told her, drying the ends of her hair with my towel. "I thought you were hungry. Don't you want to go down and eat?"

"Yeah," Abby said, but she didn't move and I saw her yawn.

"How about if I go ask Aunt Gerda if I can bring something up for you?"

"No. No, Matty." She was scrabbling off the bed, catching her toes in the hem of the nightgown, her eyes wide and frightened. "Don't leave me."

"Take it easy, Ab. I won't leave you. We'll both. . ."

And then there was a knock and Aunt Gerda came in with a tray. "I thought this might be easier tonight," she said. There were two bowls of soup and a plate of bread and two glasses of milk on the tray.

She put it on the dresser and I pulled over the chair so Abby could kneel and eat right there while I sat on the end of the cot.

"Tomorrow you can see everything," Aunt Gerda said. "The Ericson children will probably come over. Kristin does, most days, and sometimes her little brother comes, too." She picked up a brush from the dresser and began to brush Ab's hair.

"And can we have the tea party?" Ab asked.

"Abby," I said. "Don't talk with your mouth full."

Aunt Gerda smiled. "I'll tell the children about the tea party when I go back downstairs. That way they can look forward to it."

I kept my head bent finishing my soup.

"All done?" Aunt Gerda asked, taking my empty bowl, putting it with Abby's on the tray.

"It was great," I said. "Thanks."

"You're welcome." She drew the blue curtains closed. "Into bed now, Abigail. You too, Matthew."

"Can't I carry the tray downstairs for you?"

"I'm perfectly able to do that myself. But thank you for offering."

I waited till Ab got between the sheets then tucked her in. "Goodnight. God bless," I said the way Mom always used to say, the way I'd said every night since she died.

"Goodnight, Matty." Abby held her face off the pillow so I could more easily kiss her cheek.

I wriggled myself into the squeaky cot.

"And who's going to tuck you in, you big, capable boy?" Aunt Gerda said softly. She came over, smoothed my sheet, touched my face. "Goodnight and God bless. And you, dear little Abigail."

I watched as she took the tray and carried it to the door. "Can you get the light, Matthew?" she asked.

I nodded.

"Sleep well."

I clicked off the lamp and listened to her footsteps going downstairs.

"Matt?" Abby whispered. "Are you there?"

"Of course I'm here, goose. Put out your hand."

I took it and held it tight.

"She's nice, isn't she, Matt?"

"Real nice," I said. And I did think she was nice — weird but nice.

Soon I felt Abby's hand go limp and her little snoring sounds start. Through the darkness I tried to see my mother's painting but I couldn't. It was good, though, to know it was there. Tomorrow I'd take some others from the portfolio and prop them up where we could see them, too.

I don't know if I went to sleep and if it was the small squeak of the screen door downstairs that wakened me. Maybe I was awake already. Ab's hand had slipped from mine.

In the room below, someone was talking.

Aunt Gerda, talking to herself? Or to Derek? But weren't there two voices? Someone must have come calling.

I got out of the cot, tiptoed to the door and eased it open.

The stairs were flooded with light, so was the living room/shop downstairs and the outside porch.

Aunt Gerda stood in the open doorway. She was wrapped in a gray blanket that trailed on the floor behind her and she had one arm raised, like an Indian chief, or a minister praying.

"Goodnight, Edwin," she called softly.

Edwin? That was the name of one of the dolls.

From outside came a child's voice.

"Goodnight, Mother."

What? Who was that? Not Edwin, that was for sure. My legs were weak suddenly and I had to hold on to the wall.

"Goodnight, Fern. Goodnight, George."

Two voices answering, tiny, distant as if from another planet. "Goodnight, Mother."

I stepped back, closed the bedroom door, and leaned against it, my heart pounding. Then I crept back onto the cot as close to my baby sister as I could get, and lay there, shivering in the dark.

3

I SLEPT late, and it was Abby who woke me, tugging at my nose, bouncing on my cot till it squeaked and creaked.

"Wake up, Matt. Wake up." She had already opened the curtains and the room was filled with sunlight.

I groaned and put my arm across my eyes.

"Come on, Matt. I have something to show you. It's outside, out in Aunt Gerda's garden, but you can see it from the window."

I was coming awake now, remembering Aunt Gerda and where we were, remembering the dolls and the way they'd said goodnight. The cold feeling came slithering back inside me. I bit my knuckles. They couldn't have talked. I'd been dreaming. Or else Aunt Gerda had called goodnight into the garden and then answered herself in a tiny doll voice. Sure! Abby did that all the time.

"Do you want to go for a walk, Teddy?" she'd ask.

"Oh yes, please, Mommy Abby." That was supposed to be Teddy.

Now I let her pull me up, then get behind and make train noises as she pushed me over to the window. Abby hadn't sounded this chipper in a long time. I could tell she was beginning to feel safe here. She was, but I wasn't.

"Look!" She pointed outside.

The rain had disappeared as if it had never been and the morning sparkled. Beneath the window was an overgrown vegetable garden and a shed with a sloping roof.

"Down there, Matt," Abby said. "You're not looking in the right place."

Now I saw a swing hanging from the branch of an old tree. The seat sloped at one end and moved a little in the breeze.

"A swing, Matt. Can I try it?"

"We'll see," I said.

Abby's hair spiked in all directions and there was stuff in the corners of her eyes.

"First, go wash and put your clothes on," I said. "Match things up the way Mom taught you. Then we can go downstairs."

"Yippee." She began pulling a tangle of pants and shirts from her duffel.

I turned to stare out of the window again while she got dressed. Sometimes I thought how much easier it would have been if I'd had a little brother instead of a little sister. He and I could have horsed around in our underwear even. With a little sister I had to be polite. Still, I knew I wouldn't trade Ab for anybody in the whole world, not anybody.

What was that?

I stood high on my toes. There was something else down there, way back in the corner behind the swing. I stretched, putting my face close to the glass. It was a wooden cross, white, new painted. A grave! Whose?

"Matt?" Abby held a pair of rolled together yellow socks. "Do these match these?" She arched her back and stuck out her stomach so I could see her blue shorts and her blue and yellow striped T-shirt.

"They'll look great, Ab," I said. "Good job."

How could I fix it that she wouldn't see that grave and remember two other graves, the two crosses that marked them? I couldn't. I couldn't protect her from remembering.

While she washed I dressed, and then she waited for me. We helped each other make the bed and cot.

"Matt? You won't let Aunt Gerda put me in a room by myself, will you?"

"I won't, Ab. But you have to promise not to pull my nose in the morning."

"Can I pull your hair? You're hard to wake up."

"No. Not my hair either. Are you ready? Let's go."

"Can I see Mama's picture first?"

"Sure." I opened the portfolio, found the self-portrait and propped it on the dresser. Mama smiled out at us. I wondered how long it would take for the ache that came when I looked at her to stop. Maybe it never would.

"We can keep this here if you like, Ab. Do you want to?"

Abby nodded. Her shoulders drooped and her face looked awfully small as she stared up at me. "Matt? Tell me again what we're going to do."

I sat on the edge of the cot and she sat, too, and I put my arm around her shoulder and squeezed her tight.

"Well, as soon as I can I'm going to find an art dealer, a really big, important one. We'll keep some of the pictures for ourselves. . ."

"The one of Mom and the one of me, and you, and the one of Tetley," Abby said.

"Yes." Tetley was Mrs. Valdoni's dog. "Those. Whatever we want. The rest we'll sell. We'll get thousands and thousands of dollars and we'll . . ."

Abby interrupted, her eyes on my face. "You said thousands and thousands and thousands before, Matt. You forgot one."

"Thousands and thousands and thousands," I agreed. "A lot. We'll tell the guy who buys them that first we want to show them in a big gallery, an exhibit it's called. That way everyone will be able to see Mom's work and admire it. She'd like that. And then he'll give us the money, and we'll put it in a bank, and it will be ours so we don't have to depend on anyone but each other."

"And we'll buy a house . . ." Abby had her wide-eyed, story-listening look again.

"We'll buy a house . . ."

"And get a kitty cat . . . and live happily ever after." Abby finished with a sigh of satisfaction.

"Right."

I knew it wouldn't be this simple or easy, but I knew too that the paintings were our legacy from Mom and that this was what she would have wanted for Ab and me as soon as we got things together.

"Maybe we'll like it here and stay forever and give Aunt Gerda the money," Abby said.

"Maybe." I sort of doubted it. We went downstairs.

The living room/kitchen/shop was empty, except for Derek who still stood on the platform, wearing his unfinished jacket. Sun streamed through the screen doors where Aunt Gerda had stood last night in her trailing blanket. Or where I'd dreamed I'd seen her stand last night . . .

"I like this little house," Abby said, clutching Teddy and jumping down the last two steps of the stairs. It kills me the way Abby jumps, with her feet together and her knees bent and her mouth set in this little tight line as she concentrates. You'd think she was in the Olympics or something.

"Hi, Derek," she said. "Have you had breakfast?" And then she ran past him. "Oh look, Matt. I can play shop in here for real."

"No kidding." I followed her across to the long wooden counter at the front end of the room, being careful not to look at Derek. Underneath the counter were glass cases that held packets of sugar and faded boxes of cereal and dusty cans of soup. There was lots of space behind the glass, lots of emptiness. Aunt Gerda didn't keep a big stock but it looked as if she kept what she had for a long time.

A big white freezer chest against the wall hummed up a storm. At the kitchen end were a stove and a sink and cupboards painted blue. There was a couch on the other side, several big wicker baskets, a sewing machine. The walls were cf rough paneling, painted white, and the ceiling was low and paneled, too. By the front door was an old-fashioned trunk, banded in metal, and above the counter a framed picture of President Kennedy and a clock with OVALTINE printed around its face.

"Aunt Gerda?" Abby called, running across to the screen door. Her voice was as high as a bird's.

From outside came an answering call. "Abigail? Matthew? I'm out here, with the children."

Abby turned her shining face up to me. "Now we'll get to meet the other dolls."

Great, I thought. I took hold of her arm. "Listen a minute, Ab. Aunt Gerda is very old. She's even older than our grandmother would be if we had a grandmother. She thinks those dolls are real . . . remember, Mr. Ericson told us? I don't want you to believe her." It bothered me that Derek was listening to this. But of course he wasn't. Not really.

"Oh Matty!" Abby looked sorry for me. "You are so silly. I know they're not real. That's just Aunt Gerda's pretend. She's just *playing*. Come on!"

"Quit pulling at me," I said. "You're all the time pulling me or shoving me. I've got legs, you know. I can walk by myself." I unlatched the screen door.

Abby danced ahead, Teddy safely tucked against her chest, but I followed more slowly. What was *my* problem? Abby knew the dolls weren't real. Did I think they were? Of course not. That had just been Aunt Gerda talking to herself last night. So why was I so scared of them?

Aunt Gerda stood on the grass with the dolls swaying gently around her. I saw that they moved easily on their poles in those center holes. All it took was a little puff of wind. See? I told myself. Last night you thought they could move by themselves! You thought they could talk *and* move. See?

A stronger little whisk of wind rustled the metal signs and made the cardboard pieces flap against the trees. The dolls swung slowly to face us and Abby gasped and held Teddy up to cover her eyes. She spoke around him.

"Oh, Aunt Gerda," she said in a heartbroken voice. "What happened? What happened to your dollies?"

4

THE DOLLS were covered from head to toe with blobs of purple paint. I took a step closer. No, not paint, something sticky and mushy . . . and not covered head to toe, either. All their faces were clean, spared somehow or washed already by Aunt Gerda.

"Oh criminy, that's awful," I said. "What *is* that stuff on them?"

Aunt Gerda's face was grim. "Plums. Ripe plums." She pushed back her hair which was hanging, gray and wispy around her shoulders, and gestured toward the road. "Someone stood there and threw them."

Someone with a good aim, I thought. Or someone who came all the way in here, so close it was impossible to miss.

"That's mean." Abby ran forward to take Aunt Gerda's hand. "Why would anyone do such a mean thing?"

"I'm afraid not everyone around here likes me, or the

children," Aunt Gerda said. "A few things have been happening. We had a . . ." She stopped and I had a definite feeling that whatever she'd been going to say had been scary, too scary to tell us about. "A few days ago Derek had that paint thrown on him," she went on. "Now this." She stroked Ab's hair. "Don't worry about it, my dear. We'll get the children cleaned up."

"Is that why you don't like to leave them?" Abby asked, looking up at her. "Is that why you didn't come to meet us?"

"Yes. I watch over them carefully, but we're all so vulnerable at night. I wish I could afford to put up a high fence and a gate and . . ."

"When we get our picture money," Abby began and then glanced guiltily at me. Aunt Gerda hadn't seemed to notice.

I looked more closely at the dolls. What a mess. How in the world would she ever get them cleaned up? And they were so weird; no wonder not everybody liked them. I wasn't too crazy about them myself. Although they were probably uglier today than ever with plum pulp stuck on them, they'd be ugly at any time. The painted eyes on their wooden faces were too far apart so that each eye seemed to look in a different direction. And why were they all smiling? Couldn't one or two of them have had different expressions? At least?

They were like sextuplets, or whatever you call seven of a kind. Only their fake-looking hair and their clothes were different. I'd never seen such clothes. They could have come out of a museum. All of the girls had purses and jewelry and one wore a red felt hat with a wet feather in it on her yarn curls. I tried not to shiver.

Something blew against my leg and I bent to pull it off. It was a white plastic grocery bag. Right away I remembered the three figures walking single file along the road last night.

"Clay Greeley," Mr. Ericson had said. And his two friends, somebody and somebody. I'd forgotten their names. The heavenly twins.

I opened the sack and peered inside. Half of a rotten plum was squashed on the bottom. But it was silly to jump to conclusions. These bags were used in just about every market. There must be millions of them around. No need to think this was the "nothing good" Clay and his friends had been up to.

"Yukko!" Abby lifted one foot. A plum oozed on the sole of her shoe, the stain spreading up onto the white top. She came hopping toward me, Aunt Gerda following behind.

"I'm just sorry this had to happen on your first day here," Aunt Gerda said and stopped. She lifted a hand to shield her eyes from the sun, looking beyond us in the direction of the road.

"Well," she said dryly. "Here come the vigilantes."

"Vigilantes?" I turned in time to see two cars pull up and stop on the other side of the road, across from the house. A woman and three men got out of the first car and two more men and a woman joined them from the second. There was something purposeful and a little scary about the way they marched, in double file up the path.

"They're not really vigilantes," Aunt Gerda said in a voice that she seemed to be making loud on purpose, so they'd be sure to hear. "It's just that they act as if they were."

"What's a viggie lantern?" Abby whispered to me, and Aunt Gerda said: "A person who takes the law into his own hands, Abigail."

Abby gave me a glance more puzzled than ever and I wasn't sure I knew myself.

The six of them had stopped a few feet away from us and one man stepped out in front of the group. He was about Mr. Ericson's age, nice enough looking, with hair dark and straight as Abby's. He wore a tweed sports coat with elbow patches, cords, and comfortable, worn loafers.

"Good morning, Mrs. Yourra," he said.

"Good morning, Mr. Terlock." Aunt Gerda made a funny little bow in his direction and another toward the people on the path.

"I see someone paid you a visit during the night." Mr. Terlock gestured at the dolls, who turned on their poles as if to include everyone in their painted smiles.

"A rather unpleasant visit," Aunt Gerda said.

"I'm sorry, Mrs. Yourra, but I can't say I'm surprised," Mr. Terlock said. "You know very well how the canyon people feed about your dolls. Unpleasantness is bound to occur."

Abby tugged at my arm and I bent toward her. "I

don't see anything in their hands," she whispered. "Aunt Gerda said they had the law in their hands. Where is it?"

"I'll explain later," I whispered back, straightening, anxious not to miss a word of what was going on.

"I'm presuming none of you had anything to do with this particular nastiness." I couldn't tell if Aunt Gerda meant it or if she was being sarcastic.

"I promise you we did not," Mr. Terlock said. "This kind of thing is not our style."

There was a mixed chorus of "certainly nots" from the group on the path.

One of the women spoke: "You're lucky it wasn't anything worse, Gerda."

"I've already had worse, Violet," Aunt Gerda said.

Who are these two young people?" the other woman asked. She was young with a sharp, pointy face. She wore a plaid jacket and jeans that were tucked into tall leather boots.

"They're relatives of mine. They've come to live here," Aunt Gerda said, moving a step closer to Ab and me and putting her arm around our shoulders.

"They're going to be living *here*?" The sharp, pointy-faced woman had a sharp, pointy voice to match.

"Yes," I said. "From now on."

"All the more reason to listen to us, Gerda," Mr. Terlock said. "We've come again to try to convince you to get rid of the dolls. You've lived in peace in this canyon for a lot of years. The trouble only started when you and Joseph insisted on putting these . . .

these . . . " His hand swept again toward the dolls. "Making these dolls and displaying them outside."

"I will not get rid of my children, Mr. Terlock," Aunt Gerda said in a voice so fierce that I could hardly believe it when Mr. Terlock smiled. "I will not get rid of them however many times you ask."

"They are not children, my dear Gerda."

The woman, Violet, interrupted. "They're idols. Heathen idols."

"Whatever they are, they are ugly and frightening," Mr. Terlock went on. "People have to live in this canyon. *We* have to live here."

"And you have to sell property here, Mr. Terlock. I understand completely," Aunt Gerda said.

"Yes, I do have to sell property here. This is a desirable area." He gestured up and down the road. "But you and your dolls do not do anything to improve land values. I had a couple just last week who wanted to buy up at Tor Peak. When they drove past here the lady asked if you kept these carvings out here all the time and I had to say 'yes,' Mrs. Yourra. They didn't buy."

"You yourself don't mind, though, do you, Mr. Terlock?" Aunt Gerda asked. "I hear you've bought the old Patterson place and the Jennings ranch."

"That has nothing to do with why we're here," another man said. "My kids have to pass this house on their way to school. Their mother has to drive them. They won't come on their own."

"I'm sorry to hear that," Aunt Gerda said. "But who

is filling their minds with fear? Not I, certainly. We would never harm them. If they want to come by, I'll introduce them to the children. They can see for themselves how friendly we are."

The man gave a disbelieving bark of a laugh. "Oh, sure."

"This is my property," Aunt Gerda said. "I will keep my children with me, and I will keep them wherever I want to keep them. There is nothing that says I have to do otherwise. If there was a law, you would have already found it."

"Would you consider moving elsewhere?" Mr. Terlock asked. "I would be willing to give you a fair market value for your home here."

"My home is not for sale," Aunt Gerda said. "And now if you will excuse me." She made that polite little bow again, then stood, stern and proud.

Mr. Terlock said, "I think you will be sorry." What funny lips he had, so thin and pale that they were almost invisible. Like lizard lips.

Aunt Gerda's shoulders stiffened. "Is that some kind of a threat? I don't take easily to threats."

Mr. Terlock didn't answer. Instead he pushed his way through the group and led them again, back down the path. We stood, silently, till the two cars swung around on the narrow road, turned and roared away.

"Are they bad people?" Abby looked anxiously from me to Aunt Gerda.

"Probably not," Aunt Gerda said. "They just want what they want. And they don't much care how they get it. Now," She turned toward the dolls, "let's think about something important. I'm afraid all of the children's clothes will have to be washed. Some of them may even be ruined completely."

"I'll help." Abby smoothed her hand back and forth along Aunt Gerda's arm. "Don't worry. I'm a good washer."

"Thank you, dear. We'll have to bring them inside, though. I can't possibly embarrass them by undressing them out here."

Another white bag had wrapped itself around the base of the tree. I picked my way through the plum pocked grass and pulled it free, rolled it up, and pushed it inside the first one. I didn't see a third bag, but if there was such a thing it could have blown anywhere. And anyway, I wasn't so sure anymore that Clay Greeley and his friends were the ones who'd messed up the dolls.

"We'll bring the children in one by one," Aunt Gerda said. "Now, let's see. Fern! I know how important it is to you to look nice. You will be first."

She took Fern around the waist and lifted her up, straight out of the platform.

I thrust the plastic bags at Ab. "Hold these, Ab. Aunt Gerda, I'll carry the doll."

"It's perfectly all right, Matthew. I'm strong. And I'm used to this," Aunt Gerda said, but I grabbed Fern around the waist and Aunt Gerda let her go.

Man, was Fern heavy! Heavier than Abby. She swayed dangerously and I set the pole on the grass to get a better hold of her, then took her again and began walking. She felt hard and solid. Well, of course. She was a block of wood. What had I expected? Suppose, when I put my arms around her she'd been soft and squishy in the middle, like a person? What if I'd heard her stomach gurgle?

Baloney! Double baloney!

I staggered with Fern up the path, Aunt Gerda and Abby behind.

"Get the screen door for me, Ab," I puffed. "But don't come in with that gucky shoe."

"I'll just get a platform for Fern so she can stand," Aunt Gerda said, passing me. "I keep some spares in the service porch. That way I don't have to haul one in from the yard every time I need it."

I leaned Fern against the counter. Her stubby legs in their white, spattered stockings were shorter than the center pole and she began to tilt sideways. I got her in time. Her left eye watched me and she smiled with delight. The opening of the screen door must have been enough to move Derek because he had turned to face us. "You quit grinning," I told Fern. "And you, Derek, don't you be so nosy."

Oh no! Now I'd started talking to the dumb dolls, too. But they were so lifelike! I thought of the children who had to be driven to school because they were afraid to walk past them. Not much wonder.

Aunt Gerda came through the back door from the service porch then, wheeling one of the big spools.

Together she and I eased Fern's pole into the

platform. It was like putting a patio umbrella into its stand except that a patio umbrella doesn't smile and wink at you. Wink? Of course Fern hadn't winked. I'd probably blinked, that was all.

"There now," Aunt Gerda said with satisfaction. "We'll get you out of these messy clothes now, Fern, and you'll feel better."

Abby came padding across the room in her yellow socks.

"Should I take off Fern's shoes, too?" she asked, and Aunt Gerda said: "Please."

The shoes had straps with buttons and I had to help. Aunt Gerda eased off Fern's black shoulder purse and set it on the counter top. Then she turned to me. "Matthew? I'm going to have to ask you to wait outside. Fern is very modest."

"Oh . . . well . . . sure!" I could feel my face getting warm. "I'll just wait on the front porch."

The heavy wooden front door had been open all the way. I'd bumped it when I carried Fern in. Now it had swung forward, and when I went to push it back, I saw the piece of paper pinned to it. The paper was ruled and had three holes punched in the margin and a torn border as if it had been ripped out of a notebook. Printed on it in red were the words:

GET OUT OF THE CANYIN AND TAKE YOUR CREEPY GHOST CHILDREN WITH YOU. WE MEAN BUSNESS.

I pulled it off the door and read it again. Two words

· 38 ·

spelled wrong. Not that that was much of a clue. The world was filled with bad spellers. Mrs. Valdoni was terrible. She told me once she couldn't spell her married name for the first three years. But surely Mr. Terlock wouldn't write a note like this? And a real estate agent or property buyer, whatever, would surely know how to spell "canyon" unless he was faking it.

I was still looking at the note, hoping for a clue that wasn't there, when a voice called out in back of me. I almost jumped out of my skin. Had the vigilantes come back? Or was it one of the dolls . . . the ghost children? My neck hurt as I creaked it around to peer behind.

A girl sat on a too-small bike at the end of the path, balancing with her feet on the ground on either side.

"Who did this to Gerda's kids?" she asked. "I swear, this is the worst." She walked forward, straddling the bike. I couldn't believe the way she did that, holding onto the handlebars, spinning to lay the bike on the ground. Now she was running up the path.

"Oh, George!" she said to a doll who wore weird-looking knickerbocker pants. "Just look at you! And Arabella! The dress Gerda made for you just last week! It's ruined. She must be sick about this." The dolls seemed to listen, smiling their never-ending smiles. "But where's Fern?" she asked then. "What happened to her?"

She glared accusingly at me, hands on hips.

"Fern's inside," I said. "Aunt Gerda's cleaning her up."

"Oh. And you're Matthew, of course. I'm Kristin. It was my dad who brought you and your sister from the bus stop. Slim Ericson. I don't know why he's called 'Slim.' He isn't slim at all."

"Only Aunt Gerda calls me Matthew. I'm really Matt."

She nodded, staring hard at me. I was staring hard at her, too.

"I thought you'd be taller," she said. "Gerda told me you're a year older than I am, but I think I'm definitely bigger."

I stood as big as I could. "No way," I said. But she did have really long legs. That was how she was able to do that neat thing with the bike. Or maybe her legs only looked long because her shorts were so short and because the man's white shirt she wore almost hid them entirely.

"Anyway, hi Matthew." She ran up the front steps, pulling off the bent-out-of-shape tennis hat she wore, letting her long blonde hair tumble down. "What have you got there?" she asked.

I was still holding the note and I gave it to her. "This was on the door."

She read it and handed it back. I hoped she hadn't noticed that she definitely was taller than I was.

"Dorks," she said, drumming her fingers on the porch rail. "I guess all this happened last night."

"Yes. We didn't hear anything."

She turned to push open the screen door and I said: "Wait a sec. I don't think we should tell Aunt Gerda about the note. Not yet anyway. She's upset enough."

Kristin nodded. "Aren't you coming in?"

"On, no. Aunt Gerda wants me to wait outside."

"How come? You mean, in case the dorks come back?"

I shrugged. No way was I going to tell her I wasn't allowed to see a girl doll in her underwear.

I heard Kristin speak to Derek as she went past. "Well, I see you escaped. I suppose you had your turn already with all that paint. That's a sharp-looking jacket Gerda's making for you."

I shook my head. Another one who talked to blocks of wood. She said something to Aunt Gerda then and I heard the high little polite pipe of Abby's voice. They were all talking now, and I recognized a word here and there. "Truck" and "Mom has something . . ." and "cold water." Maybe they'd put a robe on Fern and I'd be able to go back inside. For now though, I'd have to wait.

I sat in one of the rockers.

The long grass in the front yard moved softly in the breeze, and the dolls moved, too, in a stiff little dance. I tried not to watch them or to think about them either.

High in the sky a hawk hung, circled, flew out of my sight. A bluejay hopped down to the yard, found a plum pit and took off with it. Abby had left the two plastic bags on the other chair and I got up, rolled them into a ball and went down the path. The road on either side of Aunt Gerda's lay sun-filled, dusty, empty.

I walked round the side to the back yard. Here was the old shed, tilted as crazily as the house, and beside it the vegetable garden I'd seen from the window. Summer squash lay tangled in the long grass, some as long as blown up yellow balloons. A clothes line with pins stretched between two trees. And there was the swing. I inspected the ropes before I let myself look at what I knew I'd come round here to see.

The grave wasn't overgrown like the rest of the yard. The grass had been carefully shaved away from the rectangle of earth. Beneath the cross was a vase of flowers, wilted but not yet brown; I remembered the roses Abby and I put on our mother's grave. They'd be dust by now.

The cross had an inscription.

I stepped closer, careful not to put my feet on that neat patch of earth. Burned into the wood were the words:

HERE LIES HARRIETTE, DEARLY BELOVED DAUGHTER OF JOSEPH AND GERDA YOURRA. REST IN PEACE.

I bit at my knuckles. Harriette? So there'd been eight children, then, and it was the last one who'd died. I walked backward, needing to get away. What did I mean, it was the last one who'd died? Dolls don't die.

5

"Matt? Matt? That was Abby calling from the front of the house.

"I'm coming," I yelled, but she was coming, too. I didn't want her to see that grave, though she'd have to, wouldn't she, sooner or later? And I guess nothing is supposed to be as frightening when you face up to it. That's what Mrs. Valdoni had said when I didn't want to go to the mortuary after Mom died.

"We're going to have breakfast," Abby announced, appearing round the corner. "Aunt Gerda says she forgot we hadn't eaten yet and what do we want. She says Kristin can eat with us, too." Abby had put her shoes back on and I bent to tie the laces.

"Good," I said. "Do you want to try the swing for a minute, Ab?"

"Yes! Aunt Gerda says we won't have the tea party today. Not till we get all the dolls looking nice again."

I nodded and held the wooden swing seat so she

could climb onto it, pushing to get her started.

"I can do it myself. I can. Don't push anymore," she ordered, so I stood back and let her pump her skinny legs up and down while I thought about how to handle this.

"We'd better go in and get that breakfast," I said after a while. "But I want to show you something first."

I took her warm little hand as we walked toward Harriette's grave. It wasn't hard to know exactly when she spotted the cross. Her fingers tightened around mine.

"One of the dolls is buried here," I said in a matter-of-fact way. "I guess something happened. Aunt Gerda probably had a pretty funeral for it, the kind we had at home for your china horse when it broke. Remember?"

Abby stood sucking on the fingers of her other hand.

Just don't remember Mom's funeral, Abby, I thought. Don't remember the wet churchyard, the rain dripping from Mrs. Valdoni's umbrella, the sticky, brown mud. "I bet Aunt Gerda put those flowers there," I said. "Do you remember we brought flowers for the china horse?"

Abby stared up at me with her big, dark eyes. "His name was Snowy, Matt."

"I know. We wrapped the pieces of china in a tissue and put them in a shoe box."

Abby was nodding now, really into the storytelling. She looked at the grave. "Is Aunt Gerda's dolly in a box down there?"

"I expect so. Her name was Harriette."

"Did she break?"

"I guess." For the life of me I couldn't think how a wooden doll with no joints could break, but I wasn't going to say that to Abby. She skipped along beside me as we walked back to the house. So the doll's grave hadn't bothered her that much after all. Not as much as it had bothered me.

The plum-pocked family swung gently to watch us as we passed. Abby stopped. "You poor things. If I had the person who did this to you I'd . . . I'd just spit on him. I would. Do you think it was those viggie-lantern people, Matt?"

"I don't know, Ab. I have no idea. But I wish you wouldn't talk to the dolls as if they're people. Would you please quit doing that, Ab?"

"How come you sound so mad?" Abby asked. "You don't get mad when I talk to my teddy."

"That's different. Come on."

In the kitchen, Kristin was scooping yogurt from a cardboard tub into three blue bowls. An opened can of raspberries was on the table and she spooned some of the fruit on top.

"Yumbos," Abby said, smacking her lips and climbing into a chair. Derek beamed from his stand and Fern stood by the sink, her back to us. Aunt Gerda knelt in front of her, her mouth full of pins.

Fern wore a blue dress now, the hem partly pinned up, the rest hanging down to cover her feet. The dress had a white lacy collar and it was too big everywhere. Aunt Gerda had the waist nipped in and there were great pinned folds on the shoulders.

"Is that one of your own dresses, Aunt Gerda?" I asked, but before she could take the pins from her mouth to answer, Abby spoke for her.

"No. Aunt Gerda goes to the dump. She finds things people have thrown away and she washes them and keeps them for her children."

I could tell I was going to have to get mad at her for calling them children, too. But not right now. Right now I was wondering how long the clothes Ab and I had would last. When they wore out would Aunt Gerda expect *us* to wear dump clothes, too?

Ab pointed with her spoon to a wicker hamper. "Aunt Gerda has a whole *basketful* of stuff. It's amazing the good things people throw away." Her voice was such an exact imitation of Aunt Gerda's that it made Kristin laugh. Abby kills me too, the way she can mimic grown ups.

"Aunt Gerda doesn't find many boy things, though," she went on. "She'll have to make them and it's hard for her because she doesn't see well enough to sew these days. Aunt Gerda's got jewelry, too. A bag full of it."

Fern had spun around to face us now and Abby put down her spoon. "Ooo, she's so pretty in that dress. Was Harriette that pretty?"

My warning glance came too late.

"What happened to poor Harriette?" Abby asked.

"We saw the grave," I said quickly. "We just wondered."

Aunt Gerda took the pins from her mouth and stuck

them in the red pincushion she wore like an oversized watch on her wrist.

"Harriette met with an accident. It almost broke our hearts. And yes, Abigail, she was very pretty. Very pretty and very sweet."

In the silence I heard the clink of Kristin's spoon on her bowl. Her hair swung forward hiding her face. What did *she* think of all this? Did she think it was loony tunes, too?

"My Snowy met with a accident," Abby said. "He fell off the table."

"Snowy was a horse," I explained.

Kristin raised her eyebrows. "And he fell off the table?"

"A china horse," I said.

"What kind of a accident was Harriette's?" Abby asked. "Did she fall too?"

"Ab! Maybe she doesn't want to talk about it," I said.

Aunt Gerda jabbed a pin in and out of the pincushion. "That's all right, Abigail. However, I don't ever discuss it in front of the other children. Harriette *was* their sister, after all."

Abby nodded wisely, looking from Fern to Derek.

"Well, I'm sure you haven't had enough to eat, Matthew dear, or you either Abigail," Aunt Gerda said.

Not to change the subject or anything, I thought.

"There's cereal in the glass case under the counter," she went on, "and milk in the refrigerator. Take whatever you want."

"I like living in a little shop," Abby said as she and

I chose a box of Crispie Cornballs from the display case. I wiped the dust from the package on the leg of my jeans. "Do you want some, Kristin?"

Kristin shook her head. "No thanks, I'm full."

As soon as I tasted the cereal I knew why she'd turned it down. Maybe ten years ago this stuff had been fresh. Abby didn't seem to notice.

By the time we'd finished and washed the bowls, Fern's dress had been pinned all the way around. Her wooden legs and feet were very pale and smooth as silk. Someone had painted her toenails pink. Looking at them gave me the creeps.

Aunt Gerda repinned the plastic butterfly clip that held Fern's hair back from her face. "Maybe the white beads and earrings, Fern dear. What do you think?"

It seemed to me we were all listening, waiting for Fern's answer which, thank goodness, didn't come.

"Shall we search through the jewelry bag, Abigail, and see what we can find?"

"Yeaa!" Abby clapped her hands.

"And Matthew. I'm sure you don't want to look through a bag of jewelry. So why don't you go out to the shed. There's a bike there for you."

"A bike?"

"It was your Uncle Joseph's. Here!" She took a key from a hook behind the counter and gave it to me.

I turned it around in my hand. "I've never had a bike, Aunt Gerda," I said slowly. "I'll take good care of it. Thanks. Thanks a lot."

"You're welcome, dear. Kristin? Can you show him where the shed is?"

"Can I go too, Aunt Gerda?" Abby asked. "I want to see Matt's bike. I'll look for Fern's jewelry after."

"Of course, dear."

Ab bounced up and down, as we walked to the back. "Maybe I can get a bike, too, Matt. In the dump, maybe."

"Maybe." I unlocked the door.

The inside of the shed was dim and smelled of damp. Dust floated in the pale sunbeams that poked through the two windows. The bike was balanced on its kickstand way in the back. I saw that there was a rusted lawnmower in the shed, too, and a chair with torn canvas and a bunch of tools. On the floor were several thick blocks of wood, and sawdust was everywhere. It puffed up around our feet as we walked through it. A dingy bed sheet was draped over something on a workbench.

"Have you been in here before?" I whispered to Kristin.

She shook her head. "This is where your uncle made the children." Kristin was whispering too, and I knew why. There was something strange in here, a feeling, a too quiet quiet. Silly, I told myself. This was my uncle's workshop, period. A place like my mother's studio with its easel and piles of canvases and tubes of paint.

Abby stood close to the door. "I don't like it in here," she whined. "It's scary."

"It's O.K., Ab. It's O.K."

I lifted the kickstand with my foot and wheeled the bike to the door without looking to right or left, edging

Kristin and Abby out ahead of me. The air felt good. I took a breath of it and locked the door behind us.

Kristin pointed down at the bike. "You're going to have to pump the tires, Matt."

The bike was an old three-speed with shiny black paint. The handlebars hadn't a speck of rust and the rims and spokes of the wheels had been coated with some kind of preserving grease. I loved it. But Kristin was right. Both tires were perfectly flat.

"All I need is a pump," I said. "Do you have one, Kristin?"

"No. But I saw one in the shed, on the pegboard at the back."

"Oh." There was a bell fastened to the bike's handlebars. I tried it and it worked. *Ching, ching, ching.* I let Abby ring it while I spun the pedals and checked the chain. I pummeled the seat and rubbed the sawdust off it with my elbow. Then I rang the bell again.

"Well," I said at last. "I guess I'd better go get the pump."

"I don't want to go in there again," Abby whispered.

I didn't either. But I wasn't going to let Kristin see what a wimp I was. "Stay here with Kristin, Ab, and hold the bike. I'll be back."

I unlocked the door and grinned back at them. See? See how brave? I may be small but I'm spunky.

Inside, I walked fast, grabbed the pump off the wall, hurried back past the workbench. Almost in spite of itself my hand reached out, lifted a corner of the stained sheet. Why was I doing this? Just get out, I told myself. Get out. But then my eyes saw the block of wood, the pale, soft wood that was beginning to turn into one of the dolls.

There was the rounded shape of the head, the small curve of the neck, the slope of the shoulders, the waist, the legs, still blocked together. No face, though, and no arms or hands or feet. Sweat cold as ice trickled down inside my shirt as I dropped the sheet and ran for the door.

6

"MATT? ARE YOU O.K.?" Kristin asked.

"Sure I'm O.K."

I worked the pump a few times to try it, whistling carelessly, then bent to unscrew the valve from the front tire. What had I seen in there? Just a piece of wood, a doll Uncle Joseph must have started before he died, three years ago. Don't get carried away, Matt!

My hand was shaking so much I had trouble screwing pump and tire together, but I did and began filling the tire up with air. When it was filled, I started to work on the back one. Abby had to have a turn, too, of course, puffing and panting and gritting her teeth.

I patted her on the shoulder. "You did great, Ab."

Kristin flashed me the nicest smile.

I tried the bike then, riding round the side of the house and up the path to the porch where Aunt Gerda stood, leaning on the railing.

"How is it?" she asked.

I gave her the thumbs up sign, then rang the bell. "Perfect. I can't believe it's mine. I asked for a bike three Christmases in a row, but Mom couldn't handle it, and I was saving, too, but . . ."

I rang the bell again instead of finishing. No point in going into the way our money had disappeared after Mom's medications started. "It's a terrific bike," I added. "They don't build them like this anymore." I wasn't sure about that, but I'd heard people say it about old cars and I thought it would please Aunt Gerda. It did.

She watched while I wheeled Abby down the path, Ab ringing the bell so fiercely that a bunch of blackbirds screeched up from the trees. The dolls watched, too. Then Kristin tried the bike. I was happy to see that her feet didn't touch the ground when she rode, especially since I was having trouble even reaching the pedals. Maybe I could lower the seat a bit.

"Abigail?" Aunt Gerda said. "I've poured all the jewelry on the table. Do you want to come in now and help Fern decide?"

"Yeah!" Abby gamboled up the path.

How was I *ever* going to get her to stop thinking of the dolls as people when Aunt Gerda talked about them this way? As if Fern had any say in which jewelry they put on her!

I looked at my aunt waiting for Ab on the porch and I was filled with all kinds of mixed up feelings. There was gratitude. What would we have done without her? Her letters had cheered Mom up. The little bits and

pieces of money she'd sent had helped with the groceries and the rent, and I could see now that she'd
probably had to sacrifice to send it because this shop
wasn't exactly a gold mine.

I remembered the way she'd said "come" when
Mom died, how loving she'd been with us last night.
But I knew I was scared of her too, the way you are
when you sense someone isn't like everyone else.
When you sense the someone is different. I wished
Blinky was here so I could talk this over with him.
Blinky was always real easy to talk to. Maybe I should
call him? Or Mrs. Valdoni? But I'd have to find a phone
someplace, and anyway, what could I say? How could
I explain this?

Aunt Gerda put her arm around Ab so they could go
in the house together, but Ab turned, stiffened her
little legs and called back to me: "Don't go off somewhere without me, Matt. Promise?"

"Promise," I said.

"I'll cry if you go," she said.

"I won't, Ab. I'll be just out here in front, where you
can see me if you come on the porch."

She nodded. "O.K."

"You're really nice to her, you know it?" Kristin
said.

I shrugged. "Abby's O.K."

"I'm not nearly that nice to Fee."

"Fee?"

"My little brother, Frank Edmund Ericson."

"Fee's probably got both a mom and a dad," I said.

"Yes." Kristin gave me a strange, soft kind of look, then pulled her white hat from the pocket of her shorts and jammed it back on her head. She picked up her bike and straddled it. I thought it was so cool the way she did that, like a cowboy on a horse.

We rode up the road a bit and back. Part of the time I could see the roof of the shed where the doll lay on its carving board. I could see the sun gleaming black on the side windows and I imagined how hot it would be in there now, and the smell of the sawdust. It would be even hotter under the sheet. Quit it Matt! Turn it off!

Cars passed us, heading into the canyon. I noticed how they slowed at Aunt Gerda's to stare at the dolls. They'd be wondering what they were or, if they'd seen them before, what had happened to them. Some of the people were probably admiring them, others would be annoyed like Mr. Terlock and think they ruined the beauty of the canyon. A few of the drivers waved to us as they went by. One guy rolled down his window. "Hey Kristin," he yelled. "How come you're not operating your stall today?"

"I'm taking a vacation," Kristin said.

"Too bad." The guy grinned. "I was planning on buying."

"I might open later," Kristin said. "Catch you on your way out."

"What do you sell in your stall?" I asked when he'd whizzed past in a cloud of dust. "Lemonade?"

Kristin rolled her eyes. "Give me a break! No, not lemonade." But she didn't tell me what.

"Lot's of cars," I said when a couple more had passed.

"It's Saturday. On Saturdays and Sundays people pour in here. They hike and picnic and look at the art and stuff. The canyon's full of artists and they put out their paintings every weekend. Dealers come all the time."

I stared at her. "Real dealers? Important ones?"

"I guess. They come up from L.A."

I rode ahead of her, made a wide arc and came back. Real dealers! Imagine if I put out Mom's art and one came and saw the canvases. Imagine if he said: "These are incredible. A new, wonderful talent." I'd ask Aunt Gerda if I could set up a table, or maybe she had a workbench . . . my mind flicked to the workbench in the shed. Not that one.

Abby came on the porch, saw me and waved.

"She's checking," Kristin said softly and I nodded.

We'd stopped in front of the house. It was getting hotter by the minute now and I peeled off my T-shirt and tied it round my waist.

"I have to go," Kristin said. "Duty calls."

Would she let me share her stall if I asked? Maybe I could bring over some of Mom's paintings and then, when people stopped for whatever they bought from her, they'd see them. Did I dare suggest it? Now? And there were a bunch of other things I wanted to know, too, if she'd tell me.

"I was going to ask you something," I said.

"Yeah? What?"

I ran my hands over the greasy handlebars of the bike. Maybe it was too soon to bring up about the paintings. I'd show them to her first, explain about Mom. "Well . . ."

I stared beyond her to the dolls standing still as statues on the grass. Should I ask what happened to Harriette? Or if she'd ever heard the dolls talk? Or . . .

Another car drove by with a screech of its horn.

"I have to go," Kristin said impatiently. "I'm losing customers by the minute."

"Do you know this guy, Terlock?" I blurted out.

"Gene Terlock? Sure. He lives farther back in the canyon. He's got no kids, but I think he and his wife are pretty rich. They own a bunch of houses. He's one of the crowd that wants to get rid of Gerda."

"I know. He was here this morning. With his vigilantes."

Kristin made a face. "He was here again?"

"Do you think he could be the one who messed up the dolls?"

Kristin stared hard at me then slowly shook her head. "I doubt it. It's not . . . not businesslike enough. I think Gene Terlock would always do things properly, you know. He'd come out with some kind of papers and tell Aunt Gerda she had to leave by sundown."

I nodded. "Of course, maybe he did it this way so nobody would suspect him."

"Maybe."

"Well, how about Clay Greeley?" I asked. "Do you know him?"

"I sure do. The Greeleys live down the road. There's just Clay and his dad. How do *you* know him?"

I told her about the three guys last night and I propped up the bike and sprinted to the porch for the two white plastic bags. "These stink of plums," I said.

Kristin took the bags, looked inside, sniffed at them.

"Of course, somebody else could have done it," I said. "One of the vigilantes or . . ."

Kristin interrupted. "Somebody *could*, but I bet Clay and those two geek friends of his *did*. That's just like Clay Greeley. I swear, he's such a bully. One time he got hold of Fee and he pushed his head down and made the poor little guy eat grass before he'd let him up."

"Why?"

"Just cause Clay Greeley thought it was funny. I got him in school, though. I punched him out good." Kristin scratched at a mosquito bite on her leg.

"You punched out a boy?"

"Sure. I'd punch out any boy any time I felt like it. That Clay's slime time. Little kids, old ladies . . . want to go get him?"

"Now?" I asked.

"Sure now."

"I'd have to take Ab."

"You could tell her we have to go someplace and we'll be back in half an hour."

"No. And anyway, I'd want to take her. I wouldn't leave her here with . . ." I stopped.

"Are you afraid of the dolls, or Gerda?" Kristin's voice was cold as stone.

"Well, I'm not afraid, exactly. It's just . . ."

Kristin glared at me. "Great. You're just like everyone else. You think Gerda's bonkers and you're scared she might hurt Abby or something. That's it, isn't it?" A bee bigger than any I'd every seen came buzzing around our heads. I swiped at it and it took off.

"I know she wouldn't hurt Ab," I said. "But she does act kind of funny."

"Wouldn't you if you were here all alone with only a bunch of dolls to talk to? If hardly anybody ever came in your shop anymore, and you had no money, and nobody to turn to, and the phone company took out your phone, and you can't pay the electric bill, and you think one of these days you're going to lose your house and you'll have to go live in an old people's home?"

"Listen," I said feebly, trying to hide my embarrassment. Were things *that* bad for Aunt Gerda? And still she'd sent for us?

"No, you listen. Gerda's just the sweetest, kindest person in the whole world. She came to our house every day, every single day, when Mom caught chickenpox from Fee or me, and we were all sick. My mom's left Fee with her a bunch of times. Do you think my mom would leave Fee with a crazy lady? You have some nerve, Matt O'Meara."

I was getting pretty mad myself. "Why don't you just cool it," I said. "My mom left me in charge of Ab. I look out for her, that's all."

We were glaring at each other now and I wished I'd let her go when she'd wanted to. I'd never ask to share her stall. I'd set up one of my own. "I thought you had to go," I said pointedly.

A big, fancy station wagon with wood trim pulled up outside the house.

"It's Mr. Stengel," Kristin muttered. "He's a friend of Gerda's."

"Oh. My mistake. I thought you said she didn't *have* any friends," I said, in a rotten sneering way I can pull out if I try.

It was wasted on Kristin. She was walk-straddling her bike down the path, calling, "Hi, Mr. Stengel" to the man who was getting out of the car.

He wore a white suit and a pink shirt and he was the smallest, most perfect little old man I'd ever seen. I tried not to stare, but it was hard. This guy wasn't much bigger than I am.

Kristin dropped her bike at the end of the path and I followed and propped mine beside it. I was still holding the bags and I jammed them into my jeans pockets.

"Hello, Kristin." The man's gaze went past her to the dolls. "What on earth . . .?" His voice was strange, too, high and squeaky.

"It happened last night. Some slime time did it."

Mr. Stengel took out a pink handkerchief and wiped the top of his head, which was bald and perspiring. "This is terrible. How is poor Mrs. Yourra?"

"She's upset. But she'll be O.K. This is Matt. He and his sister are living here now."

Mr. Stengel had a warm smile that crinkled his eyes and made furrows on his smooth forehead. "Hello,

Matt. Mrs. Yourra told me you were coming. She was looking forward to it. What a shame someone had to do this!" He tut-tutted, looking at the dolls, then held out his hand for me to shake. "It looks like they're starting to harrass your aunt again," he said. "Sometimes I think her life would be easier if she got rid of the dolls."

"She never will, Mr. Stengel," Kristin said. "You know that."

"I know. It's too bad people have to be so cruel."

Kristin looked directly at me. "They can be cruel all right."

Aunt Gerda and Abby had come out on the porch and Mr. Stengel went up and spoke softly to Aunt Gerda and shook hands in a grown-up way with Abby. Even from here I could see Ab was overcome.

We all sat on the porch, Aunt Gerda and Mr. Stengel in the rockers, the three of us on the steps.

Aunt Gerda brought out lemonade.

"Have you told the police what happened, Mrs. Yourra?" Mr. Stengel asked.

"I see no point in it. The Sierra Maria police haven't been too sympathetic to me or the children. They have had complaints, of course, and then there was that petition Gene Terlock produced to have me remove the children from the front yard. The police didn't seem to understand when I told them the children like it out here where they can see the traffic passing."

We sat silently, watching the cars and campers cruise by. Aunt Gerda sighed: "I wish people wouldn't take it out on the children, though. I can handle anything: words scrawled on the wall, letters. But the children are so innocent."

There was another silence as we looked at them, standing in their innocence. I wormed my hand under the bags in my right-hand pocket and touched the hate filled note. There'd been others like this, then. This one wasn't the first.

"Ah, well." Aunt Gerda smiled shakily at Mr. Stengel. "Are you out on an art hunt today, Mr. Stengel?"

"Indeed. I've heard that a very good young artist has just moved into the cottage on Tor Point." He glanced at his watch. "In fact, I have an appointment for a showing. I should be on my way." He drained the rest of his lemonade and set the glass on the wicker table.

I thumped mine down on the porch steps. "You . . . ah . . . you buy art?" Something strange seemed to have happened to my breathing.

"That's right." Mr. Stengel smiled his crinkly smile. "Are you interested in purchasing some, young man?" He stood and whipped a card from the pocket of his jacket.

HAROLD STENGEL: BLACK ORCHID GALLERY
3424 LA CIENEGA BLVD., LOS ANGELES

"Actually," I said, "my mom is an artist. She was. She died."

"Do you remember the painting in my living room,

Mr. Stengel?" Aunt Gerda asked quickly. "The one of the beach and the house on the cliff?"

"Indeed. Certainly." There was something in the smooth way he answered that made me think he didn't remember it at all and was just being polite.

"I could show it to you again," I said. "And we have others."

"I would definitely be interested, Matthew, but not today. I'm overloaded with appointments." He helped Aunt Gerda up. "Now Mrs. Yourra, do you have any of those wonderful cans of clams left? I can't find them anywhere but in your shop. And I could use some more of that Tate and Lyle syrup for my morning pancakes and that English jelly." He took Aunt Gerda's arm and they went in the house, she so big and Mr. Stengel so small. I decided that must be pretty much the way Kristin and I would look if we stood together.

"You know what?" Kristin whispered. "I think Mr. Stengel comes because he likes Gerda . . . you know, LIKES her. I just figured that out. Wouldn't it be great if he wanted to marry her? Wouldn't it be super? He's rich, PLUS he's nice."

"But they're so old," I said. "Both of them."

"So?" Kristin was glaring at me. "What about it?"

For a minute there she seemed to have gotten over being mad at me. Now I could see she was getting ready to begin again.

"Nothing about it," I said quickly. "It would be great."

I went slowly inside, watching as Mr. Stengel made

his choices and Aunt Gerda put them in a brown paper sack. Did I dare? Did I? She was making change out of a black purse when I ran up the stairs and grabbed the portfolio.

"Wait till he sees these!" I told Mom's portrait. "He's talking about a new young artist! Just wait till he sees your pictures." I came out so fast I skidded on the rug.

Downstairs, the screen door slammed and Aunt Gerda called: "Matthew? Mr. Stengel is leaving now."

"Too late," I told Mom. "But don't worry. Next time I'll be quicker."

We all stood at the bottom of the path, waving as he left, and I called "come back soon" louder than anyone.

"I've got to take off, too," Kristin said and I went with her to her bike.

"I'm sorry I got mad at you," she said. "It's just Gerda has it so rough, and you were so nerdy about her."

"I was not."

"O.K., O.K. Anyway, do you want to go tomorrow and tackle that creep Greeley?"

"I don't know if I can," I said. "I mean, Abby . . ."

"Oh sure. Abby."

I glanced at Kristin suspiciously. Did she think I was only using Ab as an excuse? I couldn't tell what she was thinking as she gazed up at the sky where the hawk was somersaulting again.

"I'm not afraid of Greely, if that's what you're trying

to say," I told her. "Anyway, we're not sure if he's the one who did it."

Kristin shrugged. "Well, I'm going. You can come if you want."

"Why are *you* going? She's not *your* aunt."

"She's my friend. That's just as good. And I've known her a lot longer than you have."

"Well, I'm going too then. I'll fix it somehow with Ab."

"Fine. Do you want to come to church with us?"

"Church?" I paused. "I don't know. Does Aunt Gerda go?"

"We used to pick her up every Sunday but not anymore. She won't leave the children."

"Oh. Well, I'll have to see. I'll skip it for tomorrow though. Thanks anyway."

"I'll come by after lunch then." She turned from me and walked toward the dolls. "Bye, kids. See you tomorrow."

I waited, half expecting to hear a chorus of "byes," knowing how crazy it was but expecting it anyway. But the only sound was a high distant shriek and I saw that the hawk had swooped and was streaking up into the sky carrying something small and furry in his talons.

7

THAT NIGHT I asked Aunt Gerda where I should keep the bike. I had no lock and there was no way I was going to have it outside where anyone could steal it. "Should I bring it in the house?" I asked, hoping and hoping she wouldn't say: "Put it in the shed, Matthew. That door has a lock."

"It will be perfectly safe on the porch," she said instead. "I plan on being out there all night."

"All night? Till morning?" I asked, sounding stupid and probably looking stupid, too. Mrs. Valdoni and I had sat up all night with Mom three times, but that was different.

Aunt Gerda was opening a can of Dinty Moore Beef Stew, emptying it into a pot on the stove. "I won't leave the children unprotected again," she said.

"But . . ." Didn't she know she couldn't sit up with them every night? She'd have to sleep sometime.

It was as if she knew what I was thinking because

she smiled. "Don't worry, Matthew. You don't need as much rest when you get older. And I'll be quite comfortable. I may doze off, but I'll be visible anyway, right there under the porch light."

That was one of the things that was worrying me. Would she be safe? What was to stop someone from skulking out there in the darkness and throwing plums at her? Or from doing something worse?

"Why don't we just bring the dolls inside," I said. "That would be easier." I gave a fake smile. "They'd be company for Derek and Arabella." Derek smiled at me from his stand by the couch. Aunt Gerda and Abby had worked all day on Fern's dress and now she was outside again and Arabella stood in her place.

Arabella was pinned into a flowered sundress that left her wooden shoulders and arms bare, and Abby was busily trying hats on her, standing on a stool to reach, standing back to get the effect. I'd almost protested when she got a hand mirror so Arabella could see herself, but what was the use? I decided I'd wait till we were alone and remind Ab again that this was only play.

Aunt Gerda stirred the stew with a wooden spoon. "I have considered bringing the children in," she said. "But that would be like submitting to these people. What right have they to tell me what to do on my own property? Why should the children have to move?"

"But I'm worried about you being out there." I lowered my voice so Abby wouldn't hear. "Look, why don't I sleep outside, too. Just in case." The thought of the night, the dolls moving restlessly in the dark made me shiver, but that was silly. They'd be no more frightening in the night than in the day.

Aunt Gerda touched my hand. "No, Matthew. A boy needs his sleep and I'll be perfectly fine. But thank you. Now . . ." She lifted the pot from the stove and spooned stew into three blue bowls, steam rising, wafting in my direction.

"It smells great," I said.

"Yes. We won't go hungry. There's enough food in the shop to do us for a long time."

Since hardly anyone's buying, I thought, except maybe Mr. Stengel and a few old friends. Still, it was a relief to know there was lots to eat.

She pointed to the zucchini and onion salad on the table. "And we always have the garden."

"*I'd* like to learn how to garden," I said.

"See?" She gave me another smile. "They can't get *us* down."

Later that night she came in our room to hear my little sister's prayers and to tuck us in. Then I read *Goodnight Moon* twice to Ab, watching and waiting for her eyes to close, which they usually do by the time we get to "goodnight mittens." Tonight, too.

I lay very still then, listening. Was Aunt Gerda outside already? No, because I could hear her talking softly to someone in her bedroom across the hall. Was it to one of the dolls? Nervousness twitched inside me and it was hard not to be scared, hard not to listen for a change of voice if a doll should answer. I tiptoed across to our door and opened it.

The house was so old that nothing fitted properly, and I could see light gleaming through the crack underneath and through the space at the side of Aunt Gerda's door. I could hear through that space, too, when I got closer.

"I wish you were here to share things with me, Joseph. Nothing was ever as hard when you were with me, not even Harriette's death. I'm strong, though. I'm strong enough to handle this. But now it's not only myself and the children. I have Matthew and little Abby. They're dear to me already, as dear as their mother was to us. This is the only home they have now, Joseph. I won't let anyone force us out of it."

There was a squeaking sound, as if she'd risen from a chair with sagging springs, and then her footsteps coming quickly in my direction.

I stood, numbed. No time to dash back across the hall. She'd find me for sure. I pressed myself against the wall where I'd be behind the door when she opened it. I heard her come out. If she closed the door now, there I'd be. What would she think of me, spying on her like this? What did I think of myself? Not much.

She left the door open. Through the gap by the hinges I saw her walk along the hall. She was carrying a gray blanket, and round her shoulders was the kind of navy pea coat that sailors wear in Seattle. I flattened myself against the cold plaster and held my breath till she disappeared down the stairs. Then I slid out of my hiding place. It wasn't that I'd meant to listen, I told myself. I'd just wondered who she was talking to, and now I knew. It wasn't to one of the dolls, it was to her dead husband. Was that any better?

But then I glanced into her room and saw the photograph on the wall. The man with the stiff collar and the stiff mustache that did nothing to hide his gentle smile would be Uncle Joseph. She'd been talking to his picture the way I do to Mom's. I'd never thought I was crazy, had I? Great the way I'd decided *she* was.

All in all I didn't feel real good about myself as I got my little alarm clock, set it by the light from the landing and got back into my cot.

Even though we'd left the curtains open and some light from the landing came round and under the door, the room was pretty dark. I thought about the tool shed below. The half-finished doll was probably a girl since they would have wanted a girl to replace Harriette. Her name would start with an "I," since "I" came after "H." Isabel? Iris?

I punched up my pillow, molded it around my head and tried to make myself think about nice things, like Mr. Stengel's beaming at me: "These are your mother's paintings? They're wonderful. She was truly a magnificent artist."

But I couldn't get the thinking to work and I turned over and drifted into sleep.

It was the alarm that woke me at 3 A.M.! I stifled it on the second ring, before it could waken Ab. 3 A.M.! The time I'd set it for. I got up, pulled on my jeans and sweatshirt and went quietly out of the room. The house was filled with light. What was it Kristin had said about the electric bill? There'd be a big one this month all right.

When I stood at the top of the stairs, I could see Derek and Arabella. Aunt Gerda must have moved them so they could stand together because they sure as heck hadn't moved themselves.

Derek's jacket and T-shirt were off and his chunky polished chest and stomach were bare. His skin gleamed as if it had been polished. It wasn't skin, of course, but wood, so it could have been polished. Maybe he'd smell of lemon, like Mrs. Valdoni's furniture.

Arabella had added white lacy gloves to her outfit and there was a sparkly pin on the front of her sundress. I couldn't decide if Aunt Gerda's dolls were creepier dressed or undressed. The two of them smiled their welcomes at me as I came down the stairs and I scared myself because I almost said "hi" to them.

Through the screen door, I saw the lighted porch and the spotlight at the bottom of the front yard that shone toward me like a great, white eye. Crickets chirped a noisy chorus and from somewhere close came the hollow hoot-hoot of a night owl.

As soon as I pushed open the door Aunt Gerda rose from her chair and the pea coat slipped from her shoulders. "Matthew? What's the matter? Are you sick?"

I shook my head.

"Abigail?"

"We're fine." I couldn't see the dolls on the grass but

· 71 ·

I sensed their sightless eyes watching me. Shivers ran up and down my skin. "It's my turn for guard duty," I said. "You go in now and get some sleep."

"Oh, Matthew!" She'd been working on Derek's jacket and she stuck the needle in the lapel and put the pile of fabric on top of her sewing box on the table. "Come here, Matthew!"

The door banged behind me as I went closer and let her take my hands. "My dear, this is the sweetest thing. You actually wakened yourself and came down here . . ." Her eyes brimmed with tears.

"It's O.K.," I said, embarrassed suddenly. "You go get some sleep now. I don't mind."

"I'll do no such thing. But I was just going to make myself a cup of hot chocolate. Would you like some? I'd be glad of your company."

"Sure. That sounds great."

We made it together, carried it back to the porch and sat quietly in the rockers drinking it. I told myself there was a little night breeze now and that was what I was hearing, moving nervously in the trees. It wasn't the dolls whispering. It wasn't. I made myself take a sip of hot chocolate and then sit back. "I was wondering," I said. "Why don't you get a dog, Aunt Gerda?"

"We've had dogs. Our last one was Laird. When he was twelve years old he was hit by a car, right there in front of the house. Poor old Laird! There's so much traffic in the canyon." She shook her head. "I'd never risk another dog, not unless the yard was fenced, and for now that's out of the question."

"I could build us a fence."

She smiled. "I could help."

There was no traffic in the canyon now, nothing but the monotonous cry of the owl, the crick-crick of the crickets, the night pressing itself against the light around us.

"We had a dog called Jim when your mother was a little girl and stayed with us here in the summers. Every day, when she'd take her sketch pad and go up in the canyon, Jim went, too. He lay behind the door for weeks, after she went home. I guess that dog missed her just as much as we did."

The rockers bumped gently on the wooden porch as we moved back and forth. I thumbed away a tear that had started a slow trickle down my cheek. Aunt Gerda picked up Derek's jacket and stood. "I have to try this on him. You just sit there quietly with your memories, dear Matthew. I'll be back in a minute."

I found a tissue in the pocket of my jeans and blew my nose. How long did it take Jim to come out from behind the door? How long did it take him to understand Mom wasn't coming back? Weeks? Months? I know, Jim. I know. I blew my nose again and rocked to ease the pain.

Inside I could hear the murmur of Aunt Gerda's voice as she talked to Derek.

Criminy! I'd forgotten that I was out here in the dark, alone with the dolls. I sat up stiff and straight and peered into the darkness.

Aunt Gerda pushed open the door. "It's going to fit

beautifully, thank goodness." She lowered her voice. "Derek can be difficult."

I nodded. In a strange way I was beginning to understand why she talked to the dolls and treated them as if they were real. It was so lonely here, so silent and still. And it must be extra hard for her, being alone all the time since Uncle Joseph died. Was Kristin right that Mr. Stengel "liked" her?

"I was thinking," I said hesitantly. "Mr. Stengel is very nice."

"Yes." She searched in the sewing box for a thimble. "Do you know when he'll be back?"

"He's coming more often now that he has this . . . this new interest." I thought I saw the flicker of a smile in her eyes. "Now he comes about every two weeks. I guess he's hoping I'll change my mind."

So Kristin *was* right after all. But Aunt Gerda wasn't jumping into anything.

"I don't think he remembered Mom's painting," I said.

"I imagine he sees a lot of paintings. It's probably hard to remember every single one. We'll make sure he sees all of them next time and we'll make sure he remembers."

"That's what I was thinking." We smiled at each other.

I watched her take the pins from the lapel of the jacket and begin to sew with small, fine strokes. Sleep was beginning to fill my eyes, making it hard for me to keep them open. A yawn swelled like an explosion in my throat. I tried to hide it but Aunt Gerda saw and laughed. "Go, dear Matthew. Go to bed. And thank you."

"If you're sure. If there's nothing I can do."

"I'm sure."

I got up and leaned over to hug her. She smelled of chocolate. "Well anyhow, you're not alone anymore," I said. "You've got me now . . . and Ab."

She patted my cheek. "That's right. And we'll take care of each other. Goodnight, Matthew."

"Goodnight."

I opened the screen door and almost fell over Derek. He was standing just inside, as if watching us, or listening.

"What . . ." I stepped back, the door bumping and slapping itself against my face. Derek grinned at me through the mesh.

"Aunt Gerda," I stuttered. "Derek . . ."

"Oh, I should have warned you. Is he in the way?"

I heard the rustle as she stood up, but I didn't turn. I didn't want to turn my back on Derek.

"I moved him so he'd be closer for his fittings," she said.

"Oh." But when had she moved him? When she'd gone inside, while I'd been sitting on the porch. Of course. But I hadn't heard anything. I hadn't even heard the roll of the spool across the floor. Maybe I'd been too deep in my thoughts. Of course, that was what it was.

"Well, goodnight again," I said edging around Derek, careful not to brush against his smooth, wooden chest.

But how silly I'd been to panic like that. I could just see the way Kristin would raise her eyebrows if she knew. Well, she wouldn't know.

Even so, as I went up the stairs I kept checking back over my shoulder. Just in case Derek was coming after me.

8

KRISTIN HAD said she'd be here at two so we could ride over to Clay Greeley's. We were going to warn him. If he was the one messing with Aunt Gerda and the dolls, he'd better lay off. But Kristin came earlier with her parents and Fee. I was on the porch, polishing my bike, keeping busy so I wouldn't get too nervous about going to Greeley's, when her dad sounded the horn.

Aunt Gerda and Ab came out right away and Kristin introduced us all. Then her mom told Aunt Gerda how sorry she'd been to hear about the children. She meant the dolls, of course, not Ab and me. I was getting used to the children not being us. She and Kristin walked over to admire Derek's new outfit and Arabella's sundress and Mrs. Ericson said Mr. Ericson had a nice pair of gray pants that were too small for him since he'd put on weight, and she thought they could be altered to fit George, and she'd bring them over.

Mr. Ericson said he'd fit into the pants as soon as his

diet started working and Mrs. Ericson poked his stomach and asked, "What diet?" The way they talked to each other was so friendly and loving it made my throat ache. Had Mom and Dad talked to each other like this? It hurt that I couldn't remember.

The grownups went inside then and Kristin and Fee and Ab and I sat on the porch steps.

"I've got a tortoise," Fee told Abby. "His name's Giant. I painted my phone number on his shell so if he gets lost he'll know where he lives."

Abby sat up. "I know *my* phone number. It's six three six, four nine three two."

"That's not our number anymore, Ab," I said gently. "That was at home. We don't have a phone here."

"Oh." Ab stuck her fingers in her mouth and Fee said, "You can share mine if you like." He told her his number and the two of them began rhyming it off, giggling and making faces.

"Are we going to Greeley's early?" I asked Kristin. "I thought you said two."

"I did. It's just, we stop by here some Sundays on the way home from church so Mom and Dad can buy a bunch of groceries from Gerda."

"They *do*?"

"Yeah. She doesn't have much, of course. But Mom says every little bit helps her. She's too proud to take money for nothing. I think my dad has tried."

I nodded. "Your parents are nice. You're lucky."

"I know. Anyway, I'll be back for you around two."

"O.K."

Two was hours away, and I was jumpy already!

She was back at ten after. Ab and I were waiting for her at the end of the path.

"Abby wanted to come," I explained to Kristin who raised her eyebrows. She didn't have to say "Oh really?" Her eyebrows said it for her. I didn't say: "She doesn't like me to leave her. I can't help it." I hoped my spread out hands said that for me.

"Well, anyway let's go. Clay Greeley will be out at his stall. At least we'll have no trouble finding him." Kristin took off, riding like fury down the road and I took off after her, standing to pump the pedals, Abby in the bike seat behind me, clutching handfuls of my T-shirt. "Hold tight, Ab," I ordered, and I knew I was glad to have her with me even if I wasn't exactly sure why. Maybe I don't like to be separated from her either.

Kristin had said it wasn't far to the Greeley house but it seemed far, riding in the loose soft dirt at the edge of the road to stay clear of the traffic. It was hot, even in the shade of the hedges and Abby's little hands were sweaty through my shirt. My legs felt weak. How humiliating if I had to stop and rest while Kristin raced ahead! She'd think I was slowing because I was scared. Well, I was scared. Scared enough to want to turn tail and jet out of here. I wished Blinky and John were with me. I'd even settle for Knock Knock. The four of us had stood up to the Rawlins gang on the playground that time. Well, Blinky and John and Knock Knock weren't with me now. It was just me and Kristin. I made myself put on a spurt of speed and lessen the gap between us.

And then we swung round a bend in the road and I saw Kristin come to her special brake stop with both feet dragging in the dirt. We were there.

The Greeley house sat in the middle of a bald brown yard, small and poor and neglected. Not newly poor the way Aunt Gerda's was. This one had been that way since the beginning, more like a shelter for animals than a house for people. Part of the roof had caved in and the wooden wall had patches of peeling paint, crusty as scabs.

The best looking thing around was the stall that had been set up inside the front yard, parallel to the road. I saw it and thought, that's the kind I'll have when I start to sell Mom's paintings. If Mr. Stengel doesn't buy them all first. Mine will be sturdy and strong like this, the three clean planks held up by nice saw horses on either end.

There were two customers in front of the stall and three guys behind it, selling. It wasn't hard to figure them for Clay Greeley and the heavenly twins. I stopped and held the bike while Ab stepped onto the pedals and then to the ground.

"Oh, look Matt!" She was gone, running from me to a cardboard box with a hand-lettered sign: RABBITS FOR SALE. $2. Someone had done a drawing of a rabbit with long floppy ears on the side of the box.

By now the two customers were walking back to their car and Clay Greeley had spotted us. He said something to one of the twins and the three of them began tittering and staring in our direction.

"Hi, Kristin," Greeley called. "Who are your friends?"

"Don't worry about it. This isn't a friendly visit," Kristin said.

"Let me do this," I whispered.

"Did you think I was coming to just stand around and be quiet?" she whispered back. "Think again."

Now I was getting a good look at Clay Greeley and I was deciding that he wasn't that scary after all. I don't know what I'd been expecting. A monster maybe, straight out of an old Maurice Sendak book, or a dude in a black leather jacket with a switchblade behind his ear.

This guy had a face that was round as a pumpkin and covered with freckles, and his hair was pumpkin colored too, soft and short and feathery. I sighed with relief. Clay Greeley wasn't even that big. The twins had long pale faces and pale eyes. Mrs. Valdoni would have said they looked sickly, and if they'd lived in our building she'd have told their mother to give them cod liver oil. Cod liver oil was Mrs. Valdoni's answer to everything.

I stopped to look in the rabbit box which had an old piece of heavy screening laid across the top. "Isn't he darling, Matt?" Abby breathed.

"Go ahead, pick him up, kid. Make yourself at home," Clay Greeley called. "It pays to let the customers check out the merchandise. That's what a wise man once told me." He waved to Kristin and me, inviting us closer. "What can I do for you two?"

Kristin had edged herself ahead of me somehow and I stepped beside her so the two of us were in front of the stall, facing the other three in back.

"If you're the one who's bugging Mrs. Yourra, you can stay away," I said. "I'm Matt O'Meara and I've come to live with her. Me and my sister." I jerked my head in the direction of Ab who was sitting beside the box now, the rabbit in her lap. Little as Ab is she'd managed to lift the screening off. I lowered my voice. "If you guys have plans to hassle my aunt anymore just forget it. I'm there now."

"Oh wow!" One of the twins nudged the other with his elbow. "Oh wow, this guy is maxi tough. We have to look out for *this* guy."

"That's right," I said.

There was a wooden crate filled with avocados on the stall in front of me. The sign said AVOCADOES, FOUR FOR A DOLLAR. I wondered if avocados was spelled right because if it wasn't that might be a clue, but I couldn't tell because I didn't know how to spell it myself. There were some small, bumpy-looking colored rocks marked CRYSTALS, DIFFERENT PRICES, and there were lemons, 10 CENTS EACH, and oranges tied in plastic sacks, the kind I'd found in Aunt Gerda's yard.

"Any *plums* for sale?" I asked.

"Plums? Plums?" Clay Greeley grinned at Castor or maybe Pollux. "Do we have plums?"

"Not anymore." The twin grinned back.

"What he means is, we had plums," Greeley said.

"We got trees in back. But we used them all up. And what's left are all rotted out."

"Or the birds got them," the other twin said, his pale eyes wide and innocent.

"Course, sometimes we clean up what's lying on the ground," his brother said. "We like to keep Clay's place neat and tidy."

Kristin jabbed a finger toward Clay Greeley. "We don't want any rotten plums or anything else at Gerda's," she said. "You're such a smut, Greeley. You give me a big, fat pain."

"Aw. He's real worried about that," Castor or Pollux said.

"Yeah," Greeley's grin spread. "I won't be able to sleep tonight I'll be so worried."

"*I* won't be sleeping tonight," I said. "You come near Aunt Gerda's and I'm going to get you. I mean it. Leave her alone."

Greeley and I were almost eyeball to eyeball now, with both of us leaning across the stall and suddenly I realized that he *was* scary. You just didn't notice it at first. The scary things were his eyes. They didn't go with the round, freckled face and the big, gummy grin. His eyes were adult eyes, the kind of adult who doesn't like anything or anybody. Tough, mean, cold. My heart started hammering.

"So what if we want to get rid of your crazy old aunt," Greeley said. "You can't stop us. We do what we like. And if you want to help her you'll tell her to get out of our canyon."

"And take her ghost children with her?" I asked. So they *were* the ones. "Write her another letter, why don't you?"

"This bozo's real brave," one twin told the other.

"Well, he'd have to be, wouldn't he, living up there with the witch and the talking dolls."

I glanced nervously over my shoulder at Ab but she was playing with the rabbit, totally absorbed.

Kristin took over. "She's not a witch and the dolls don't talk. That's the dumbest . . ."

"Yeah? Clay Greeley's cold gray eyes stared into mine. "Don't tell that to the twins. They *heard* them."

"Oh sure," Kristin said sarcastically.

"We heard them all right. And we weren't the only ones. Billy Jackson was with us and Card Killander."

"Sure," Kristin said again. "Great bunch there. And what were the dolls saying, Pollux?"

"He's Pollux." Castor thumbed toward the other twin.

"Go ahead and tell them what you heard," Clay Greeley ordered.

"You want me to?"

"That's what I'm telling you, isn't it?" Clay said impatiently.

"Well, it was real dark. It was about one in the morning and we were just walking past, on the road . . ."

"One in the morning and you were just walking past on the road?" I raised my eyebrows the way Kristin does and tried to sound disbelieving, because I knew I didn't want to hear this and didn't want to believe it if I did hear it. I didn't want to know. The sun beat down on us, white and burning, but that coldness was creeping under my skin again. I spread my fingers hard on the edge of the stall.

"The doll way in back was saying something about the moon and lightning . . ."

"And about a flower, and death . . . that was the worst," Pollux said. "The flower and death part."

"And then another one, the one with the yellow hair that we threw the paint . . ." Pollux stopped and I knew he'd been talking about Derek and that they were for sure the ones who'd splashed the paint all over him and who'd done the other stuff, too. I wanted to face him with that, with what he'd just said, but I couldn't interrupt him now. Not when he was telling me this about the dolls.

Castor shivered. "Anyway, the one with yellow hair by the path said 'Goodnight' in this creaky, croaky kind of voice. It freaks me out just thinking about it."

"He said '*Sweet* goodnight,' that's what he said," Pollux corrected. "Get it right."

"O.K. Sweet goodnight. But it still freaks me out."

My teeth were clenched so tightly my jaw hurt and my fingers spread on the table had gone numb.

"And did you say goodnight back?" Kristin asked, grinning. "I bet you did. You're such a dork, Pollux."

"I'm Castor, and I didn't say a word. I took off like a bat out of daylight. We all did."

In the silence a truck pulled in behind us and a

· 85 ·

woman got out and came over. "I'll take ten of those lemons. Here's a dollar."

Clay Greeley put the lemons in one of the plastic bags, took her dollar and said, "Our oranges are very nice today, too, ma'am." Nice, polite, freckle-faced little pumpkin head Clay Greeley.

The woman shook her head. "I'm up to the gazoos in oranges of my own, but thanks anyway."

Clay put the money in a red wooden cigar box and said, "Come again."

The woman was gone and we were left standing in silence. I swallowed to get my voice under control. "So, if you think the dolls talk, stay away. Then you won't have to hear them. Come on, Kristin."

I swung around and almost stepped on Abby who was right behind me holding the rabbit. "Can I get it, please, Matt? Please, please. It's two dollars."

"I tell you what," Clay Greeley said before I could speak. "Because you're this nice guy's sister and to welcome you to the canyon you can have it for free."

"Truly?" Abby was squirming, too happy to stand still. The bunny nestled against her neck. "Matt?"

"You can't have it, Ab. Put it back."

"But Matty . . ."

"Oh, he's so *mean*," one of the twins said. "He's mean to his little sister."

"Matty . . . can't I . . ."

"Put it back, Abby. Aunt Gerda didn't say we could bring home a rabbit. And besides . . ." Besides, I didn't want her taking anything from this guy, or buying anything either.

· 86 ·

"We have to go right now, Abby," I said instead. I took the rabbit, settled it in the box, and put the screen back on top.

"You *are* mean," Ab whispered. "He said I could have it."

I grabbed her hand and pulled her toward the bike, "Well I say you can't." This was all I needed, to have Ab start whining.

Behind us, I heard Kristin speaking to Clay Greeley. "So you're selling crystals now, too, Greeley. Thanks a lot. I really appreciate the competition."

Then Clay Greeley's voice. "All's fair in business, Kristin. And even if it wasn't . . ." I heard his laugh.

Abby kept her face turned from me as I lifted her into the bike seat.

"Listen," I whispered. "We'll ask Aunt Gerda, and if she says it's O.K., we'll get you a bunny somewhere else, all right?"

She kept her face turned away. "I wanted this one."

"Kid?" Clay Greeley called. "Little girl?" Abby looked back. "Don't worry about not taking the rabbit. If nobody buys him, my old man and me'll just put him in the stew pot."

Abby gasped and clutched at me. Her eyes were terrified. "He says . . ."

"I heard what he said. He's just trying to scare you. Don't listen to him, Ab."

I could hear their awful tittering as we rode away and I was filled with helpless rage. Clay Greeley had known I wouldn't let Ab take a rabbit from him and he'd known telling her about the stew would scare her to death. He'd like doing something like that . . .

Kristin was still yelling back at Greeley. "Remember the time I beat you up in school, Clay Greeley? Do you want me to do it again?"

"Aw Kristin, you're scaring me. I *let* you hit me the last time cause I'm so polite. Next time I'm going to forget you're a girl."

Abby was whimpering and gulping in the seat behind me. As soon as we got round the bend in the road I stopped, lifted her down and knelt beside her. Kristin stopped, too.

"Ab," I said. "I'm sorry you couldn't have the bunny. But those boys aren't nice. Kristin and I think they're the ones who did the bad things to Aunt Gerda's dolls."

"She wouldn't want you to take a bunny from them," Kristin added.

Tears rolled down Abby's face. "But he's going to *kill* it."

"No he's not," Kristin said. "He's not going to kill anything he can sell for two dollars. Not Clay Greeley."

"Come on, Ab," I said. "Let's go home and see the dollies."

There was a stream of traffic now and we walked single file, pushing the bikes, Abby in the middle, me in front.

"So now we know for sure they did it," Kristin said. "He just about admitted it. And all that baloney about the dolls talking. Did you ever . . .?"

I stopped her with a nod down at Ab who scuffed along with her head bent, her fingers in her mouth.

"I guess you sell crystals?" I asked Kristin in a light, ordinary voice.

"Yeah. Kristin's crystals. My dad and I find them when we hike back into the mountains. Then I purify them with fire and water so they have good vibes. I'm going to give you one, Abby, a rose quartz. They're pretty, all sparkly like diamonds."

Ab took her fingers out of her mouth. "A fire and water one?" she asked with interest.

"Sure."

I stared back at Kristin. "You *purify* them?"

Kristin winked. "My dad told me the tourists would go for that and he was right. They sell great. Course, now Clay Greeley's getting to the tourists first. What did you think of him, Matt?"

"He's sick," I said.

A string of motorcycles was passing, throttles open, motors roaring. Kristin raised her voice over the noise. "My mom says we have to excuse him for what he is. His dad drinks a lot and he's never there. Clay's mom died when he was real little so there's nobody . . ." She stopped and gave me a quick apologetic glance.

"It's O.K.," I said. "And you don't have to be a creep just because your mother died."

"I know that."

It was too noisy now to talk, but not to think and I didn't want to think. All that stuff about the dolls talking. Clay and the twins were making it up, of course. But what strange words they'd heard the dolls say. Were they smart enough for that? And hadn't I heard the dolls myself, or thought I'd heard them?

I stopped, grabbed Ab's shoulder so she wouldn't step out into traffic and faced Kristin . . . "I have to ask you something. Have *you* ever heard the D-O-L-L-S T-A-L-K?"

I spelled out the last two words and Abby swung around and beat my stomach with her fists. "I hate it when you do that, Matt. What did you say? Tell me."

I held both her little fists in one hand. "Quit it, Ab."

"No. I never heard the D-O-L-L-S T-A-L-K," Kristin said, spelling too. "Because D-O-L-L-S can't T-A-L-K. O.K.?"

"I hope not," I said. "Because if these do we're in big trouble."

"And if you start believing they do, *you're* in very big trouble," Kristin said.

Right then I wasn't sure what I believed.

9

I'D TOLD Clay Greeley I wouldn't be sleeping at all tonight and I'd meant it, because then I'd been determined to take my turn outside. But Aunt Gerda had refused my offer and settled herself on the porch instead. And man, was I glad. The thought of the dolls, standing in the darkness talking to each other was enough to turn my bones to mush. Still, I set my alarm again for three. Every night that Aunt Gerda sat up I'd go down and be with her for a while. That I'd do. And I'd make the hot chocolate and bring it out to her. It wouldn't be so bad, I told myself. I wouldn't be alone.

So when something woke me I thought it must be the alarm, and through my sleep I felt for the clock on the floor beside my cot. It wasn't ringing, though, and when I held it close to my eyes I saw that it was only twenty minutes after one. What had wakened me then? Something. What? I was getting used to the way my heart could start hammering for no reason at all.

I lay listening. Nothing but Abby's soft little snores. But something was wrong, something was missing. Then I knew what it was. There was only silence. Where were the crickets? Why wasn't the owl hooting its monotonous, hollow hoot? Had they taken the night off?

I got up, went cautiously to the door and opened it. The stairs and the house below were filled with light. When I crouched I could see the bottom part of the screen door to the porch and the light shining in from there too. I could also see a little of the curve of the front tire of my bike that I'd propped at the side. Aunt Gerda gave a short rustle of a cough. Nothing wrong. Nothing to worry about.

I crossed to the window. Before we got into bed I'd closed the blue curtains and now I tugged them open. The back yard was dark with just the shaft of white light from the front lying across the vegetable garden, touching the side of the shed. What? I put my face against the glass, then raised the window so I could see better. Was the shed door open? It couldn't be, surely. Didn't Aunt Gerda keep it locked?

I stood, biting my knuckles, trying to think. What was in the shed that anybody would want? Not the rusted, broken-down lawnmower. The bike wasn't there anymore. Maybe the tools. The doll? The thought of that half-finished doll filled me with dread. But why would anybody want to steal her? Why?

I put on my jeans and sneakers, checked on Ab, then went quietly down the stairs. From their stands,

Bethlehem and George watched me. How come the dolls always seemed to be turned facing me? Why was I always looking at their fronts and not their backs?

"Quit staring, will you?" I muttered and hurried past them, outside.

Aunt Gerda smiled up at me from the rocker. "I thought you might come down, Matthew, and I'm sure I should scold you. But it's just so nice to see you and to know you care about me. Sit down for a few minutes, dear."

She leaned forward and lifted a pair of pants off the other chair. "Kristin's mother sent these over with Slim. She was quite right. They will be perfect for George."

I hovered, uncertain. The night air was cool on my bare chest, the sweat cold on my forehead.

"Aunt Gerda . . . I was going to come anyway but . . . something woke me and when I looked out at the back . . . I think the door to the shed is open. Did you leave it that way?"

"No."

The crickets were chirping again, filling the night with their racket. Did crickets stop singing when someone walked close to their homes in the long grass or the zucchini plants? Had someone been out there? Clay Greeley with his old, hard eyes? The long, pale, heavenly twins? Or maybe the vigilante leader, Gene Terlock, tired of businesslike methods, ready to scare Aunt Gerda out any way he could.

Aunt Gerda stood. The pea coat had been loosely

round her shoulders and now she put her arms through the sleeves and buttoned the coat. I hadn't noticed the flashlight by the side of the chair till she picked it up and turned it on. We certainly weren't going to see much by its light. The battery should have been changed months ago. "Matthew, I want you to stay here. I'm going to go back to the shed and check."

"I'm going with you," I said. "No way are you going there alone." I thought she was about to argue and I couldn't help wishing she would. But then she said, "Very well. Just lock up. I have a key."

She waited while I clicked the front door closed and tried the knob, then went down the porch steps ahead of me. In the shadowy garden beyond the lights the dolls stood very still. I heard the faint creak as one of them turned on its pole, the faint creak as it swung back. Oh boy, I thought. Now's the time for a dog, if ever there was a time, a big toothy dog that could leap ahead of us into the darkness. If only we had a dog, or a great heavy club, or . . . One of the Morton Salt signs had fallen across the grass and I picked it up. The top part looked like a rusted tin flag. The bottom was a sturdy stick with a pointed end. It rattled as I carried it and Aunt Gerda looked back at me, saw it, and nodded her approval.

We were round the side of the house now, the pale spot of the flashlight moving like a torn spiderweb in front of us. Aunt Gerda raised the beam and I saw the shed, the darkness inside the half-open door. The door creaked as she pushed it all the way back. "Who's in here?" she asked.

Only silence answered us.

She stepped forward. I stepped behind her, scuffing through the sawdust on the floor. If I'd been brave, I'd have gone ahead, carrying my Morton Salt banner pointed forward like a lance. O.K., I wasn't brave. I made myself small behind Aunt Gerda's bigness, peering around her as the faint light poked into the shed. The tin flag on the end of my lance rattled and I tried to steady it with both hands, felt it shake even more as I saw the empty, bare workbench, the sheet in a bundle on the ground. Iris was gone.

Aunt Gerda gave a little groan, ran forward, picked up the sheet and held it to her face. The flashlight was smothered against her and I took it and made it jump in all directions. There was no one here.

"Do you think someone stole her?" I whispered. "Or did she . . .?" Did she what? Get up and go for a night walk on her own? Get real, Matt. She wasn't even a she, yet, just a lump of timber.

"Who would take her? Who would do such a thing and why?" Aunt Gerda's voice was strong and harsh.

I wanted to say that I knew who, or suspected anyway, and that it was probably done to be mean, to hurt, to take the heart out of her. Instead I moved the beam of the flashlight in the direction of the windows. One had been pushed up and hung at a cockeyed angle on its cords. There was a gap of about twelve inches at the bottom, enough for someone to crawl through, maybe someone pale and sickly and skinny. I saw the white, gouged out wounds at the bottom of the old wood. It had been forced open against the lock. The someone had come in, taken Iris, opened the door and walked out with her. She'd been too bulky to fit through that twelve-inch opening, so he'd made it easy for himself.

Aunt Gerda was striding toward the window and I hurried after her. "Isn't there a light in here?" I whispered.

"There is. I took the bulb for the house a long time ago."

I gave her the flashlight and she shone it through the opening. On the path below lay an iron bar. "Maybe there'll be fingerprints on that," I said. "We can take it to the police." And I thought, when they hear what's missing they'll probably have a good laugh. Missing blocks of wood are probably not very high on their crime list.

The faded flashlight beam drifted around the outside yard, tangled in the grass, shimmied along the shine of the clothesline and then Aunt Gerda gave a gasp, so filled with horror and pain that my heart lurched.

"What?" I whispered. "What is it? Do you see someone?"

"Oh no," she said. "Oh no."

Then she was pushing past me, going fast, taking the flashlight and leaving me alone in the darkness, still saying "Oh no, oh no."

I scurried after her. Don't leave me here. I don't like the dark. I don't like this place. Where was she going anyway? Not back to the house, down toward the bottom of the garden. Damp bits of things stuck themselves against my legs as I followed. My tin flag shook and rattled. A snail shell scrunched under my shoe and some part of my mind recorded that the crickets were quiet again, lying hidden, listening to us blundering through the night. My elbow bumped the swing seat, sending it swaying backward into darkness. "Ouch," I said. "That hurt."

And then I saw the hole in the ground where the grave had been, the earth mounded carelessly on one side, the white cross still standing straight. HERE LIES HARRIETTE, DEARLY BELOVED DAUGHTER . . . But not anymore.

"Oh no," I whispered, like an echo of Aunt Gerda. "Oh no."

Harriette was gone too.

10

I GOT AUNT GERDA inside and upstairs and then went to make her hot chocolate. When I came back with it she was in bed and I sat in the big chair under Uncle Joseph's photograph, letting her be quiet, letting the shaking stop. If only mine would stop. There's something about a grave, disturbed, dug up, that is unholy, even though it's just a doll's grave. And to Aunt Gerda it was worse. That was her child in there, her Harriette.

The clock by her bed ticked louder than my heartbeats. I put down my empty cup.

"Would you like me to leave now so you can sleep? I'll stay out on the porch for a while if you want."

"Thank you, Matthew, but the damage is done. They went in back while I watched in front. They got what they wanted. I don't think they'll come again. Not tonight."

"Will you be all right?"

"Yes. And I think I need to be alone for a while. Goodnight, dear Matthew."

"Goodnight."

I tucked her up the way she'd tucked us up every night since we'd come. She wore what looked like men's pajamas with the sleeves rolled up. The pins were out of her hair and it spread, gray and loose on the pillow. On the very top there was a little bald spot that you couldn't see when she had it piled up. That bald spot almost did me in and I felt tears in my throat. How could they do this to her? I hated them, *hated* them. Hadn't I warned that Clay Greeley to stay away? He was going to get it now all right.

"Try to sleep," I whispered to Aunt Gerda. "And we'll find Harriette and Iris . . ."

"Iris?" she asked wearily.

"The part-finished . . ."

"Oh, you mean Isadora."

"Yes. We'll find them both," I said and tiptoed out.

Before I got into the cot I closed our bedroom curtains tight again and lay, listening to the crickets. The watch crickets. Let them stop chirping and I'd be up in a flash. I closed my eyes, but opened them again when the pictures began coming behind my lids. The heavenly twins digging, pulling Harriette up from the earth, dirt falling from her like drops of water.

Or maybe she'd been in a coffin. Probably. Aunt Gerda and Uncle Joseph wouldn't have just opened a hole and tossed her in. He'd have made the coffin out there in the shed, cutting the wood, hammering the nails the way they did in old Western movies. So the twins and Greeley would have taken the coffin up and opened it, just to make sure that Harriette was inside. Her happy face would have smiled up at them because even when a doll died it would still smile, wouldn't it? Now I was seeing Gene Terlock leaning on the spade, his thin lips stretched in a lizard grin. I hoped the doll smile scared the heck out of him — I hoped he or the twins got heart attacks on the spot.

Thinking about the dead Harriette almost gave me a heart attack myself. Were her eyes open or closed? I curled myself small and cocooned the blanket around me. Greeley and the twins probably carried the coffin along the road on their shoulders the way Mr. Valdoni and Mr. Novis and Archie Shultz and I had carried Mom's. What had they done with Isadora? Tied her on top? If it was Mr. Terlock, he could have put them in his car. Would a coffin fit in a car? But I hadn't heard any car . . .

I jammed my fist against my eyes to stop the thoughts coming, but they wouldn't stop. Sometime I slept, but my dreams were bad, too, and I was glad when Abby woke me to morning and sunlight.

"Can we ask Aunt Gerda about the rabbit?" she demanded right away.

"Not today, Ab," I said.

"But why?"

"Because Aunt Gerda isn't feeling well. And besides, isn't Kristin bringing over the crystal for you?"

"Oh yeah! That's right. I didn't know she was bringing it today."

"She said she would."

I decided it must be pretty nice to be only five and easily distracted.

Sometime in the middle of the night I'd realized that I should get up early and fill in Harriette's grave so Aunt Gerda wouldn't have to look at it and Abby wouldn't see it. But when I went outside I found Aunt Gerda had already done it.

She seemed calm enough as she mixed water and powdered milk in a pitcher but I saw the twitch in one of her eyes and noticed how her hands trembled. Pour Aunt Gerda. Poor doll mother.

Kristin came after eleven. She'd wrapped the crystal in green tissue paper and I let her give it to Ab before I told her what had happened in the night.

"So what are you going to do about it?" she demanded, facing me angrily with her hands on her hips.

"Something," I said vaguely, as if I didn't know. But I did know and I knew when. This time, though, Kristin wasn't going to be in on it. Aunt Gerda was my aunt. This was my cause.

"I swear, Matt O'Meara," Kristin began in a disgusted voice, "if you *don't* you're . . ."

I interrupted her. "Kristin? Could you tell me how Harriette died?" Aunt Gerda had said, "I don't want to talk about it in front of the children," so I lowered my voice and turned my head in case the dolls could read lips.

"Harriette was shot," Kristin said. "Shot first, and now kidnaped. It's not fair."

I picked up my Morton Salt sign and rammed the

point into the wooden step. "Shot? By Greeley?"

"No."

"By one of the vigilantes?"

"No. It was back a while, about six years ago when there was still hunting up here in the canyon. Two guys with rifles drank too much beer and they wandered down here and shot up a bunch of stuff."

Kristin looked up and pointed and I saw that a tin C AND H SUGAR sign tacked to the wall had a rusted hole through the middle. "There used to be a weathervane on top of the house, a rooster crowing. I can sort of remember it. They shot that, too, and then, well, one of them shot Harriette. Three times."

"But did it matter? Couldn't Uncle Joseph take the bullets out and patch her up? I mean, she isn't human."

"One went through her heart, one through her lungs, one went in her leg," Kristin said solemnly.

"But she didn't *have* a heart or lungs. I can see the *leg*, but . . ."

"Joseph and Gerda believed she had. And how do you know she hadn't?"

"Because she was a doll," I said. "Give me a break, Kristin."

Kristin shrugged. "You asked how she died and I told you."

I glanced across at the dolls and I could have sworn they were all leaning toward us, trying to hear.

Kristin jumped up. "I have piano practice. If I don't go home, Mom'll kill me."

"Thanks for bringing the crystal for Abby," I said.

"That's O.K." Kristin hesitated. "We are going to do something about this, aren't we, Matt?"

"I'm thinking about it," I said. I was thinking about nothing else.

Sometimes Abby refuses to take a nap. I hoped it wouldn't be that way today because today I was going to break my word to her, my promise to never leave her alone. While she slept I was going to go to Clay Greeley's. If Harriette and Isadora were there I'd bring them back somehow.

I left as soon as Abby fell asleep. Aunt Gerda was sitting at the kitchen table adding columns of figures in a red ledger. George and Bethlehem stood behind, as if reading over her shoulder. Crikes! George was wearing reading glasses!

"I . . . I didn't know George wore glasses," I said.

Aunt Gerda put a finger on the page to hold her place and turned around. "He doesn't, usually. Abigail found those in one of the bags and I'm really glad. They'll make it easier for him. His eyes have been looking a little weak lately."

I wanted to say "the paint's fading," but I didn't. There were things I couldn't say to Aunt Gerda.

"Well, I'm going for a ride," I told her. "Will you listen for Ab? I'll try to be back before she wakes up."

"Enjoy the sunshine, Matthew. And take your time."

The canyon was quieter today with only the birds

chirping at me from the trees and the small hum of the telephone wires. There was a smell of honeysuckle in the air. But I was in no mood to enjoy any of it. I rode faster than fast so I'd have no time to get more nervous than I was already, and in case I tried to change my mind and chicken out on this. That was possible. With every minute I could feel part of my fierceness ebbing away. Was I rushing into this too fast? After all, I wasn't certain about anything. Maybe I needed to think this out some more. I slowed down, but I got to the house too quickly anyway.

Clay's stall was gone from the front yard now and without it the old, tumbledown place looked worse than it had before. I rang the doorbell twice but no one came, not even when I banged on the wood. The front window was so dirty I couldn't see anything through it even though I put my face up close to the glass. I banged on it, too, before I let myself realize that there was nobody home.

"Shoot," I said under my breath. "Now what?" And I tried not to admit that I was more relieved than disappointed. The door was locked when I tried the handle.

"Locked," I said out loud. "Wouldn't you know?" I was feeling better all the time. I'd tried, hadn't I? That was all anybody could expect. I'd even try some more.

I walked round the side of the house. The stall was there, placed neatly against the back wall, still set up the way it had been on Sunday with its crates of lemons and avocados and bags of oranges. The cardboard signs were stacked flat. They'd just carried everything around here, and I guessed that next week they'd carry everything back.

In a netting wire cage was the rabbit. I poked a finger through the mesh and he sniffed cautiously at it with his soft nose. "Hi," I said. "Hi, rabbit." Someone had given him fresh water and there was a stub of carrot poked through the netting. So he hadn't gone in the stewpot after all. Kristin had been right. Next weekend he'd probably be out in front, for sale again, too.

I walked all the way to the scrubby back hedge, kicking a path for myself through the rotted plums. Ants crawled over my shoes and up my legs. There was no place to hide Harriette or Isadora out here. They had to be inside and I couldn't get inside. I'd have to come back some other time.

And then I saw the open back door to the house. It hung on broken hinges, inviting me inside. Maybe I hesitated for ten seconds, thinking about breaking and entering or whatever it's called when you go in some-body's house without their permission. Whatever it was, it had to be against the law. But look what Clay Greeley had done last night, I told myself. That was against the law too and a heck of a lot worse than just taking a quick look inside his house. I decided there was no way I could wimp out of this and feel O.K. about myself. So I edged through the door.

The inside back porch was filled with old boots and shovels and gardening tools. I picked up one of the shovels and examined it. The blade was thick with dirt. This could be the one they used to dig up Harriette, I thought. But there was no way to be sure.

The small living room was the grungiest room I'd ever seen and the kitchen was worse. Pans of yellow scummy water sat on the floor. I figured they'd been there since it had rained, catching the drips from the leaky roof. Flies buzzed around pans and plates, gummy with food. One glance told me that neither Harriette nor Isadora was here either.

The smell in the bedroom almost made me gag but I forced myself to go in, to pull down the stained sheet and blanket on the tumbled bed in case the dolls were beneath them. No dolls. I yanked a pile of dirty clothes from underneath the bed, poked them back in. I checked through the mess in the closet. Nothing.

I was rushing now, trying to figure how long I'd been here, knowing I was in an inside room with no way out if Clay Greeley or his father came back. I'd be trapped. And what reason could I give for being in the bedroom? In the living room I could maybe bluff something, but not in here.

At the far end of the room was a blue curtain on a pole. My heart was chug-a-lugging the way it does when I start to panic. I didn't want to take the time to look behind that curtain, I wanted out of here, now and fast. But suppose the dolls were back there? What was the sense in leaving without checking?

I hurried across, rattled the curtain open on its rings, and stood staring. Behind was a single bed and a small, wooden chest of drawers. The bed was smoothly and perfectly made, the way I guess a bed in an army barracks would be, with the sheets crisp and white and knife edged, and the corners folded in, neat as envelopes. There wasn't a wrinkle or a bulge. No need to check if the dolls were in *that* bed. They weren't.

The top of the dresser was bare except for a picture of a sad-looking lady in a cheap plastic frame and two pieces of purple crystal that could have been the ones I'd seen on the stall on Sunday. Those drawers were way too shallow to hold the dolls. I turned back toward the other bedroom and looked into the depressing, disgusting mess. Then I pulled the curtain, shutting myself in the corner. This was Clay Greeley's space. I knew it. The only place he could find for himself in this yuck of a house. Maybe he'd tried with all of it and given up. After his mother died? After his dad started drinking?

Some feeling of pity trailed inside of me but I pushed it away. What did I care how hard things were for Clay Greeley? He'd still been rotten enough to do what he did last night, and the other times, too. I jerked up the bed cover and bent to look underneath. Nothing but bare, clean boards and a sharp smell of disinfectant. I was just about to straighten up when I saw the edge of red beneath the dresser. Whatever it was had been pushed well back and it was hard to reach, but I got it out. The Indian Head cigar box that Clay Greeley had used for his cash yesterday on the stall. Should I open it? If he'd hidden it this carefully there might be more inside than money, a clue maybe, something.

I opened the lid. Inside were dollar bills, neatly stacked, and a pile of quarters and dimes. I picked up the bills and ruffled through them. In the middle, with four singles on top and five beneath were six fifties. Three hundred dollars! Where would Clay Greeley get that kind of money? And in fifties? Not from selling oranges and lemons and avocados. Not from crystals, either, I was pretty sure. So where?

There was something else here, too, folded in the bottom of the box. It was an ad clipped from a magazine. PACKAGE DEAL, it said. WANT PEACE AND QUIET? AIR YOU CAN BREATHE? SOLITUDE YOU CAN TOUCH? BUY YOUR OWN LAND IN BEAUTIFUL WASHINGTON STATE. BUILD YOUR OWN LOG CABIN. IT COSTS LESS THAN YOU THINK. CALL US.

There was an area code and a phone number. The paper was almost worn through at the creases, and I could tell it had been handled a lot. I folded it, put it back with the money on top, and slid the box under the dresser again. Peace, quiet, solitude.

I had too much to think about, too much to puzzle over, but not here. Not in this dangerous room in this dangerous house.

I left the way I'd come in, grabbed my bike, and put plenty of space between me and the Greeleys' place before I slowed. And all the time my legs were pumping my brain was pumping, too. Had somebody paid Greeley to hassle Aunt Gerda? Gene Terlock? But why? Because he was too much of a businessman to do it himself? Plots from books I'd read and TV movies I'd seen jumbled around in my head. The land was valuable, not just nicely situated in the canyon. There was gold in the ground, or oil.

But if Clay Greeley had taken the dolls, where were they? At the twins' house? Of course Clay could have dumped them. I imagined the two dolls floating through the night in some dark river, Harriette's drowned face, water bubbling up through the bullet holes in her heart and lungs, and I wished I didn't have such a good imagination.

11

AUNT GERDA was sitting on the porch when I got back. I asked her if Ab was still napping and she said yes, so I flopped down in the other chair beside her. She looked terrible and I wished more than ever that I could have found Harriette and Isadora and brought them back for her.

"I bet you're real tired," I said, pulling off my Mariner's cap, fanning myself with it. "Would you like me to rub your neck? I'm pretty good at that. Mom used to like it."

Aunt Gerda gave me one of her nice smiles. "Thank you, Matthew. But I don't think a neck rub's going to help today." She picked up an envelope that lay on the table. "This just came." It was from the Water and Power Department and the typed note inside said that unless the bill was paid in full in the next three days all utilities would be shut off. The bill was for $364.22.

"Three hundred sixty-four dollars and twenty-two cents," I gasped. "That's so much. There must be a mistake. I used to write our checks for Mom, you know, at the end, and our electric bill was about twenty-five dollars. In fact, didn't you send us money once to pay?" She had sent it one month when we were going to have *our* electricity disconnected. I remembered perfectly.

"This one's for four months," Aunt Gerda said, her left eye twitching. "And I can't blame them. They've given me lots of warnings."

"You don't have the money?" I asked hesitantly, afraid to hear her answer.

"No. I'm not even close."

We sat quietly rocking while I tried to think.

"Ab and I have a hundred and thirty-eight dollars," I said. "You can have that and . . ."

"Matthew," Aunt Gerda sat forward in the chair. "I feel bad that I asked you and little Abigail to come here. It was irresponsible, things being the way they are. I just couldn't bear to think of the two of you going into some place . . . maybe being separated. Your mother loved you so. Children shouldn't be separated. But I'm sorry I brought you into the middle of this."

"Don't say that," I told her. "Your letter was the only good thing we had when Mom died. We were so scared."

She went on as if talking to herself, as if she hadn't heard me. "I don't know why I'm always such an optimist. I thought we'd muddle through." She swept a hand around the yard at the ever-smiling dolls.

They're optimists, for sure, I thought. Grinning and smirking as if everything's O.K.

· 111 ·

"The children and I don't need much," Aunt Gerda said. "I expect we could do without electricity. People did in the old days. We don't miss the phone at all. In fact, we're better without all those hateful calls. But I'm not sure if we could do without water, and of course, what would happen to the freezer? A lot of the food we use is in there."

She looked directly at me, and I saw that her eye was still twitching. "And, Matthew, if we have no lights to turn on, they'll come when it's dark, and take the rest of the children the way they took Harriette and Isadora."

"No, they won't. We'll stop them. We'll get candles and lamps."

Her gaze was fixed somewhere on the sky above the trees. "I've nothing left to sell, Matthew."

"Wait," I said, excited suddenly. "We have Mom's paintings. Sure. When Mr. Stengel comes . . ."

"You're a kind, loving boy. But I'm not sure the paintings would bring in enough money to save us. And besides, I wouldn't want you to give up what you have left from your mother . . . not for me."

"For all of us," I said. "This is our home now, too. You said that. And Mom would want us to. She would." What did Aunt Gerda mean, anyway, that the paintings wouldn't bring in enough money? Of course they would. We had just three days to sell them. Three days. I'd have to get going on it right away.

"I think I'll go see if Ab's awake," I said and went upstairs.

Abby wasn't, but she rubbed her eyes and smiled at

me when I spoke her name. It kills me the way Ab smiles first thing like that. No wonder Mom called her Sunshine.

I opened the portfolio and laid the paintings edge to edge along the cot and on the bottom of Ab's bed. The colors glowed in the sunlight, the blues, the reds, the yellow and browns of Mom's *Woods in Autumn*, which was nothing but leaves splattered in a vivid blaze across the canvas. We'd gone to Blake's Glen that day, the three of us, with a picnic. It was before Mom got so sick, while she could still do things. I'd carried the picnic bag and our jackets, because it had gotten so warm we'd had to take them off. Mom had her paints and easel and canvas, and Ab blundered along, wading through the leaves clutching Sweetie Pie, her old bald-headed doll, and the tartan blanket that had gone with us on so many picnics.

Looking at the painting now I could smell the dry, peppery dead leaf smell and hear the crunch as they crumbled under my feet. There was a little river and we'd sat on sun-warmed rocks and dabbled our feet in water that was clear as ice. Ab had dropped Sweetie Pie and screamed when the doll began spiraling downstream, and I'd had to wade in deep to get her. The remembrance of Sweetie Pie changed, turned into Harriette in another unknown river. I shivered. No, don't think about Harriette, don't let thoughts of her float into the good memories.

I set *Woods in Autumn* aside. "We won't sell this one."

Ab pointed at the painting of Tetley, Mrs. Valdoni's

dog, asleep at the bottom of the apartment house stairs. "And not this one, either. Where's the one of you and me?"

"Here." I put it on the "keep" pile.

Ab looked at the framed picture on the wall. "And that one's Aunt Gerda's."

"Yes."

"And not Mom's picture of herself, huh Mattie? We'll keep that one for ever and ever, won't we?"

"For ever and ever."

I slid the other paintings back in the portfolio.

"Who's going to buy them, Mattie? Will we get this much money?" Ab spread her arms wide.

"I hope so." I buckled the straps, then took Abbie's spread apart hands. "Listen, Ab. This is a secret, yours and mine. Aunt Gerda might try to stop us selling the pictures if she knew."

"Why?"

"Because she thinks we're selling them to give *her* the money, and in a way we are. But it's for us, too. It'll be such a great surprise for her. So don't spoil it. O.K?"

"O.K."

"That means you, too, Teddy," I told him. "Not a word."

Abby hadn't even asked how we were going to do this wonderful thing and I wasn't sure myself. But I knew I would. And when I'd told Ab it was for us as well as Aunt Gerda, I'd meant it. This was our home too — the only one we had. No one else was going to get it.

I stayed behind when she went downstairs and I found the card Mr. Stengel had given me and slipped it and some change into my pocket.

"I thought I'd ride Ab and me in to take a look at the village," I told Aunt Gerda. "How far is it?"

Aunt Gerda was fixing red earrings in Cleo's ears, and she said "Excuse me a minute, Cleo" before she turned to answer me. "About two miles."

"You don't need me for anything?"

"Nothing."

I'd just noticed that Cleo's ears were pierced. Unbelievable!

Abby stopped stringing red beads on a piece of thread to stare up at me, delighted.

"We're going someplace now? Are we going to . . ."

I warned her with a finger on my lips.

"Can I bring Teddy?" she asked.

"Sure. But let's go."

She tried again on the way out. "Aunt Gerda? Me and Matt have a terrific secret."

"You do?"

"Ab," I said. "We're *going. Now.*"

"You're really good at keeping secrets," I told her as I lifted her onto the bicycle seat.

"I know," she said.

The front door of Clay Greeley's house was open as we passed. Someone was home, Clay maybe. Did he carry his meals in behind that curtained corner? Did he count his money? Did he read his leaflet on how to build a log cabin and dream of going somewhere clean where he could breathe? Or did he sit in there, smiling that horrible smile, thinking of how clever he'd been to steal Harriette and Isadora? I gritted my teeth. That was more likely. If he only knew, nobody needed to hassle Aunt Gerda, not him, not the vigilantes, not anyone. The bills were going to drive her out sooner or later.

I spotted an Esso gas station with two wall phones right on the road, close to town.

"You watch the bike and hold Teddy," I told Ab and fished Mr. Stengel's card from my pocket.

"Are you calling Mrs. Valdoni?" Ab asked.

"No."

"Who then?"

"Give me a break, will you?"

I was dialing now, listening to the phone ring.

It was a woman who answered. "Black Orchid Gallery."

"Mr. Stengel, please."

"I'm sorry, he isn't in today. May I take a message?"

"Oh, no. I'm a friend of his and he told me to call. When will he be back?"

"I expect him tomorrow, around noon. Would you like to leave your name, sir?"

I thought I heard a smile in the way she said that "sir" as if she knew I wasn't as grown-up as I was trying to sound.

"That's O.K." I said. "I'll come in tomorrow at noon."

Black Orchid Gallery, La Cienega Boulevard, Los

Angeles. Where the heck *was* that? It might as well be on the moon for all I knew.

I pushed the bike over to where a mechanic in greasy coveralls was working with his head stuck inside the open hood of a car and Ab skipped along beside me.

"Excuse me. Could you tell me how to get to La Cienega Boulevard?"

He didn't move and his voice came up muffled from the depths of the motor. "No such place around here."

"Yes there is." I tried to poke Mr. Stengel's card down in front of his eyes.

His head turned and he looked up at me. "You're talking L.A."

"Yes."

When he straightened I saw he had HENRY in red stitching on the pocket of the coveralls. He eyeballed me good, then said: "Are you kids planning on riding bicycles down there?" I guess this guy was what people mean when they say "deadpan." His face, his lips didn't move as he talked and he was slow, slow, slow. Mrs. Valdoni would have said the dead fleas were dropping off him.

"It's probably too far to ride," I said. "How can we get there?"

"You could rent a limo."

He didn't smile, but I guessed he was joking. "Seriously," I said.

Henry gave me back the card with his big, greasy thumbprint right in the middle of it. "You'd take a bus into L.A. and transfer." He jerked his head toward a glass cubicle with OFFICE printed above it. "Come on inside."

There was a big city map tacked on the wall and Henry stood, considering it. I saw the crisscrossings of freeways and streets.

"Here's La Cienega."

My heart flopped. Never in a million years would Ab and I be able to find our way there.

"Here's how you do her." His finger made the trip again. "You're not planning on going, just the two of you?"

"No," I said. "We'll have somebody with us." And I thought, we'll have Teddy. Ab won't leave *him* behind.

"O.K. then." Henry tore a piece of paper off a yellow pad and wrote down a bunch of stuff, looking back and forth at the map.

"The L.A. bus leaves this corner every day at ten minutes past the hour," he said, giving me the paper. "I've put down what to ask when you get to the terminal, and you'd better take this." He rummaged around in a drawer and pulled out a folded Los Angeles County map.

"Thanks a lot."

"I have a bunch of bus schedules somewhere too." He found them and gave me one. "Are you kids new around here?" he asked. "I don't recall seeing you before. Where do you live?"

"With our Aunt Gerda and the children," Ab said.

Henry's deadpan face didn't change. "You mean, you're living out in the Yourra house?"

I nodded. His eyes went from me to Ab and back.

"Little girl?" he asked, slow as pancake syrup. "Do you like gum?"

"Yeah," Abby breathed.

"Well here." Henry fished in the pocket of his coveralls and held a palm full of change toward Ab. "Take the pennies. There's a gumball machine over there. How about getting a few pieces for everybody?"

Abby picked out the pennies with greedy little fingers. She never once looked at me and I knew why. She loves gum and she was afraid I'd stop her. I'm on to Ab's little tricks. But I didn't say anything because I had a feeling Henry was getting her out of the way for some reason and that I ought to know for what.

"I don't like the idea of you two kids out in that house," he said softly as Ab ran for the gum machine. "That Mrs. Yourra's real strange and . . ."

"She's O.K.," I said.

"Maybe she's not the one I'm worrying about," Henry went on.

"You're worried about the dolls? Everybody is, but . . ."

He held up a hand. "I'm not saying I'm not worried about them and that you shouldn't be. There's something not right about those dolls. But I'm talking now about practical things. The canyon people want rid of your aunt and there's some would go to just about any lengths to get her to leave."

"You think I don't *know* that? Criminy . . . that Mr. Terlock . . ."

"Do you know someone tried to burn her out a year or so ago? Slim Ericson was passing and saw smoke and got the house wet down till the fire engines arrived. If it hadn't been for him, the whole place would have been ashes and your Aunt Gerda with it."

Beyond him I could see Ab working intently on the gum machine.

Henry kept on talking. "There was a big fuss because they found an empty gas can and I think the attention scared off whoever set the fire. But just a couple of months back somebody broke all her windows and when she came out they threw a rock at her. It cut the side of her head.

I shivered. "Did they ever find out who did it?"

"No," Henry said.

Abby was coming back. She dropped two or three of the gumballs, picked them up, wiped them on her skirt.

Henry was watching her, too. "Look!" His deadpan voice speeded up. "If you get scared, if anything happens, call, O.K.?"

He stopped as Abby tugged at his arm. She held out the gumballs. "You take the red ones. They're the best and you can have them 'cause it's your money."

"You're sure it's not because these are the ones you dropped?" Henry asked.

"Uh-uh," Abby said, offended.

"Well, thank you little girl."

"I'm not little girl. I'm Abby and he's Matt."

"We've got to go," I told Henry. "Thanks for the gum and the other stuff."

"I'm here just about all the time," he said.

"Thanks," I said again.

I helped Ab up onto the bike. Her hands were full of gumballs and I had to persuade her to let go of them and drop them in her pocket so she could hold on to me. Behind me I could hear her singing "Jingle Bells," happy as a lark. I was glad she hadn't heard.

In bed that night I studied Henry's directions, marked the route on the map and checked the timetable. And I worried a lot. Suppose we did get to Mr. Stengel's studio? Suppose he did buy the paintings and we did get a lot of money, what then? The money could save Aunt Gerda and the house. And the children. And forevermore we'd have to be on guard, the way we were now, because money wasn't going to change how the canyon people thought.

Henry's words kept coming back, however hard I tried to shut them out. I got out of bed and checked how far it would be for Ab and me to jump from the window if there was another fire. I should get a rope or see if there was a ladder and leave it outside against the wall. But a person could come up a ladder as well as down. A person could come while we were asleep, step over the windowsill into our room. I wondered if a thrown rock could hit us in bed. Would flying glass come through the curtains?

"Look after Abby," Mom had said. She'd wanted us to come to Aunt Gerda's, but she hadn't known how dangerous things were. Shootings, fires, rocks. Maybe I'd have to get Ab out of here. But the first thing was to sell the paintings. Without money I had no choices.

I went downstairs again at three because I'd promised myself I would.

"Abby and I didn't see much of the village yesterday," I told Aunt Gerda. "I think we'll go in again today."

She looked at me vaguely, then said: "Did I tell you Kristin came by? She said she'd be over in the morning. She said maybe you and Abigail would like to go crystal hunting with her."

"Oh." Should I put the trip off for another day? No. Every day here, every night, could be dangerous.

Around us and in front the lights blazed. If I looked into the dark beyond I could see the pale floss of Derek's hair and the sliced edge of his checkered pants.

"I love this canyon," Aunt Gerda said dreamily. "I've always loved it and soon I'll have to leave it."

I started to comfort her, to say "maybe not," but the words wouldn't come. It would be better if she *did* leave. If we all left. All of us except the dolls. But would she go without them?

"At night, sitting out here, I think about Joseph and a time when we were young," she said softly. "We had such plans, the two of us. We'd have children, lots of children, and they'd run free, and we'd teach them about nature. For a time it seemed as if it wasn't to be and I have to admit that I took that hard."

The dolls moved gently on their poles, seemed to sigh along with the little wind. The steady roll of Aunt Gerda's rocker was as soothing as a lullaby.

"And then Joseph began making the children for me.

First there was Arabella, and a pretty little thing she was. She was made from love. Joseph told me, and it was true, Matthew. It was true, but after we lost Harriette, the life seemed to go out of him, and then he started Isadora and, well, he died before she was finished so I lost her, too. It's a great blessing that I have the others." Her hand came out briefly and touched mine. "And now I have you and little Abigail."

She'd never give up the dolls. There was no point in thinking that she would.

"Ah well. Forgive me for being so mournful, Matthew. It's this time of morning. There's melancholy in the air. I shouldn't inflict it on you. I'll keep going as long as I can. All else is in God's hands."

I don't know how long we sat together, quietly, with just the sounds of the crickets around us. My eyelids were heavy and I thought that, worried or not, I'd be able to sleep. I was just wondering if I'd sat with Aunt Gerda long enough, if I could leave now, when she spoke again.

"Matthew? I have to go inside for just a minute. Would you mind being here with the children till I get back?"

"No. I don't mind. Go ahead."

"You're not afraid of the children are you?" she asked gently.

"Of course not," I lied.

"I'm glad. Some people are, you know. They don't understand."

I nodded to show that I did, which was another lie.

"The children like you a lot," she said.

Oh criminy! "They told you that?" I asked.

Aunt Gerda patted my shoulder. "They told me."

"Oh, well good." For a minute I thought about standing up and shouting "thanks, you guys." Maybe I was going nuts myself.

Aunt Gerda stepped down onto the path. "I'll be back in a few minutes, children," she said. "Matthew will be here."

"I'll be here," I echoed. See? I *was* going nuts.

When she went inside, I sat back in the chair, rocked and tried to relax. A moth flapped itself too close to the hanging light bulb, retreated, flapped back.

"You turkey," I muttered. "Do you want to fry?"

Your Aunt Gerda would have been ashes, Henry had said. I rocked harder and hummed a little tune under my breath. She'd be back in a few minutes. No sweat.

I was glad, anyway, that she'd told me about Uncle Joseph and how he'd come to make the dolls. Then they'd both started pretending they were real. Easy to see how that could happen. They were ghost children all right.

Something rustled in the tired shrubbery below the porch and I sat up, my heart pecking inside my chest. I thought I heard a click, like a gun being cocked. But that had to be my imagination, too. I'd be such an easy target here, under the light. I'd be a sitting duck. I scrunched down as far as I could go.

How long had Aunt Gerda been in there? More than a few minutes. Where in heck was she?

And then, plain as plain from the darkest part of the yard came a little girl voice.

"We like you a lot, Matthew."

This time I got out of the chair slowly, edged myself behind it.

"Did . . . did somebody say something?"

"We all like you a lot, Matthew." A boy's voice this time, high and babyish. "We like Abigail, too."

I backed against the house, staring into the darkness.

It wasn't my imagination, not this time. There was no one here except me and them. No way to reason myself around this one. The dolls had talked.

12

THE DOLLS had absolutely and definitely talked.

"There's something not right about them," Henry had said in his deadpan way. He wasn't kidding. And neither were the twins; they'd heard the dolls, too.

Shootings, a fire, rocks, kidnapings, and now a bunch of dolls that talked like people. I couldn't stop shaking. The dolls talking had finished it for me. So what if they liked me? Ab and I were leaving.

Lying in bed, I made mental lists. First we'd need money. I'd go into the Black Orchid Gallery the way I'd planned, and when I'd sold the paintings, I'd give half to Aunt Gerda because we owed her a lot and because . . . well, just because. Was she a witch? Don't think about that, Matt. Don't think about it. I'd call the airport and book Ab and me on a flight to Seattle. I'd call Mrs. Valdoni too. She'd take us in, temporarily, till we got things together. We'd find a secret place, the two of us, where nobody could get to us or separate us.

I remembered Clay Greeley's mountain cabin. How much would something like that cost? I'd fish and we'd have a garden like the one here, except there'd be no dead dolls buried in ours.

But first, the money.

When it began to get light outside, I heard Aunt Gerda come in, heard the door of the bathroom close behind her, and I grabbed Mom's portfolio and ran quickly downstairs with it. Curving wide, keeping as far from the dolls as I could, I hid it in the high weeds by the hedge. Then I turned and said:

"You guys?" My voice sounded like Jell-O. "I know you saw me do that, but don't tell her, O.K.? She'll try to stop me and I'm selling the paintings for all of us, for you guys too. So keep your mouths shut."

Arabella's purse slipped from her shoulder to hang, swinging from her wrist, and I jumped at least six inches off the ground before I turned and raced for the front steps. Just let Ab and me get safely out of here. Safely and quickly.

There was instant oatmeal with canned peaches for breakfast. I glanced quickly at the glass case under the counter. Yep. This was the last can of peaches and Aunt Gerda was giving it to us. Witch or not, she was kind and good. Well, soon she'd have money. Soon she could buy herself a whole caseful of canned peaches.

"Ab," I said, "hurry up and finish. We're going for another bike ride this morning and I want to leave early."

"Do I have to go?" Abby got up and fished the last

slice of peach from the can with her fingers. "Aunt Gerda's starting a new skirt for Cleo today. And she said Kristin's coming over. She's going to show us where to find crystals. And I want to help make Cleo's skirt. You go, Matt. I'll stay."

That's right! Kristin was going to come. So? I couldn't worry about that. What I'd do was call her from Henry's gas station. But what was this baloney about Ab wanting to stay, without me? I could hardly believe what I was hearing. *Ab* telling me to *go* somewhere and she'd stay. Little nervous Ab. And naturally it would be just at a time when I didn't want her to stay.

I told myself it was great that Ab was so much better. I'd wished for a long time that she'd stop clinging and hanging on to me because that was no good for a little kid. But I felt a bit let down, too. This was the first time in two years that Abby hadn't wanted to be with me. Anyhow, she couldn't stay. It would be a while till Kristin got here. There was no way I was going to leave her behind with Aunt Gerda and the talking dolls. No way.

"You have to come," I said sharply. "So don't argue. Just go and wash your hands. You're not supposed to stick your fingers in the peach can. And wash your bowl and spoon while you're at it."

Aunt Gerda gave me an apologetic glance. "Abigail? When I told you last night you could help with Cleo's skirt and that Kristin would be over, I didn't know Matthew had other plans. Cleo's skirt can wait till tomorrow. That's all right, Cleo, isn't it?"

Don't answer, Cleo, please. Not in front of Ab.

"You and I will cut out the pattern when you get home, my dear," Aunt Gerda said. "And Kristin can take you to look for crystals any day, all summer long. Matthew really wants your company."

Abbie gave me a doubtful glance. "Truly, Mattie?"

"Truly," I said.

Ab smiled. "O.K."

The Ovaltine clock said ten minutes to eight when we left. Aunt Gerda was busy now washing down the front of the glass cases so I didn't think she'd come out on the porch to see us off. Still, I was careful to check before I pulled the portfolio from its hiding place. All clear.

"Why did you hide Mom's paintings out here?" Ab asked in a loud voice. "Where are we taking . . ."

"Sh!" I said. "It's part of the secret. Remember?" I lifted her onto the seat of the bike and balanced the portfolio across the handlebars. Teddy was jammed inside my shirt with his furry head sticking up under my chin. He and the portfolio kept slipping, but I couldn't think of a better way to carry them.

"We're going to Los Angeles," I told Ab over my shoulder. "Remember Mr. Stengel? He might want to buy some of Mom's paintings."

"Oh boy," Abby said. "Will he give us all the money today?"

"Could be."

"Oh boy," Abby said again.

I didn't try to talk to Ab as we rode. The wheels of the bicycle sizzled and burned on the road, singing their own scary song: "We all like you a lot, Matthew, a lot, a lot." I pedaled harder.

Henry was in his little gas station office.

"We're on our way to the bus," I told him. "Can I leave the bike here till we get back?"

"Sure."

I tried to keep my eyes steady when I looked at him and push that tiny, little girl doll voice out of my head in case the memory would show and I'd turn into a lump of Jell-O again. "We like you a lot, Matthew. We like Abigail, too."

Henry made a big point of getting up and looking behind us. "I don't see that adult person who was supposed to be with you."

"It's different than I said. But I know what I'm doing."

He nodded, then slid a piece of paper toward me. "Write down where you're going on La Cienega." When I'd written it he folded the paper and put it in his top pocket. "What time will you be back?"

"Three or four. It depends how long it takes."

"I guess this trip is important?"

"Yes." I fished a dollar bill out of my pocket. "Can you give me some change? I have to call somebody."

"Who?" Abby asked.

"Ab?" I asked. "How come you're always asking me who I'm calling? You don't have to know."

Henry grinned. "Why not use the phone in here? As long as it's a local call. Is it?"

"Yeah."

"Well, go ahead then. Sis and I'll wait outside." He winked at Abby. "So he can be private. Big brothers need privacy sometimes, you know."

"Thanks," I said. I propped the portfolio against his desk, found the Ericsons's number in his phone directory and dialed.

It was Fee who answered and I had trouble getting him to go for Kristin. I guess little brothers can give you a hard time, too.

At last she came. "Hi," she said. "What's up? Where are you calling from, anyway?"

"From Henry's gas station," I said.

There was a long silence. "What are you doing there? I was just getting ready to ride over to Gerda's. Did she tell you I was coming?"

"Yes, but . . ."

"If you don't want to go find crystals that's O.K. I thought Abby might like it. Maybe she'd still want to go."

"Ab's with me," I said.

Henry's desk was covered with a sheet of dirty glass. Underneath it he'd pushed business cards, ads for pizza, and pictures of baseball players. I ran my fingers around the outline of Fernando Valenzuela. "We have to go to L.A.," I said.

"L.A.? What for?"

To get money to escape, I thought. "We like you a lot. We like you a lot."

"We have business there, that's what for," I said.

"*Business*? Is Gerda with you?"

"No. And don't tell her. She doesn't know."

"Are you going on the bus?"

I nodded, then said "Yes." Kristin sure was a snoop! I was beginning to wish I hadn't even called her. "I just wanted to tell you we wouldn't be going for the crystals, that's all."

"L.A.'s really big," Kristin said. "My dad says it's a jungle. Are you sure you can get wherever you're going? I mean, you don't even know . . ."

"I can get where I'm going and . . ." I swung around, facing the road outside. Now I could see through the glass wall of Henry's office. "Oh no!" I said.

"What? What's the matter?"

"We've missed the bus, that's what's the matter," I said furiously. "It's just pulling away from the stop." I felt like slamming down the stupid phone. What a great way to start the day! Why had I bothered to call her anyway? Why had I talked so long? Why was I yelling at her?

"Matt?" Kristin's voice was anxious.

I covered Fernando's smiling face with the flat of my hand. "Yes?"

"Nothing," Kristin said and hung up the phone.

Henry and Ab were at the gum machine when I went back outside.

"Why didn't you call me?" I asked Henry. "We missed the bus."

He shrugged. "Seemed like you were in the middle of an important call. Anyway, there'll be another bus in an hour. Relax, Matt."

"A whole hour wasted," I said pulling out the timetable to check, though I knew he was right. *Depart Sierra Maria Canyon, 10 A.M.*

Henry went on giving Ab more pennies. I swear, he was spoiling her useless.

"Relax," he said again glancing over at me. "You'll live longer."

I decided that if relaxing had anything to do with living longer Henry would make it to a hundred and ten.

I gritted my teeth and walked out to the front to watch for the next bus. So what if it wouldn't be here for a whole hour. I kept checking the time, walking up and down, warning Ab to be ready to come when I said the word.

It was ten minutes to ten when I saw someone on a too-small bicycle pedaling fast from the direction we'd already come. Kristin!

She came to her skidding stop beside me and pulled off her mashed-up white hat. "Good," she said. "I made it in time."

"In time for what?" I asked suspiciously.

She smiled. "In time to go with you."

13

I TRIED TO argue. "This hasn't anything to do with you, Kristin."

"You're on the trail of Harriette and Isadore, aren't you?" she asked, squinting up at me from her seat on the bicycle.

I held out the portfolio. "We're going to Mr. Stengel's studio. I'm hoping he'll buy these. I'm not on anybody's trail."

Kristin tapped the bicycle pedal with her foot, spinning it in a blur of silver. "Well, since I'm here, I might as well go along. Mom and Dad and Fee are at a swap meet in Glendale. They're going to lunch at McDonalds after. So . . ." she shrugged.

"Look," I said. "It'll be boring for you."

"Uh-uh. And I can help you find Mr. Stengel's place. I mean, I know my way around. And I can help you get a good price. Since I started selling my crystals, I'm a terrific bargainer. Sometimes I can get people to come up, oh, maybe five dollars more than they offered to begin with."

"Wow," I said. "A whole five dollars."

"You don't have to be sarcastic," Kristin said coldly.

"Sorry."

Ab came running over then. "Hi, Kristin. How come you're here?"

"I'm going, too," Kristin said, and Ab said, "Goody. Can we go look for crystals tomorrow, then?"

"We'll see," Kristin told her, and then I spotted the bus coming and I grabbed Ab's hand. "Come on. We don't want to miss this one too."

Kristin dropped her bike right there, wheels spinning. "Keep an eye on this for me, O.K., Henry?" she yelled.

"Be careful," Henry called after us. "Got your map, Matt?"

"Yeah." I patted my back pocket, and wanted to add: And now we've got Kristin, too. Kristin who knows everything.

Except that pretty soon I discovered she didn't know a thing, either about riding on a bus or getting to L.A. She didn't know you had to have the correct money for the driver. She'd never thought about having to change buses, or needing a transfer.

"You've never ridden on a bus before, have you?" I asked.

"Yes I have. I rode the schoolbus for two years."

Oh brother, I thought. Big deal. But I knew better than to say it.

"So how do we know where to get off this one and where to get the other one?" she asked. If I hadn't known better, I might have thought Kristin sounded nervous.

I pointed to the map. "We get off here, at Broadway and First. Then we take a Number 3, north, to Sunset and La Cienega."

"Oh. But how do you *know* that?"

"I read the map and the timetable," I said casually, and I saw something on her face that I'd never seen before. Kristin was impressed! I could hardly believe it. She was impressed with me! Hey, I thought, she's just a little canyon mouse. And I couldn't help grinning.

"What are you grinning for?" she asked suspiciously.

"Nothing." I said, and I decided I was glad she'd come after all.

"I took buses a lot in Seattle," I said comfortingly. "You get to know how to do it."

We did it well, and when we finally got off at Sunset and La Cienega I figured we only had four blocks to walk.

It was still only 11:30 though, and I couldn't see Mr. Stengel till 12. We walked slowly along a street that was lined with galleries till we came to the Black Orchid.

"We're too early," I said.

The gallery right next to it had BLAKELY: FINE ART in antique-looking gold print across the window.

I stood looking up at its sign. "Why not?" I asked out loud. "We don't have to sell the paintings if we don't want to, but I wouldn't mind seeing what they'd offer for them in here. Do you want to come in too, Kristin?" I frowned discouragingly.

"Sure," Kristin said. Kristin definitely is not easily discouraged and I had a feeling she'd already forgotten that she'd never have made it this far without me. I pushed open the heavy glass doors, easing the precious portfolio through.

We were standing in a large bare room that had polished wood floors and a single black line drawing on each of its white walls.

Ab pointed. "That one's nice."

Immediately a tall, thin man standing at the back came toward us. "You have good taste, young lady," he said. "That's a Hokusai."

"I like these, too." Ab was looking at three paintings of stick people and a stick dog and a house with smoke coming out of its chimney. She would like those! They were exactly the kind of drawings she always did herself.

"They're neat," Kristin said.

The man turned and his face softened. "Yes. But those are not for sale. They're too valuable. By the way, let me introduce myself. I'm Kevin Blakely. My partner Phoebe and I own the gallery. Is there something else I can show you?"

"Actually, we have some very nice paintings we'd like to show you," I said and held up the portfolio.

"They're even prettier than Mr. Hokey whatever," Abby said, and the man grinned.

"Well, in that case, I'd better not pass on seeing them. Come this way."

The three of us followed him into a little cluttered back studio office and I took Mom's paintings out of the portfolio and placed them carefully on the desk.

Mr. Blakely began going through them, holding them delicately by their edges, examining them slowly at first, then going faster and faster. When he'd seen them all, he put them back in a neat pile and smoothed his hair, though it didn't need smoothing.

"Um," he said. "Yes. Very nice." Before I could ask him *how* nice and if he'd be interested in buying some of them, he said to Abby: "I have chocolate cookies. Would you like one?"

"Oh, yes, please," Abby said.

He took a package from a drawer.

"About the paintings," I began, but he was too busy with the cookie package to talk to me.

"You can just tear it," Abby told him hopping impatiently from one foot to the other. I swear I'm going to have to do something about Ab. She's getting to be a real greedy little kid.

Mr. Blakely gave her the whole package.

"You want me to do it for you, Abby?" Kristin asked and Abby passed it over.

"So, do you like the paintings?" I asked.

"As I said, they're nice," he told me. "But they're frankly not our style. We go in for more classical work — woodcuts, prints, etchings, that kind of thing. If you want to sell them, you might try the Art Mart, two streets over."

I raised my eyebrows. "The Art Mart? It doesn't sound too great."

"They do handle more . . . well, more popular stuff."

"Mom made the pictures," Ab said, her mouth filled with cookie. "She died." Ab's eyes can go from happy to sad in the space of one second. "Matt and I look after ourselves now. There's just us. And Aunt Gerda."

"Oh." Mr. Blakely looked from Ab to me and then to Kristin. "Kristin's our friend," Abby explained.

Mr. Blakely said, "I see," then tapped his fingers on the desk and began sorting through the paintings again. He pulled out one of a garden filled with daffodils that Mom had done last spring. I remembered the day. "This one is pretty," he said. "I could give you . . . oh, fifty dollars."

"Wowee!" Abby said, smiling happily up at me. "Fifty dollars, Matt."

"It's worth a lot more," Kristin said quickly. "Sixty at least."

I slid the paintings back in the portfolio. "Thanks. But I don't think we're that desperate to sell. Let's go."

Abby started to protest, but I grabbed her shoulder and nudged her ahead of me toward the outside gallery and the door to the street. Kristin and Mr. Blakely followed behind us.

"I'm sorry I can't do better," Mr. Blakely said.

Abby stopped and pointed to the three stick paintings. "I could make you another one like this," she offered. "And then if you wanted, you could buy it for fifty dollars."

Mr. Blakely smiled down at her. Adults always smile

at Ab. "My little boy sent those to me. He lives with his mother in Montreal. I don't see him very often."

"Is that why they're so valuable?" Abby asked.

"That's why." He spoke to me. "If you want to change your mind later, Matthew, and let me have the daffodil . . . "

I interrupted. "That's O.K. But thanks for looking at them." I was wondering if he'd have offered to buy any of them if Ab hadn't spilled that Mom had done them and that she'd died. Did that mean the paintings weren't any good? Naw. It was just that they weren't his style.

I pushed open the door and held it with my back so Kristin and Abby could come through.

"It's not that the paintings aren't good," I told Kristin. "It's just that they aren't his style. That's what he said."

Kristin nodded.

I wished she wasn't with us.

"It's five minutes to twelve," I added. "We'd better hurry."

The Black Orchid Gallery was a lot bigger and grander than the Blakely Gallery. Mr. Stengel's big square showroom had an all-white floor and white walls with strange, modern paintings, pale and transparent, on the walls. I decided standing in here was like standing inside an ice cube.

A woman with silver hair and big, flat silver earrings came out from the back.

"Hello," she said, smiling mostly at Ab, but at Kristin and me, too.

"Hi," I said. "I called yesterday. Mr. Stengel gave me his card." I fished it out.

"Oh yes. I'm sorry, but he isn't in yet. Would you like to wait?"

"Please," I said.

She stood for a minute, then she said: "Unfortunately, I'm interviewing this morning for a new part-time secretary to help me out, so my office is a bit chaotic. Never mind. I'm sure it will be perfectly all right for you to wait in Mr. Stengel's room."

She led us through an outer office where a young man was typing so hard he didn't even glance up and where two women sat in black leather chairs, leafing through magazines and looking nervous.

"Here you are." She opened an inside door and motioned toward a gigantic white couch, then said, lowering her voice, "I hope you don't have to wait *too* long. But Mr. Stengel is a bit of a Tom Tardy."

"We can wait," I said.

Mr. Stengel's room was white as the gallery, except that here the floor was covered with carpet, thick and pure as new snow. There was a big dark red desk with a phone on it, and a dark red phone book and a golden clock. Behind the desk was an oversized leather chair. I tried to imagine little Mr. Stengel sitting there. He'd be lost.

There were more pictures on these walls and I walked around examining them. There were garden scenes with ladies carrying parasols and one of a field filled with rows of haystacks, rows and rows and rows. I thought they were a bit like Mom's pictures and I decided we might have a good chance here.

We sat for ages. I figured it had to be after noon, way after. Fortunately Ab still had the package of cookies to keep her happy and Kristin prowled around, looking at the pictures, counting the haystacks in the field, asking me to guess how many, asking me if I'd ever seen a haystack.

I passed the time by picking Ab's crumbs out of the deep white carpet and trying to stay calm. What if Mr. Stengel didn't want the paintings either? What if he said they were nice in that give-away, not interested kind of voice? What then? Then Kristin would feel sorry for me again and I'd hate that.

The door opened and I thought Mr. Stengel had arrived at last. "Finally," Kristin breathed, but it was just his secretary again. She was carrying a pile of ledgers and she walked to a door that I'd already noticed behind Mr. Stengel's big desk. I guess it was kept locked, because she began messing around with a key, trying to get it in the lock which she couldn't see properly because of the pile of stuff she was carrying. The top ledger began to slip.

I jumped up. "Here." I saved it, took the key from her, opened the door.

"Thanks, honey," she said.

Inside, paintings were stacked against the walls. There were several glass pedestals and a big white statue of a lady holding a mirror. All this I saw in one glance that took the statue in and let it go again. Because there were two other things in the room.

It wasn't possible. How . . . ?

And then Abby's voice chimed up beside me: "Oh look, Matty. Mr. Stengel has a dolly, too." Behind me Kristin gave a loud, disbelieving gasp.

Nobody needed to tell me that that was the missing Harriette who stood balanced on her pole against the wall, her face shiny clean and smiling above a white draped sheet. Beside her, formless and blank, was Isadora. Upright like this she could have been one of those mummy cases you see in a museum. The two of them — here. We'd found the missing dolls after all.

14

MR. STENGEL's secretary opened a file drawer and slid the ledgers inside.

"Don't say anything about the dolls," I whispered to Kristin and I put my fingers to my lips to make sure Ab got the message too.

"There," the secretary straightened. "Thanks for your help."

"You're welcome. Those are interesting-looking dolls. Where did Mr. Stengel find them?"

"Oh, some elderly lady has a bunch of them. Her husband made them and Mr. Stengel has been trying to get her to sell to him. I guess she finally gave in and sold him these two."

I sensed Abby about to speak and I gripped her arm and squeezed a warning.

"They're genuine folk art," the secretary went on.

"According to my boss, they're almost priceless." She stroked Ab's cheek with her finger. "By the way, my name's Itsy, like Itsy Bitsy Spider. Do you know that song?"

Ab glanced at me for permission to answer and when I nodded she nodded, too.

"It's fun, isn't it?" Itsy asked, and Ab checked with me again before she nodded for a second time.

"Where did you say Mr. Stengel got the dolls?" Kristin asked.

"I believe it was somewhere in Los Angeles County. I think he said it was out on the way to Palmdale. They're pretty strange looking, huh?"

"Really!" I said. "Is it O.K. if we still wait for Mr. Stengel?"

Itsy smiled. "Fine. I expect he'll be here any minute."

I steered Ab toward the white couch. As soon as the door closed behind Itsy, she said in a sulky way: "You squeezed too hard, Matt. I wasn't going to say anything."

"Sorry, kiddo," I said.

Kristin leaned against Mr. Stengel's big desk and fanned herself with her hat. "Can you believe this Matt? What did she mean Gerda sold them? She never did. What a liar Mr. Stengel is."

"Maybe he bought them from somebody else," I said. "Somebody who stole them." I thought for a minute. "Somebody who stole them *for* him, because Mr. Stengel wanted them so much and Aunt Gerda wouldn't sell." I immediately got a picture of Clay Greeley's cigar box, the fifty dollar bills piled neatly inside.

"Oh man!" Kristin sighed. "And we all thought Mr. Stengel was so nice. I even hoped Aunt Gerda would *marry* him. He sure had me fooled."

"Is he not nice, Matty?" Ab asked all agog. "*I* thought he was nice."

"I think he fooled all of us," I said. I remembered the way Aunt Gerda had said: "He comes a lot oftener now that he has this new interest." I'd thought she meant in her. She'd meant in buying the dolls. But he'd fooled her, too. She would never have dreamed he'd take them.

"I'll just bet he was the one all along," Kristin said. "The one trying to force her out of her house and into an old people's home."

"She wouldn't have been able to bring the dolls with her . . . "

"And she'd sell to him," Kristin finished. "What a sleaze ball! And what about Clay Greeley? I know Mr. Stengel always stopped at Clay's stall. He kidded about what a good businessman Clay was. He must have figured out how greedy he was, too. I bet he paid that creep Greeley to do everything. You know, to make life hard for Gerda."

"And in the end to dig up Harriette," I said.

Kristin squeezed her hat in her hands as if she had Clay Greeley by the neck. "How *could* he? A nice lady like Gerda."

"All's fair in business," I reminded her. "Isn't that what Clay said?"

"So what should we do next, Matt?" Kristin asked. "Should we try to steal them back? But how could we get them past Itsy Bitsy Spider?" She nodded in the direction of the outer office.

I turned toward the windowless room where we'd seen the dolls. "And how do we get in there to get them? The door's locked."

"Can we go home now?" Abby asked. "I don't like it here."

"Not yet, Ab." I was looking at the leather phone book on Mr. Stengel's desk. "I've just thought of something," I told Kristin, picking up the directory, leafing through its pages. There were lots of names listed under G, but no Greeley. One number under G was listed with only the initials, C.G.

"Yeah," Kristin breathed.

She stood next to me as I dialed. At the other end the phone rang and rang. At last someone picked it up and a groggy bad-tempered voice asked: "Yeah?"

"Is Clay there?"

"No he ain't. And don't call no more. I'm not Clay's answering service and I'm trying to sleep."

The slam of the receiver almost took my ear off.

"Greeleys'?" Kristin whispered. I nodded.

Behind us Abby bounced on the couch and chanted: "No more monkeys jumping on the bed. One fell off and broke his head." Abby doesn't stay worried for long, thank goodness.

I hadn't heard the door open. I hadn't heard his feet on the carpet or seen him because my back was turned as I talked on the phone. But there was Mr. Stengel beside us.

"Hello," he said heartily. "Kristin, isn't it? And you're Gerda's grandson. And this is your little sister."

"Mrs. Yourra's our great aunt, not our grand-mother," I muttered, as if it mattered.

"So what brings you here, my friends?"

"You stole her dolls," I said.

I hadn't meant it to come out like that. I'd thought I'd trap Mr. Stengel, make him admit to what he'd done, but the words wouldn't stay inside my mouth. I wished I had them back, safely hidden. Why had I blurted them out like that? Maybe he had a gun. Maybe he'd try locking *us* up in that room. But how could he, with people in the other office? I didn't know, but I wasn't sure there was anything he couldn't do.

"My dear boy." His glance flickered to the locked door, then back to me.

"I saw them." My voice shook. My legs, too. "We think you got Clay Greeley to steal them for you."

"Clay Greeley?" It was as if he'd never heard the name in his life. But Clay's number was in his phone book and that proved something.

Abby came over and pushed her hand into mine.

"Sit down, all of you," Mr. Stengel's voice even had a smile in it. "We can discuss this matter intelli-gently."

"We don't want to sit down." I heard the shake in Kristin's voice too and that gave me a sort of courage.

"It's O.K.," I said. "We have to find out about this."

Mr. Stengel had already seated himself behind the desk and I noticed how big he looked there, how important. The chair must have been specially made to be higher so he'd seem that way.

Kristin and I sat on the couch with Ab between us. I kept hold of her hand.

"I want to level with you," Mr. Stengel said. "Then perhaps you'll understand why I did what I did. You'll see it was best for your aunt in the long run."

"I'm sure!" I hoped he understood I was being sarcastic, not agreeing.

"And that's why you were so sneaky and pretended to be her friend," Kristin added. I could tell she was trying to help me out and I had to admit I was glad she was here, that it wasn't just Ab and I.

Mr. Stengel was wearing a white suit with a black shirt and there he sat, big and important and calmy smiling. But I decided he wasn't as calm as he pretended to be when he took out a black handkerchief and wiped his brow.

"Your Uncle Joseph was quite a craftsman," he said. "Unfortunately, he was a poor businessman and your aunt was not left in good shape financially. I offered to take one or two of her dolls to help her out, but . . . . "

"And she wouldn't, so you stole them," I said. He didn't seem to hear.

"But she said she wouldn't split up her family. So

· 149 ·

she wouldn't sell." He spread out his little hands. "Maybe you could help me convince her. I'd take all of the dolls. I'd give her $500 for each one. That would be . . . " — he put his fingers together and stared at the ceiling — ". . . thirty-five-hundred dollars."

"What about Harriette and Isadora?" Kristin asked.

"Who?"

I pointed to the locked door.

"All right. With another thousand dollars for them she'd have forty-five-hundred. She could pay her bills and . . . "

"And she wouldn't have to worry about getting hit by a rock, or having stuff dumped on her dolls, or another fire." I stopped. Better not push this too far. Better pretend to believe him and wait till we got out of here before I started accusing him.

"Weren't you scared you'd burn up all those valuable dolls along with Aunt Gerda when you set the fire?" Kristin asked.

"My dear young lady, I didn't set the fire. And I made sure those boys knew to start it well away from . . . " Mr. Stengel stopped and gave Kristin a smile and me a sly look. "Uh-oh. You almost got me there."

Those boys! Clay and his friends. They'd even set a fire for him.

"And you turned all the canyon people against her." I said angrily, forgetting that I shouldn't accuse him yet.

Ab scrunched back and whispered, "Matty?" I squeezed her back and took a deep breath. "It's O.K., Ab."

"You made them all think she was crazy," Kristin said. "You're such a creep."

Uh-oh. Now Kristin *had* said too much. I tensed the muscles of my legs, ready to run. I'd lift Ab, shove Kristin ahead of me. But Mr. Stengel was still smiling. Maybe he'd been called a creep a few times before. He smoothed the wood on his desk with delicate fingers. "You have to remember, Gerda brought a lot of that on herself. She couldn't resist having the dolls talk."

I stared at him. "What do you mean, having them talk?"

"Oh, you must have heard them. Old Joseph had them all wired for sound. There are speakers in those bases where the dolls stand. He and Gerda would have them put on plays for the two of them in the evenings, and he made it so they'd say goodnight to her and call her 'mother.'" Stengel clicked his fingers. "All Gerda has to do is push the play buttons in the recorders she keeps in the trunk by the door. There's one for each doll."

"*That's* what Clay Greeley and the twins heard," Kristin said to me. "No wonder they were scared."

That's what I'd heard, too, and no wonder *I'd* been scared. Relief flooded through me. Tape recorders. Buttons. I remembered the click I'd heard the night they'd said "We like you. We like Abby, too," and I almost laughed out loud, even though there wasn't much to laugh about except what a wimp I'd been. "I suppose she can change the message anytime she likes?" I asked.

"Of course. Gerda always did the doll voices. She

was good at it. There was a time when Joseph even wanted to do a doll opera and take the show on the road. But Gerda had a voice like a sick cat." His grin invited us to mock Aunt Gerda too, and I realized he thought we'd softened up because we'd been asking questions about the tape recorders and acting interested.

"So what do you say, my friends?" he asked. "Partners? Remember, it's for Mrs. Yourra. And there'd definitely be something in it for the three of you." He jumped up and came round the desk, small again, down to his normal size. "As a matter of fact, there could be a great deal in it for all of you."

I stood too and Abby scrambled up beside me. I wanted to say: "Never!" But there was still the fear, the knowing that we weren't out of here yet.

"You think we'd go in it with you . . . you . . . you thief?" Kristin asked. "You must be crazy." Shut up, Kristin, I thought. Just shut up.

"So? So what do you plan on doing then, young lady? Going to the police maybe? Telling Mrs. Yourra? I advise you, don't any of you try to lock horns with me. You won't win."

My heart was thumping and I was really frightened now. Mr. Stengel was small, but all at once I could feel the evil. We had to get away. I headed for the door, pushing Ab ahead of me. "Let's go."

"Wait," Mr. Stengel said.

I froze. What if I looked back and he had a gun pointed at us? What if he said "Go where? You're not going anywhere."

"You forgot something," he said.

I turned. He was holding Mom's portfolio. How could I have forgotten it? I'd been ready to walk out of here and leave it behind.

"I suppose this is why you came," he said, his mouth a tight line, his eyes tight, too. I'd never seen anybody so terrifying.

"You wanted me to look at these paintings. Well, I'll tell you something. I've seen some of this work before and it's worthless."

He opened the buckles before I could guess what he was going to do, and even if I'd known I don't think I could have moved to stop him. Not then. He had one of the paintings in his hand now, staring at it with an offended look on his face, dropping it on the floor. It fluttered, in slow motion, drifting like an autumn leaf, the colors blending, twisting . . .

"Oh no!" Abby pressed her fist against her lips.

Mr. Stengel turned the portfolio upside down. The pictures fell and Abby and Kristin ran to scoop them together.

"Why did you have to do that?" Kristin asked. "These belonged to their mother."

Mr. Stengel smiled. "I know."

"You're a horrible man," Ab said fiercely. "Matt and I hate you."

I knelt beside them, helped slide the pictures carefully back inside the portfolio, took Ab's hand. "Let's go," I said again. This time Mr. Stengel didn't call us back.

Itsy looked up at us and smiled as we went through

the front office. "Your patience paid off, then."

"Yes."

Ab snuffled and rubbed her eyes.

"What's the matter?" Itsy asked with a frown. "Are you all right?"

"She's fine," I said.

"She will be when we get out of here," Kristin added.

I took a gulp of fresh air when we reached the sidewalk. We were out. Safe. Free. But what now? What should we do? Would the police believe us? And even if they did, what if they came and Stengel had moved the dolls someplace else?

"Can we go home now?" Abby asked.

I nodded. "Yes."

"I vote we find a phone booth and call my dad," Kristin said. "We can tell him to come down here right away and get the dolls, and punch out Stengel and . . ."

"You said he's not home," I reminded her. "Weren't they staying wherever they went till the afternoon? The afternoon could be too late."

We were passing the Blakely gallery now. Through the big glass front I could see Kevin Blakely with a young woman who was probably Phoebe, his partner. They were talking and laughing and holding coffee mugs. He saw us and waved and I began to wave back. Instead I pushed open his door.

"Matt?" Kristin asked, but I was already inside.

"Will you help us?" I asked Mr. Blakely.

"If I can. Is something wrong?" He looked hard at

me, then turned to his partner. "Phoebe you can mind the shop for a while, can't you? Come and sit down, kids."

We did. And we told him the whole story.

15

THE FOUR of us went back to the Black Orchid Gallery.

"I've come to see the dolls," Kevin Blakely told Mr. Stengel.

Itsy hovered nervously by the door. "They insisted on walking right in, Mr. Stengel. I'm sorry."

Mr. Stengel didn't rise from his power place behind his desk. "That's all right, Itsy." He dismissed her with a nod of his head. "What dolls are you referring to, Kevin?"

It was Kristin who pointed to the locked door. "He's referring to the ones in there."

"And Aunt Gerda didn't sell them to you either," I said. "You stole them." I felt braver now that Kevin Blakely was with us. Much braver.

"You're not going to say you don't have them, are you?" Kristin asked.

I pointed, too. "Make him open that door, Mr. Blakely. You'll see."

Mr. Stengel rubbed the edge of his desk the way he'd

done before. Maybe the feel of it gave him comfort, or courage. He smiled at Kevin Blakely, not bothering to even glance at any of us. "I found the dolls up in Sierra Maria Canyon," he said. "I borrowed them to show to an interested party. If the price on them is right, I believe the owner will be willing to sell the rest. These two were discards."

"That's a lie," I said, getting braver all the time.

Mr. Stengel didn't look at me then, either. It was as if everyone in the room except Mr. Blakely was invisible. "I have them more or less on consignment, Kevin. See what you think," he said and unlocked the door. And there was poor, dead Harriette and lumpy Isadora. It was such a relief to see that they were still there, that he hadn't somehow magicked them away.

Mr. Blakely examined the dolls carefully. "Yes," he said. "I remember a dealer discovered some like these in Nevada not so long ago. As I recall the artist there didn't want to sell either."

"And what a loss that would have been to the world of art." Mr. Stengel shook his head. The holy expression on his face made me want to throw up. Surely Kevin Blakely wouldn't be fooled by this "all-for-art" talk? Please don't be fooled, Mr. Blakely.

"And you took these from her house without her knowledge?" he asked Mr. Stengel.

I butted in. "From her yard. From her property."

"She's an old friend, Kevin," Mr. Stengel said. "She doesn't know what she has here. When she does, I'm sure she'll see reason. Naturally I wasn't planning on keeping them."

Mr. Blakely looked at him for the longest time, then shook his head and turned to me. "What would you like to do about this, Matthew?"

"I'd like to take them home."

And that's what we did, Kristin and Ab beside Mr. Blakely in the front of his car, me in the back where Harriette and Isadora lay. I touched Harriette's cheek, warm and smooth as silk, and I discovered I wasn't afraid of her at all.

Art people have come from all over to see the dolls, now that we've been on TV and in the papers. A New York City dealer offered $40,000 for Derek alone.

"Derek is not for sale," Aunt Gerda said.

Of course he isn't. Derek's her child. And now Harriette, her dead daughter, is safely at rest again in her backyard grave.

Mrs. Valdoni wrote saying how terrible all this was and were we all right. Knock Knock and Blinky and John sent a letter. They took turns writing the sentences. They all said I was lucky, and they wished they were in California, that nothing fun like this ever happened in Seattle. All it ever did there was rain. Knock Knock didn't even send a joke.

But I kept thinking that though this publicity was nice, we still didn't have any money. We were famous and poor.

And then Kevin Blakely brought out Mr. Corbin Samuelson, a wealthy art patron. Mr. Samuelson said he'd like to offer us an art endowment. The dolls would be left where they were. "Move them and you lose the soul the artist put into them," Mr. Samuelson said. "The house will stay, and I can arrange funds for the permanent upkeep of the dolls. And for your upkeep too, Mrs. Yourra, as honorary curator."

"What about Matthew and Abigail?" Aunt Gerda asked. "I'm getting old and . . ."

"For Matthew and Abigail also, in perpetuity," Mr. Samuelson said.

Abby stared. "In *what*?"

"It simply means the home will be here for you too, for both of you, as long as you need it," Mr. Samuelson explained.

"I would, however, like to put the dolls in a temperature-controlled glass encasement." That's the way Mr. Samuelson talks, as if he has a sock in his mouth.

Aunt Gerda clapped her hands. "The children will love that, I'm sure. They hate the cold."

"Can you believe these canyon people?" Kristin asks me, endlessly. "Now they're trying to say they liked Aunt Gerda and the dolls all the time. It's sickening."

"Sickening!" I raise my eyebrows and shake my head the way she does.

"And where do you think Clay Greeley went?" she asks.

The police are interested in that, too. They've been here, checking things out, questioning everyone about both Clay and Mr. Stengel. I told them Clay left. I know he did, because I saw him go.

It was a couple of days after we found Harriette and

Isadora. I was taking Henry's map back and there was Clay Greeley, waiting at the bus stop and carrying a big, old duffel bag.

I took the map in to Henry, came back out, and Clay Greeley was still there.

Part of my mind said skip it, leave it alone, everything's finished. But this wasn't finished. You stood up to Mr. Stengel, I told myself. You can do this, too.

I cycled across the road.

Clay Greeley watched me come, standing there with that same grin on his round pumpkin face. He'd had his hair cut even shorter and the sun made a red shadow around his head.

"Going someplace?" I asked.

"That's right."

"On your own?"

His grin widened. "See anybody with me?"

"No. But . . ." I didn't know what else to say. "Will you be coming back?"

The grin disappeared. "Never." He bit off the word with a snap of his lips. "Would you come back, if you were me?"

"I . . . I guess not," I said and turned away. I was glad he was leaving.

I'd told Kristin only that I'd seen him go. Just that. And each time she asks, "Where do you think he went?" I shrug. "Beats me!"

I've never told her either about going to his house on my own and what I found there.

It's funny how I have secrets about Clay Greeley. It's as if I have some kind of understanding of him, an

· 160 ·

understanding I can't figure out myself.

"And can you imagine, my Mom's still sorry for him? Kristin says. "She thinks Mr. Stengel used him and that Clay was only a kid. *I* think he was a slug."

"Your mom's nuts," I say. But sometimes I imagine Clay Greeley in a clean, quiet place, in a bed with the sheets tucked neatly in. It's easier to think of him like that, and I'm not sure I want the police to find him.

The twins, of course, say they know nothing about stealing dolls and that they wouldn't go near those dolls if they were paid for it. I think they were paid and they went. But there's no way to prove it.

Aunt Gerda tried to keep Mr. Stengel out of it, for old times' sake, but she couldn't. He's big news. I guess he's going somewhere, too, because Mr. Blakely read in a posh art magazine that the Black Orchid Gallery is up for sale. He told me that the Art Dealers Association of California had sent a letter to all its members saying that Mr. Stengel is no longer connected with them. That means they threw him out.

Mr. Blakely says Mr. Stengel's finished as a dealer. The association will never give him references and without references he won't be able to open a new gallery. As far as I'm concerned, it serves him right and the punishment is not half bad enough. Kristin says he should be locked up for life. I think so, too, and maybe the police will get him even though Aunt Gerda won't press charges.

"I don't think Harold Stengel would ever have taken any of my living children, Matthew," she says.

Not half he wouldn't.

It's almost the end of summer now. Aunt Gerda and I sit out on the porch a lot at nights, when Ab's gone to bed. We talk quietly. Behind their partly finished glass walls the dolls listen and smile.

"Have you ever wondered, Matthew, what people mean by valuable?" Aunt Gerda asks me one night. The cold is beginning to creep in and the trees along the canyon road are tinged with orange and yellow. The crickets have disappeared.

I have wondered about valuable a lot. Mom's paintings line my room now, and Abby's room, too. There are some on every wall of the house. Once I'd hoped we'd have an exhibit of her work. We have one. Here. And it's as if she's still with us.

Aunt Gerda rocks peacefully. "Do those people think the children mean more to me now that I've discovered they're worth a lot of money? Am I supposed to love them more? How foolish."

I know she's speaking about Mom's paintings, too, and trying to comfort me, but I don't need comfort. I began to understand the day I saw the pictures in the Blakely Gallery, the pictures that were priceless because they were done by someone Kevin Blakely loved.

I stretch out my hand and Aunt Gerda takes it and we rock peacefully together. It's nice here with her.

Pretty soon she goes in to make the hot chocolate and I sit, smelling the cool night smells. There's no need to be afraid for our future anymore. No need to be afraid of anything.

And then, from behind one of the half walls of shining glass I hear a faint little voice:

"All's well that ends well, Matthew."

I stop rocking, stare unbelievingly at the dolls, then quickly over my shoulder. Aunt Gerda is carrying a pan of milk to the stove. She must have switched on a tape as she passed. I hadn't heard the click, though.

One of the dolls begins to sing an old-fashioned warble of a song, true and sweet:

"For he's a jolly good fellow . . ."

Another one joins in, and another, singing as softly as bells chiming:

"For he's a jolly good fellow,
And so say all of us."

Hadn't Mr. Stengel said Aunt Gerda couldn't sing? He must have made a mistake.

"For he's a jolly good fellow,
For he's a jolly good fellow . . ."

I could go in, look at the tapes, check that they're moving, but I don't. Maybe I don't want to know. Or maybe I know already. Instead I just sit back in my chair and enjoy the singing.

THE PANS

When *Gilligan's Island* premiered in September 1964 on CBS-TV, critics greeted it with accolades such as "inept, moronic, humorless" (UPI)... "preposterous" (*New York Times*)... not to mention "the worst"... "trite"... "the actors should know better."

VS.

THE FANS

Yet this humble little sitcom about seven castaways on an uncharted Pacific island shot up the Nielsen ratings chart, becoming the sleeper of the season and one of the most successful syndicated comedy series of all time—still seen twenty-five years later by over 2.5 million viewers every day. Gilligan and his buddies have infected the collective consciousness of a generation.

It's time to join the castaways once again, with...

THE UNOFFICIAL GILLIGAN'S ISLAND HANDBOOK

The Unofficial GILLIGAN'S ISLAND HANDBOOK

A CASTAWAY'S COMPANION TO THE LONGEST-RUNNING SHIPWRECK IN TELEVISION HISTORY

JOEY GREEN

WARNER BOOKS

A Warner Communications Company

Library of Congress Cataloging-in-Publication Data

Green, Joey.
    The unofficial Gilligan's Island handbook: a castaway's guide to the longest-running
shipwreck in television history / Joey Green.
        p. cm.
    ISBN 0-446-38668-5
    1. Gilligan's Island (Television program)   I. Title.
PN1992.77.G53G74   1988
791.45'72—dc19   87-24208
                                                                                     CIP

Cover design by Carmine Vecchio

Designed by Giorgetta Bell McRee

For my little buddies,
Amy Sue, Douglas, and Michael

CONTENTS

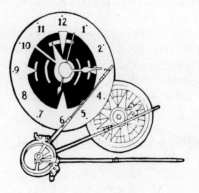

INTRODUCTION

don't know about you, but watching *Gilligan's Island* always leaves me with a slew of unanswered questions: Why did the crew and passengers of the *S.S. Minnow* bring along so much luggage for a three-hour tour? Why can't the castaways build a simple raft with the Professor's expertise? What are the odds of all those people visiting the island, returning to civilization, and then somehow forgetting to report the castaways to the authorities?

While *Gilligan's Island* hardly deserves academic exploration, intelligent dissection, or critical appraisal, I decided that the show's infinite flaws and discrepancies have remained the subject of speculative cocktail party banter for far too long. The time had come for some concrete answers. And that's exactly what *The Unofficial Gilligan's Island Handbook* attempts to provide. But I'm afraid it doesn't stop there.

You see, there's a lot more to *Gilligan's Island* than meets the eye. While *Gilligan's Island* makes no pretense of being intelligent comedy, the parallels between *Gilligan's Island* and Luigi Pirandello's *Six Characters in Search of an Author,* William Shakespeare's *The Tempest,* Daniel Defoe's *Robinson Crusoe,* Thomas More's *Utopia,* and William Golding's *Lord of the Flies* would undoubtedly make interesting fodder for a doctoral thesis of questionable merit.

Perhaps *Gilligan's Island* brilliantly dilutes otherwise unpalatable literary and philosophical themes to make them accessible to a wider audience than Pirandello, Shakespeare, Defoe, More, and Golding could ever hope to reach. Maybe the deceptively lowbrow and predictable *Gilligan's Island* is cleverly layered with hidden meaning ambitiously addressing key social issues and philosophical themes, luring captive and unsuspecting viewers into the realm of political and social consciousness. Or perhaps, after carefully combing every episode five or six times, I've simply lost my grip on reality.

This book is more than just a transparent excuse for me to immerse myself in the innocuous world of *Gilligan's Island.* It's a dangerously obsessive regression. And that, as we shall see, is what *Gilligan's Island* is all about.

Joey Green
New York, 1987

Just sit right back and you'll hear a tale,
A tale of a fateful trip;
That started from this tropic port,
Aboard this tiny ship.
The mate was a mighty sailor man,
The skipper, brave and sure;

Five passengers set sail that day,
For a three-hour tour (a three-hour tour).
The weather started getting rough,
The tiny ship was tossed;
If not for the courage of the fearless crew,
The *Minnow* would be lost (the *Minnow* would be lost).

The ship set ground on the shore of this,
Uncharted desert isle;
With Gilligan, the Skipper too,
The Millionaire, and his wife;
The Movie Star, the Professor, and Mary Ann.
Here on Gilligan's Isle.

CHAPTER 1

SIT RIGHT BACK AND YOU'LL HEAR A TALE

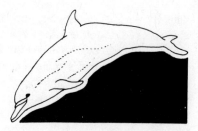

I n the spring of 1963, Sherwood Schwartz, former head writer on the Emmy Award–winning *Red Skelton Show,* conceived his story of seven characters marooned on an uncharted, uninhabited Pacific Island, unabashedly using Daniel Defoe's *Robinson Crusoe,* one of the top ten best-sellers of all time, as his model. The passengers and crew aboard the *S.S. Minnow,* a small sightseeing vessel, would be shipwrecked on an island about two hundred miles southeast of Hawaii. Each week the castaways would find themselves in a peculiar situation, in which Gilligan, the lovable but bumbling first mate, would somehow manage to ruin their chances of being rescued.

Remembers Schwartz, "My agent of some seventeen years said, 'Who the hell is going to look at the same seven people on the same island week after week? It doesn't make any sense. Nobody's ever done a show like that.' Of course, anytime anybody ever rejects something with the answer 'Nobody's ever done anything like that,' to me, that's a positive, not a negative. To him it was a negative, and he quickly said, 'Of course, if you want me to try to sell it . . . ,' and I said, 'No, it's hard enough for anybody to sell something they believe in,' so I called another guy who wanted to represent me." Less than forty-eight hours after his new agent showed United Artists–Television the ten-page mimeographed outline, they advanced him the money to develop the show.

The title for *Gilligan's Island* had been plucked from the Los Angeles telephone directory. "I could have called it *Thompson's Island,* but that's lukewarm water," recalls Schwartz, who holds master's degrees in both zoology and psychology. "I could have called it a crazy name, such as *Mukenmire's Island,* but that's burlesque. I wanted a real name that would connote comedy without hitting you in the face, and it took a long time just to find that. I also believe in hard letters. . . . I think they're more memorable than soft letters."

In the outline, Schwartz described the seven intentionally cliché characters who would be shipwrecked on the island. "There's a great deal of sociological implication in *Gilligan's Island,*" he explains. "It takes a group of very carefully selected people who represent many different parts of our society and shows how in a circumstance—being shipwrecked together—they have to learn to get along with each other. I mean, none of these people had anything in common with each other, and that's quite deliberate."

It took Schwartz many months of hard thought to wind up with those seven people. "Some of the people are named by name," he explains. "I didn't want to do that. I didn't want anybody to have a name because I wanted everybody to be just 'the millionaire.' Nobody ever called Gilligan anything but Gilligan, or the Skipper anything but the Skipper. They had names, never to be used. The Professor was the Professor. But you couldn't keep calling Dawn Wells the sweet little girl next door, so she had a name, Mary Ann. But they were all representative rather than people, and that was deliberate." In fact, Schwartz deliberately named the boat, the *S.S. Minnow*, after FCC president Newton Minow, as a personal dig at the man he felt had shipwrecked network television.

In a meeting with William Paley and Frank Stanton, who were then running CBS, Schwartz described *Gilligan's Island* as a social microcosm. "Mr. Paley blanched and said, 'I thought this was a comedy show,'" recalls Schwartz, "and I quickly said, 'It's a funny microcosm.' It almost cost me the show, because I have since learned that when you're describing a comedy show, you do not use a literate phrase."

The costly $175,000 pilot took six days to film in a remote section of Kauai, Hawaii, and was finished on the day Kennedy was assassinated. CBS, which had become a partner in producing the show with United Artists, absorbed much of the cost. Bob Denver, Alan Hale, Jr., Jim Backus, Natalie Schafer, and three others (whose identity Schwartz still refuses to reveal) were cast for the pilot.

Schwartz's first choice for the role of Gilligan was Jerry Van Dyke, who, represented by Schwartz's original agent, was advised to take a different pilot. "The only other person I ever talked to was Bob Denver," remembers Schwartz. "William Morris got in touch with me and said they had a perfect guy." Denver had played beatnik Maynard G. Krebs on *The Many Loves of Dobie Gillis* for four years.

"The Skipper was the hardest role to cast," remembers Schwartz, "and I couldn't cast that to save my neck. It was just so hard. I knew that the Skipper would be yelling at Gilligan most of the time, and as it turned out, hitting him with his hat and carrying on against him, so I needed somebody who would be so lovable and warm that you knew he loved Gilligan no matter how much he yelled at him. I wrote a special test scene, which wasn't even in the pilot, that laid it on so thick that if anybody could survive that scene, he would be the one to

4

be the Skipper. Actor after actor failed [including Carroll O'Connor]; they all turned black—except for Alan Hale, Jr." Hale, son of movie actor Alan Hale, had starred in two unmemorable television series, *Casey Jones* and *Biff Baker USA,* and had hitchhiked from St. George, Utah, where he was doing a picture with Audie Murphy, to screen-test for the part.

Jim Backus, the voice of Mr. Magoo, and star of television's *I Married Joan* and *The Jim Backus Show,* had worked with Schwartz in both radio and television and had originated the Thurston Howell III character while performing for *The Alan Young Show* in the late 1930s. "I'd been doing 'the rich boy' for my own amusement," recalls Backus. "The kind of guys from Yale and Harvard with Larchmont lockjaw. No one had ever done this. So I went on and the response from the people who heard the show was great, but the NBC censor department sent down word that I couldn't do that character any-more. We asked, 'Why not?' And they said, 'Well, it sounds like Roosevelt.' Strangely enough, that's what it is. I call it my Groton accent. They called the character Hubert Updyke the Third, which is a little kind of a jokey name, and he had about a five-minute spot on the show and just tore the place down. The writers found it so easy to write for him. We originated all the rich jokes."

Natalie Schafer, an accomplished actress of stage and screen who was once a protege of Gertrude Lawrence, had played Eleanor Carlyle, Lana Turner's mother, in the television dramatic series *The Survivors.* When Schafer, reluctant to move to California to do a series, read the script for *Gilligan's Island,* she thought, " 'Oh, I don't have to worry about that, it'll never go.' And my agent called me, saying, 'Listen, Natalie, we can get you good money, and you can go to Hawaii where you've never been, and this'll never sell. You don't have to worry about it.' So I did it."

Once the pilot was made, the troubles began. Virtually everybody at CBS liked the premise—except for Jim Aubrey, then network presi-dent. "Jim's idea of the show was very different from mine," recalls Schwartz. Aubrey bought the show believing the renamed *Gilligan's Travels* would only shipwreck the seven people aboard the charter boat in the first episode. "Then the little boat takes some other people on another adventure," remembers Schwartz. "I used to say, 'Jim, that's a different show. That's not my show.' And he said, 'Well, you can't keep the same people ...,' and I was back to my [first] agent again."

Schwartz finally convinced Aubrey to allow him to keep the seven castaways shipwrecked on the island until the ratings slipped. Aubrey agreed, insisting that Schwartz add a one-minute trailer to the end of the pilot film, featuring coming attractions to the second episode in which Gilligan and the Skipper unwittingly take two escaped bank robbers on a cruise around Hawaii and get chased by the Coast Guard.

United Artists, the coproducers, also tried to stymie Schwartz. Schwartz felt that the only way he could establish who these people were and what they were doing on an island was with an opening song. But without explanation, Dick Dorso, then United Artist president, forbid him to do so.

A completed version of the *Gilligan's* pilot, without a song, was shipped back to New York. Schwartz appended a note indicating that the finished product did not represent his original thinking. The CBS brass rejected the film, without any explanation, and Aubrey went ahead and authorized another series about a charter boat, *The Baileys of Balboa,* which was later canceled after twenty-six episodes.

For all purposes, *Gilligan's Island* was dead, so Schwartz now wrote the song that he'd been insisting was the only solution to the problem. He then viewed the assembled film footage, reedited it, and rushed a new version to Manhattan, where it was shown to a test audience. "This is the pilot I had in mind," he wrote in an accompanying memo.

The results were so phenomenally high that CBS dismissed them, claiming there was something wrong with the audience. They retested the show twice more. Again the audiences indicated that the show would be a hit. All this testing took place in the final week of the selling season while CBS was locking up the 1964–65 schedule—a schedule that still didn't include *Gilligan's Island.*

At the eleventh hour, late one afternoon, Aubrey conceded and firmed the show. Then, with unusual tenacity, CBS officials began to dilute their latest acquisition, and Schwartz found himself attending more meetings. "The network demanded complete changes in characterization of all the characters after it was sold, after the audience testing went through the roof," Schwartz told *TV Guide.* He was told no one would identify with a Hollywood actress, to find a character who would fit a larger audience. He was told no one would understand a billionaire, to make him a wealthy man. He was told that the professor was wooden, without flair.

"The major battle that was fought and won was to keep the seven characters intact," Schwartz told *TV Guide.* "Without them, the show could not have succeeded. Unfortunately, the pilot show is the one that meddlers have several months to analyze. The more something is analyzed, the more faults are found, whether actual or imaginary. I dare say, if one had a year to play with a show, and enough experts saw it, you'd have nothing left."

"My mother was very sick," remembers Natalie Schafer, "and I was asked to go down to Puerto Vallarta for the holidays. I went, and we were all at cocktails one day when they brought me a telegram. Everybody thought Mother had died, and I opened the telegram and burst into tears. They came over and said, 'Don't worry, we'll get you home,' and I cried, 'The series sold!' "

Meanwhile, a set was built in the middle of a lake in Hollywood's CBS Studio Center, at a cost of about $75,000, complete with artificial palm trees, a blacktopped lake, transplanted tropical plants and flowers, and a man-made stream and waterfall. After the lake bottom was blacktopped and the water poured in, it leaked, so it had to be emptied, fixed, and refilled. The palm trees were pine poles plastered over to simulate bark, with fronds and coconuts nailed on. On the sound stage at CBS Stage 2, the concrete floor was covered an inch thick with two tons of grainy sand before a lush collection of authentic palm trees, flax, exotic birds, carpet grass, and cut magnolias were put in place along with the castaways' huts.

Back at CBS, the network brass managed to win several skirmishes. The actors who played Ginger Grant, the Professor, and Mary Ann in the pilot were discharged and replaced by Tina Louise (who had been appearing with Carol Burnett on Broadway in *Fade Out—Fade In*), Russell Johnson (who played Marshal Gib Scott in the television western *Black Saddle*), and television newcomer Dawn Wells (Raquel Welch purportedly tried out for the part as well). Two extra days of shooting the new trio boosted production costs. For this last-minute revamping, Zuma Beach, a picturesque stretch of sand on the California coast, was improvised for Hawaii.

The new shooting, plus continued CBS vacillation, resulted in a great scurry to get the first show into the can. "Jim Aubrey still didn't like the show," Schwartz told *TV Guide*. "Three scripts were written, but with a new show, everybody has to approve the scripts before you can start shooting. Well, if Jim didn't like the show to begin with, it was predictable he wouldn't like the scripts. He didn't care for seven people on an island, and all these scripts were about seven people on the island."

What eventually reached the air late in September was a pastiche of three separate shows, including half of the pilot, welded together by the CBS group think. "The first episode was meant to be the second episode," says Schwartz, who wanted the pilot to air first. "They're already on the island and trying to get off, and it didn't make any sense. The actual pilot was the Christmas episode [Episode 12], where I managed to salvage two-thirds of the original pilot as a remembrance of how grateful they all were at Christmastime that they weren't killed in the original wreck." (Schwartz has refused to donate the only existing copy of the pilot to the Museum of Broadcasting to protect the identities of the three replaced cast members.)

The first episode, an incoherent hodgepodge of primitive sight gags, pratfalls, and lowbrow humor, incensed the nation's television critics. "It is impossible that a more inept, moronic, or humorless show has ever appeared on the home tube," wrote Rick DuBrow of UPI. Jack Gould, in *The New York Times,* called it "quite possibly the most preposterous situation comedy of the season." In naming the show the worst comedy on the air, syndicated columnist Hal Humphrey added: "*Gilligan's Island* is the kind of thing one might expect to find running for three nights at some neighborhood group playhouse, but hardly on a coast-to-coast TV network." Terrence O'Flaherty of the San Francisco *Chronicle* wrote: "It is difficult for me to believe that *Gilligan's Island* was written, directed, and filmed by adults.... The cast is heavily larded with actors who should know better. I can only assume they were motivated by avarice alone." Added *Variety*: "The series tries so hard to be funny that it loses all sense of spontaneity and, indeed, of humor. Everything that happens seems manufactured and deliberate, so that even the trite-and-true pratfalls have the appearance of being dictated by a computer."

In truth the first episode, heavy-handed and contrived, strains pathetically for laughs. The cast members seem unnatural. They've yet to establish harmony or genuine rapport, and they don't really immerse themselves in the make-believe.

"I resented the criticism," admits Schwartz, "because they were criticizing an episode that I had had terrible fights about with CBS over not putting on the air. I wanted to put the reconstructed pilot on the air first, because I wanted the public to see how these people got on the island, particularly because we knew in advance the public reaction to it, because we had the statistical information from the testing. But the network was adamant."

Undaunted by the reviews, Schwartz merely expressed anger at the critics, who, he claimed, didn't understand what the show was attempting. Schwartz's greatest fear was that the criticism would undermine the show before it had a chance to blossom. "Most of the cast had little faith in the show to begin with," he recalls, explaining why the cast didn't own profit participation in the show (decisions they all would later regret). Schwartz gathered the cast, told them his previous three shows were all in the top ten within six months of his arrival, and assured them they'd make the top ten, placating most of his players.

One of the exceptions was Tina Louise. "I was ashamed when I saw the first show," she told *TV Guide*. "In this medium, you perform, everyone performs. There's no such thing as a real moment, an honest reaction, because the show is like a cartoon. You're not acting, not the way I studied it. I wouldn't watch it if I wasn't on it." Louise still says, "It was a very highly stylized kind of situation, which cramped my style, I would say. But you learned that you had to work within those confines and have fun with it, and that's what I learned."

But to the consternation of the critics and despite the continued CBS interference, *Gilligan's Island*, sponsored by Crest at a cost of about $40,000 a minute, was a success with the viewers, never dropping out of the top forty.

One afternoon in November 1964, CBS messengers delivered three-foot-square packages wrapped in burlap and tied with hemp to homes all over Hollywood. The boxes, labeled *Gilligan's Island* Cast-away Kit, contained snake-bite antidote (a pint of Canadian Club), malaria cure (a split of champagne), a carton of cigarettes (for smoke signals), hardtack (a stale bagel), canned K rations (for instant banquets), *Gilligan's Island* weather reports (the sunny Nielsen ratings for the previous month), and an invitation to a shipwreck costume party celebrating the show's unexpected success.

The next night, some two hundred members of the local press corps were shuttled via jeep-driven, twelve-man lifeboats from the gates of the old Republic lot in North Hollywood to CBS Stage 2. Inside, critics who had blasted the show drank screwdrivers served in coconut shells, feasted on barbecued spareribs and fried rice, watched two sarong-clad dancers from Central Casting give hula lessons, and mingled with the cast and producers, who tried to explain how their show was pushing the bounds of situation comedy.

By late February, the shipwrecked septet had navigated into the third position in the Nielsen ratings, emerging as the sleeper series of the year, confounding critics and columnists.

Schwartz explains some of the reasons for his show's popularity: "Kids had a reason for watching it, adults had a reason for watching it, professors had a reason for watching it, sex maniacs had a reason for watching it. That's why I think the show has lived the way it has. Its demographics to this day are extraordinary... one-third children, one-third women, one-third men."

"We always did long scripts and jammed them into the half hour, which, I think, is another reason why it was a real success," offers Bob Denver. "It was very fast. Things are happening all the time. If you turned away, you missed a gag or you missed a joke."

"It was just goddamn funny," quips Jim Backus.

"It reached children and adults," says Natalie Schafer, "and it made people laugh at a time when there wasn't very much on television to laugh about. It brought comedy into people's lives."

"There was a wonderful chemistry between the people," says Dawn Wells. "I think you could have recast the show and not had it work. There's a magic that happened with Bob and Alan. A magic."

"We just all work together well," adds Tina Louise, "and there was a certain quality that I guess I brought to the character so that it was more than just being a redhead standing there. There was just a certain spirit that kind of connected."

"I suppose there's something in kids that hits their imagination about being on a desert island, and being not alone but in a group, and always being somehow protected," says Russell Johnson. "It's a safe kind of wonderful fantasy."

"Everyone needs a little nonsense in their lives, and that's what Gilligan's Island was," says Alan Hale, Jr. "Escape," agrees Dawn Wells. "I think that was the joy of the show. You put your feet up and didn't have to think."

"They say familiarity breeds contempt," Schwartz told TV Guide. "I think it breeds viewers, if you can get people familiar with your pattern. People watch for patterns, not the same thing each week, but the general outline. They want to keep seeing the same kind of thing. Shows that go all over the place—all you have to do is look at the anthologies—go down the drain, one after another. If you come into people's homes, you're their friends. They want you to be who you are, they don't want you to change. What they want to change is the dialogue, the story, and the scene."

Sociologically, Schwartz intended for the island to be seen as a microcosm, to demonstrate that to survive, people must drop their differences, respect one another's individuality, and consolidate their efforts. "Again, it's not only a social microcosm," says Schwartz, "it's an international microcosm where eventually the Irish and the English have to learn to live together, where the Arabs and the Jews have to learn to live together, where the United States and Russia have to learn to live together—because we're all on the same island. It's a show that operates on many, many levels." Of course, on Gilligan's Island, the castaways' differences are merely limited to socioeconomic class, intellect, sex, and profession. They still share major similarities: a common race, religion, ethnic origin, and nationality. Seven WASPs stranded on an island, where women are treated like second-class citizens, hardly constitute a microcosm worthy of in-depth sociological study.

Of course, most viewers weren't capable of such simple analysis, primarily because they were children—if the fan mail was any demographic indication of the show's original audience. In fact, elementary school teachers would recommend the show to their classes as one of the few on television that children could watch; it is a harmless comedy void of violence or blatant sex.

In a Philadelphia school, clips from *Gilligan's Island* were used to test educational television. Children of equal ability and age were divided into two classrooms. One class was shown a television clip of the Professor revitalizing a battery on *Gilligan's Island,* while in the other classroom, a teacher demonstrated the same experiment. The children learning from the Professor far outperformed those taught by the teacher, blazing the trail for educational television.

Shooting *Gilligan's Island* was not all fun and games. "In the wintertime the lagoon was not a fun place," remembers Bob Denver. "One morning we were down there, and there was ice along the edge. I said, 'I can't go in there! It's gotta be like forty-two degrees!'...I wore a wet suit underneath the outfit, but it didn't do any good."

"We had a scene with a dummy trunk-branch on a tree [Episode 29]," recalls Alan Hale, Jr. "I was up in the tree, and it was on a cable and it was supposed to break because of my weight. Well, it timed a little differently, and it threw me. I fell backwards from this tree twelve feet up in the air, down onto the stage, and I broke my fall with my arm. I didn't realize I had fractured my wrist, but I didn't tell anybody because it was near the close of the season and I didn't want to hold up production."

Animals often created havoc on the set. Jim Backus, bitten on the hand by a macaw, was obliged to take an antitetanus shot on the set, and Russell Johnson once sat at his makeup table petrified while a loose tiger casually walked behind him.

During the filming of one episode, Bob Denver was supposed to barricade himself inside the Howell's hut, sit on the bed, notice a lion sitting next to him, and run back out the door [Episode 60]. But when Denver looked at the lion, recalls Schwartz, "he let out a yell and jumped off the bed—which he wasn't supposed to do, since lions don't like quick movement or loud noises. So as he left the bed, the lion sprang at him."

"The thing that fascinated me more than anything was Bob's

reaction," says Dawn Wells. "I mean, I would have been a pile of butter on the floor. He ran, and realizing that the lion was coming, he turned around with a karate chop to practically hit the lion."

"Nah!" says Denver. "I was preparing to put my hands up and catch it." Fortunately, the bed was on casters, so it rolled out from under the lion, who fell on the floor.

After the first few episodes of the show were broadcast, a Coast Guard lieutenant brought Schwartz a couple dozen telegrams sent to Hickam field and Vandenberg Air Force Base from viewers who, taking the show seriously, asked the United States to send a destroyer to rescue the seven castaways. "Here's a show that had music to it, a laugh track in it, and yet," laughs Schwartz, "they believed it to the extent that they were concerned about those people on the island."

Throughout the first season, permanent exile seemed imminent. No one knew whether the series would stay on the air, and if so, whether Tina Louise would stay with the show. Finally, CBS, faced with *Gilligan's Island*'s overwhelming ratings, renewed the show.

In the second season beginning in September 1965, the show was filmed in color and switched to Thursday nights at eight o'clock up against *Daniel Boone* on NBC and *The Donna Reed Show* on ABC. The show's opening, originally shot at the Honolulu basin, was refilmed in color at the Long Beach Marina. But the most noticeable change occurred in the opening song's lyrics. The words "the rest" were replaced with "the Professor, and Mary Ann." Originally cast as second-billed costars and credited at the end of the show, the Professor's and Mary Ann's increasing popularity demanded top billing. "I had expected a bigger part," says Russell Johnson. "That came in the second year. The first year was kind of nothing until the audience discovered this guy, and the word got back somehow, and they said we've got to make the Professor a little more."

"I think that originally Ginger was signed before the Professor and Mary Ann," recalls Dawn Wells, "and I think her contract stated she was in fifth place and no one after her. Then I think the second year, when the show was definitely seven characters equally, there was a contract renegotiation." Wells fondly recalls exchanging flowers and birthday gifts with Russell Johnson with cards signed "Love, the rest."

In September 1966, for its third season, *Gilligan's Island,* switched to Monday nights at seven-thirty, began to lose its audience to a new show on NBC, *The Monkees.* In early 1967, two weeks after announcing the cancellation of *Gunsmoke,* William Paley, needing a show to fill the eight o'clock half-hour time slot, decided to cancel *Gilligan's Island* to make an hour available to save *Gunsmoke.* "People ask,

'How'd you get off the island?'" says Alan Hale, Jr. "I say, 'We got fired—that's how we got off the island.'"

Having been seen by three generations of television viewers, all seven cast members continue to receive worldwide fan mail and recognition. "I've only met one person so far who said they never saw it," says Bob Denver. Alan Hale, Jr., has been recognized as the Skipper in India, Thailand, and Japan. Dawn Wells was once recognized by a German couple while touring Ludwig's castle in Bavaria.

"You're typecast for the rest of your life, you know, but you look at it the other way—that people are still enjoying it, kids are still laughing and still scratching," says Bob Denver.

"I consider the Skipper a friend of mine," says Alan Hale, Jr., who, having lived most of his life in his father's shadow, still revels in the role of the Skipper. Hale and Jim Backus, who had been typecast most of his life, didn't resent being typecast as much as other members of the cast.

Natalie Schafer, who immediately after *Gilligan's Island* received rave notices for playing a sadistic lesbian in *The Killing of Sister George,* couldn't get another part on the screen. "When I was up for a different part [on television], the new network kids said, 'We can't put Natalie Schafer in another kind of part at five o'clock, and at six o'clock *Gilligan's Island* goes on. It wouldn't be believable.' I don't agree. I think audiences would be fascinated by people who change their personality and play something else."

"I think [*Gilligan's Island*] hurt me in some ways," claims Tina Louise. "But you can't knock success, I guess. You know, it certainly made everybody know me."

"You know, it's a double-edged sword," says Russell Johnson. "It really was fine while it was on and caught everybody's fancy and that kind of thing, and then, after the show went off the air, I couldn't get arrested as a heavy."

"I had a difficult time breaking the Mary Ann image at first," recalls Dawn Wells. "That's the reason I went back to the stage."

As one of the most successful syndicated comedy series of all time, *Gilligan's Island's* popularity spurred ABC to air an animated version in September 1974 entitled *The New Adventures of Gilligan,* which featured many of the original cast members providing the voices of the individual characters.

In 1978, after eleven years of reruns, all but one of the seven original cast members returned to make *Rescue from Gilligan's Island,* a two-hour, two-part NBC movie broadcast on October 14 and 21. "I felt that a lot of people—especially since there had never been a final episode—were curious about those seven people [eleven] years later," says Schwartz. Tina Louise, still furious with the show for typecasting her, demanded too much money. "As much as I wanted to get together with everybody for old times' sake—I thought, well, that'll be fun—I was afraid of confusing the casting agents," explains Louise. "I thought if they paid me something worthwhile, then I'll say, 'Okay, well, I'm doing this for the money—I do have a child to support—and I'll overcome my emotional hesitations.'" She was replaced by newcomer Judith Baldwin. Part one, said *Variety* of October 18, 1978, "was like viewing Saturday morning kidvid on Saturday night.... It was hard to figure where the script would go in the second part, even harder to care."

But once again, bad reviews didn't stop the show from going through the ratings roof, and the next year a second movie, *Castaways on Gilligan's Island,* was put together as a pilot for a new series. Having been shipwrecked again on the island, the crew is rescued again, but the idea of an island hideaway hotel dawns on the millionaire, providing a *Love Boat* framework. Said *Variety* of May 9, 1979, "When all was happily resolved, one could only hope that the terribly out-of-date 'Gilligan's' concept had had its last hurrah, before Bob Denver has to play the title role as a grandfather."

A third movie, *The Harlem Globetrotters on Gilligan's Island,* was produced in 1981, but ratings were so low that plans for a continuing weekly series were temporarily suspended. They have yet to be reignited. In September 1982, CBS began airing another animated version entitled *Gilligan's Planet,* where the castaways are marooned on another planet. Many of the cast members again provided the voices.

Schwartz wrote a script for a fourth movie in which the castaways learn that a nuclear war has destroyed the world. "I went around spouting the plot every time I got a chance because you never know," reveals Denver. "The networks hear it and they think they made it up, and the next thing you know it's on. But he had a script on that whole premise. The seven of us think it's destroyed and we get married. Gilligan marries Mary Ann and they have a baby boy. And the Professor marries Ginger and they have a baby girl. And then there's like a *Blue Lagoon* sequence where the kids grow up, so when Gilligan's son is twenty, he sails off to see whether the world is really destroyed, and of course it isn't. They heard it on the radio, and Gilligan broke it just before the disclaimer came on." Schwartz couldn't sell the idea to the networks.

Still, *Gilligan's Island* continues to make its mark on popular culture.

Mad magazine published a *Gilligan's Island* parody; a student at UCLA wrote a graduate thesis on *Gilligan's Island;* a band recorded the *Gilligan's Island* theme song to the tune of Led Zeppelin's "Stairway to Heaven"; and in the fall of 1982, members of the *Harvard Lampoon,* dressed in black and seated on stools, performed an episode of *Gilligan's Island* ("Seer Gilligan," Episode 55) as an existential play in beatnik [inflection] for one week at Harvard's Experimental Theatre. In November 1986, all seven castaways attended Sherwood Schwartz's seventieth birthday party; the January 1987 issue of *Emmy* magazine published an essay explaining how each of the castaways represented one of the seven deadly sins; several comedians perform monologues on *Gilligan's Island; It's Gary Shandling's Show* and *The Bob Newhart Show* have included segments devoted to the *Gilligan's Island* mythos; and a 1987 novel, *The Broom of the System,* refers to a theme bar called "Gilligan's Isle." By the fall of 1987, *Gilligan's Island* had attained such cult status that an episode of the television series *Alf* aired in which the puppet Alf dreams he is a castaway on the island; Bob Denver, Alan Hale, Jr., Russell Johnson, and Dawn Wells all guest-starred in the dream sequence.

In the 1987 movie *Back to the Beach,* Bob Denver guest stars as a bartender who, after woefully recalling life as a castaway, is dragged off by Alan Hale, Jr., for another three-hour tour.

Gilligan's Island is a phenomenon filled with paradoxes. Despite contemptuous reviews, *Gilligan's Island* has remained one of the top hits of syndication for the last twenty years. In 1986, Nielsen reports indicated that *Gilligan's Island* was being seen by over 2.5 million people every day. For whatever it's worth, Gilligan, the Skipper, the Millionaire, his wife, the Movie Star, the Professor, and Mary Ann have infected the collective consciousness of a generation. Hopefully, scientists will someday discover a vaccine.

CASTAWAYS' CORNER

How did you react to the criticism?

BOB DENVER: "You know, it's like a reviewer's delight, any kind of show like that. I think they assume you're trying to do something beyond what it is. And you're not. You're just doing something very simple." By the time he saw the reviews, "we were already picked up for the second year, so it was okay whatever they said."

ALAN HALE, JR.: "Fortunately, I've had thick skin for years."

JIM BACKUS: "It was an easy, easy thing to ridicule. Johnny Carson used to say they were going to make *Gilligan's Island* into a comedy. I think it has more lasting power. It's exactly what it is, what it started out to be.... I thought the ensemble acting was very good."

NATALIE SCHAFER: "I expected it. I never thought it would go on. I thought it was dreadful in the beginning.... I don't think they got maybe the directors who had the sense of comedy that it needed, but it later became more acceptable."

TINA LOUISE: "I only wanted to stay in it for a year. You know, I really didn't want to put three years of my life into it. It's just that it became such a big hit, you know, there was no choice. I kept being asked back. And I had a contract; I couldn't get out anyway."

RUSSELL JOHNSON: "I was offended. I still am...I mean, I was trained in the method; I'm a Stanislavsky actor. It used to bother me. It still does bother me when people take shots at it. But I understand it

16

now. I mean, we're not curing cancer. We're not doing *Hamlet.* We're doing *Gilligan's Island."*

DAWN WELLS: "I don't think it bothered us at all because we were in the top ten. I think we just sort of laughed our way to the bank."

CASTAWAYS' CORNER

What was the message of *Gilligan's Island?*

BOB DENVER: "I guess, you know, truth and honesty and all the rest of it. I mean, all the values. Try to keep that, you know, in the forefront. It wasn't trying to change anybody's mind or do anything like that....It was mainly just fun. Just to have fun."

ALAN HALE, JR.: "I don't think there was any message at all. I think it was just such a misnomer, 'deserted island.' We were there; it wasn't deserted. And who deserted it? Nobody who was there....The big thing about it was nonsense. Everybody has to have nonsense in their lives."

JIM BACKUS: "I think it left a message of plain decency without being cloying. I don't think we ever went to cute. The message was delivered with very deft hands—if there was any message, in fact. For kids growing up, I think it kind of says that the good guys wound up good and the bad guys got punished....It's a lesson that all people from different places can live together and work together and be very happy."

NATALIE SCHAFER: "That all kinds of people can live together if they want to and with great care for each other."

TINA LOUISE: "It's just fun. It's not offensive to anyone."

RUSSELL JOHNSON: "I used to work with people who said, 'You want a message? Call Western Union!'...As far as I'm concerned, it's just plain damned fun. And fantasy. Just wild and crazy dreams. The effect of the show was a nonviolent good time. I suppose if you want to look for a message, you could talk about survival and the spirit of man, but you can't play those things, you just play the moment."

CHAPTER 2
SeVeN STRANDeD CaSTAWAYS

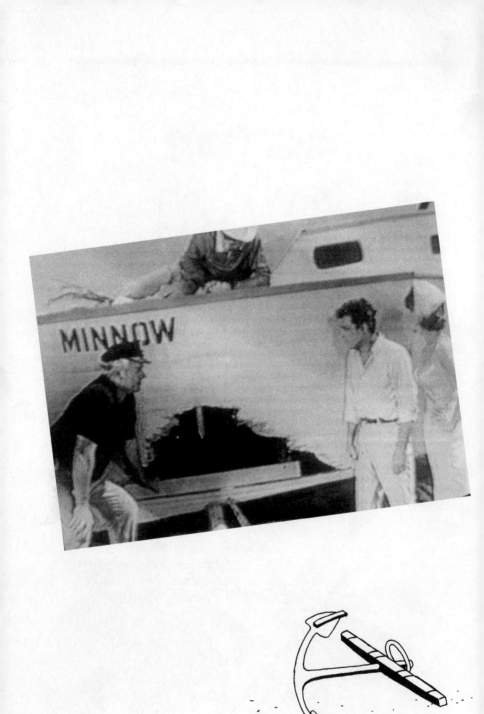

Skipper Jonas Grumby and his first mate, Gilligan, had been running an excursion boat, the *S.S. Minnow,* from Honolulu, Hawaii, offering three-hour tours for an undisclosed price that included a free lunch served aboard the boat.

On a Tuesday in September 1964, the *Minnow* left Honolulu harbor carrying five passengers: millionaire Thurston Howell III, his socialite wife, Lovey Wentworth Howell, movie star Ginger Grant, Professor Roy Hinkley, and country girl Mary Ann Summers. The Howells were aboard for a pleasure cruise; Ginger jumped aboard the boat to escape from some sailors who were chasing her; the Professor took the cruise to be alone, to write his book, *Fun with Ferns;* and Mary Ann had won the trip on the *Minnow* from a contest on a local Kansas radio station.

The day the *Minnow* set sail, the radio operator issued weather information from the previous day, making no mention of the approaching tropical storm. When the *Minnow* got out to sea, the storm flared up, and the tiny ship was tossed. As the *Minnow* neared a reef, the Skipper ordered Gilligan to throw the anchor overboard, which Gilligan did—neglecting to make sure it was securely tied to the ship. The crew and passengers of the *Minnow* would have otherwise endured the storm and returned to Honolulu, but instead the Skipper lost control of the ship, Gilligan threw the blowtorch overboard, and the ship's compass broke. In fact, Gilligan fell overboard, and the Skipper fished him out. After drifting at sea for three days, the *Minnow* finally picked up a current and drifted to the shore of an uncharted island that couldn't be found on any of the Skipper's navy maps.

GILLIGAN

"I've done it again? I only wish I knew what I was doing!"

—Gilligan

Perhaps the greatest mystery on Gilligan's Island is why Gilligan's fellow castaways don't kill him. In virtually every episode the lovable but bumbling first mate inevitably manages to ruin the castaways' chances of being rescued. When he's carrying water buckets, a ladder, or a bucket of glue, he's invariably a walking time bomb. And whenever he tries to help, he always ends up doing more harm than good. Yet while Gilligan gives the word "klutz" new meaning, the other castaways willingly tolerate his thick-witted buffoonery.

The only obvious explanation for Gilligan's survival is that he's won the affection of his fellow castaways and level heads prevail. Of course, the Skipper's "little buddy" also does most of the unpleasant chores on the island—which undoubtedly puts him in better standing with the others. He's always stuck digging that new well, building another rescue tower, carrying water buckets, working as the Skipper's slave, or caddying for Mr. Howell, to whom he's always "Gilligan, my boy." His lackadaisical subservience obviously makes him indispensable.

For a servile castaway, Gilligan is extraordinarily content on the island. To him, it's a playground paradise. After all, the *Minnow's* sole crew member may be a mighty sailor man, but he's also a naive kid at heart. He's got everything he needs on the island: attention, freedom, adventure, and above all, a loving substitute family. Even his favorite

22

rock 'n' roll group, the Mosquitoes, shows up. The only things he really misses are "television, hot dogs, and licorice whips."

Gilligan is clearly a case of arrested development. Like Jethro Bodine of the *Beverly Hillbillies,* Gilligan didn't make it past the sixth grade—at least not psychologically. He can't tie his own shoelaces, and he's always recalling his grammar school days (he was in the play *Our Friends in the Forest,* had a pet turtle named Herman, and his best friend was pigeon-toed Walter Stuckmeyer). Growing up, Gilligan once worked in a gas station and served as president of his eighth-grade camera club. Back home, his best friend is Skinny Mulligan.

We never learn anything about Gilligan's family life (other than the fact that he has a brother, and his father is short with a mustache and glasses) or where he grew up (although he was born in a small town in Pennsylvania), but on the island the Skipper acts like a father to him. In fact, they're such good buddies that they share the same hut, sleeping fully dressed (including their shoes and sailor hats). Of course, Gilligan rarely follows the Skipper's orders. He'll do anything to avoid work. He's much happier lounging around the island, listening to rock 'n' roll on the radio, climbing trees, exploring the island's many caves, taking care of a new pet, or continually starting the great American novel. The only work he doesn't seem to mind is work done for the Howells—for money.

Despite his unpardonable bungles and dim-witted blunders, Gilligan often proposes surprisingly clever ideas. His unspoiled, childlike imagination enables him to offer simpleminded yet perfectly applicable solutions to a number of problems. Whenever Gilligan excitedly shares these ideas or warns the castaways of impending danger, they either ignore him or chastise him for exaggerating. While he can be remarkably superstitious and astoundingly clumsy, for all the rescues Gilligan ruins, there are just as many times when Gilligan saves the castaways' lives—albeit accidentally. Beyond his lovable personality, he also displays a redeeming love for animals. He always has a pet— whether it be a duck, frog, parrot, monkey, or homing pigeon.

While it's difficult to completely understand why his fellow castaways don't kill him for all the rescues he ruins, there's one far more baffling question that remains unanswered: Is Gilligan his first or last name?

ACTOR BOB DENVER:

"I've heard [Gilligan called] schlepp, nerd, you know, I've heard all those. He's just a catalyst....He always screwed up the rescues, you know—that's what the kids love the best—and a lot of times it wasn't his fault....It was just circumstances, and I think a lot of kids understood that because a lot of times they get blamed for stuff they didn't do....A lot of kids tell me that. 'That happens to me all the time! I didn't do it, and then I get blamed! And it turns out it wasn't my fault!'

"They just like him because, you know, they feel superior to him. They also kind of identify with him because he gets picked on. There are a lot of shows where he left to live in a cave because he couldn't stand it."

24

CREATOR SHERWOOD SCHWARTZ:

"To this day, almost every time I see Bob Denver we still argue. He thinks Gilligan is his first name, and I think it's his last name. Because in the original presentation, it's Willy Gilligan. But he doesn't believe it, and he doesn't want to discuss it. He insists his name is Gilligan."

GILLIGAN:	What are we going to do?
SKIPPER:	The first thing we must do is remain calm and cool. You won't get hysterical, will you?
GILLIGAN:	Right.
SKIPPER:	And you won't panic.
GILLIGAN:	Right.
SKIPPER:	And you won't be afraid.
GILLIGAN:	Wrong.
SKIPPER:	Wrong?
GILLIGAN:	Two out of three's not bad, Skipper.

● ● ●

PROFESSOR:	These batteries are rechargeable.
SKIPPER:	Professor, how can we recharge batteries here on the island?
GILLIGAN:	We don't even have a charge card.

| SKIPPER: | Gilligan, I should have known better. Asking you to help is like putting a fire out with gasoline. |

| SKIPPER: | Gilligan, why must you repeat everything that I say? |
| GILLIGAN: | It's easier than thinking up things by myself. |

SKIPPER:	Oh, sure, but where do we start? Knowing Gilligan, that ticket could be anyplace.
GILLIGAN:	No, it couldn't, Skipper. It's not in my pocket because I looked.
SKIPPER:	Great. Where else couldn't it be, Gilligan?
GILLIGAN:	Well, let's see. It couldn't be in that tin box buried down at the base of that big palm tree by the lagoon.
GINGER:	I didn't know there was a tin box buried under that tree.
GILLIGAN:	There isn't. That's why it couldn't be there.

SKIPPER:	Wouldn't Benjamin Franklin have been interested had he been here?
GILLIGAN:	Who?
SKIPPER:	Benjamin Franklin.
GILLIGAN:	I don't remember anybody with that name sailing on the *Minnow*.
PROFESSOR:	He experimented with electricity one hundred and fifty years ago.
GILLIGAN:	Oh, it was a lucky thing he wasn't here with us.
SKIPPER:	Huh?
GILLIGAN:	No man like that could have ever lasted through the storm. Unless he worked out with dumbbells and took vitamin pills and things like that.
PROFESSOR:	Gilligan, Benjamin Franklin is dead.
SKIPPER:	Exactly.
GILLIGAN:	He's dead? I didn't even know he was sick.

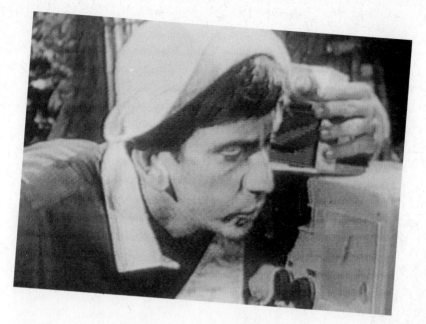

PROFESSOR: Luck, Gilligan, is all in the mind.

GILLIGAN: Professor, with my mind, I need all the luck I can get.

GILLIGAN: With all the time on this island, it will be good to be on dry land again.

SKIPPER: Why didn't we think of that before? Everything grows from seeds.

GILLIGAN: Not everything.

SKIPPER: Yes, Gilligan, everything. Orange trees grow from orange seeds. Apple trees grow from apple seeds. And watermelons grow from watermelon seeds.

GILLIGAN: Yeah, but birds don't grow from birdseed.

SKIPPER: What are the odds on that?

PROFESSOR: Well, a million to one.

SKIPPER: Oh, fine. A million to one. What could be worse than that?

GILLIGAN: A million to none.

SKIPPER: Gilligan, look at that mess. And it's all your fault!

GILLIGAN: Oh, well, Skipper, it won't take very long when all three of us pitch in to clean it up.

SKIPPER: All three of us?

PROFESSOR: All three of us?

GILLIGAN: Yeah. Me, myself, and I.

RESCUES GILLIGAN RUINS

- He explodes all the castaways' signal flares. [Episode 3]
- He breaks the transmitter after establishing contact with the *Vagabond Lady,* a pilot passing over the island. [Episode 4]
- He sends off a wild duck, forgetting to attach a message to its leg. [Episode 7]
- As the Skipper's about to issue a Mayday call over the repaired transmitter, Gilligan drops firewood on the transmitter, breaking it. [Episode 12]
- He breaks the mirror that the castaways are about to use to signal a government search plane. [Episode 18]
- He punctures and deflates a weather balloon and then cuts it up into squares for use as fabric. [Episode 20]
- He gives the Skipper amnesia as the navy's about to hold maneuvers offshore, causing him to lock the castaways in a cave as the ships pass the island. [Episode 30]
- He drinks the phosphorescent marker before the Professor can send it out on a raft. [Episode 32]
- He covers the castaways with glue and feathers before they can be spotted by a NASA space probe's camera, which he then breaks. [Episode 40]
- He sets his watch according to Manila time, causing the castaways to miss the opportunity to be rescued by the Soviet navy. [Episode 45]
- He uses the castaways one remaining signal flare on the Skipper's birthday cake. [Episode 53]
- He seals an open telephone cable before it washes back out to sea, preventing it from eventually corroding and requiring a repair crew's attention. [Episode 53]
- He puts a rabbit's foot inside a robot that the castaways send to Hawaii, inadvertently demagnetizing the robot's receptor spools and jamming the SOS message the castaways recorded. [Episode 57]
- He imprisons himself and the other castaways in a cave, allowing a plane to pass overhead before the Skipper and Professor can spell out a rescue message with phosphorescent rocks. [Episode 83]
- He allows a helicopter to take off from the island. [Episode 84]
- As he's about to be spotted while flying with a jet pack, he flies into a cloud, causing a rainstorm, which causes the search to be called off. He launches the same jet pack without strapping it to his back, losing it forever. [Episode 95]

29

THE SKIPPER

"The first thing I do when I get back, I'm going to sink my teeth into a nice thick juicy steak."
—Skipper Jonas Grumby

Jonas Grumby, the good-natured skipper and old sea dog, is the castaways' benevolent and benign leader. The Skipper, brave and sure, continually urges the castaways to work together and is always looking out for them—particularly Gilligan. His most important tool is his captain's hat, which he claims represents leadership, gives him authority, and reassures his fellow castaways that everything's under control.

The Skipper's naval career is sketchy. He served in the navy and fought in World War II in the South Pacific, earning the rank of captain, although we never learn what destroyer he served aboard or for how many years. He had three ships shot out from under him by the Japanese fleet, and while being strafed on Subchaser 307 by enemy fighters, a mile off Guadalcanal, he converted the ship's radio into a transmitter. He was the best poker player in all of the Seventh Fleet and led the navy band for five years aboard his ship. In fact, in his sea chest, he still keeps a rather peculiar memento from his naval years: a bottle cap from the first bottle of beer he opened with his teeth (when someone hit him in the head with it during a barroom brawl in Singapore in 1947).

The Skipper met Gilligan in the navy, where Gilligan saved his life by pushing him out of the way of a depth charge that had broken loose and was rolling down the deck of their destroyer. After retiring, the Skipper used his commission to buy the *S.S. Minnow* and began offering three-hour excursion tours from Honolulu harbor. Gilligan, naturally, became his first mate. Of course, the only way the Skipper can get any work out of Gilligan is to threaten him or give him a direct order, although he usually winds up the victim of Gilligan's clumsiness and retaliates by hitting him in the head with his cap.

While the Skipper thinks of Gilligan as the son he never had, we never learn if he was ever married or if he has any daughters of his own. The Skipper does have a great, loving admiration for his dearly departed "Pop," whom he describes as "kind of a world traveler." His father had two sayings that the Skipper says he'll always remember: "Hurried work is worried work" and "A job not well done is not a well-done job." In fact, one of the Skipper's most prized possessions is his gold pinky ring that has been in his family for over two hundred years.

Of all the castaways, the Skipper has the hardiest appetite. In high school he played the line on the football team, and now, in his mid-forties, he weights about 220 pounds. If the castaways ever get rescued, the Skipper says, "I'll go straight to an Italian restaurant and have eight or ten pizzas, six dozen meatballs, and two miles of spaghetti, and then I'll have dinner."

While the Skipper considers himself a stabilizing force on the island, his susceptibility to superstition often undermines his credibility. During his many years at sea, the Skipper witnessed a number of peculiar superstitious rites unique to various South Pacific islands and their tribal natives. Consequently, he vehemently believes the legends on which these superstitions are based, and he's always warning Gilligan about them and falling prey to them himself.

Still, the Skipper is a benevolent leader, and he'd avidly subscribe to the words of Benjamin Franklin, who at the signing of the Declaration of Independence declared: "We must all hang together, or assuredly we shall all hang separately."

ACTOR ALAN HALE, JR.:

"The Skipper lent himself to certainly being a nice fellow, a bumbling fellow, of course. He had a perfect foil in Gilligan, and he could blame his own shortsightedness on Gilligan. But he dearly loved Gilligan. They really were good friends. Between the two of them, nothing ever seemed to dovetail. The only thing that did dovetail was their everlasting friendship. They really were fond of each other."

31

SKIPPER:	C'mon, little buddy, I think we better have a little talk.
GILLIGAN:	Did I do something wrong, Skipper?
SKIPPER:	Of course not. Sit down. Here, take my chair.
GILLIGAN:	What do you want to talk to me about, Skipper?
SKIPPER:	Gilligan, you've never had three million dollars before, have you?
GILLIGAN:	Uhhhhh, no, sir, I haven't.
SKIPPER:	I didn't think so. Well, let me tell you something. You're going to find a big change in some of the people around here.
GILLIGAN:	What do you mean?
SKIPPER:	Well, take this morning for example. Number one, the Professor never offered to build you a fire before, right?
GILLIGAN:	Right!
SKIPPER:	Number two, Mary Ann never offered to fix you a special breakfast before, right?
GILLIGAN:	Right!
SKIPPER:	Number three, Ginger never offered to fix you lunch before, right?
GILLIGAN:	Right! And what about number four?
SKIPPER:	Four? Number four?
GILLIGAN:	I never sat in your chair before, right?
SKIPPER:	Right.

SKIPPER: Gilligan, why don't you stop that? You don't know anything at all about space.

GILLIGAN: I know one thing about it. You take up more of it than I do.

SKIPPER: Very funny. Gilligan, there are three types of space. There's the space up there, the space down there, and the space between your ears.

SKIPPER: I like him. Gilligan is a friend of mine.

PROFESSOR: But you do admit that he annoys you from time to time.

SKIPPER: But I don't dislike him. I mean, it's just that I'd like to kill him every now and then.

THE MILLIONAIRE

"No one can pull the wool over my eyes. Cashmere maybe, but wool, never."

—Thurston Howell III

Thurston Howell III, blustery billionaire and one of the world's richest men, inherited all his money from his father. He met his wife, Lovey, during his college years at Harvard. They were married in 1944, eloping in the middle of the night. Howell remembers it as the day Consolidated General jumped seventeen points. Although they've been married twenty years (at the time of the shipwreck), they both admit that the last five years of their marriage haven't exactly been a picnic. Still, Howell can be remarkably sentimental and romantic with Lovey.

Howell, known in New York as the Wizard of Wall Street, has been convicted six times on antitrust suits and investigated every year for income tax evasion. He owns and attends the board meetings of anywhere between six and twelve corporations, including Howell Steel Company, Howell Chemical Company, Howell Industries, Howell Enterprises, Howell Aircraft, Howell Battery Company—all run under the umbrella of the Howell Corporation, where Howell, as chairman of the board, has five thousand employees and an office on the second floor. He also owns several oil companies, a Manhattan apartment building, and he's even backed a few Broadway plays. Both Howells have seats on the stock exchange—although we never learn which one.

Howell is egotistical, pompous, and aristocratic. He prides himself on being a Harvard graduate and a registered Republican. He has homes in Palm Beach, Paris, Newport, New York, Monaco, and all fifty states. The Howells, welcome with open arms at the White House, Buckingham Palace, and the Kremlin, don't associate with people who aren't in the social register, and they refuse to travel anything but first-class, making it difficult to understand why they took a cruise on the *S.S. Minnow* in the first place. Of course, Howell had gone on some inexplicable outings well before the cruise; he once went tiger hunting in a zoo, and while on safari in Africa, he accidentally trapped four of his native guides. (Howell, incidentally, owns a ranch in Africa that declared itself its own nation.) In any case, the Howells brought along more than enough luggage to qualify for first-class passage; Thurston has twenty suitcases just for himself, and he left their car double-parked with the engine running at the marina.

Despite his breeding, Howell displays little tact. He harshly blames the Skipper for the shipwreck, and he's always trying to break the castaways' laws, to shrewdly outnegotiate or bribe the others, and to harbor the island's valuable resources for himself. The Howell family crest may read "honesty, fidelity, integrity," but Thurston is sneaky, untrustworthy, conniving, greedy, and corrupt. Yet when it comes to the lives of his fellow castaways, he's always exceptionally generous and redeemingly altruistic—usually offering huge sums of money to save them. Otherwise, he's motivated solely by avarice. After all, the Howell family crest pictures crossed dollar bills on a field of Swiss banks.

His grandfather, Thurston Howell I, killed himself during the 1929 stock market crash by leaping out a window. Howell seems to have also inherited his grandfather's cowardice, letting his wife fight for him, and sleeping with a teddy bear—which even the Skipper and Gilligan find unusual. He even passed out when Lovey had her ears pierced.

While Howell refuses to give up his daily golf game, he isn't exactly the healthiest specimen on the island. At home he may skeet shoot, fox hunt, and play polo, but he always catches cold in damp places, takes a red pill at lunch and another pill at dinner, and he has seen a stomach specialist who told him to keep away from cholesterol, starches, and lousy food. He also has two allergies: to gold (his hands convulse when he's near anything over twenty-four karats); and to Ginger's perfume (which makes him sneeze).

Howell refuses to do manual labor, preferring instead to hire Gilligan to work for him. He usually spends his day relaxing with Lovey on the bamboo lounge chairs outside their hut, napping, sipping exotic tropical drinks from tall bamboo-shoot drinking glasses, listening to the radio for the hourly stock market report, and golfing in the afternoon with Gilligan as his caddy. He reads the same copy of *The Wall Street Journal* every day and finds it comforting that the market neither goes up or down.

ACTOR JIM BACKUS:

"[Howell's] bark was worse than his bite. The Howells have that wonderful indifference that only the rich can have....They assume everyone has it as good as they do. And Mr. Howell really was a naive jerk when you get right down to it.

"But I also base it a little on Jack Benny...his naivete, which is what I was trying to get in Mr. Howell...Jack, who was—God knows—one of the best-known people in the world, had all the money he could possibly have, all the standing and recognition. And we used to be rehearsing or having lunch or something, and he'd come in, and he'd say, 'I had the most marvelous shower,' 'I had a wonderful shave today.' And if you stop and think about it, it's a very nice thing. So, he naturally assumed that everyone had the same thing he did.

"And [Howell] couldn't see that, you know. [But] he was a generous man, and he was, of course, madly in love with Lovey. And you never could see him cheating, even though he had the pick of the ladies."

LOVEY:	It was so wise of you, Thurston, to insist that the boat be repaired. It won't be long now before we're home.
HOWELL:	And not a moment too soon. I've already missed twelve board meetings of six of my corporations. Or is it six board meetings of twelve of my corporations?
LOVEY:	Poor Thurston, you do have problems.
HOWELL:	It is rather difficult being rich. If it wasn't for the money, I'd rather be poor.

HOWELL:	Gilligan, my boy, let me tell you something. Look behind every successful man, and you will find a woman.
GILLIGAN:	Yes, sir.
HOWELL:	Just make sure his wife doesn't find her.

GILLIGAN:	You're really a very thoughtful husband, Mr. Howell, going to all this trouble to make a pillow for your wife.
HOWELL:	Well, of course, I want her to have the comforts of home. You see, she's been a true friend. A devoted companion. She has the one quality that every man wants in a wife.
GILLIGAN:	She's loyal?
HOWELL:	No, she's an heiress. She's loaded.

• • •

LOVEY:	Oh, darling, I always knew you had a heart.
HOWELL:	Yes, remind me to speak to the Professor. There must be a painless way to turn it back to stone.

SKIPPER:	Mr. Howell, hard work never hurt anybody.
HOWELL:	Well, it never helped anyone either.

HOWELL:	Do you think I began a dozen international corporations by stooping to thievery?'
PROFESSOR:	Well, of course not.
HOWELL:	Shows how naive you are. How else do you get to the top of the corporate ladder?

PROFESSOR:	I'm afraid that headhunters have moved on to the island, and you know what that means.
HOWELL:	Property values go down like a shot.

THINGS A HOWELL DOESN'T DO

- A Howell never does any work requiring manual labor.
- A Howell never runs in the face of danger (he walks very quickly).
- A Howell never travels anything but first-class.
- A Howell never allows his golf game to be interrupted.
- A Howell is never wrong.
- A Howell never goes back on his word.
- A Howell is always first.
- A Howell never carries petty cash (tens and twenties).
- Nobody rushes a Howell.
- A Howell is a servant to no man.
- A Howell is never chicken ("pheasant perhaps, but never, never chicken").

HOWELLS' POCKET MONEY

How much cash did the Howells bring along?

A solve-it-yourself mystery.

The clues:

- He offers a Japanese sailor $50,000 to return them to civilization, which the sailor refuses. [Episode 15]
- He offers the castaways $100,000 each for their share of a treasure chest, which the castaways later refuse to accept. [Episode 16]

- He offers a $10,000 cash reward to anyone who finds Lovey's brooch, and never makes good on the offer. [Episode 22]
- He buys fifty carrots from Mary Ann for $50,000; eight turnip plants for $4,000; and wild lettuce for $3,000. [Episode 28]
- Lovey throws an undisclosed sum of money into a cave to entice Gilligan to return to camp. [Episode 33]
- Lovey claims that her husband only brought along "a few paltry hundred thousand." "That's petty cash," admits Howell. "Back home, that's interest on my interest." [Episode 44]
- He tries to bribe Gilligan with a pile of thousand-dollar bills. [Episode 61]
- He offers one million dollars to the castaway who gets him off the island, starting the contest by tearing a one-hundred-dollar bill in half, and never awards the money. [Episode 62]
- He stuffs the pockets of his dummy with $100 and $50 bills. [Episode 63]
- He leaves a roll of money in a cave to appease a voodoo witch doctor. [Episode 73]
- He offers headhunters $50,000 to release him, but they refuse. [Episode 78]
- He gives $50,000 to kidnapper Norbert Wiley in ransom money. [Episode 80]
- He offers game show contestant George Barkley $30,000 to help them off the island, which Barkley refuses. He later finds the $10,000 cash prize Barkley lost. [Episode 84]
- He offers hunter Jonathan Kincaid $500,000 to call off a hunt, which Kincaid refuses. [Episode 86]
- He offers a $10,000 cash reward for any information leading to Gilligan's whereabouts. [Episode 89]
- He throws an undisclosed sum of cash into the lagoon while aboard a space capsule. [Episode 90]
- He offers a one-million-dollar cash reward to Birdy to help rescue them, sending a thousand-dollar bill with a carrier pigeon. [Episode 96]
- He offers the Papuan native king, Killiwanni, $100,000 to rescue them. [Episode 98]

HIS WIFE

"I don't know how we're going to explain to our friends that we spent several years with people who aren't even in the social register."
—**Lovey Howell**

Lovey Wentworth Howell, the vacuous, birdbrained, socialite wife who's more concerned with next Saturday's dinner engagement than being rescued from the island, is the world's most socially prominent international hostess. She hates having to sit out the social season on a tropical island paradise. She misses the opening of opera, the horse show, debutante balls, weddings, charity balls, benefit luncheons, serving the Daughters of the Revolution, or matchmaking. And she's far more comfortable socializing with royalty than with her fellow castaways (the Howells know Britain's royal family, have been skeet shooting with Prince Phillip and the Duke of Albania, and have spent time in Monaco with Princess Grace and the Duke of Troy).

As the island's matriarchal leader, Mrs. Howell rarely displays any leadership qualities beyond establishing some sense of decorum. While Ginger and Mary Ann come to her for motherly advice, Lovey primarily concerns herself with decorating her hut and seeking answers to questions of etiquette, including: "Whatever does one say when one meets an astronaut?" "Whatever shall I wear when we're rescued?" and "What does one wear to deliver a ransom?" While aristocratic, Mrs. Howell can also be remarkably noble and generous. She donates her furs and perfumes to help the others, and whenever the castaways sew together a ship's sail, a banner, or a curtain from old clothes on the island, they're inevitably using the Howells' wardrobe.

The Howells met while they were both in college, where Lovey was queen of the Pitted Prune Bowl Parade and a nurse's aid. Thurston proposed to her at a French restaurant in Manhattan, and they eloped in the middle of the night. For a wedding gift, Lovey's father gave the newlyweds what he thought was a football stadium—until he discovered that Dustbowl, Oklahoma, was two hundred acres of phony oil property. Lovey not only inherited her wealth and birdbrain from him, she inherited her diamond brooch, which has been in her family since Queen Isabella gave it to Columbus. While the Howells pledged never to delve into each other's romantic past, we do learn that Lovey once dated Mark Marancy Vandergray and used some underhanded trick to dump him. While Thurston is undoubtedly devoted to her, Lovey occasionally displays jealousy toward Ginger and Mary Ann.

Still, Mrs. Howell maintains social convention on the island, insisting that the castaways adhere to the accepted rules of conduct and civilized behavior. The Howells dress appropriately for every occasion, including dinner each evening. Without Lovey's guiding presence, the castaways would inevitably falter from the dictates of society and fall victim to the unspeakable barbarisms of impropriety.

ACTRESS NATALIE SCHAFER:

"The part was written as a Pasadena lady who was very, very stodgy.... It was just 'yes dear, no dear, yes dear,' and I was getting very bored with this when we did the pilot, and finally I said, 'I'd like to meet with the writers. I'd like this to be a kind of a Dulcy.' Well, I met with five young writers, and I said this, and there was a deadpan look on their faces, so I realized they didn't know of the George Kaufman book Dulcy. So I

42

went to Samuel French and sent them all copies of *Dulcy,* and then I went to the management and said, 'I would like something to do with my own wardrobe. Let me do one week of designing and buying and planning my own wardrobe. If you don't like it, we'll talk about it.' Well, of course, then I came on with the pants and the pearls and the hats and the gloves, and as you'd walk on the screen, you couldn't possibly be a straight Pasadena lady.

"Apart from the fact that we were so rich and everything, we had an affection that I think people want in their lives and in their marriages. And I think [Lovey] was just a lady who had taken being rich for granted—it never meant a great deal to her because it was always there—and who loved putting on fancy new clothes and having Mr. Howell approve, and I think she adored him.

"I think she wanted to have all these people around her, loving her. I think she liked to be loved, and I think she liked to help,the people. They were all different from anybody she'd ever met in her social life and at the country club, and it was very amusing to her. She thought she could teach them a way of life, and she didn't realize that when they got back—if they did get back off that island—[the others] wouldn't go back to being millionaires. They'd have to work. And this is something she didn't quite understand....But there were a lot of things she could help them with, and that was kind of fun—being a little bit maternal with everybody."

HOWELL:	Lovey, have I got news!
LOVEY:	(*preoccupied fixing her hair*) News?
HOWELL:	Yes, I've discovered a gold mine on the island!
LOVEY:	Oh, that's wonderful.
HOWELL:	There's only one complication. I don't think we'll be able to mine the gold.
LOVEY:	Oh, that's dreadful.
HOWELL:	You see, the Skipper found a raft, and it looks like we're going to be rescued.
LOVEY:	Oh, that's wonderful.
HOWELL:	So we won't have time to mine the gold.
LOVEY:	Oh, that's dreadful.
HOWELL:	You see, Gilligan has to work all day on the boat for the Skipper....Lovey!
LOVEY:	Oh, I'm sorry, Thurston. Where were we? Dreadful or wonderful?
HOWELL:	Well, it's dreadful....If that boy has to work day and night, it's dreadful.

LOVEY: Quite right, Thurston.

HOWELL: You know what would be wonderful? It would be wonderful if you would go down to that mine and help that boy dig!

LOVEY: Oh, dear, we're back at dreadful again.

LOVEY: You know, I really wouldn't mind being poor, if it weren't for just one thing.

HOWELL: What is that, my dear?

LOVEY: Poverty.

LOVEY: I often wish I was alone, especially when I'm by myself.

HOWELL: Can you imagine, people actually lived in caves like this?

LOVEY: Where were the servants' quarters?

HOWELL: (*teaching Lovey how to play golf*) Now the first thing you use, my dear, is your driver.

LOVEY: My driver? Don't be silly, darling, you know perfectly well my chauffeur is back home. I believe his name was Charles, wasn't it?

HOWELL: No darling, I'm talking about clubs.

LOVEY: Of course, he drove us to all the very best clubs.

GILLIGAN: Mrs. Howell, I might blow up.

LOVEY: Oh, don't you dare get angry at me.

GILLIGAN: I mean, blow up for real. I drank some—

LOVEY: Oh, that's why you don't feel a thing. You've been dipping into Mr. Howell's private stock. Demon rum is your worst enemy.

GILLIGAN: Mrs. Howell, I didn't drink rum, I drank nitroglycerin.

LOVEY: Oh, mixed drinks are even worse.

LOVEY: Thurston, I never knew there were so many different kinds of smells in the world.

HOWELL: Oh, yes, there's so many things we take for granted. The fragrance of a wet Rolls-Royce after an April shower.

LOVEY: The marvelous aroma a brand-new sable coat.

HOWELL: Or the heady intoxication of the stock market when it first opens in the morning.

LOVEY: I do so miss the smells of simple everyday living.

THE MOVIE STAR

"If we had to get marooned on an island, why couldn't we pick Manhattan?"
—**Ginger Grant**

Any man worth his weight in hormones would give his right arm to be stuck on an island with Ginger Grant, the alluring and sexy actress, reminiscent of Marilyn Monroe, who persists in worrying about her gowns, her appearance, her career, and Hollywood gossip.

Ginger, a self-proclaimed tease, follows a fascinating moral code. "Everyone says I have an open mind," she admits, having dated an extensive list of swingers, including a medical student, a basketball player, and a safecracker. While Ginger's extraordinarily flirtatious and shapely, she never tried to advance her acting career on the casting couch. On the island, she may be easily bribed by Howell, but she's obviously unwilling to have an affair with him to further her career. Yet she's always willing to use her seductive powers or acting ability to help her fellow castaways. She coquettishly diverts any visitor to the island, and she eagerly suggests plans of action based on parts she's played in movies. Yet while considerably sex-starved, Ginger never displays promiscuity beyond an overly passionate French kiss.

As for her acting career, Ginger boarded the boat just after her last performance. She lives in Hollywood, California, and has an agent whose name we never learn. She once sang in a club in Waikiki, Hawaii, played a nurse in one episode of *Ben Casey*, and had minor roles in a remarkable number of Hollywood pictures for someone of her age. Up until the shipwreck, Ginger was scheduled to play the lead role of Cleopatra in the Broadway production of *Pyramid for Two*—a part she's convinced would have rocketed her to stardom. We never learn anything about her family (aside from the fact that she has a sister) or background prior to her acting career.

Since she only brought one gown with her, Ginger sews other gowns together from Mrs. Howell's remnants and fabric that washes ashore. She even makes one dress from Gilligan's duffel bag. As for any other talents, Ginger can't swim and she can barely cook. She's always assisting the Professor (the only man on the island she truly desires), entertaining the other castaways with her singing and acting, or nursing the other castaways back to health. In fact, her one regret in life is that she didn't pursue a career in nursing.

While Ginger shares the same hut with Mary Ann, they aren't exactly best friends. While they live, swim, fish, take mud baths, cook, sew, and do the laundry together, there is an unspoken rivalry between them—perhaps grounded in their diverse upbringings and opposing sexual mores. Still, they both share a curious indifference toward being relegated to sexist roles.

ACTRESS TINA LOUISE:

"The show really kind of came together when [director] Dick Donner got on the show. He kind of let all the characters go in the directions that they should go, because it was a little bit confusing in the beginning when John Rich was directing. I had been told [Ginger] was a Marilyn Monroe/Lucille Ball character, and he sort of wanted to make it Eve Arden. And I didn't want to go in that direction. So there was a difference of opinion. When Dick came on, everything got clear, and the show really took off when the characters were delineated. I think my suggestions proved to be correct that people didn't want to see a big beautiful doll, you know, talking out of the side of her mouth. This wasn't about to go. When they let me do it the way I thought it should be, things fell into place. I mean, every little girl wanted to dress up and play Ginger."

MARY ANN: I don't see how you can exercise anyway in that dress. It's so tight. I'm surprised it doesn't cut off your circulation.

GINGER: Honey, in Hollywood, the tighter the dress, the more the girl circulates.

GINGER: Ooh! Look, Mary Ann! A framed picture of my favorite movie star!

MARY ANN: Oh, really? Who is it?

GINGER: Me.

MARY ANN: Oh, Ginger, I think the plan is impossible.

GINGER: Why? A girl can get a man to do all kinds of things for her.

MARY ANN: I know, but robots aren't human.

GINGER: Neither were some of the guys I went out with.

GINGER: Well, the way I practice the gentle art of persuasion, three's a crowd. As a matter of fact, sometimes even two gets to be a little crowded.

GINGER'S MOVIE CREDITS
What movies has Ginger starred in?
A solve-it-yourself mystery.
The clues:

- *The Hula Girl and the Fullback* (her most memorable film, for which she created her own hula dance).
- An unnamed movie in which "he loved her with a burning passion, and she loved him like a flaming fire."
- An unnamed movie in which she picks a lock with a bobby pin.
- An unnamed jungle movie in which everyone gets lost, nobody finds them, and they all die. (The movie had a happy ending, says Ginger, since it made three million dollars.)
- An unnamed movie starring Rock Hudson as the wealthiest man in the world, who loses all his money and jumps off a cliff.
- An unnamed movie in which one of the lines was "None proclaim their innocence so loudly as the guilty."

- An unnamed movie in which a native man and woman throw themselves into a volcano to appease its appetite.
- An unnamed movie in which a couple on a big boat is married by the ship's captain.
- *Belly Dancers from Bali-Bali,* filmed in the South Pacific, in which Ginger snaps the hero out of a zombie trance by doing a native dance. (Gilligan saw the movie three times.)
- *Rain Dance of Rango-Rango,* in which Ginger performs a rain dance.
- An unnamed movie in which she plays a psychiatrist who reforms a criminal who later returns to crime.
- *Mohawk over the Moon,* the story of an Indian astronaut.
- *Sing a Song of Sing Sing,* a musical in which two cellmates stage a fight to get out of jail. (Gilligan saw the movie three times.)
- *San Quentin Blues,* in which the prisoners made so much noise that the guard had to open the door.
- Ginger would have had the leading role in *Standing Cow, Daughter of Sitting Bull* if she had known how to shoot a gun, and she was up for a part in *The Land of the Vampires,* but had the wrong bloodtype.
- Her repertoire of slinky songs includes: "Let Me Entertain You," "I Wanna Be Loved by You," and "Alouette."
- She was once voted Miss Hourglass for having all her sand in the right places, winning a loving cup.

THE PROFESSOR

PROFESSOR: I have an idea that may well be instrumental in securing for us deliverance from our enforced isolation.
GILLIGAN: Not only that, we might get rescued.

If you were stranded on an uncharted island, the person you'd most want with you would undoubtedly be the Professor. Without Professor Roy Hinkley, Ph.D., the other six castaways would have long since lost contact with civilization, been captured and devoured by cannibals, been decapitated by headhunters, or died from malnutrition or a seemingly endless variety of rare tropical diseases.

Dr. Roy Hinkley, a high school science teacher and well-known scout leader, is a handsome research scientist with all the answers to nature, but without a clue about sex. He's actually the only levelheaded person on the island, a bookworm who rarely displays his emotions— in short, a shipwrecked Spock. While the Professor may not have a poetic personality, he always seems to have the most sensible solutions. He is clearly the castaways' guiding light and silent leader. He's unquestionably the most intelligent castaway, preferring to sit quietly in the background and let the others think the Skipper runs the island. But when it comes to judicial affairs, life-threatening matters, or possible rescue attempts, the Professor unobtrusively assumes leadership.

The Professor has a B.A. from USC, a B.S. from UCLA, an M.A. from SMU, and he received his Ph.D. from TCU at the age of twenty-five. He has six degrees in all, including a master's degree in psychology, and he spent seven years writing his Marine Biology paper. He spent two years on an anthropological expedition in Egypt, · and back home (wherever that may be), he is the number one man

51

on his chess team. Oddly, we never learn where the Professor teaches. In any case, the Professor originally took this cruise aboard the *Minnow* to write his book, *Fun with Ferns,* but since being shipwrecked he has been keeping a chronicle of the castaways' adventures on the island, which he thinks might someday make a good book. On the island, he demonstrates expertise in a remarkable repertoire of subjects, including botany, medicine, dentistry, chemistry, agriculture, astronomy, psychology, physics, law, anthropology, Latin, and tribal native languages.

In his first week on the island, the Professor discovered five different mutations of ragweed. He can synthesize almost anything from the indigenous plants on the island, identify nearly any local native tribe merely by their headdress or costume (displaying full knowledge of their customs and culture), and speak fluent Marubi, Papuan, and Katubi, to name but a few.

In fact, the Professor has mastered such a remarkable control of the English language (employing exotic scientific terms and unique phraseology) that even his fellow castaways can't understand what he's talking about (clearly demonstrating that Howell wasn't admitted to Harvard on academic merit alone—unless his high school grades severely outshined his Verbal SAT scores).

Of course, the Professor is fallible. He doesn't always have the answers, and at times he displays all the traits of a bumbling, absentminded inventor. As a Renaissance man, he shows surprisingly little knowledge of sex, sea navigation, or the world of high finance.

Although constantly pursued by Ginger and Mary Ann, he remains oblivious not only to their needs and desires, but to his own. Whenever the castaways build a raft or find a similar vessel, he always insists that the Skipper and Gilligan, as the only experienced seamen on the island, make the journey alone—despite the fact that they're the two responsible for the shipwreck and the many subsequent rescue failures. And if he were such a remarkable scientist, the Professor could easily fix the boat or design a suitably strong raft.

Still, the Professor is the only rational person marooned on the island, and without his scientific skills and leadership ability it is unlikely that the castaways would ever stand a chance of survival, let alone rescue.

ACTOR RUSSELL JOHNSON:

"He's a square. He embodied everything that is, or is supposed to be, honorable. And he's straight and true and asexual. I mean, he is a person that's hard to find really. Genuine and not a phony bone in his body....

"How did the Professor know all of that?... The answer to that was: it's in the script, that's how he knew. You just have to believe the Howells could pull out of their trunks any damned thing they wanted, and the Professor was able to figure out all these things. And kids believe that, they want to believe that."

PROFESSOR: Do you know what it would take? It would take a polyester derivative of an organic hydroxide molecule.

HOWELL: Watch your language! You're in the presence of a lady!

PROFESSOR: Well, kissing on the mouth is far from sanitary. It can lead to all sorts of bacterial transfer.

GINGER: You certainly make a kiss sound romantic. Like germ warfare.

THE PROFESSOR'S LIBRARY

- *The Carpenter's Handbook*
- *Chemistry*
- *The Criminal Law*
- *Four-Masted Schooners I Have Known*
- *Hamlet* by William Shakespeare
- *The History of Tree Surgery*
- *How to Tell a Mushroom from a Toadstool* by the late Dr. Morton Kepstone
- *Integrated Calculus* by Zimmerman
- *A Million Ways to Make a Million*
- *Navy Regulations*
- *Physics*
- *Psychology*
- *Rare Tropical Plants*
- *Tropical Diseases*
- *Volcanoes and Their Destructive Powers*
- *A World of Facts*
- *The World of Insects*

MARY ANN

"The first thing I'll do when I get back home is bake an apple pie, milk the cow, feed the chickens." —**Mary Ann Summers**

Mary Ann Summers, a sweet, naive country girl modeled after Pollyanna and Dorothy from *The Wizard of Oz,* is a well-meaning clerk from Winfield, Kansas, where she worked in the Winfield General Store. She has an Aunt Martha and Uncle George, was a member of the 4-H Club, and worked a farm by herself. We learn very little more about her.

Mary Ann is gentle, kind, and exceptionally warmhearted. She has a soft spot in her heart for Gilligan, and while the Howells' marriage provides the castaways with stabilizing parental figures, Mary Ann's strong moral character guides the castaways' ethics and principles. She's the most honest, homespun, and down-to-earth person on the island. She can't be corrupted by Howell at any price, and while she envies Ginger's talent and glamorous lifestyle, the Howells' wealth, and the Professor's inquisitive mind, she frowns on Ginger's vanity and morals, the Howells' greed, and the Professor's myopic vision. Still, she accepts everyone as they are.

While remarkably squeamish, Mary Ann displays rugged instincts. She farms the island and cooks all the castaways' meals, displaying remarkable culinary skills and resourcefulness. Thanks to Mary Ann, the castaways eat amazingly well, nourished with a hot helping of moral principles.

ACTRESS DAWN WELLS:

"There's a lot of me in Mary Ann. There's a side of Dawn that's very Mary Ann. I think Mary Ann is very strong of character. I think she's very principled. I think she comes from a background of work ethics. I think she's very positive and very optimistic. I think she's much more naive than Dawn Wells, of course, even than Dawn Wells was at that age....

"There's a goodness to Mary Ann that I find a tremendous responsibility for....I mean, she was kind of an idol to young girls of that time. And the questions these young girls started asking me [while speaking before a group of about three hundred in Lubbock, Texas]—about boys, about drugs, about sex, about God. I was all of a sudden so aware of the responsibility that I had to these children."

MARY ANN: Ooh, here's an old slave bracelet an old boyfriend in high school gave me.

GINGER: Ooh, how can you bear to part with it? Doesn't it do something to you?'

MARY ANN: Yeah, it turns my wrist green.

GINGER: I've got samples of all my cosmetics, including one perfume guaranteed to drive any normal man wild.

MARY ANN: And to think I wasted all my time in Kansas using honey behind each ear.

GINGER: Honey? Did you attract many boys that way?

MARY ANN: Not very many boys, but lots of flies.

CHAPTER 3
AN UNCHARTED DESERT ISLE

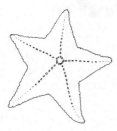

ccording to the Skipper, Gilligan's Island is located 250 miles southeast of Hawaii at 140 degrees longitude and 10 degrees latitude [Episode 18]. The Professor, however, insists that the island is located 110 degrees longitude and 10 degrees latitude [Episode 21]. Unless their calculations are incorrect, the castaways are shipwrecked on a floating island whose continually shifting location clearly explains why the island remains uncharted.

While there isn't any game on the island, there are woodpeckers, monkeys, gorillas, a six-foot spider, owls, and parrots. As far as food goes, the island offers bananas, mangos, coconuts, papaya, pineapples, guava, watermelon, blackberries, blueberries, avocados, pears, and grapes. The seas around the island provide the castaways with halibut, tuna, mackerel, flounder, and swordfish. There are a number of caves, an underground cavern of fresh water, a geyser of natural helium, a quicksand pit, a gold mine, a mud bog, a mountain range, and a volcano—not to mention waterfalls and streams that lead to a lush lagoon. The island would be an idyllic tropical paradise, if it weren't always being used as a test site for missiles.

VISITORS

For an uncharted island, an astounding number of visitors, tribal natives, and animals drop by. What's the likelihood of all these people visiting the island and either refusing to rescue the castaways or returning to civilization with acute amnesia?

- Wrongway Feldman
  [Episodes 5 & 24]
- A Japanese sailor still
  fighting World War II [Episode 15]
- Gangster Jackson Farrell
  and his accomplice [Episode 17]
- Two gangsters from
  the Indigo Mob [Episode 17]

- A jungle boy [Episode 19]
- Surfer Duke Williams
  [Episode 21]
- A native headhunter
  [Episode 23]
- Cannibals [Episode 26]
- A parrot [Episode 27]
- Famous painter Alexandri
  Gregor Dubov [Episode 34]

- A family of three natives
  and a native suitor, Haruki
  [Episode 37]
- An exiled Latin American
  dictator, Pancho Hernando Gonzales
  Enrico Rodriguez, of Equarico
  [Episode 39]
- Two Russian cosmonauts
  (Ivan & Igor) [Episode 45]
- A rock 'n' roll band,
  the Mosquitoes (Bingo, Bango, Bongo,
  and Irving) [Episode 48]
- Wealthy socialite Erika Tiffany
  Smith [Episode 51]
- A robot [Episode 57]
- A lion [Episode 60]

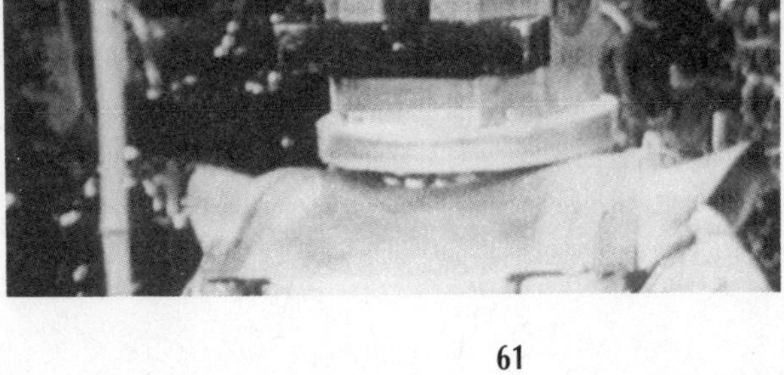

- Mr. Howell's look-alike [Episode 62]
- A spy disguising himself as a ghost [Episode 63]
- Mad scientist Boris Balinkoff [Episodes 65 & 77]
- A Russian spy, Gilligan's double [Episode 70]
- Movie producer Harold Hecuba [Episode 72]
- A voodoo witch doctor [Episode 73]
- Famous butterfly collector Lord Beasley Waterford [Episode 75]
- Three native headhunters [Episode 78]
- Compulsive kidnapper Norbert Wiley [Episode 80]
- Ginger look-alike Eva Grubb [Episode 82]
- Game show contestant George Barkley [Episode 84]
- Big game hunter Jonathan Kincaid and his assistant Ramoo [Episode 86]
- An actor disguised as Tongo the Ape-man [Episode 88]
- Three Kapuki natives [Episode 91]
- Native girl Kalani of the Matoba tribe and three Matoba natives [Episode 94]
- A homing pigeon [Episode 96]
- A native king, Killiwanni of the Papuan tribe, and two natives [Episode 98]

GREAT FINDS

Is it possible for the island to be home to such a wealth of natural resources? Could all these remarkable things be found on the island, fished from the lagoon, wash up on shore, or fall from space?

- Marubi headdresses [Episode 1]
- An inflatable raft from the *Minnow* [Episode 9]
- A gold mine [Episode 9]
- A tiki [Episode 10]
- A treasure chest filled with cannon balls [Episode 16]
- An air force test missile [Episode 18]
- A geyser of helium [Episode 19]
- A hot-air weather balloon [Episode 20]
- A newspaper dated April 10, 1906 [Episode 27]
- A box of Jewel Crackers [Episode 27]
- A lucky stone [Episode 29]
- A gallon of chocolate and a gallon of vanilla ice cream [Episode 29]
- A crate of magician's props [Episode 33]
- An unmanned spacecraft intended for Mars complete with live camera [Episode 40]
- A crate of silent movie equipment [Episode 43]
- A World War II mine [Episode 50]
- A crate of coconuts packed with pages of a recent newspaper [Episode 52]
- A telephone cable [Episode 53]
- Seeds that when consumed enable telepathic mind reading [Episode 55]
- Two crates of grenades and ammunition [Episode 58]
- A hot-water geyser [Episode 61]
- A 200-function pocketknife [Episode 70]
- A crate of radioactive seeds [Episode 71]
- Magic rings [Episode 77]
- A government attaché case [Episode 79]
- A totem pole [Episode 91]
- A prehistoric stone tablet [Episode 93]
- A jet pack [Episode 95]
- A crate of molding plastic explosive [Episode 97]
- A crate of old clothes rejected by the Salvation Army [Episode 97]
- A crate of sixteen decks of playing cards with all the numbers washed off [Episode 97]

63

NATURAL DISASTERS

The castaways certainly experience their share of problems, from invading cannibals to a vitamin deficiency. But is it really possible to experience all of these acts of God?

- An approaching tropical storm [Episode 2]
- A blight [Episode 7]
- A water shortage [Episode 14]
- A test missile targeted for the island [Episode 18]
- A gorilla that captures Mrs. Howell [Episode 22]
- The island is sinking [Episode 42]
- An approaching typhoon [Episode 46]
- A deadly bug that bites Gilligan, causing everyone to think he will die in twenty-four hours [Episode 49]
- An active World War II mine that threatens to explode [Episode 50]
- A volcano on the island that threatens to erupt [Episode 61]
- An allergic reaction to Gilligan experienced by the castaways [Episode 64]
- A vitamin C deficiency [Episode 66]
- A meteor that crashes on the island and emits cosmic rays that will cause the castaways to die of old age within a week [Episode 68]
- A bat that bites Gilligan, causing him to think he is turning into a vampire [Episode 69]
- An unknown ailment that, after turning Gilligan's hair white, causes both him and the Skipper to go bald [Episode 76]
- A bump on the head that causes Gilligan to see everything upside down [Episode 78]
- Lightning that strikes Gilligan, getting a rock bowling ball stuck on his hand [Episode 89]
- Lightning that strikes Gilligan a second time, turning him invisible [Episode 89]
- An unmanned space capsule that falls from orbit and lands on the lagoon [Episode 90]

MAPS

The series provides viewers with three maps of the island—all of which offer conflicting topographical information.

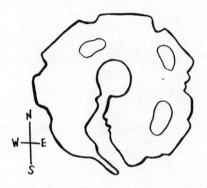

The Professor's map of the island [Episode 58].

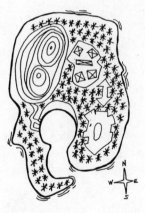

Butterfly collector Lord Beasley Waterford's map of the island [Episode 75].

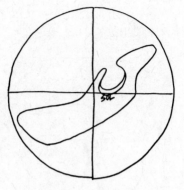

The island as seen by U.S. astronauts orbiting the earth [Episode 90].

CHAPTER 4

NOT a SINGLE LUXURY

For seven castaways stranded on a desert isle, the crew and passengers of the *S.S. Minnow* sure have a lot of luxuries.

The inventory of the *S.S. Minnow* alone includes: a toolbox (containing a saw, machete, rope, chisel, hammer, crowbar, ruler, hand drills, pliers, screwdriver, hatchet), one box of matches, a pistol, blankets, a flashlight, binoculars, a large ax, six shovels and picks, a deep-sea fishing rod, tackle, fishing nets, wood and nails from the wreckage, engine parts, a brown nail keg, a large wooden barrel, several wooden buckets, a radio, a transmitter, a fire extinguisher, a barometer, a thermometer, a sand dial, an oxygen tank, a hot-water bottle, a frying pan, a black kettle, a spatula, wooden crates, a life preserver, a dozen raincoats, a first aid kit, a picnic basket, two diving masks, and a wet suit.

Of course, you don't have to be a Nobel laureate to realize that each castaway brought an excessive number of belongings for a three-hour tour. "The kids think they've really figured out something, you know," says Bob Denver. "I think we discussed what we were going to do with it. I remember there was something about a freighter being sunk off the island and we got all the clothes from the freighter. There were all different ideas, and then we said, 'Aw, the heck with it. Let's make it one of those things people look at and go, "Wait a minute! What?!? How can that be?" ' "

Aside from the clothes in his duffel bag, Gilligan brought along his pocketknife, bubble gum, baseball cards, a deck of cards, his library card, his bank book, a calendar, two marbles, seven cents, his lucky charm, a rabbit's foot, a secret-compartment spy ring, Yogi Bear bottle tops, a chrome yo-yo, the wheels from his skateboard, a Manny Moose wristwatch, a high school graduation ring from Girls High, and comic books (including *Fossil Face and Davie Davis*). The Skipper brought a duffel bag of clothes, his sea chest, a checkerboard and checkers, a two-headed coin, a windbreaker, and his naval dress hat.

Of course, the Howells dress for almost every occasion. When searching through the jungle, they wear matching khaki safari outfits and pith helmets. When sneaking about the island, they wear matching Burberrys and Stetson hats. They both dress for dinner and have seemingly endless wardrobes.

"Instead of a three-hour tour where they had all these clothes...," says Natalie Schafer, "it should have been maybe a three-day tour."

"That is a satiric comment," explains Schwartz. "What that says is that rich people have it good no matter where they are. They will get things that nobody else can get. Somehow that happens."

Mr. Howell brought twenty suitcases, including a briefcase (filled with stocks, certificates, IRS forms, and checkbooks), a steamer trunk, at least $500,000 in cash, a copy of *The Wall Street Journal,* a solid-gold camera, a second camera and flash, binoculars, a large net, solid-gold suspenders and butane lighter, a money changer, an alligator-skin briefcase (filled with bottled medication), his teddy bear, an Indian headdress, a chef's hat, two fencing outfits with masks and sabers, a bottle of brandy, and several bottles of champagne. Lovey brought a typewriter, a cuckoo clock, an anniversary clock, her social calendar, her furs (fox, beaver, chinchilla, mink, and sable), a hairdryer, jewelry (her engagement ring, emeralds, pearls, rubies, earrings, a diamond brooch and bracelets), a makeup case, and nine bottles of perfume (including Gold Dust #5, Warm Afternoon, Happy Hours, and Foggy Nights).

As for the others, Ginger only brought one gown, a purse, a makeup kit (containing a framed photograph of herself), a script to *Pyramid for Two,* and a horoscope magazine. The Professor brought one suitcase with a change of clothes, a jacket, pajamas, books [see "The Professor's Library" in Chapter 2], a hat, rubber gloves, a magnifying glass, and a slide rule. Mary Ann brought one small suitcase of clothes and a sewing basket.

Once the castaways exhaust the provisions from the *Minnow,* they must fend for themselves. Fortunately, the island provides them with fresh tropical fruit, and the surrounding seas provide them with fresh fish. The Professor cultivates a vegetable garden and claims that the breadfruit he grows is so rich in vitamins that they could live on it forever. Gilligan usually starts the fires, and Mary Ann generally does the cooking. The castaways even make coffee from fish, although—thankfully—we never learn how.

For water, the castaways initially dig a freshwater well, but when that dries up, Gilligan accidentally locates an underground cavern filled with fresh water. They build a shower and a bathtub, and the Professor invents seaweed shampoo. The men, continually clean-shaven, share a single straight razor; Howell obviously brought along a three-year supply of razor blades for himself. As far as toilet facilities go, we never learn whether the castaways use a latrine or an outhouse. Feminine hygiene is another boldly ignored topic.

When the castaways first land on the island, they build a communal hut before building separate huts, sharing a highly adept skill for bamboo construction. They can build almost anything from bamboo and woven palm-fronds: huts, tables, chairs, furniture, cages, pedal-powered appliances and machines. They build a pedal-powered washing machine, a pedal-powered electrical generator, a hand-cranked phonograph (using the *Minnow*'s steering wheel for a turntable), a pedal-powered dentist's drill, a wooden stage with curtains (sewn together from old clothes), a hot-air balloon (sewn together from raincoats), and the world's first pedal-powered bamboo car. They're also able to

make paint from berries, and the Professor makes candles and wicks. [A complete list of the castaways' inventions can be found in Chapter 6, following each episode's plot summary.]

"Sherwood gave the effects department so much lead time to build everything, they always came up with stuff that was just outrageous," remembers Bob Denver.

"I just remember that those prop guys came up with the damnedest things," recalls Russell Johnson. "They used to make me laugh. They were so wonderful. The property department for *Gilligan's Island* was one of the most creative departments in that whole show. . . . They had things with coconuts and water that could make electricity. I mean, it astounded me how the hell they did it. And then they had to explain to me how to make them work."

The castaways' huts, while far from luxurious, are hardly as primitive as can be. The life preserver from the *Minnow* hangs on the door to Gilligan and the Skipper's hut, which contains a bamboo telescope, hammocks, a table, and the castaways' water supply. The Howells live luxuriously in their own secluded hut furnished with bamboo beds, lounge chairs, partitions, a cuckoo clock, pottery, a vanity table, and a chandelier made from coconut shells. Howell has his own golf course, and at one point they even build their own exclusive country club. Orange curtains, two blanket-covered beds, a vanity table, makeup mirror, two bamboo chairs, a table, bureau, and the pedal-powered bamboo sewing machine fill Ginger and Mary Ann's hut. The Professor's hut contains purple curtains, food lockers, a bed, table and chairs, and the Professor's improvised laboratory equipment.

While the castaways also have a seemingly endless supply of paper, pens, and pencils, the radio remains their only contact with civilization. The radio's batteries, made by the Thurston Howell Battery Company, die after just a few weeks on the island, but fortunately the Skipper finds rechargeable batteries from the *Minnow*. The radio provides the castaways' sole diversion. Gilligan enjoys lounging around the island listening to rock 'n' roll; Howell listens for the stock market reports; Lovey listens to "Uncle Artie's storytime"; Mary Ann follows soap operas and, together with Ginger, an exercise program; and of course, they all listen to the news, which oddly always seems to pertain to their plight.

The castaways, basking in luxuries they either brought along or built for themselves, appear more than capable of getting off the island. Perhaps a collectively held subconscious conflict keeps them forever marooned on this tropical island paradise. Or is their fate simply dictated by the show's premise?

NEWS LEARNED FROM THE RADIO

- The Vagabond Lady, a lone pilot circling the globe, will be passing over the island. [Episode 4]
- Wrongway Feldman has returned to civilization without being able to recall the island's location. [Episode 5]
- A navy destroyer has been dispatched to search the area for stranded castaways. [Episode 12]
- Howell's oil company in Oklahoma struck a geyser. [Episode 13]
- The air force plans to use the island as a test site for a new missile. [Episode 18]
- The jungle boy has landed safely on a United States aircraft carrier. [Episode 19]
- Surfer Dick Williams has returned to Hawaii with amnesia. [Episode 21]
- The navy will be holding maneuvers offshore. [Episode 30]
- Someone Ginger knows won the Miss America contest. [Episode 38]

ANNOUNCING

- NASA scientists report life on Mars. [Episode 40]
- Gilligan has the winning number in the Argentinian million-dollar sweepstakes. [Episode 41]
- The castaways' film has won first prize in the Cannes Film Festival. [Episode 43]
- The Howells are broke. [Episode 44]
- Erika Tiffany Smith can't recall the island's location. [Episode 51]
- Horace Higgenbothem of Horner's Corners, Kansas, has eloped with Sybil Wentworth. [Episode 54]
- The robot walked to Hawaii, but when scientists check its voice, the castaways' message is scrambled. [Episode 57]
- A fleet of one hundred destroyers is to comb the area that claimed the *Minnow*. [Episode 59]
- A Mr. Howell look-alike has taken Howell's place and is spending all his money. [Episode 62]
- The minister who married the Howells is a phony. [Episode 67]
- Movie producer Harold Hecuba is making a movie version of *Hamlet*. [Episode 72]
- Lord Beasley Waterford, preoccupied with his butterfly collecting, hasn't reported the castaways to the authorities. [Episode 75]
- Game show contestant George Barkley won't be able to collect his prize winnings. [Episode 84]
- The Maritime Board decided that the shipwreck was the Skipper's fault. [Episode 85]
- Hunter Jonathan Kincaid has had a nervous breakdown after a shooting match. [Episode 86]
- An orbiting spacecraft will be directly over the island. [Episode 90]
- A fleet of ships will be in the area searching for a lost jet pack. [Episode 95]

MARY ANN'S RECIPES

COCONUT CREAM PIE

¾ cup honey (or 1 cup sugar)
½ cup flour or 4 tablespoons cornstarch
½ teaspoon sea salt
2 cups coconut milk, scalded
3 duck eggs, separated
2 tablespoons coconut butter
1 teaspoon vanilla
1 cup shredded coconut
1 baked 9-inch pastry shell

Mix together ½ cup honey, flour, and salt; gradually stir in milk and cook over boiling water 10 minutes, stirring constantly until mixture thickens. Stir small amount into slightly beaten egg yolks; then gradually pour into thickened milk and cook about 2 minutes, stirring constantly. Add butter and vanilla and cool slightly. Stir ½ cup shredded coconut into cream filling. Turn into baked pastry shell. Cover with meringue made by gradually beating remaining ¼ cup honey into stiffly beaten egg whites. Sprinkle with ½ cup coconut. Bake in moderately hot oven (400° F) 5 to 8 minutes, or until delicately browned; chill. If made with 2 eggs, use 1 cup honey. If desired, omit meringue and serve with whipped cream, sweetened.

GILLIGAN'S FAVORITE DRINK

⅓ papaya juice
⅓ pineapple juice
⅓ coconut juice

Mix together in a tall bamboo-shoot drinking glass and serve.

HOMEMADE GUAVA JELLY

4 cups water
1 quart guava
1 cup honey

Add 4 cups of water per 1 quart of guava and cook until soft. Turn cooked fruit into a jelly bag of canton flannel or several thicknesses of cheesecloth and allow to drain; shift pulp occasionally to keep juice flowing. Return drained pulp to kettle, barely cover with water, cook slowly about 25 minutes and drain again. This juice is usually kept separate from first extraction and made into jelly by itself. Measure juice (not more than 4 to 6 cups) into a deep kettle. Boil fruit juice rapidly 5 minutes; skim if necessary, then add ¾ to 1 cup of honey, stirring until dissolved. Cook rapidly until jelly test is obtained: Lift a full spoon from the boiling syrup, hold it about 12 inches above the kettle, and pour contents back into kettle. At first they pour like water; later the drops flatten out into a thin sheet, which, when the jelly reaches the finishing point, will shear away from the edge of the spoon, leaving it clean. The total time of boiling will be 30 minutes.

Pour hot jelly into sterilized glasses, filling them to within ¼ inch of the top. Cover jelly with a thin layer of hot but not smoking paraffin. On second day, cover with another thin layer of paraffin. The combined layers shouldn't be more than ⅛ inch thick. Cover with tin lids or paste heavy paper over top. Label and store in cool, dark, dry place.

BREADFRUIT MUFFINS

2 cups breadfruit
2 teaspoons baking powder
1 teaspoon sea salt
2 beaten turtle eggs
1 cup coconut milk
½ cup sour cream
¼ cup papaya oil

In a bowl combine breadfruit, baking powder, and salt. In another bowl combine sour cream, eggs, milk, and oil. Add egg mixture to breadfruit mixture. Grease 1 muffin tin liberally. Pour in batter to fill ⅔ of each cup. Bake at 375° F for 20 to 25 minutes. Use a toothpick to test for doneness. Remove tins to a rack. Let stand for five minutes. With a greased knife, cut around each cup. Invert and tap to remove muffins. Serves 6.

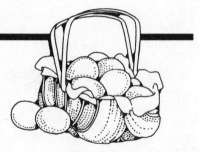

COCONUT MILK PANCAKES

1 cup sifted flour
1 teaspoon baking powder
½ teaspoon salt
2 teaspoons honey
1 beaten duck egg
1 cup coconut milk
1 tablespoon coconut oil
¼ cup melted butter

In a bowl combine dry ingredients. In another bowl combine egg, milk, honey, and oil. Add gradually to the dry ingredients; stir until batter is lumpy. With a large spoon or ladle drop batter onto a hot greased griddle. Cook until bubbles appear on the surface. Turn; cook until brown. Remove pancakes from griddle. Brush each pancake with melted butter. Serve with hot syrup. Makes 6 to 8 pancakes.

WATERMELON PIE

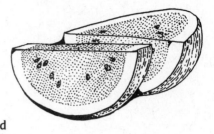

Pastry for two-crust pie
5 cups watermelon
1 cup honey
¼ cup flour
⅛ tablespoon salt
1 tablespoon grated lemon rind
1 tablespoon grated orange rind
2 tablespoons butter

Place watermelon in a pot, bring to a boil, stirring constantly. Boil for 2 minutes. Press pulp through a sieve to remove seeds. In a bowl combine honey, flour, butter, and salt. Add to fruit mixture. Blend in lemon and orange rind. Mix well. Line a 9-inch pie pan with pastry. Fill with fruit mixture. Cover with slitted top. Seal edges. Bake at 425° F for 45 minutes. Yields one 9-inch pie.

CHAPTER 5

AS PRIMITIVE AS CAN BE

SEX

nyone who has ever watched *Gilligan's Island* for even just one episode can't help but wonder if there isn't any hanky-panky going on in those huts. Even when she's not acting the part of seductress, Ginger provokes even the youngest male viewers. And Mary Ann isn't too far behind. Why then aren't they continually pregnant?

"I would think if it really happened, then Mary Ann and Ginger would have ended up in the hay with somebody," says Natalie Schafer. "It seemed that to be on that island all that time without any Hay Department was a little bit farfetched."

"In the European version, we'd all be in the hut together," says Dawn Wells, laughing.

♥♥♥♥

After all, Ginger, a self-proclaimed swinger, is obviously sex-starved. She tries to seduce almost every man who visits the island, and whenever she asks one of the men to rehearse a scene with her from one of the many scripts she brought along with her on the cruise, it's an exceedingly passionate love scene.

Of course, Ginger may be sex-starved, but not desperately enough to lower her standards to sleep with the Skipper. She often flirts with Thurston Howell III, but life on the small island would be hellish if either of them stirred Lovey's wrath. She's always assisting and admiring the Professor, the only man on the island she really desires, but he's oblivious to her needs.

GINGER: Professor, when you were in your teens, didn't you ever go to a drive-in movie?

PROFESSOR: Once. But the curvature of the screen and the fidelity of the sound made it impossible to enjoy the picture.

GINGER: Let me start again. In your hometown, didn't you ever meet a girl whose house had a porch swing?

PROFESSOR: As a matter of fact I did. Oh, but she was quite impossible. I tried to start intelligent conversations, but all she was interested in was hugging and kissing. Kissing and hugging.

Ginger thinks of Gilligan as "a shy, frightened fawn" and "kind of cute," but whenever she tries to seduce him, he usually backs away, accidentally banging his head into a palm tree and knocking himself unconscious. Gilligan can't even understand that Ginger usually has ulterior motives when she tries to seduce someone for the benefit of the others. "Gilligan," she tells him, "there are some things about life that you just don't understand." But Gilligan isn't as ignorant as he seems; he's merely petrified by sex. Besides, he's too busy thinking about food to be bothered with any other primitive instincts.

GINGER: (*seductively*) Gilligan, look into my eyes. Now what do you see?

GILLIGAN: All I can see is a little black thing in the middle of a little green thing in the middle of a white thing.

Mary Ann has a soft spot in her heart for Gilligan, and she lets her feelings be known, coyly telling him how sweet he is. She's always willing to take care of him, cook for him, and nurse him. She considers herself much too young for the Skipper, and too different from the Professor, but when Lovey tries to matchmake a marriage between Gilligan and Mary Ann, the two show romantic interest in each other. Yet the romance never materializes.

Curiously, whenever Ginger makes a move on the Professor, Mary Ann gets rather catty. Perhaps Mary Ann's jealousy in these situations stems not from any feelings she has for the Professor, but rather from her own amorous feelings for Ginger. After all, Ginger and Mary Ann share not only the same hut, but also an inability to find sexual satisfaction with any of the men on the island. They do spend an inordinate amount of time together cooking, sunbathing, and doing the chores. Whenever a man visits the island, Ginger and Mary Ann simultaneously express physical affection toward him, perhaps implying latent receptiveness to a ménage à trois.

"The fraternity boys were really crazy about Mary Ann," recalls Dawn Wells. "Mary Ann is the fourteen- and fifteen-year-old boy's fantasy.... I would expect the male to be attracted to the sex image, the glamour girl that Tina was, but I think there is a part of Mary Ann that is obtainable. I think you as a young man feel that you could talk to her, and that she might go to the senior prom with you."

"Everybody likes a different type," explains Tina Louise. "It depends on what you can cope with, you know, how far they let their fantasies go. Some people can't cope with someone who is sensual."

"I guess that Ginger movie star scared more guys off than she attracted," speculates Bob Denver.

The Skipper, a navy man who has seen more than his share of ports of call, blatantly lusts for both Ginger and Mary Ann—who, understandably, want nothing to do with him. While he's certainly amiable, likable, and good-natured, the Skipper is physically unattractive and old enough to be the father of both. Could the Skipper and Gilligan possibly be homosexual lovers? While they served together in

the navy, the Skipper and Gilligan are so homophobic they each sleep fully dressed.

SKIPPER: Ginger, I've got a problem. I've got a real problem. You're a girl, right?

GINGER: Well, if you're not sure about that, you have got a problem.

Lovey and Thurston Howell III are the only ones who see any action on the island. Thurston Howell III may lust for the two girls, but Lovey seems to have him on a tight leash. Still, he wouldn't mind an extramarital affair with either of the girls—especially Ginger (whose affections he could undoubtedly buy by promising to produce her films upon their return to civilization).

"I think [Howell] would flirt up until the moment of truth, and he would back off," says Jim Backus. "That's my own conception. He was very flattered when someone said something nice to him. Of course, we only see him on the island. We don't know what kind of guy he's going to be on the outside."

Of course, there's absolutely no form of birth control on the island. The Professor might synthesize some formula from tree sap or invent some sort of bamboo device, but given his questionable track record, who would trust it to work? Since Lovey has obviously reached menopause, it's unlikely that Howell is carting around a suitcase full of condoms. The only possible birth control available to the castaways is the rhythm method.

While the Skipper can legally perform marriages on the island, the need never arises. On an island that's as primitive as can be, there doesn't seem to be anything very primitive going on. "You're watching the show on one day," explains Schwartz. "God knows what they're doing on the other six."

CASTAWAYS' CORNER

Who was the island's leader?

BOB DENVER: "I don't think anybody, because there was always bickering, somewhere along the line. I'm sure Mr. Howell thought he was, and the Skipper thought he was, and Gilligan thought he was, and the girls probably thought at certain times they were, and the Professor—I don't know if he ever wanted to be the leader, but he was, you know.... Nah, I don't think we showed that."

ALAN HALE, JR.: "In many ways, validly, you could say the Professor was really the leader. It was astounding with all the things that he fancied and certainly dreamed up, if you will, and put us on the brink of coming back, but met failure again. Yes, if you will, perhaps the pecking order, as they say—I suppose I was the biggest bear of all."

JIM BACKUS: "Ginger. Because when called upon, she used her wiles as a very attractive lady, and she had more native street intelligence. The Howells were insulated, so you'd leave them out. The Skipper was a big, naive goof. Gilligan is the clown. And Ginger is a girl who obviously came up through Broadway, and you have to be smart, that's all. She had native shrewdness, and she was just smarter than the rest of them. The Professor was in his ivory tower. We thought he was the leader. He might be the leader, but somewhere along the line, it was instigated or promoted by Ginger."

NATALIE SCHAFER: "I think the team of Mr. and Mrs. Howell was very important. One alone wouldn't have been.... I thought everybody contributed to what Sherwood really wanted: a mixed-up group of people who got on."

TINA LOUISE: "The Professor certainly kind of held it together. He came to the rescue, you know, in terms of common sense. I don't feel that Bob ran it. He charmed the audience, but I certainly don't feel that he ran it. I feel everybody kind of...I would say between Skipper and Mr. Howell and the Professor, in terms of common sense."

RUSSELL JOHNSON: "I would say the Skipper. I think in the long run he was the real boss. I came into my own when there was a problem. When there wasn't a problem, he was the boss. When there was a problem, then I, in a sense, decided a lot of things....I mean, the Howells were too crazy to be listened to, and Ginger and Mary Ann were young women and not to be listened to in terms of society. So I would say certainly the Skipper ran the show."

DAWN WELLS: "I guess the Skipper. But Howell controls everything, but there was the Professor."

POLITICS

"The Declaration of Independence" and "The Communist Manifesto" are the unacknowledged cornerstones of the castaways' loose system of governance. While the castaways adhere to the principle that men are by nature endowed with certain inalienable rights (among them "life, liberty, and the pursuit of happiness") and that government is created by contract to serve the welfare of the people, the general system under which they agree to be governed is left to evolution and deduction and is never stated specifically in a formal basic document. In short, their utopia remains both literally and metaphorically unnamed.

Essentially, the island operates according to the system of direct democracy. Each castaway has the right to vote, participate, and influence the decision-making process. The castaways compose a self-governing entity, democratically organized and responsible for their own survival and for effectuating rescue. General meetings are ruled by consensus and empowered with improvisation, debate, and flexibility of action. Decisions are executed by volunteers or assigned according to ability.

LOVEY: Well, I think we should be selected the democratic way. According to our social position.

SKIPPER: Well, as your Skipper, I know there's only one choice. This unpleasant duty's got to fall on only one man. Mr. Howell.

HOWELL: Me? Wait! You're the Skipper. It's your duty.

SKIPPER: But you're an executive. You know how to handle these manners in a businesslike way.

HOWELL: Well, that's different—if you want it handled in a businesslike way.

SKIPPER: Then you'll handle it?

HOWELL: Yes, I'll dictate a letter and send it out in triplicate.

While decisions are reached democratically, the castaways live according to the Marxist ideal, "From each according to his ability, to each according to his needs." Economically, socialism prevails. The castaways share the island's natural resources equally, and currency is never issued—although Howell is constantly trying to bribe someone. Permanent jobs are assigned by ability, and when special needs arise, the castaways assume jobs according to both ability and need. The castaways take responsibility for each other's health; meals are served around a communal table; housing is allocated according to age, marital status, and seniority; and furniture is provided according to seniority and need. The castaways' society most closely resembles the Israeli kibbutz.

While the castaways dismiss the Skipper's claims to military authority and Howell's claim to rule by the hierarchy of social privilege, they never officially appoint an executive leader or create a judicial system. They do elect Gilligan president for a short term [Episode 6], but while the Professor actually may be the castaways' silent leader, the

Skipper considers himself the leader, always training Gilligan to replace him. When Gilligan and Mr. Howell dispute the ownership of a discovered treasure chest, the Professor insists upon presiding over a legal trial [Episode 16]. Otherwise, the castaways generally abide by cosmic law.

PROFESSOR: Now, Mr. Howell, we all gave our word that we'd obey the law.
HOWELL: I know, but...
PROFESSOR: And we agreed to accept the Skipper as sheriff and Gilligan as his deputy.
HOWELL: I know, but...
PROFESSOR: And we must agree to obey their authority and to accept the penalty if we break the law.
HOWELL: But the whole thing sounds so darn democratic.

Democratic decision making does not always prevail, however, and inequities flourish. The men often conceal information that should be considered public or reach decisions without consulting the others. While anarchy often ensues, a common enemy—the struggle for survival or a possible rescue—always unifies the castaways against internecine squabbles. Despotism results only from foreign invasion.

While the castaways' governance system is astoundingly progressive, their system of sexual inequality appalls a modern sensibility. The men often forbid the women to participate in the decision-making

process and relegate them to sexist roles. For instance, when Ginger volunteers to help lure the headhunters away [Episode 47], Gilligan chauvinistically tells her, "A woman's place is in the hut."

"Yes, it's the way the women were treated," admits Alan Hale, Jr. "The men exceeded them in intelligence and we showed it."

While Lovey would rebel against Mr. Howell's chauvinism, Ginger and Mary Ann displayed very little independence. "I was a slave from Kansas," laughs Dawn Wells. "I'm the secretary that makes coffee. That would be a real issue now."

"It's nothing I'd want to do again," says Tina Louise. "But it's always interesting to represent, you know, different characters."

Schwartz flatly denies any intentionally sexist overtones. "We had several episodes where the women refused to be treated like women and all moved to the other side of the island [Episode 20]," he says. "It was a recognized factor in those years, so we dealt with that, and they demanded equal rights, and that was a long time ago, long before this country was ready for equal rights."

MARY ANN: You men keep promising to build us a hut, and you won't keep your promises.

GINGER: We think that women should have the same rights as men.

HOWELL: Did you hear that Lovey? Women should have the same rights as men! (*Laughs*) You're not laughing, Lovey.

LOVEY: Thurston, you've been promising me you'd build us a hut of our own for weeks now.

HOWELL: Well, I'll get to it by and by.

LOVEY: But I'm not asking for anything elaborate. Just a little split-level hut or a palm-tree penthouse.

PROFESSOR: Well, I'm afraid you women are going to have to face the facts. Historically, it's the man who decides what should be done.

MEN: Hear! Hear! Hear!

LOVEY: Haven't you ever heard of Lysistrata?

GILLIGAN: Yeah, isn't that a mouthwash?

CASTAWAYS' CORNER

What kind of government is on the island?

ALAN HALE, JR.: "I think very much so it was democracy. We would get an idea, but we always had...a round-table discussion with all of us. And if there was anything on the radio that would possibly benefit us, we were all listening."

JIM BACKUS: "A benign welfare state. It could be a welfare state because we all shared, and no one's voice seemed to be bigger than the other, and Mr. Howell went along with it in the end."

NATALIE SCHAFER: "What kind of government was going on on the island? Certainly silent."

RUSSELL JOHNSON: "I think there's no doubt about the fact that it was socialism. You know, I mean, it was, in a sense, share and share alike with the two capitalists being a problem—but going along."

CREATOR SHERWOOD SCHWARTZ: "In truth the show illustrates both. There is a socialistic community because they're living together. Nevertheless, the wealthy guy always has the best of things because that's how life is."

RELIGION

For seven people marooned on an island, the castaways display surprisingly little philosophical or theological despair. The shipwreck fails to provoke any spiritual anguish, and the secular castaways remain strangely unaffected, refraining from both existential and religious quests. Curiously, they never question their fate or pray for cosmic intervention.

We never learn the castaways' religious affiliations or beliefs. While they basically adhere to the Ten Commandments, they never practice any religious rituals other than primitive superstition and voodoo. For all we know, Gilligan worships childhood; the Skipper reveres superstition; Howell venerates money; Lovey adores the social calendar; the Professor worships knowledge; and Ginger bows to the silver screen. Only Mary Ann, adhering to a strict morality, displays even a slight hint of a complex system of religious beliefs. But for all their books, the castaways don't have a Bible on the island.

Perhaps the castaways are nothing but unwitting pawns in a metaphysical chess game where they allegorically represent the Seven Deadly Sins: sloth (Gilligan), anger (the Skipper), greed (Howell), gluttony (Lovey), lust (Ginger), and envy (Mary Ann). While optimism and hope pervade the island, the castaways, failing to affect an ontological oneness with their fate, forever remain metaphorically marooned.

THE ARTS

If the castaways devoted as much attention to getting themselves off the island as they do to staging musical extravaganzas, they'd easily find themselves back in civilization. The energy and materials they expend on building elaborate stages and sets could be put to much better use staging their escape. Yet for a variety of irrational reasons, the castaways choose instead to stage a theatrical version of *Cleopatra* called *Pyramid for Two* [Episode 11]; form a primitive orchestra [Episode 26]; hold a beauty pageant for "Miss Castaway" [Episode 38]; form rock 'n' roll bands [Episode 48]; and stage a musical version of *Hamlet* [Episode 72]. Ah, culture.

CHAPTER 6

NOW THIS IS THE TALE OF OUR CASTAWAYS

CASTAWAYS' CORNER

What's your favorite episode?

BOB DENVER: "I never really had a favorite episode. No, I can't think of one. They were really fun to do because each one was a little bit different than the other one, you know, so it was not like doing a series where you basically lived in the living room or the kitchen and the four sets you have. We did big special effects gags, and consequently every week you'd read the next week's script, you know, and go, 'Ohhhh! They've topped it again! Look what we're doing! More craziness!'"

ALAN HALE, JR.: "When we did the takeoff on Sherlock Holmes [Episode 69]. The Professor was Sherlock, and I was Dr. Watson. Fun! Delight! We all came off with the British accent, and I mean it was rather wonderful. And dear little Mary Ann was the old hag with the teeth missing and everything. And of course, Gilligan did his vampire, Dracula and all."

JIM BACKUS: "The favorite episode that I had was a dream sequence. We shot it on the *Gunsmoke* set, and I dreamt I was an old prospector coming down from the mountains with the gold to be assayed [Episode 41]. And I had a donkey. A lot of people say it was one of the best comedy performances they'd ever seen. It gave me a chance to really go to town, and a lot of it was ad-libbing and improvisation as we went, too."

NATALIE SCHAFER: "I loved doing Cinderella [Episode 87]. I think that was the thing I enjoyed the most because it was so farfetched."

TINA LOUISE: "There was one where we made a movie, that was, I think, just a classic episode [Episode 43]. And then I liked singing, 'I Wanna Be Loved by You,' that episode [Episode 96]. I liked the Eva Grubb one where I got to play two characters [Episode 82]. I also liked the one where I played another three characters, where I was Italian and Marilyn [Episode 72]."

RUSSELL JOHNSON: "I remember one story that was written for me with Zsa Zsa Gabor, because it was my story [Episode 51]."

DAWN WELLS: "I loved the one where I got to play Liza Doolittle a little bit; I think it was the Dr. Jekyll and Mr. Hyde segment [Episode 81]. I loved the one where I got to play Ginger [Episode 92]. I thought that was fun. It was fun working with some of the guest stars, watching the comedy with Phil Silvers and Don Rickles....I learned so much."

CREATOR SHERWOOD SCHWARTZ: " 'The Little Dictator' [Episode 39]. That's my favorite episode because it's a very important truth about life....Time and again, political overthrows wind up with a worse dictator than the guy who started....My second favorite is the one with Phil Silvers called 'The Producer' [Episode 72]. And I think that's a brilliant episode in terms of the marriage of opera with Shakespeare....More kids know about Shakespeare from that episode than from any other source."

THE RATING SYSTEM

Sunk ⊗

Sinking ⊗⊗

Waterlogged ⊗⊗⊗

Afloat ⊗⊗⊗⊗

THE FIRST SEASON

1: TWO ON A RAFT ⊗

Writers: Lawrence J. Cohen & Fred Freeman
Director: John Rich

After being shipwrecked and hearing the radio report their disappearance, the Skipper and Gilligan plan to set sail on a raft to find help. When the Professor finds a native headdress and arrowheads in one of the caves, he warns the Skipper and Gilligan that a tribe of Marubi headhunters may be on one of the nearby islands. Still the Skipper insists on making the trip.

The Howells come by and ask the Skipper to contact their stockbroker, but when the Skipper refuses, insisting that he'll be too busy just arranging for a rescue party, Howell insists that he'll go on the raft—until he realizes that he can't bring along all his luggage. The girls bring Gilligan and Skipper leis strung with pineapple and banana for good luck.

When the two set sail, Gilligan neglects to hoist the anchor, runs back to shore for it, and then walks into the lagoon after the raft. When the Skipper tries to pull Gilligan aboard, he falls into the lagoon.

After three days adrift at sea in calm waters, Gilligan (who's eaten all the food, including the tropical leis and the shark repellent the

Professor prepared for them) finds a bottle containing a note from castaways on a deserted island—which he wrote. Suddenly a shark attacks, devouring Gilligan's paddle and parts of the raft. Finally, a rainstorm flares up, sinking the raft.

Gilligan and the Skipper swim to the shore of an island. Convinced that they've traveled hundreds of miles, the Skipper orders Gilligan to start a fire to dry themselves. Meanwhile, Mary Ann sees smoke on the other side of the island, and the Professor, assuming it's the Marubi headhunters, runs to warn the Howells, who are in the middle of their golf game. The girls show up with five large conch shells, which, when sounded, will serve as their warning system.

Meanwhile, the Skipper finds footprints in the sand, convinced that they too belong to Marubi headhunters. The Skipper and Gilligan, hearing the wail of the passengers' conch shells, camouflage themselves as trees.

Meanwhile, the Professor finds a cave and rigs a trap for the Marubis by tying a vine to some of the rocks over the cave's entrance, leading it around a tree and along the ground where he covers it with palm fronds—which, when triggered, will cause an avalanche to block the cave. Later, when the Professor sees two trees moving, he shoots an arrow into one of them, and sounds his conch shell to warn the others.

The Skipper and Gilligan find the cave, and Gilligan suggests that they set up a trap by tying a vine to some of the rocks over the cave's entrance, leading it around a tree and along the ground, where they could cover it with palm fronds. While debating the merits of Gilligan's plan, the Skipper realizes that the trap has already been set—by the Marubis. Deciding that the cave offers them the safest hiding place, they go inside.

Soon after, the Professor leads the other castaways into the cave. A fight erupts in the darkness, throwing both Gilligan and the Professor from the cave, ending the misunderstanding. The Professor runs inside to tell the others, and when the fighting stops, Gilligan runs back into the cave, tripping over the vine and setting off an avalanche of rocks that traps the castaways inside. When the castaways dig themselves out of the cave, Gilligan emerges, disguised as a Marubi native, and scares them away.

COMMENTS:

- We never learn where the five passengers sleep on the island for the three days they're there.

TROPICAL INVENTIONS:

- Raft with sail
- The Professor's shark repellent
- Bow and arrow
- Conch shells as warning signal
- Mr. Howell's golf clubs (clam shells tied to bamboo poles with an avocado pit for a ball)

CASTAWAY QUIZ #1:

What did the Howells miss on account of the shipwreck?

(For answer, see page 359)

2: HOME SWEET HUT ⊗

Writers: Bill Davenport & Charles Tannen
Director: Richard Donner

While the Skipper cooks breakfast, a downpour breaks, and the Skipper, predicting a major storm, suggests that the castaways build a communal hut. While the men work on the hut, Gilligan, carrying two water buckets suspended from a large pole, makes a nuisance of himself. When he empties the water into a large barrel, he forgets to replace the cover, and the Skipper accidentally falls in. When Gilligan runs  to get a ladder for the Skipper, he pulls it out from under the Professor, who is knocked to the ground unconscious. Gilligan slams the ladder into Howell, spilling a bucket of the Professor's black, gooey weather-stripping concoction all over Mr. Howell. When he backs up again with the ladder, pinning the Skipper up against a bamboo supporting beam, the Skipper chases him, accidentally falling into the lagoon.

That night, after the communal hut is built, Gilligan and the Skipper are awoken by the Howells' loud bickering—which wakes the other castaways as well and incites them to each build his own hut by taking away their contribution to the communal hut. The Howells take the doors; the Professor takes the roof; the girls take the walls. The Skipper insists that they've got to work together as a group.

The next morning, while Gilligan and the Skipper build their own hut, Mr. Howell stops by to announce the completion of Howell Manor, inviting Gilligan and the Skipper to a "plantation warming party" later that night, and borrowing the machete from Gilligan. The Skipper tells Gilligan to stop lending out the tools, but when he leaves, Ginger seductively asks Gilligan for rope, which he resignedly hands over. When the Skipper discovers that Gilligan has given away his rope, he orders Gilligan to round up all the tools he's lent out. While at the Professor's hut, Gilligan pulls one palm leaf and an entire wall falls down. When Gilligan shows the Professor what he did, the remaining walls collapse. When Gilligan shows up at the girls' hut, he tries to help them open the front door, and their entire hut falls down. When the Skipper and Gilligan pay a visit to Howell's hut to reiterate the need for a community hut, Gilligan sits on Howell's hammock, collapsing his hut.

When the storm breaks, the castaways, gathered in the community hut, clutch one another in fear of their lives. When the storm stops, they hug each other and revel in the success of their group effort. When the Skipper opens the door and steps out to take a look, he falls into the lagoon, where the hut is now floating. Gilligan throws the Skipper a line, but falls in himself.

The next day, under clear skies, the castaways start building their own huts once again. When Ginger comes along to seductively ask Gilligan for the tools, he resignedly hands them all to her, carrying the toolbox for her.

COMMENTS:
- Rather than build a communal hut, the castaways could easily take shelter from the storm in one of the caves on the island.
- If the castaways can build a hut to withstand a tropical storm and float in the lagoon, they could certainly repair the *Minnow.*

TROPICAL INVENTIONS:
- Huts
- The Professor's weather-stripping concoction
- Bamboo paintbrushes
- Woven hammocks

CASTAWAY QUIZ #2:
What provisions does the Skipper cook for breakfast?
(For answer, see page 359)

3: VOODOO SOMETHING TO ME ⊗

Writers: Austin Kalish & Elroy Schwartz
Director: John Rich

While Gilligan sleeps standing guard, the Skipper brings the others out to the campfire and wakes Gilligan, causing him to fire a gun. The Skipper fires one of the castaways' flares in the hopes of signaling a passing boat (as they do every night), startling Gilligan, who fires off the castaways' last bullet. The Skipper lectures Gilligan on the importance of sentry duty, and when he leaves, Gilligan falls asleep again.

The next morning, after Gilligan admits that he fell asleep on the job, the Skipper informs the others that someone broke into the supply hut during the night and stole their food supplies and flare gun. The Professor suggests an immediate search, and the Skipper tells Gilligan that he thinks they've been under a voodoo curse ever since being shipwrecked.

The Professor and the Skipper leave Gilligan to guard the others with the unloaded gun and a rabbit's foot. While Mary Ann shares her fears, Ginger makes herself up to lure the intruder. They find Gilligan setting a rope trap, and while warning the girls how to avoid springing it, he traps himself. Later, while checking up on the Howells, who've barricaded the window of their hut, Gilligan hears the Skipper calling and runs out to find him hanging from the rope trap.

That night while standing guard, Gilligan hears sounds from the jungle, and checking the supply hut, he's attacked by an unseen intruder. The Skipper and the Professor run to his aid but find nothing, and after Gilligan describes the monster that attacked him, the Skipper expresses his fear that they've all been cursed by voodoo.

The next day while searching the island, the Professor tries to allay Gilligan's superstitious fears. When they split up, Gilligan trips and slides down a long, natural shoot into a mud bog. While he swims in the lagoon to wash off, a chimpanzee emerges from the jungle and steals his clothes.

While the Skipper builds a huge fire to chase off the demons, the Professor returns to camp without Gilligan. As the Skipper organizes search parties, he spots a chimpanzee wearing Gilligan's clothes. Convinced that Gilligan has been turned into a monkey by a voodoo curse, the Skipper speaks to his little buddy, takes off its clothes, and puts his Skipper's cap on its head. The monkey runs off into the jungle, and the Skipper chases after it.

Meanwhile, Gilligan, walking back to camp wrapped in palm fronds, stumbles over the boxes of signal flares. When he suddenly spots the chimpanzee wearing the Skipper's hat, he believes it's the Skipper. The monkey runs off, and Gilligan chases after him, running into the Skipper. They return to camp to find the others trying to coax the monkey to return the flare gun. Gilligan gets the gun back by giving the chimp a banana, and then accidentally fires a flare into the supply hut where the other flares are stored. When he runs in to save the flares, they all explode.

The next day, while the castaways have a luau by the lagoon, Gilligan shows up dressed in palm fronds with the monkey dressed in his clothes. After the Skipper forgives him, he stumbles into another rope trap.

COMMENTS:

- Gilligan leaves a crate of signal flares in the jungle.

TROPICAL INVENTIONS:

- Table and chairs
- Ginger's clam-shell compact (black berry eyeliner, blue berry mascara, red berry lipstick)
- Gilligan's rope trap
- Gilligan's palm-frond skirt

CASTAWAY QUIZ #3:

How many flares do the castaways have at the beginning of the episode?

(For answer, see page 359)

4: GOOD NIGHT, SWEET SKIPPER ⊗

Writers: Dick Conway & Roland MacLane
Director: Ida Lupino

In the middle of the night Gilligan wakes up to find the Skipper out by the lagoon, reenacting an attack on Guadalcanal in his sleep, converting an unseen radio into a transmitter. After Gilligan falls into the lagoon, the Skipper returns to his hut, and when Gilligan wakes him, the Skipper convinces him he was the one sleepwalking.

The next morning, after the Professor and the Skipper hear a radio broadcast from the Vagabond Lady, a pilot circling the globe, the Skipper calculates that she should be passing over the island. When the Professor suggests they build a signal fire, Gilligan, wishing he could convert the radio into a transmitter, jogs the Skipper's memory. Unable to recall any details, the Skipper tries to fall asleep to retrigger his sleepwalking, and the Professor asks Gilligan to stand guard over the Skipper. As Gilligan's about to nail a Do Not Disturb sign to the hut, the Professor stops him. When they step inside to find the girls singing a lullaby to the Skipper, Gilligan joins in, waking the Skipper.

When the Skipper, hearing the Vagabond Lady's latest broadcast, wanders off, the Professor sends Gilligan to get some tranquilizers from the Howells. Lovey brings Howell his alligator-skin briefcase filled with bottles of pills, and he hands Gilligan a bottle of tranquilizers.

While Ginger and Mary Ann cook dinner, Gilligan inconspicuously slips two tranquilizers into the Skipper's drinking cup. When Ginger finds the bottle, she slips another two pills into the Skipper's cup, and when the Professor wanders by, he slips two more pills into the cup. When Gilligan brings the Skipper to the table, the Skipper notices the bottle of tranquilizers on the table, takes two, and washes them down with the cup of mango juice laden with tranquilizers. After falling asleep at the table, the Skipper starts walking in his sleep, and as the Professor and Gilligan struggle to help him, the others admit they each put pills into his cup.

Later, when the Professor and Gilligan learn that the Vagabond Lady is an hour ahead of schedule and anxious to speak with anyone in the Pacific, the Skipper walks out of his hut and heads toward the lagoon. The Professor and Gilligan follow, but when the Skipper accidentally pushes Gilligan into the lagoon, Gilligan, swallowing a mouthful of water, yelps, waking the Skipper. The Professor hypnotizes the Skipper, and the castaways all reenact battle sounds and role-play as the Skipper calls roll.

After the Professor fixes the transmitter according to the Skipper's instructions, it still doesn't work. When the Professor and the Skipper turn in for the night, leaving Gilligan on sentry duty, Gilligan pounds the transmitter, suddenly contacting the Vagabond Lady. After returning with the Skipper, Gilligan demonstrates how he fixed the transmitter, and the back panel pops open, and the transmitter's insides spill forth as the Vagabond Lady's plane passes overhead.

COMMENTS:

- Oddly, the Professor doesn't possess the technical know-how to convert the radio into a transmitter.

TROPICAL INVENTIONS:

- Communal table
- Cooking pot
- Plates, wooden silverware, and coconut drinking cups

CASTAWAY QUIZ #4:

What is the Vagabond Lady's name?
(For answer, see page 359)

5: WRONGWAY FELDMAN ☺☺

Writers: Lawrence J. Cohen & Fred Freeman
Director: Ida Lupino
Guest Star: Hans Conried

While walking through the jungle, Gilligan discovers a propeller plane. While examining the airplane, the castaways realize it belongs to the long-lost incompetent pilot Wrongway Feldman, who suddenly appears and reveals that he's been stranded on the island for ten years. The Professor claims that he can repair the plane engine with spare parts from the *Minnow*'s engine. While the Professor and Wrongway return to his camp for some oil, Gilligan and the Skipper check the plane's rear wheel.

That night, Ginger wakes Wrongway and promises him glamorous evenings if he takes her along—but he refuses. Later, Howell offers Wrongway the vice presidency of Howell Aircraft and his teddy bear—but Wrongway doesn't wake up.

The next day, when Wrongway starts the plane, the propeller falls off. That night, after the castaways repair the propeller, an unseen stranger cuts through one of the wing's support beams with a hacksaw.

The next day, Wrongway starts the engine and noticing the cracked beam, jumps from the cockpit. Realizing that somebody sabotaged the plane, the Professor reasons that there's someone else on the island, but Wrongway suspects one of the castaways. The Skipper has the men stand watch twenty-four hours over the plane, leaving Gilligan with a bow and arrow.

The next day, when the castaways can't find Wrongway, Gilligan searches his hut and finding it a shambles, realizes Wrongway put up a fight before being abducted. While the three men search the island independently, Gilligan stumbles into Wrongway, who admits that he perpetrated the kidnapping hoax because he's afraid to fly the plane. At Gilligan's suggestion, Wrongway agrees to teach him how to fly—if Gilligan promises not to tell the others.

That night, Wrongway trains Gilligan, using a mock control panel made from various fruits. After Gilligan relieves the Professor on watch the next morning, Wrongway helps him into the cockpit, but Gilligan jumps back out of the plane, explaining that he can't fly without fruit. When the other castaways hear the plane take off, they race to the

clearing to find Gilligan lying in the sand and Wrongway flying the plane off the island.

Later, the castaways learn from the radio that Wrongway returned to New York, where he told the authorities about the castaways, without being able to recall the island's location.

COMMENTS:

- When Gilligan accidentally ignited the castaways signal flares [Episode 3], Wrongway, having been on the island for ten years, should have been alerted to the castaways' presence.

CASTAWAY QUIZ #5:

What's Wrongway Feldman's plane named?

(For answer, see page 359)

6: PRESIDENT GILLIGAN ⊗⊗

Writer: Roland Wolpert
Director: Richard Donner

When the Skipper orders Gilligan to help dig a well, Howell disputes his authority as leader of the island, and when the Professor admits that in actuality no one runs the island, Ginger proposes an election.

The Professor, officiating the election, suggests that they make it quick so they can finish the well. But Howell demands time to campaign, insisting that they debate the issues: "public transportation, coconut conservation, and high-rise dwellings." While Howell practices his campaign speech before Lovey, the Skipper practices his speech before Gilligan. Deciding to woo the voters, the Skipper gives Ginger flowers, which she recognizes as those the Professor labeled poisonous.

Meanwhile Howell offers to hire Mary Ann as a secretary for $50,000 a year, an offer she recognizes as a bribe and finds offensive. But Howell succeeds in bribing Ginger by promising to buy Hollywood and produce her next movie. She, in turn, tries seductively to entice Gilligan to vote for Howell, but Gilligan, who's campaigning for the Skipper, backs up into a palm tree, knocking himself unconscious.

While the Skipper and Gilligan try to hang a sign reading "Don't Change Skippers" on a palm tree over the lagoon, they both fall in. Later, Howell offers to make Gilligan secretary of the navy, promising to find an able-bodied seaman to tie his shoes for him. When the Skipper learns of Howell's proposition, he laughs, unintentionally humiliating Gilligan.

That afternoon, the Professor, having rigged the shower stall as a voting booth and prepared the official ballots (seven pieces of paper initialed by all seven castaways), conducts the election. After every other castaway votes, Gilligan enters the voting booth and pulls the wrong string to draw the curtains, inadvertently showering himself with water. While Mary Ann warms Gilligan, the Professor counts the ballots, tallying two votes for the Skipper, two votes for Howell, and three write-in votes for Gilligan.

Later, while sweeping up his hut, Gilligan apologizes to the Skipper, but the Skipper (who along with Howell recounted the votes four times) congratulates him, warning him to watch out for power-seekers and appointing himself Vice-President. Howell comes in to offer Gilligan a token of his esteem, solid-gold cufflinks, in exchange for the opportunity to serve as Chief Justice of the Supreme Court. Gilligan consents, and Howell says that the first thing on his agenda is to investigate the plot to overthrow the President that he started immediately after the election.

At the Inaugural Luau that evening, as Gilligan makes his inaugural address, Mary Ann serves dinner, and the castaways talk among themselves, ignore Gilligan's suggestion that they build a well, and leave the table. The next day, after each castaway refuses to help him with the well, Gilligan ends up digging the well himself. As the other castaways watch Gilligan, Howell, insisting that Gilligan will never hit water, explains that he's working on Gilligan's impeachment—for accepting a bribe from a power-mad favor-seeker: himself. Infuriated, Gilligan resigns as President, throwing down his shovel, which strikes a spring, showering the castaways with water.

Later that day at a cabinet meeting, when Gilligan proposes that the castaways build a lookout tower, the others excuse themselves, once again leaving Gilligan to do the work himself.

COMMENTS:

- According to United States law, the Skipper would legally be the castaways' leader.
- When he loses the election, Howell refuses to make good on his bribe to Ginger.
- When Gilligan suggests that they build a lookout tower, the others, refusing to help, don't seen very eager to expedite their rescue.

TROPICAL INVENTIONS:

- A shower stall
- Paint
- A voting booth and ballots
- The castaways' well

CASTAWAY QUIZ #6:

Which three castaways vote for Gilligan for President?
(For answer, see page 359)

7: SOUND OF QUACKING ⊗

Writers: Lawrence J. Cohen & Fred Freeman
Director: Ray Montgomery

When Mary Ann serves him breakfast, the Skipper learns that all the food on the island is shriveling up because, according to the Professor, they're experiencing a blight. The Professor explains that the last seeds from his healthy plants will survive if Gilligan, who is standing in the field as a scarecrow, can keep the birds away.

Later, Gilligan falls in the lagoon when trying to catch a duck. While duck-calling through the jungle, Gilligan hears quacking through the bushes and winds up grabbing the Skipper. Using a homemade decoy (feathers tied to an old shoe), Gilligan tries to lure the duck from the lagoon—until the shoe, which has a hole in it, sinks. Gilligan wades into the lagoon and catches the duck, which the castaways then plan to fly back to Hawaii with a message tied to its leg.

Gilligan names the duck Everett, but when Howell suggests that they roast the duck, Gilligan protectively takes it into the jungle. Gilligan flies Everett like a kite, with a string tied to his leg, but when the string breaks, he uses two palm fronds to guide Everett's landing. The Professor ties a note to Everett's leg, but when Gilligan throws the duck into the air, Everett flies back to the island. When Gilligan hides Everett from the others, Everett lays an egg, and Gilligan, renaming the duck Emily, runs to tell the others, insisting that the duck can now fly—accidentally breaking the egg. The Professor attaches the message once more, but the duck isn't going anywhere—except, says the Skipper, into a pot.

That night, as Gilligan sleeps with Emily in his arms, Howell, the Skipper, and Ginger each stand by him, eyeing the duck. Falling asleep, Gilligan dreams he's Marshal Gilligan in the old West, protecting Emily. The Professor and Howell, dressed as members of a lynch mob, walk down the main street for a showdown with Gilligan. When Gilligan finds a fork and knife on his deputy, the Skipper, he forces the Skipper to turn in his star. Ginger, the saloon-hall girl, tries seductively to entice Gilligan to drink with her, but Gilligan, realizing that Ginger intends to get him drunk so she can steal the duck, refuses. Mary Ann runs in to warn Gilligan of the approaching lynch mob.

When Gilligan sets Emily free and goes out to face the lynch mob, Lovey pulls him into an alley and gives him a special gun, but Gilligan leaves her after discovering that she's carrying a jar of duck gravy. On the main street, Howell and the Professor reach Gilligan, stand before him, and fire their guns. But they miss him completely, so Gilligan retrieves his gun from his holster and chases them off. When Mary Ann runs to congratulate him, Gilligan fires his gun into the air, inadvertently killing Emily.

Gilligan wakes up screaming, and the Skipper, holding an ax, tries to calm him, explaining that he's come for the duck. Gilligan volunteers to kill the duck himself, and while the guilt-ridden castaways sit around the communal table trying to rationalize their decision, Gilligan carries over a covered plate and offers them their choice of the duck. Everyone's suddenly lost their appetite, but when they hear a sudden quacking, the Skipper uncovers the plate to reveal a feathered shoe. Emily is in the clearing, eating the blighted plants, and the Professor determines that the diseased plants aren't poisonous after all, saving the castaways from starvation.

Gilligan's kindness to animals inadvertently saved the castaways' lives, but later, when he sends Emily flying off, he forgets to tie the message to her foot.

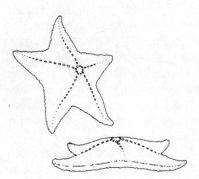

COMMENTS:

- It is highly unlikely that anyone would ever find a message tied to the leg of a wild duck.
- We never learn where Gilligan gets the coil of kite string.

TROPICAL INVENTIONS:

- Communal bamboo table
- Gilligan's duck decoy
- Bamboo bird cage

CASTAWAY QUIZ #7:

Who does Gilligan name Everett after?

(For answer, see page 359)

8: GOOD-BYE ISLAND ☺☺

Writers: Albert E. Lewin & Burt Styler
Director: John Rich

The Professor, attempting to forge nails from an outcropping of ferrous oxide he discovered on the island, drives one of his nails into a plank of wood to repair the *Minnow*. But when he hits the new nail with the hammer, the nail shatters like glass.

Later, Mary Ann and Gilligan, sampling the sap of different trees, fill a coconut shell with sweet syrup. Later that afternoon, the Professor tests another nail, which explodes. Unable to perfect the formula after two days of work, he resigns himself to defeat. That night at dinner, Mary Ann serves pancakes covered with Gilligan's syrup. When the Skipper tries to eat his, the syrup responds like rubber, sticking to the plate like glue. The Professor runs to the lagoon with his plate, discovers that the glue is waterproof, and claims that the rubber, chicle, and resin in the syrup bonded together when Gilligan heated the sap.

The next morning, the Professor and the Skipper paint a plank of wood with the glue and successfully set it in place on the *Minnow*. The Skipper announces that they will shove off the next day, ordering the girls to pack the provisions. When Gilligan asks if he can help the Skipper finish repairing the boat, the Skipper sends him off for palm leaves to make more brushes. Gilligan accidentally steps in the bucket of glue. When the Skipper tries to help him, Gilligan gets stuck to the boat, and then the Skipper gets stuck to both Gilligan and the *Minnow*.

The Howells, eventually realizing the crew's sticky situation, run to tell the Professor, who explains that the glue is insoluble—until he realizes that perfume contains the necessary chemical solvent. While Lovey goes through her perfumes, the Professor finds Ginger in her hut and grabs her to sniff her perfume. Ginger naturally misinterprets his intentions—especially when the Professor leaves with a bottle of her perfume.

After the Professor frees them, the Skipper reglues the entire boat, board by board. When Gilligan asks if he can help again, the Skipper sends him off to locate icebergs. Ginger wanders over to the lagoon, carrying his plate of pancakes, and studies his reflection, wallowing in self-pity. When he tips his plate to admire the glue's strength, the pancakes fall off. When Gilligan realizes that his glue is only temporary and that the *Minnow* will fall apart at sea, he runs to warn the others.

Meanwhile, as the Skipper prepares to launch the *Minnow*, Howell demands a launching ceremony. Just as Howell realizes he hasn't got a bottle of champagne, Gilligan runs up and frantically interrupts, explaining that the glue won't hold. When the Skipper hits the boat to prove it's just as solid as a rock, planks start popping loose. Gilligan climbs aboard to hold the ship together, but the entire boat starts flying apart. Boards start ricocheting everywhere, leaving only the frame, which then springs apart as well. Gilligan is left holding only the wheel.

That night, the Skipper, sitting by a kettle over a fire, tells Gilligan he's okay. And Gilligan tells the Skipper he's sitting on a paintbrush full of glue.

COMMENTS:

- Since the castaways only had to repair the *Minnow* to leave the island, destroying the ship left them completely stranded.
- Forging nails from ferrous oxide is a simple procedure well within the Professor's abilities.
- The castaways could have easily removed nails to repair the boat from the various crates they brought ashore.
- The castaways could have also melted down all the metal objects they brought along to forge nails.

TROPICAL INVENTIONS:

- Scooper (clam shells tied to two bamboo poles)
- The Professor's nails
- Gilligan's waterproof glue
- Mary Ann's pancakes
- The Professor's perfumed glue solvent

CASTAWAY QUIZ #8:

What perfume does Mrs. Howell use?

(For answer, see page 359)

9: THE BIG GOLD STRIKE ⊗⊗

Writer: Roland Wolpert
Director: Stanley Z. Cherry

While caddying for Mr. Howell, Gilligan falls into a deep cavernous pit. Mr. Howell looks down and sees yellow stuff on the walls, which Gilligan recognizes as gold, causing Howell to fall in after him.

Meanwhile, while fishing at the lagoon, the girls catch an inflatable life raft from the *Minnow,* and the Skipper helps them reel it in. Meanwhile, in the underground cave, Gilligan, eager to share his discovery with the others, reiterates the castaways' agreement to share everything on the island, but Howell convinces Gilligan to help him secretly mine the gold and bury it to save the others from the evils of greed.

Soon after, the Skipper tells Gilligan and Howell about the life raft, insisting that Gilligan must work day and night to help repair it. Howell tells Lovey about the discovery and asks her to help mine the gold. The next day, Howell interrupts the Skipper, the Professor, and Gilligan, who are all busy repairing the raft, to make sure Gilligan will be able to help him that evening.

That night, after the Skipper and Gilligan fall asleep, Howell wakes up Gilligan to mine the gold. While Gilligan digs, Howell weighs the bags of gold they have mined. The next morning at breakfast, to stall for time, Howell insists that before they set sail the Skipper should first test the raft. Since Gilligan's asleep at the table, the Howells volunteer to put him back to bed. Unable to understand why Gilligan is so tired and why Howell is so considerate, the castaways grow suspicious of the Howells' reluctance to leave the island.

That night, when Howell sends Gilligan off to work and pauses for a moment to count his money (which naturally makes him sleepy), the other castaways secretly follow Gilligan, discover that he's been mining gold, and start mining for themselves. After a day in the mine, the Howells (with Lovey doing all the digging) have filled fifty bags of gold, while the other castaways haven't unearthed a dime's worth. So the other castaways quit, returning their attention to the raft. The Skipper and Gilligan agree to rent mining tools to the Howells (six picks for two bags of gold), the girls charge the Howells for their meals ($740 for dinner alone), and the Professor charges Howell for candles (six for $1200, wicks not included).

The next day, when the raft is fully repaired and ready to cast off, the Professor and the Skipper tell the others that the raft will only hold the combined weight of the seven castaways and one piece of luggage each, forbidding anyone to take any gold off the island. As they board the life raft, Mr. Howell brings his golf bag as a memento, Lovey brings a bamboo handbag, Mary Ann brings a crate of homemade guava jelly, Ginger brings a box of diaries, and the Professor brings aboard a burlap sack of botanical specimens. When Gilligan casts off, the raft sinks into the lagoon, along with all the castaways' belongings. When Gilligan can't understand how the raft sank without the extra weight of gold, the other castaways each admit that they were trying to smuggle a bag of gold off the island.

That night as the castaways dry by the fire, they all promise never to be greedy again. But when Gilligan announces that he found a pearl in an oyster down by the cove where there may be hundreds more, the other castaways greedily run off to the cove. Alone, Gilligan laughs knowingly, since there are only four oysters.

COMMENTS:

- The other castaways should be suspicious when the Howells only take a golf bag and a bamboo handbag over any of their personal effects.
- The castaways should send just the Skipper and Gilligan on the raft to send a rescue ship back for the remaining castaways.

TROPICAL INVENTIONS:

- Bamboo balance
- Candles and wicks ~~To drip on mary ann's nipples~~
- Mining helmets (candles lit inside clam shells tied to metal bowls)

CASTAWAY QUIZ #9:

How much does Mrs. Howell's diamond engagement ring weigh?

(For answer, see page 359)

10: WAITING FOR WATUBI ⊗

Writers: Lawrence J. Cohen & Fred Freeman
Director: Jack Arnold

When Gilligan hurts his back digging a refrigeration pit, the Skipper volunteers to dig for a while, unearthing a wooden, hand-carved tiki, which he recognizes as Kona, an ancient native god. As the Skipper explains that according to legend whoever disturbs Kona's rest will be cursed forever, an earthquake shakes the island.

The Skipper and Gilligan bury Kona beneath the refrigeration pit, where they plan to store perishable food over it in one of Mr. Howell's sea trunks. The Howells accidentally overheard the crew's conversation, and thinking Kona must have great value, dig up the tiki after the Skipper and Gilligan leave. When the Skipper and Gilligan go to the Howells' hut to take Howell's trunk, they discover that it's locked and still packed. While searching for the key, the Skipper finds Kona in the Howells' bamboo wall cabinet.

Convinced that the curse of Kona is following him, the Skipper asks Gilligan to bury the tiki. While Gilligan carries the tiki through the jungle, another earthquake shakes the island, and a lightning bolt strikes a nearby tree. Petrified, Gilligan tosses the tiki into the jungle and races back to the Skipper. Insisting that the tiki must be buried, the Skipper forces Gilligan to search through the jungle with him where the Skipper accidentally falls in a pit of quicksand. While Gilligan busily chops down some vines to save the Skipper, the Skipper hoists himself out of the quicksand. Gilligan returns to find only the Skipper's hat floating on the surface, and jumps when he finds the Skipper standing beside him.

After searching the island all day and night, Gilligan suggests that the castaways throw a surprise birthday party for the Skipper to lift his spirits. Meanwhile, Mary Ann finds the tiki in the jungle and with Ginger, decides that it will make a great birthday gift for the Skipper.

That night the castaways surprise the Skipper with a party, birthday cake, and presents. The Professor gives the Skipper a book; Gilligan gives him his favorite pocketknife; the Howells give him a gold earring (because, as Mrs. Howell explains, "every sea captain should look like a pirate"). When the Skipper opens the girls' gift and discovers the tiki, he runs away.

The next day, while the Professor digs a pit to bury the tiki once and for all, Ginger flatters the Skipper, but severely depressed, the Skipper wanders off in a daze, accidentally falling into the Professor's pit where he discovers Kona. He jumps out of the hole and runs into a tree, bruising his head. After the Professor doctors him, the Skipper lies in bed with his head bandaged, crying out that only Watubi, a mythical witch doctor, can lift the curse.

That night, while sitting watch over the Skipper, Gilligan accidentally wakes the Skipper, who gives him his most valuable possessions from his sea chest. When he offers Gilligan his ring, Gilligan struggles to free the ring from the Skipper's finger—until the Professor takes him outside and urges him to dress up as Watubi to "cure" the Skipper.

The Professor explodes a smoke cloud, and Gilligan, dressed as Watubi, and accompanied by the sarong-clad girls, enters the Skipper's hut, dances about, throws powder in the Skipper's face, and pounds him with a drum stick. As he lifts the curse, another earthquake shakes the island, and the Skipper believes in his powers and is cured. The Skipper gets up and joyously runs out from the hut—and into another tree.

COMMENTS:

- We never learn whether the castaways ever finish building the refrigeration pit.
- Earthquake tremors on the island go unexplained.
- We never learn what finally becomes of Kona.

TROPICAL INVENTIONS:

- A refrigeration pit
- The Professor's smoke bomb

CASTAWAY QUIZ #10:

What book does the Professor give the Skipper?
(For answer, see page 359)

11: ANGEL ON THE ISLAND ⊗

Writers: Herbert Finn & Alan Dinehart
Director: Jack Arnold

Gilligan and Skipper search through the jungle for Ginger, who they find holding a script and crying because she's missing her opening night as the star in a Broadway play that she feels would have rocketed her to stardom.

After the Skipper asks Mary Ann to bring food to Ginger, Gilligan reads lines from the script to the Skipper, and Howell, walking along, mistakes their conversation as mutiny. Gilligan convinces Howell to produce the play on the island, and then when they return to civilization, on Broadway. When he agrees, Gilligan runs to tell Ginger, lifting her spirits dramatically.

Mary Ann sews the costumes, the Professor builds the stage and designs the set, and Howell directs Gilligan as Cleopatra, Lovey as her maid, and the Skipper as Mark Antony. When Howell shows too much adoration for Ginger, arousing his wife's jealousy, Lovey rebels against having to play the part of a simple servant, compelling Howell to give her the role of Cleopatra and Ginger the role of the maid—leaving Ginger traumatized.

While the Skipper rehearses, Gilligan tries to talk to him about Ginger's dilemma, but the Skipper can't be bothered and orders Gilligan to get back to work on the stage. When the Skipper enters the stage door, he walks into the ladder Gilligan's carrying, breaking all the rungs.

Gilligan decides to speak directly with Mrs. Howell, candidly explaining why he suggested they produce the play in the first place. Lovey says nothing, and when Gilligan observes that she hasn't said a word, Lovey, moved by his motives, feigns laryngitis. Gilligan immediately calls Mr. Howell and begs him to use Ginger, the understudy.

That night at the performance, Gilligan ushers the Howells to their seats. When the curtains opens, Gilligan plays the maid, the royal messenger, and the royal slave. Ginger plays Cleopatra and the Skipper plays Mark Antony. When the curtains close and Lovey exclaims "bravo," Howell, discovering that Lovey didn't have laryngitis after all, admires her nobility. "I was just being a Howell," she admits.

COMMENTS:

- If the castaways can build a stage, they can certainly build a boat to leave the island.
- The castaways build a phonograph, implying that one of the castaways brought phonograph records along on the cruise without a stereo to play them on.

TROPICAL INVENTIONS:

- Stage with curtains
- Hand-cranked phonograph (using the wheel from the *Minnow* as the turntable)

CASTAWAY QUIZ #11:

What's the name of the play the castaways produce?

(For answer, see page 359)

12: BIRDS GOTTA FLY, FISH GOTTA TALK ⊗⊗

Writers: Sherwood and Elroy Schwartz, Austin Kalish
Director: Rod Amateau

While decorating a Christmas tree on Christmas Eve, Gilligan wishes they can be rescued, and suddenly the radio reports that a navy destroyer had been dispatched to an uncharted island where a group of castaways was spotted by a small weather plane.

After building a signal fire, the Skipper recalls the shipwreck. He remembers being beached on the island and waking up Gilligan who leapt overboard onto the beach. After explaining the situation to the other castaways, the Skipper ordered the Howells to salvage the galley, while he and Gilligan explored the island. When the Skipper ordered Gilligan to climb a tall coconut tree, Gilligan knocked the Skipper in the head with a coconut and then spotted a boat and people on the other side of the island. After Gilligan slid down the tree, landing on the Skipper, he led the Skipper to the boat he spotted, which turned out to be the *Minnow* and the castaways. After the Professor fixed the transmitter, Gilligan, casting the fishing rod, hooked the transmitter and radio and tossed them both into the ocean.

The Professor comes by with the radio, which announces that the navy will soon be on the island. As the castaways sit with their luggage at the lagoon, they remember how angry they were with Gilligan the day they were shipwrecked on the island. They recall that after the Skipper and the Professor took inventory of their belongings from the boat, the Skipper and Gilligan started a fire, with Gilligan wasting most of their matches. While the Skipper built a hut, Gilligan caught over a dozen fish on the beach while the Howells watched from the deck of the *Minnow*. When Gilligan heard the radio broadcasting from inside a fish, he brought the fish back to the others and thinking another fish may have swallowed the transmitter, returned to catch more fish. The Professor tuned the radio to the transmitter's frequency and instructed the castaways to talk into the fish to determine which one had swallowed the transmitter. After finding the transmitter, the Skipper and the Professor sent Gilligan to get more firewood, and when the Professor got the transmitter working again and the Skipper began transmitting, Gilligan dropped the firewood on the transmitter, breaking it.

As the castaways sit on the beach waiting for the navy, the radio announces that castaways picked up by the Coast Guard were not from the *Minnow* as originally thought.

That night, the Skipper, dressed as Santa Claus, tells the castaways how lucky they are not to have been lost at sea, marooned on an island without any food, or stranded with enemies. When he leaves and the Skipper suddenly shows up carrying firewood, the castaways think they've been visited by Santa Claus.

COMMENTS:

- The odds on Gilligan's catching the fish that swallowed the castaways' radio, while remote, are significantly better than the likelihood of Gilligan's catching a second fish that happened to swallow the castaways' radio transmitter.

TROPICAL INVENTIONS:

- The castaways' Christmas tree

CASTAWAY QUIZ #12:

How many blankets were aboard the *Minnow*?
(For answer, see page 359)

13: THREE MILLION DOLLARS MORE OR LESS ⊗⊗

Writers: Bill Davenport & Charles Tannen
Director: Ray Montgomery

When the Skipper's dream (that a ship passes the island) recurs for the third night in a row on the third day of the third week of the third month of the year, he insists that Gilligan build a lookout tower. Gilligan points out that the Skipper dreamed that Gilligan hit him in the jaw, which hasn't happened yet. But when Gilligan practices his golf swing, he hits the Skipper in the mouth.

Later, while Howell golfs, Gilligan interrupts his concentration. Miffed, Howell bets that Gilligan couldn't possibly putt while Howell jabbers, but Gilligan gets a hole in one—twice. Howell bets Gilligan a quarter that he can't do it a third time, and again Gilligan sinks the putt. Howell bets double or nothing, and before long, night falls and they're playing by torchlight. The Skipper comes by and learning that Gilligan has won three million dollars, forbids him to gamble any further.

The next morning the Professor builds a fire for Gilligan, Mary Ann fixes him a special breakfast, and Ginger promises to fix him lunch. The Skipper takes Gilligan aside and paternally explains that people will start treating him differently now that he's rich. After the Skipper leaves to find Howell, the millionaire enters the hut with a small suitcase and hands Gilligan a check for three million dollars along with a long, complicated tax form. Howell convinces Gilligan that he's better off owning a corporation as a tax shelter, offering him the deed to one of his oil companies in lieu of a check. Gilligan signs it, transfering the ownership of the corporation to himself. When the Skipper returns, they learn that Gilligan signed the deed to two hundred acres of worthless land in Dustbowl, Oklahoma. At breakfast, while Gilligan cooks over the fire, the other castaways accuse Howell of wrongdoing. When Howell turns on the radio, he learns that the Howell Corporation has struck oil in Dustbowl, Oklahoma.

Later in his hut, Gilligan makes a list of gifts he wants to give the others: a science lab for the Professor, a farm in Kansas for Mary Ann, and a new boat for the Skipper. Ginger walks in, wearing a new dress made from Gilligan's duffel bag, and tries seductively to convince him to build a movie studio so she can star in the movie version of his story—as his wife. Gilligan backs up and falls into the water trough.

When Howell invites Gilligan to his hut for dinner that evening, the Skipper insists on accompanying his little buddy.

That evening, while Lovey fixes dinner, Howell suggests a game of chance, revealing a deck of cards, dice, and a roulette wheel made from the steering wheel of the *Minnow*. When the Skipper says he'll only gamble at pool, Howell pulls the tablecloth off the table to reveal a bamboo pool table, and the Skipper proceeds to lose twelve million dollars. Howell asks Gilligan to sign an IOU for the Skipper, payable upon demand. Once Gilligan signs it, Howell immediately demands the money—or in lieu of money, the deed to the oil company.

The next day the castaways learn from the radio that further investigation by the Howell Corporation revealed the true source of the gusher: drills had punctured the tank of an oil truck that had been buried in one of the frequent dust storms in the area.

COMMENTS:

- Gilligan and the Skipper never build the lookout tower.
- The castaways never institute any laws to prohibit gambling or fraud.

TROPICAL INVENTIONS:

- Howell's roulette wheel
- Howell's bamboo pool table

CASTAWAY QUIZ #13:

What oil company does Howell give Gilligan?
(For answer, see page 359)

14: WATER, WATER EVERYWHERE ⊚⊗

Writers: Tom and Frank Waldman
Director: Stanley Z. Cherry

While Gilligan pedals a contraption to pump the water from a fresh-water spring to irrigate the Professor's breadfruit garden, the spring dries up, ending the castaways' freshwater supply.

When Gilligan runs to stop Ginger from showering, he trips and falls into the mud. When Ginger leaves and Gilligan showers off the mud, the Skipper comes along and seeing Ginger's scarf still hanging on the bushes, hands flowers over the shower stall to who he thinks is Ginger. Gilligan reveals himself and tells the Skipper about the water shortage.

After the Professor suggests that they ration water until they find a new spring, the castaways empty their water supply into a communal water sack. When the Professor suggests they dig a new well, the Skipper puts Howell in charge of the rationing and suggests they use his new divining rod. The Professor criticizes the Skipper's supersti-tious mind, but the divining rod points to Howell's ankle where he's bootlegging a flask of water. Later, while walking through the jungle with his divining rod, the Skipper shows Gilligan a trick he learned from the natives in the Solomon Islands: sucking on pebbles to relieve thirst. Gilligan causes the Skipper to swallow a mouthful, and later when the Skipper's divining rod starts vibrating, Gilligan accidentally breaks it in two.

That night after the Skipper puts Gilligan in charge of guarding the water supply, Howell distracts Gilligan while Lovey fills a tall rubber

boot with water. Later, Ginger distracts Gilligan while Mary Ann fills a rubber glove with water. Later, when the Skipper leads the other castaways back and forces them to return the water they stole, Gilligan shows the Skipper a new divining rod he made, accidentally puncturing the water sack, depleting the castaways' entire water supply.

The next day the Professor and the Skipper ask Gilligan to leave them alone while they dig a well. When Gilligan visits the girls, who are sewing together a large sheet to catch the morning dew, they send him to the Howells, who, performing an Indian rain dance, insult him. Alone, Gilligan writes a farewell letter to the other castaways, and a frog suddenly leaps up onto the tree stump he's using as a desk. Realizing that the frog's feet are wet, Gilligan follows the frog into the jungle, hoping it will lead him to water. Meanwhile, Mary Ann finds Gilligan's note and thinking he intends to kill himself, alerts the Skipper.

Meanwhile, Gilligan follows the frog and falls into an underground cave filled with fresh water. But the walls are too steep and slick for him to climb back out. When the castaways organize a search for Gilligan, the Skipper finds Gilligan's sailor cap and falls into the hole after him—where they both start calling for help. The Howells find them first, and Mr. Howell tosses Gilligan a box of matches. When the Professor arrives with the girls, he tries to warn Gilligan and the Skipper not to light the matches (since there may be explosive natural gases in the cave), but there's a sudden explosion, and Gilligan and the Skipper are sent flying out of the cave and into a tree.

Later when the castaways celebrate Gilligan's discovery, Gilligan gives credit where credit is due—to the frog.

COMMENTS:

- While matches are a rare commodity on the island, Howell happens to have a box that he casually tosses down to Gilligan, who's sitting in a pool of water.

TROPICAL INVENTIONS:

- Bamboo pedal-powered pump

CASTAWAY QUIZ #14:

What perfume does Ginger use?
(For answer, see page 359)

15: SO SORRY, MY ISLAND NOW ⊗

Writer: David Harmon
Director: Alan Crossland
Guest Star: Vito Scotti

While collecting lobsters from the lagoon, Gilligan mistakes the periscope of a submarine for a sea monster, and as he runs to tell the Skipper, a Japanese sailor still fighting World War II surfaces to the island.

When Gilligan tells the Professor and the Skipper, the Skipper orders him to return to the lagoon, where Howell's captured by the Japanese sailor. When Gilligan reports Howell's disappearance to the Professor, the Professor explains that Howell is probably avoiding work. While Ginger searches the jungle with Gilligan, the Japanese sailor captures her, and when the Professor and Mary Ann, hearing Ginger's yell, run to the lagoon, they find Gilligan searching the water for the sea monster. While the Professor talks to Gilligan, Mary Ann disappears. The Professor sends Gilligan back to camp, where he discovers Lovey's umbrella. He returns to the lagoon with the Skipper, only to find the Professor missing.

The Professor and Howell, imprisoned in a bamboo cage, try to convince the Japanese sailor that the war ended twenty years earlier. On the lagoon the Skipper and Gilligan discover the camouflaged Japanese submarine, and realizing a Japanese sailor's on the island, the Skipper hops in the submarine to sail to the mainland, but gets

stuck trying to slip down the hatch. After Gilligan frees the Skipper with coconut oil, the Skipper orders Gilligan to captain the submarine. Gilligan submerges, pilots the submarine in circles around the lagoon, and resurfaces—unable to read the Japanese instruments.

After Howell and the Professor try to talk to the sailor, the sailor locks himself inside the women's cage, and Ginger, feigning a sprained ankle, seductively asks the sailor to help her, but he refuses to let them free. While Gilligan and the Skipper watch from the edge of the jungle, the sailor, who hasn't slept in forty-eight hours, falls asleep in a tree. As the Skipper starts tunneling the others out from their cages, Gilligan sneaks up on the sailor, grabs his bayonet and the keys tied around his neck, and frees the castaways as the Skipper continues tunneling.

When the castaways realize the sailor's gone, they run to the lagoon to see the submerged submarine cruising in circles, since Gilligan has the sailor's glasses.

COMMENTS:

- Japan never developed one-man submarines, and if it had, the Japanese sailor would have run out of fuel long ago.

TROPICAL INVENTIONS:

- Lobster traps

CASTAWAY QUIZ #15:

Where did the Japanese soldier attend college?
(For answer, see page 359)

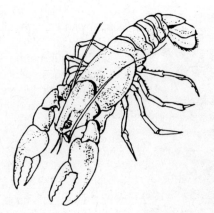

16: PLANT YOU NOW, DIG YOU LATER ⊗⊗

Writers: Elroy Schwartz & Oliver Crawford
Director: Lawrence Dobkin

While digging a barbecue pit for Mr. Howell, Gilligan uncovers a treasure chest. With the girls' help the Skipper and Gilligan try to snap the chain on the chest with bamboo poles, saw it in half with a rock of coral, and cut it with the nose of a swordfish. The Professor, searching through the caves on the other side of the island, won't return for another day.

That night no one can sleep, wondering what's in the chest. The Skipper convinces Gilligan that it's his; Howell is positive the chest belongs to him, since Gilligan was in his employ at the time. Each castaway decides to pick the lock on the chest, but when they all sneak out of their huts, they discover each other, and all agree to return to sleep.

The next morning the Skipper hoists the chest up on a vine, planning to let its own weight break it open, but before he can cut the vine, an argument ensues over the chest's rightful owner. Howell suggests settling this matter with a game of poker, but as they're dealing the cards, the Professor returns from his outing and insists upon a legal trial. The Skipper agrees to represent Gilligan; Howell will represent himself.

While practicing before Lovey, Howell realizes that he never paid Gilligan, so he offers him one hundred dollars, but the Skipper advises Gilligan not to accept the money and warns Howell not to talk to his client. While Gilligan irons his shirt, Ginger tries seductively to convince him to admit that he was working for Mr. Howell, but the Skipper overhears her and foils Howell's scheme. When the Skipper reviews the case with Gilligan, showing him how he'll signal him at the trial with his fingers, Howell overhears their discussion and files charges with the Professor against the Skipper for tampering with a witness. When the Professor explains that the Skipper has a right to brief his client, Howell offers him a $5000 bribe, but the Skipper, overhearing this exchange, files charges against Howell.

When court is called to session, the Skipper allows Howell to call the first witness, but after Howell calls Lovey to the stand, the Skipper objects that they've rehearsed Lovey's testimony, filing charges with the Professor. Lovey states that Thurston offered Gilligan a job to build the barbecue pit, but when the Skipper questions her, she admits that he didn't use the exact words "offering a job." When Howell questions Gilligan, she states that he hired Gilligan. When the Skipper objects on the grounds that Howell bribed Ginger, both Howell and Ginger file charges against the Skipper for libel and slander. When the Skipper questions Mary Ann, she claims that Gilligan was doing a favor for Mr. Howell. When Howell questions Gilligan, the first mate misreads the Skipper's hand signals (he's busy swatting a fly), and Howell objects that they're using signals.

After a half hour of deliberation, the Professor returns and announces his decision: the chest belongs to all the castaways equally—as a natural resource of the island.

Before the castaways open the chest, Howell offers the others $100,000 each for their share of the chest. The Professor cuts the vine, and the chest breaks open, revealing the chest's contents: cannonballs.

The castaways sportingly agree not to accept Howell's money, building a wooden bowling alley to make use of the balls.

COMMENTS:

- When the Professor returns from the other side of the island, he doesn't share any new discoveries with the other castaways.
- The castaways previous agreement to share the island's natural resources equally [Episode 9] should have covered this dispute, negating the need for any judicial proceedings.

TROPICAL INVENTIONS:

- Courtroom and gavel
- American flag from flowers
- Gilligan's iron (a hot frying pan filled with rocks)

CASTAWAY QUIZ #16:

What's the Professor's gavel made from?
(For answer, see page 359)

17: LITTLE ISLAND, BIG GUN ⊗

Writers: Dick Conway & Roland MacLane
Director: Abner Biberman
Guest Stars: Larry Storch, Jack Sheldon, K. L. Smith,
  Louis Quinn

One night gangster Jackson Farrell arrives by boat on the island to hide out with the loot stolen from a bank. He orders his accomplice to return to the shipping lanes so the boat will be searched and cleared before they sail for South America.

The next morning at breakfast Gilligan smells the bacon Farrell is cooking. While shooting dates from trees with a bow and arrow, Gilligan encounters Farrell, who's hidden his sack of money in a tree. After Farrell claims to be a doctor who washed ashore, Gilligan, demonstrating how he shoots dates from trees, knocks the bag of money from the tree, which Farrell explains are funds he's collected to build a hospital.

After Gilligan introduces Farrell to the girls, the men offer the "doctor" Gilligan's bed. While Gilligan gathers his things, he learns Farrell's true identity from the radio. When Gilligan tries to signal the Skipper, Farrell spots the radio, which, after falling to the ground, broadcasts a repeat news bulletin revealing Farrell's identity. Explaining that a boat will pick him up shortly, Farrell demands the castaways' cooperation at gunpoint.

When Farrell overhears the men scheming to overtake him, he has them tie each other to their beds. When Howell offers Farrell a check for $100,000 written on a piece of driftwood, Farrell refuses to accept. After freeing himself, the Skipper has Gilligan climb to the roof of a hut with a net filled with coconuts to throw down on Farrell, but Gilligan accidentally falls off the roof, missing Farrell. Ginger feigns romantic interest in Farrell, asking him to take her along, but as she caresses him, he notices that she's reaching for his gun.

When Gilligan informs the castaways that a ship's arriving on the lagoon, Farrell climbs to the roof of a hut and after looking through a telescope, explains that the Indigo Mob has arrived on the island. He forces the castaways to dress as natives, while he holds Mary Ann hostage in a hut. Two gangsters approach the camp, try to communicate with the natives, and after failing to learn anything, leave the island.

When Farrell's accomplice returns to the island, the Professor, the Skipper, and Gilligan see them off. When Farrell asks Gilligan to toss the anchor, Gilligan throws it in the lagoon, pulling Farrell's bag of loot overboard, where the propeller from the engine shreds the bills. When Farrell is unable to shoot off his waterlogged gun, the Professor, the Skipper, and Gilligan swim after Farrell, who, along with his accomplice, takes off in their boat.

While gluing the shredded bills together into one long note, Gilligan learns from the radio that the Coast Guard captured Jackson Farrell.

COMMENTS:

- The Skipper, the Professor, and Gilligan, sharing the same hut, sleep in beds, while the Skipper and Gilligan typically sleep in hammocks.
- The Howells could offer Farrell millions in exchange for his boat.

CASTAWAY QUIZ #17:

What bank did Jackson Farrell hold up?
(For answer, see page 359)

18: X MARKS THE SPOT ☺☺☺ ·

Writers: Sherwood and Elroy Schwartz.
Director: Jack Arnold
Guest Star: Harry Lauter

At the Pentagon, General Bryant puts Operation Powdercake into effect, notifying the media that the air force plans to test a missile targeted for a deserted Pacific island, destroying everything within a one-hundred-mile radius.

While building a playroom on the island, the Skipper leaves Gilligan to find the radio. The Skipper finds the Professor, who, making a mirror for the Howells, tells him to check with the girls. When the Skipper finds them exercising to a radio announcer's instructions, he inconspicuously turns off the radio and mimics the broadcast as the girls continue exercising. After revealing his practical joke, he turns the radio back on, only to discover that the batteries are dead.

While the Pentagon receives final approval to launch the warhead the next day, the Skipper finds an extra set of batteries, which the Professor declares dead. But realizing they're rechargeable, the Professor sets up several metal strips, pennies, and coconut shells filled with seawater and instructs the castaways to stir the seawater in each coconut shell, eventually recharging the batteries. When they turn on the radio, they learn that Vandenberg Air Force Base will launch a test missile at noon the next day to an isolated island 140° longitude and 10° latitude—a position which the Skipper recognizes as their island.

At the Pentagon, General Bryant, discovering a technical problem with the new warhead, suggests they remove the warhead and proceed with the launch to test the new guidance system—without announcing any change in plans to the news media.

The castaways, unaware of the new development, contemplate their impending doom. Mary Ann, feeling guilty about the way she treats Gilligan, gives him two coconut cream pies. After Gilligan finishes eating the pies, the Skipper walks in with two pies Mary Ann gave him and feeling guilty about the way he treats Gilligan, insists on giving him one. One ends up in the Skipper's face, the other in Gilligan's. While Howell rewrites his will, leaving all his money to charity, the Professor, consoling Ginger and reflecting on his own life, remembers that before the government launches a test missile, they send out a search plane. He runs to tell the others and to assure their rescue decides to finish the mirror he was working on for Mrs. Howell.

That afternoon Gilligan, standing on the roof of a hut with binoculars, spots the plane. As the Professor and the Skipper set up the mirror, Gilligan swings down off the roof from a vine, smashing into the mirror. The castaways each hold up a piece of the broken mirror to signal the plane—which has already passed overhead. After hearing the radio broadcast the lift-off, the castaways wait for the missile, which splashed down in the lagoon without detonating. Moments later the guidance system sends the missile directly for the castaways, landing on the shore.

The Professor advises the others to remain silent, explaining that only Gilligan's small enough to fit inside and disarm the missile. As Gilligan tries to circle around the missile, its nose follows him. Finally the Professor returns with tools, removes the access panel, and instructs Gilligan to crawl inside, find a green-and-yellow wire, and disconnect it without letting the end touch any other connector. Gilligan naturally crosses wires, and the missile takes off across the jungle, turns around, and races back across the lagoon and out to sea with Gilligan inside. Later, while the other castaways mourn for Gilligan, he walks from the jungle, soaking wet.

Later, Gilligan, having found the bottle containing Howell's revised will, throws the bottle back in the lagoon where Howell dives in after it.

COMMENTS:

- The Skipper and Gilligan never complete the playroom they start building.

TROPICAL INVENTIONS:

- Coconut-shell battery recharger
- The Professor's mirrors

CASTAWAY QUIZ #18:

In what banks do the Howells keep their money?

(For answer, see page 359)

(For answer, see page 359)

19: GILLIGAN MEETS JUNGLE BOY ☺☺☺

Writers: Al Schwartz & Howard Harris
Director: Lawrence Dobkin
Guest Star: Kurt Russell

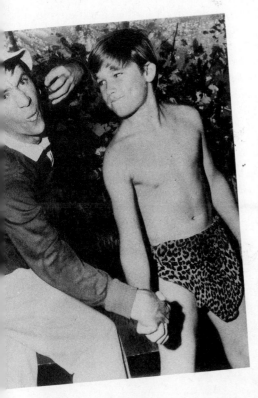

While eating a banana, Gilligan hears a wild yell and finds a jungle boy whom he chases through the jungle. Unable to catch him, Gilligan runs to tell the Professor, who's pedaling a pedal-powered fan for the Skipper. When the Skipper and the Professor express disbelief, the Skipper takes Gilligan along to find the jungle boy. Gilligan spots the boy again, but when the Skipper turns around, Gilligan's pointing at a bird, which lays an egg on the Skipper.

While Gilligan sits alone in the jungle, the boy comes along and after they play catch, the boy leads Gilligan to a natural fountain of helium. Gilligan brings the boy back to camp, where Howell is watching Mary Ann and the Skipper wash clothes. After Mary Ann coaxes the boy out of the jungle, they bombard the boy with questions—until they realize he doesn't understand a word they're speaking.

The women try to teach the boy to speak English, Ginger combs his hair, and Lovey tries to teach him manners. That night, when Lovey finds the boy sleeping in a tree, she demands Thurston's teddy bear for him.

The next day Gilligan brings the Professor and the Skipper to the helium font. When Howell comes by, eager to start a helium company, the Professor suggests that they make a balloon to carry one of them back to civilization.

Using a pedal-powered sewing machine that the Professor builds from pieces of the pedal-powered fan, Mary Ann and Ginger sew together all the castaways' raincoats. The Professor seals the seams with sap from a rubber tree, fills the balloon with helium, and with the other men constructs the balloon's rigging. When Howell, who's building the basket, calls over to the Professor and the Skipper to share an idea, Gilligan's sailor cap floats up off his head and up into the balloon, where he floats up to retrieve it. The Professor and the Skipper pull Gilligan back down, and while they check the balloon for damage, Gilligan, filled with helium, floats around, much to the jungle boy's amusement. After the Skipper squeezes the helium out of Gilligan with a bear hug, the men argue over who will pilot the balloon—until Gilligan suggests they draw straws, and the Skipper wins.

When the castaways try to launch the balloon that afternoon, it doesn't take off, so the Skipper throws off some ballast, but as the balloon takes off, the basket's bottom falls out. Later when the Professor suggests that they send the boy up in the balloon with a

note, the women object, so Gilligan suggests that they send the balloon off by itself with a note—to which all the castaways agree. After each of the castaways writes his own rescue note, Gilligan announces that he can't find the boy, and the castaways rush to discover that the jungle boy has taken off in the balloon on his own.

A few days later a radio report reveals that the boy landed safely on a United States aircraft carrier, but that the mystery will go unsolved for years since the boy can only mimic.

COMMENTS:

- Speech therapists and linguistic specialists could easily discover the boy's story in less than three months.
- The boy's existence on the island is never explained or examined.

TROPICAL INVENTIONS:

- A pedal-powered bamboo fan
- A pedal-powered washing machine
- A pedal-powered bamboo sewing machine
- A helium balloon (sewn together from raincoats and sealed with tree sap) tied to a bamboo basket.

CASTAWAY QUIZ #19:

What do the castaways name the jungle boy?
(For answer, see page 359)

20: ST. GILLIGAN AND THE DRAGON ⊗

Writers: Arnold and Lois Peyser
Director: Ray Montgomery

While serving breakfast, Ginger and Mary Ann demand more privacy from the men, refusing to serve them anymore until they build them a hut and grant them equal rights. When Howell refuses to build Lovey their own hut, Lovey leads the other women to the other side of the island to build their own hut.

The men agree that the women will be back before nightfall, and when the women arrive at the Howells' own camp site and start building their hut, Lovey predicts that the men will come crawling back to them. Back at the men's camp, Gilligan cooks a fish stew sans fish, and later while the men are cleaning their communal hut, Howell spells out a plan to scare the women back to them. Meanwhile the women, experiencing difficulty building their hut, send Ginger back to the men's camp for another hammer, where she sees the men disguising themselves as a dragon. She returns to the other women, who then plot to undermine the men's scheme.

That night as Gilligan and the Skipper, dressed as the dragon, near the women's hut and roar, the women ignore them. When the women finally see the monster, they feign fear and loudly declare their intention to kill it and send its head back to the men. Gilligan and the Skipper run, but when the women pummel them to the ground with bamboo sticks, they reveal themselves and unable to offer a reasonable explanation, are chased off.

The following night the Skipper dreams that he's a sultan served by a harem of the three women; Howell dreams that Ginger is giving him a massage, Mary Ann is giving a manicure, and Lovey is giving him a pedicure, washing his feet with champagne; the Professor dreams that he's a famous actor, being attacked outside his dressing room by the three women, who tear his clothes from his body; and Gilligan dreams that he is a bullfighter and the three women bring him presents. Gilligan awakes to find himself standing in the middle of the hut, bullfighting with his blanket.

Awoken, the other men go outside and sit by the fire, where Gilligan suggests they give in to the women. Howell makes the first move, but when he peeks into the women's hut, the women splash him with water, calling him a Peeping Tom. The women go out behind their hut, where they see another monster out in the jungle, but when they realize the men are standing behind them, they run back to them for protection. The Skipper had Gilligan examine the monster, and when the Skipper returns to protect the other castaways, the Professor realizes that the monster is nothing but a lost weather balloon. But before they can tell Gilligan, he attacks the weather balloon, puncturing and deflating it.

A few days later the Skipper gives up on trying to repair the balloon's radio transmitter, but as the Professor explains that he can repair the balloon with tree sap and inflate it again with hot air from a fire—Gilligan shows up with a pile of fabric cut from the balloon.

COMMENTS:

- In the previous chapter the castaways discovered a source of natural helium on the island, which they could easily use to fill the hot-air balloon. The Professor should have thought of that immediately before giving Gilligan a chance to cut up the fabric.
- Howell can't seem to recall how long he's been married; first it's nineteen years, then it's twenty-two years.
- The women are reunited with the men without ever being granted the equal rights they demanded.

TROPICAL INVENTIONS:

- The Skipper and Gilligan's dragon costume

CASTAWAY QUIZ #20:

When Gilligan and the Skipper disguise themselves as a dragon, who plays the front half?
(For answer, see page 359)

21: BIG MAN ON A LITTLE STICK ⊗⊗

Writers: Charles Tannen & Lou Huston
Director: Tony Leader
Guest Star: Denny Scott Miller

When the Skipper finds Gilligan fishing on the lagoon, a surfer rides up to the beach and collapses. Gilligan administers artificial respiration, and when the Skipper rolls over the surfer, he regains consciousness. Duke Williams of Topeka, Kansas, speaking in indiscernible surfer lingo, claims to have ridden a thirty-foot wave from Honolulu for five days. The Professor explains that Duke probably rode in on a tsunami—a tidal wave cause by a submarine earthquake originating off the coast of Japan. Duke insists that he'll work out, regain his strength, and surf back to Hawaii on a reverse tsunami.

The Skipper brings the muscular Duke back to his hut, and when the girls stop by to meet him, they are instantly attracted to his physique. The Howells, thinking a regal duke has arrived on the island, ask Gilligan to invite him to their hut for cocktails and dinner. When the girls, watching Duke work out on the beach, ignore Gilligan, he builds his own weights (coconut shells tied to bamboo, and a barbell made from bamboo and two heavy rocks) and while working out, traps himself under his barbell and cries for help. After Duke frees him, Gilligan once again traps himself under the barbell.

That evening the Howells welcome Duke to their hut, and after treating him like royalty, Howell calls his bluff, and Duke leaves. That night the Professor explains that, according to his calculations, "shifts in the trade winds and the tidal forces, compounded by the current pull of the sun, have caused a syzygy with the earth and made a perfect correalis effect." In short, the tsunami will return in forty-eight hours headed for Hawaii. But Duke, uninterested, leaves with the girls, and Gilligan explains to the Professor that while the men are building up Duke, the girls are knocking him down.

The next day when Duke makes advances toward Ginger and Mary Ann, the girls decide to seek Mrs. Howell's help, and later Lovey explains the situation to Howell, who, after learning how she dumped an early suitor, details a plan of action to the other men.

That night when Duke finds the Skipper waxing his surfboard, he denies any intention of leaving the island and asks for Ginger. The Skipper tells him that Ginger is with the Professor, and when Duke finds them, he watches from the bushes as Ginger kisses the Professor. Duke returns to the Skipper and asks for Mary Ann, who, the Skipper tells him, is with Gilligan. Disbelievingly, Duke finds the couple and voyeuristically watches Mary Ann kiss Gilligan. Shattered, Duke decides to leave the island, and the next morning the Professor sends him off on his surfboard as the other castaways watch from the edge of the jungle. After Gilligan climbs to the top of a palm tree with a pair of binoculars to watch Duke surf, he jumps down and lands on the Skipper.

A week later while Gilligan, the Skipper, and the Professor are listening to the radio, they learn that Duke Williams not only landed in Honolulu, but he hit his head on a rock when he beached and developed amnesia, unable to account for his whereabouts for the last two weeks.

COMMENTS:

- A reverse tsunami is as possible geologically as surfing 250 miles for five consecutive days is physically.

TROPICAL INVENTIONS:

- Gilligan's bamboo-and-stone barbells

CASTAWAY QUIZ 21:

What does Gilligan name the small fish he catches on the lagoon every day?
(For answer, see page 359)

22: DIAMONDS ARE AN APE'S BEST FRIEND ⊗

Writer: Elroy Schwartz
Director: Jack Arnold
Guest Star: Janos Prohaska

One night while trying to fall asleep, Gilligan sees a gorilla outside his hut window and wakes the Skipper who convinces him he's only dreaming. Later that night the gorilla reaches through a window of the Howell's hut and steals Lovey's forty-eight karat diamond brooch sitting on her night table.

At breakfast the Skipper, insisting that Gilligan didn't see a gorilla, orders him to get some coconuts from the jungle, where the gorilla pins him to a palm tree. When Gilligan yells and the Skipper runs to help him, the gorilla's nowhere to be seen. They return to the communal table to find Howell telling the others about Lovey's missing brooch, implying thievery. Insulted, all but Gilligan leave, and Howell, admitting that perhaps Lovey made a mistake, decides to apologize by offering a $10,000 reward to anyone who finds the brooch.

When Gilligan relays Howell's apology to the others, they refuse to accept it—until Gilligan mentions Howell's reward offer. While the Skipper and Gilligan search for the brooch, Gilligan encounters the gorilla and after describing it to the Skipper, finally convinces him of its existence, and they both flee from the jungle.

That night, feeling that his previous accusations may be inhibiting one of the castaways from returning the brooch, Howell gathers the castaways at the communal table and tells them that when he and Lovey turn out the torch lights, whoever found the brooch should simply place it on the table anonymously and take the $10,000 cash reward. When Lovey turns out the torch, she yells, and Howell relights his torch in time for the others to see the gorilla carrying Lovey away.

The next morning Howell, exhausted from having searched the island all night, finds the Professor, the Skipper, and Gilligan building a cage. While the men try to determine the gorilla's whereabouts, Gilligan, trying to think like a gorilla by acting like a gorilla, says he'd take Lovey to a cave. The other men concur and find the gorilla in a cave, guarding Lovey.

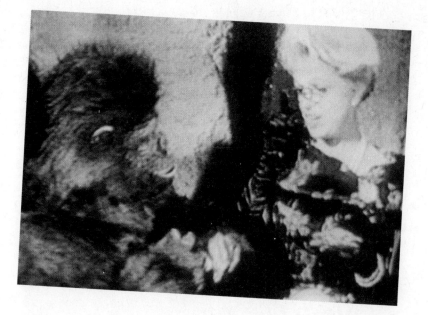

When Howell runs up to the cave, the gorilla chases him back to the other men. Gilligan fails to lure the gorilla from the cave so the other men can sneak past, and when the Skipper hits the gorilla with a club, the ape throws the Skipper over his head. The Professor explains that the gorilla considers Lovey a mate and suggests they use a net to catch it, sending Gilligan to collect vines; Howell suggests they use Ginger as bait.

After setting the trap, the Professor sends Ginger to lure the gorilla, instructing Gilligan to release the net when he snaps his fingers. When Ginger fails to lure the gorilla under the net, the Professor, suddenly inspired with a new idea, snaps his fingers, and Gilligan drops the net on the Professor and the Skipper.

The Professor explains that the gorilla, an animal attracted to sweet fragrances, was probably attracted to Lovey's perfume. When the Professor sends Gilligan to the Howells' hut to get the perfume, Gilligan, searching through her bottles, spills Lovey's perfumes all over himself. When he returns with the empty perfume bottle of Warm Afternoon, the gorilla swings from a vine, grabs Gilligan, and carries him off into the jungle, leaving Lovey behind. Later, after Mary Ann and Ginger collect flowers to lure the gorilla away from Gilligan, they return to the cave where the gorilla grabs Mary Ann's bouquet and presents it to Gilligan.

155

Later while the Skipper watches the Professor experiment with Mrs. Howell's perfumes to synthesize a stronger fragrance, Gilligan runs from the jungle and explains that the gorilla found someone he likes better—another gorilla.

COMMENTS:

- The castaways never use the cage they build to capture the gorilla.
- We never learn if the castaways ever find Lovey's brooch.

TROPICAL INVENTIONS:

- A bamboo cage

CASTAWAY QUIZ #22:

Upon their return to civilization, why wouldn't the Howells be able to collect the insurance on Lovey's diamond brooch?
(For answer, see page 359)

23: HOW TO BE A HERO ⊗

Writers: Herbert Finn & Alan Dinehart
Director: Tony Leader

When Gilligan jumps into the lagoon to save Mary Ann from drowning, she pulls him under, and the Skipper jumps in to save them both. Howell later photographs the Skipper and Mary Ann, asking Gilligan to get out of the way. After Howell asks Gilligan to take a picture of the other castaways, Gilligan dejectedly wanders into the jungle.

After Lovey psychoanalyzes Gilligan, she tells Howell and the Skipper that Gilligan needs recognition. The Skipper brings Ginger to a fallen log, slips himself under the log, and asks Ginger to call Gilligan. When Ginger leaves, a headhunter who arrived on the island by boat earlier sneaks up on the Skipper—until Ginger returns with Gilligan. Gilligan ties a vine around the log, throws it over a branch for leverage, lifts the log, and then drops it on both the Skipper and himself. When the women run to get the Professor, the headhunter begins stalking the crew—until the women return with the Professor, who lifts the log and frees the crew. When they all leave, Gilligan spots the headhunter and runs back to camp.

Claiming that Gilligan's having delusions, Lovey gives him a sedative to sleep. Later that night Lovey calls for help, and Gilligan runs to her hut to find a spider, but as he's about to kill it with a broom, he accidentally knocks his head against a supporting beam and falls unconscious.

The next day, after sending Gilligan out to pick some bananas, the Skipper brings Lovey and Mary Ann to a remote spot in the jungle and explains that he'll dress up as a headhunter, take the others prisoner, and allow Gilligan to rescue them. When they leave, Gilligan rises from amidst the banana bush where he's overheard everything. While walking through the jungle, Ginger, Mary Ann, and the Professor encounter the real headhunter. When the Howells find the girls and the Professor tied to stakes, the real headhunter captures them as well.

Unable to find the Skipper, who, dressed as a headhunter, hides in his hut, Gilligan searches the jungle where he finds the real headhunter, guarding the other castaways tied to stakes. Thinking the headhunter is the Skipper, Gilligan provokes him, allowing the headhunter to chase after him. When the headhunter runs into a tree, knocking himself unconscious, Gilligan returns to the clearing to find the Skipper dressed as a headhunter. The headhunter returns, and as Gilligan runs to save the Skipper, he trips, pushing the headhunter into the fire. The headhunter leaps up, runs into the lagoon, and swims off the island.

COMMENTS:

- While the Howells are forever snapping photographs, we never learn how much film they brought along on the cruise.

CASTAWAY QUIZ #23:

What does Lovey insist Gilligan's suffering from?
(For answer, see page 359)

24: THE RETURN OF WRONGWAY FELDMAN ☺☺

Writers: Lawrence J. Cohen & Fred Freeman
Director: Gene Nelson
Guest Star: Hans Conried

Gilligan, the Skipper, and the Professor, spying through a bamboo telescope, spot Wrongway Feldman flying his plane back to the island. When the castaways greet him, they learn that Wrongway hasn't notified the authorities of their whereabouts because he's returned to flee civilization.

As Howell tries to bribe Wrongway, he grows depressed learning current real estate values. Wrongway upsets Ginger with his stories of Hollywood. The Skipper decides to pretend he's sick so Wrongway will return to civilization for a doctor. When the Professor and Gilligan bring Wrongway to the Skipper's aid, Wrongway insists on removing the Skipper's appendix, and the Skipper, insisting he's fine, runs off. The Skipper later has Gilligan feign the symptoms of bola-bola fever and stagger up to Wrongway. Convinced that Gilligan has bola-bola, Wrongway considers returning to Hawaii.

The next morning the Professor finds a note from Wrongway explaining that he's returned to the mainland. That afternoon while the castaways sit with their packed suitcases, waiting for a rescue party, Wrongway returns with a bottle of bola-bola serum for Gilligan, having failed to notify any authority. The Skipper, the Professor, and Gilligan decide to give Wrongway a taste of civilization to chase him off the island.

When Wrongway wakes up the next morning to hear the Skipper, the Professor, and Gilligan building a city, the Skipper orders him to drive stakes. While Wrongway pedals a clay mixer, Ginger feeds him coffee made from fish. Gilligan later brings Wrongway to the Howells, who order him to chop down trees to clear the way for a freeway. That night when Wrongway shows up for dinner, Mary Ann tells him he missed it. As Wrongway tries to fall asleep, the crew talk, read, noisily eat fruit and vegetables, and swing in their hammocks above him.

Several days later the castaways hear Wrongway's plane engine start up and run to find Wrongway taking off in his plane, which the Skipper has loaded with maps of the island. Three days later, while the other castaways sit with their luggage, Gilligan finds a note in a bottle from Wrongway informing the castaways that he lost his bearings and landed on a tropical island with hula girls.

COMMENTS:

- Wrongway could not obtain bola-bola serum without seeing a licensed physician and attracting considerable attention.

TROPICAL INVENTIONS:

- A bamboo telescope
- A pedal-powered clay mixer

CASTAWAY QUIZ #24:

Who was Ginger's roommate in Hollywood?
(For answer, see page 359)

25: THE MATCHMAKER ☺☺

Writer: Joanna Lee
Director: Tony Leader

Dismayed that she's missing the entire social season, particularly weddings, Lovey longs to arrange for some social event on the island. When she sees Gilligan carrying Mary Ann through the clearing, Lovey, recalling that the captain of a ship can perform weddings, decides to matchmake a marriage between Gilligan and Mary Ann.

Lovey decides to work on Mary Ann while Thurston works on Gilligan. Howell refuses, but winds up taking Gilligan out to take pictures with his solid-gold, custom-made camera and talks to him about the benefits of marriage. When Howell asks Gilligan to take a picture, Gilligan breaks the camera. Meanwhile, Mrs. Howell, sewing while Mary Ann pedals, puts the idea of marriage in her head, explaining that since they may never get rescued, she should consider the eligible bachelors on the island.

When Mary Ann returns to her hut to find flowers on her bed, Ginger tells her that Gilligan brought them. Ginger encourages Mary Ann and later offers Gilligan cryptic encouragement, making him think Mary Ann has a crush on him. That night as Gilligan, who's been invited to the Howells' for dinner, dresses, the Skipper and the Professor, learning that Gilligan left flowers for Mary Ann, fail to convince him that he's set himself up for a major misunderstanding.

After Gilligan and Mary Ann arrive at the Howells' hut, the Howells go out to get a bottle of champagne cooling in a nearby stream, leaving the two alone. When Mary Ann thanks Gilligan for the flowers, he tells her that he left them for Mrs. Howell. When Mary Ann explains that she thought Gilligan had amorous feelings for her (which she seems willing to reciprocate), Gilligan compliments her, and they begin clumsily fawning over each other. The Howells, who've been watching from the window, decide to make their return to demonstrate true marital bliss. Lovey explains that twenty years ago that night she accepted Thurston's proposal at a French restaurant in Manhattan. Disagreeing over the restaurant's address, what they ordered, and what Lovey wore, the Howells exchange insults until Lovey says she never wants to speak to him again.

The next day Thurston moves in with the men, and Lovey moves in with the girls. At lunch the Howells sit at opposite ends of the table, exchanging snide remarks. While trying to reunite the Howells, the other castaways start fighting among themselves. The Skipper takes Gilligan aside and insists on reuniting the Howells, and after Ginger tells him she's been to the restaurant where Howell proposed, the Skipper suggests that they re-create the restaurant on the island, get the Howells there on some pretext, and fill them with fond memories.

That evening, after the Professor as the maître d' shows Howell to a table, Mary Ann seats Lovey at that same table. When the Professor as emcee introduces Ginger, who sings a slinky rendition of "Alouette," Lovey asks Thurston to hold her hand. Mary Ann sells Howell a corsage for Lovey. As chef, the Skipper gives waiter Gilligan flaming shish kebabs of turtle meat, which the Professor serves to the Howells. The Skipper then gives Gilligan a tray of soup to bring to the Howells, and while Ginger dances a hula dance, Gilligan, trying desperately to pass behind her, winds up stumbling backward and spilling the soup on the Skipper.

The next day, after they're reconciled, Lovey tells Thurston that she wants to match up another couple—the Professor and Ginger—bringing him to tears.

COMMENTS:

- While Mary Ann and Gilligan express amorous feelings for one another, a romance never materializes.
- While the castaways previously built a hand-cranked phonograph using the wheel of the *Minnow* as the turntable [Episode 11], we now see a brand-new record player that either (a) mysteriously washed ashore, or (b) one of the castaways forgot they'd brought along.

TROPICAL INVENTIONS:

- A French restaurant in the Professor's hut.

CASTAWAY QUIZ #25:

In what French restaurant did Lovey accept Thurston Howell's marriage proposal?
(For answer, see page 359)

26: MUSIC HATH CHARM ⊗

Writers: Al Schwartz & Howard Harris
Director: Jack Arnold
Guest Stars: Paul Daniel, Russ Grieve, Frank Corsentino

When Lovey finds Gilligan beating on a drum, she decides that the castaways should form their own symphony orchestra. Meanwhile on another island, natives, hearing what they believe to be enemy war drums, prepare to attack.

Lovey, deciding what the orchestra should play, asks Thurston, who's been trying to swat a fly, to be the conductor. Meanwhile the Skipper, eager to be the conductor, searches for a baton, and when Gilligan helps him pull a branch from a tree, he rips the Skipper's pants. While helping Ginger build a xylophone from bamboo, Gilligan teaches Mary Ann how to play the saw. Later when Lovey finds Howell practicing his conducting, the Professor walks by carving his flute. While Howell conducts the Professor on the flute, the Skipper insists on conducting the Professor—until they wind up fencing with their batons.

Later that afternoon on the castaways' stage, Lovey conducts the castaways in playing "The Blue Danube." The Skipper plays the conch shells and the *Minnow*'s foghorn; Howell plays the triangle; Gilligan plays the drum; the Professor plays the flute; Ginger plays the xylophone; and Mary Ann plays the saw. While Gilligan plays a drum solo, natives land on the island. When the Skipper catches a native scout, the castaways spot hordes of natives standing on a hill, run to each end of the island, and wind up hiding in a cave. That night as the castaways freeze in the cold cave, the Professor, recalling that primitive tribes are exceptionally superstitious, suggests that they pose as gods with mystical powers to scare off the natives.

After retrieving the radio, the Professor and Gilligan frighten the natives with the radio, but Gilligan trips, breaking the radio, and the natives capture the Professor. The Skipper and Gilligan then return to the clearing with the flashlight, and when the Skipper wakes the natives and turns on the flashlight, which Gilligan forgot to load with batteries, the natives capture the Skipper. When Howell and Gilligan return to the natives with the fire extinguisher, Gilligan sprays his head white and passes the extinguisher to Howell, who, discovering it empty, is captured by the natives.

After returning to the cave, Gilligan brings the women to the clearing, and unable to find the natives, they return to camp to find the natives dancing to the men's music. Gilligan and the girls join the men on stage and play their instruments. When the natives leave the island without the castaways, Gilligan beats his drum, alerting natives on yet another island, who prepare to attack.

COMMENTS:

- Natives on distant islands could not possibly hear Gilligan's drumming from such a distance.

TROPICAL INVENTIONS:

- Gilligan's drum
- Ginger's bamboo xylophone
- The Professor's flute
- The Skipper's conch-shell horns

CASTAWAY QUIZ #26:

How much money did Howell donate to the New England Philharmonic to keep them in New England?
(For answer, see page 359)

27: NEW NEIGHBOR SAM ⊗

Writers: Charles Tannen & George O'Hanlon
Director: Thomas Montgomery

While collecting firewood, the Skipper and Gilligan overhear a gang of criminals and return to camp to tell the others. The Professor suggests they sneak aboard the gangsters' boat and sail back to Hawaii. When the men scout out the situation, they send Gilligan back to camp, where he helps the women set up a trap in their hut, which the Skipper later walks into. The Skipper and Gilligan hear noise, hit the ground, and hide under palm fronds. When the Professor walks over them, a fight ensues until the men realize they're fighting each other. Passing the entrance of a cave, they overhear the gangsters and decide to return to camp to warn the others.

The castaways stay up all night, trying to decide what to do. An hour before dawn, Ginger suggests that they do what Gary Cooper does in *Beau Geste* when the Arabs are about to attack: prop up the dead men with guns in their hands. Gilligan runs to get Howell's clothes so the castaways can make dummies to prop up in the hut's windows. At sunrise the castaways hear the gangsters coming, see the bushes moving, and discover a parrot walking into the clearing. The

men go outside and pick up the parrot, who says his name is Sam. The Professor claims that since parrots only repeat what they hear, there must be gangsters and a boat.

The men try to get the parrot to talk, and the Professor explains that the parrot was obviously associated with the men whose names he keeps repeating: Artie, Louie, Gus, and Sid. The word "boat" provokes a reaction from the bird, and when Howell privately provokes a reaction from the word "jewelry," he brings the bird back to his hut to show it Lovey's jewels to provoke a reaction. The parrot picks up Lovey's diamond engagement ring and runs through the hut. When Gilligan and Ginger come by to get the bird, the Howells tell them that Sam ran away, and when Gilligan asks to borrow the bird cage, Howell gives him a basket, which he doesn't realize contains the bird.

Later when Gilligan and the Skipper find Sam in the basket along with Mrs. Howell's diamond, they realize that the parrot squawks when they say the word "jewel." The castaways follow the parrot through the jungle to a cave where the Professor finds a newspaper dated April 10, 1906, which reports that bandits robbed an art museum—a story, the Professor claims, that the parrot was obviously reciting. The parrot begins digging up something in the cave, and the men find a box of Jewel Crackers. "Sam wants a cracker," says the bird.

COMMENTS:
- While the Professor claims that parrots only repeat what they hear, he later insists that the parrot was reciting from a newspaper article it somehow read.
- The castaways never explore how the parrot got on the island or who read him the newspaper article and hid the box of crackers in the cave.

TROPICAL INVENTIONS:
- Dummies (constructed from coconuts, bamboo, and Mr. Howell's wardrobe)

CASTAWAY QUIZ #27:
What newspaper does the Professor find?
(For answer, see page 359)

28: THEY'RE OFF AND RUNNING ⊗

Writer: Walter Black
Director: Jack Arnold

After the Skipper loses everything he owns to Howell in a turtle race, Howell suggests they stake his yacht against Gilligan's services as a houseboy, but the Skipper refuses.

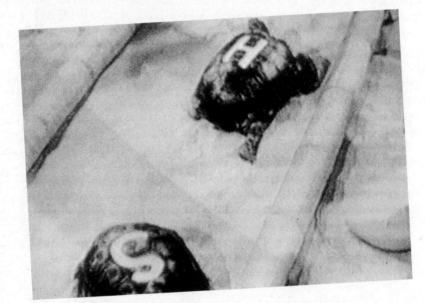

When Gilligan frees the Skipper's turtle, the Skipper discovers that his turtle is attracted to carrots, and Gilligan insists that the Skipper bet his services. After the Skipper tells Howell he's willing to race, Howell has Ginger seduce Gilligan to discover what the Skipper has up his sleeve. When the Skipper and Gilligan later ask Mary Ann for a couple of carrots, they discover that Howell bought all fifty carrots for $50,000, all eight turnip plants for $4,000, and the wild lettuce for $3,000. Later while trying to train the turtle using seaweed, the Skipper discovers that the turtle is attracted to moss. At the race, Howell's turtle wins (since Gilligan fed the turtle moss all afternoon), and Howell takes Gilligan as his houseboy.

After Howell orders Gilligan around his hut, Gilligan helps Lovey wind her yarn. When the Skipper visits Gilligan at the Howells' hut, Gilligan offers the Skipper his pocketknife to bet with Howell, but the Skipper refuses. When Gilligan pleads with Howell to race turtles for his pocketknife, Howell accepts the challenge, and as Gilligan runs to tell the Skipper, Lovey asks Howell to let the Skipper win.

After reading Mary Ann her horoscope, Ginger tells the Skipper that according to his horoscope, the sixteenth is his lucky day. The Skipper agrees to race Howell on the sixteenth—the next day. That night after Lovey surreptitiously switches the turtles in their pens, Howell sneaks out and switches them again (thinking he's switching them in favor of the Skipper). When Gilligan informs the Skipper that Howell switched the turtles, the Skipper, only wishing to win honorably, orders Gilligan to help him switch the turtles back where they belong. When Howell learns that the Skipper switched the turtles back, he has Gilligan switch the turtles again.

The next day when the turtles race, Howell's turtle wins again, and Gilligan gives Howell his knife. Later Howell, holding a pebble in one of his two outstretched fists, bets the Skipper to guess which hand it's in, and when the Skipper guesses incorrectly, Howell gives Gilligan back, explaining that when it comes to Gilligan, the winner is the loser.

COMMENTS:

- Mary Ann steps out of character by selling the castaways' communal vegetables to Howell.

TROPICAL INVENTIONS:

- Turtle pens
- Turtle racetrack

CASTAWAY QUIZ #28:

What does Gilligan name the Skipper's turtle?
(For answer, see page 359)

29: THREE TO GET READY ☺☺

Writer: David P. Harmon
Director: Jack Arnold

While digging a bait trap, Gilligan finds a clear stone that the Professor recognizes as a cat's-eye, but which the Skipper recognizes as the Eye of the Idol, entitling Gilligan to three wishes. He wishes for a gallon of ice cream, and as the Skipper and the Professor debate the superstition's merits, Gilligan finds a gallon of chocolate ice cream floating in the lagoon.

While the castaways eat the ice cream, the Professor insists the ice cream fell from a freighter or plane. The Skipper asks Gilligan to save his last wish to rescue the castaways from the island, and Gilligan wanders the island trying to decide what to do with his second wish. The Skipper, trying to father Gilligan, chases him from his hut. Ginger cuddles with the first mate in a hammock and tries to coax him to wish he's a movie star so he can pick his costar. When he chooses Lassie, Ginger tosses him out of the hammock. Howell stands Gilligan on his head, picks up the stone, which has fallen to the ground, and wishes for money—which fails to appear. When Howell returns the stone, the Skipper explains that only Gilligan can use the wishes. Gilligan demonstrates by wishing for vanilla ice cream, and Mary Ann suddenly brings him a gallon of vanilla ice cream.

When all the castaways gather at the lagoon to leave the island, the Professor insists they're not going anywhere. When Gilligan realizes he lost the stone, the Skipper splits everyone up in search teams. The Howells search through a pile of oysters; the Skipper and Mary Ann search around a bird's nest; Gilligan searches the ground; Ginger and the Professor search the cave. While climbing out on a branch, the Skipper falls from a tree; the Howells find a pearl in one of the oysters; and Ginger finds the Eye of the Idol. Later at the lagoon when Gilligan loses the jewel again, the Skipper finds it in his little buddy's sneaker. When the castaways finally persuade the Professor to join them, Gilligan wishes the castaways off the island, and the small peninsula of land they're standing on breaks off the island and floats out into the lagoon.

The Professor later explains that digging the bait trap loosened the small peninsula. Gilligan throws the stone into the jungle, and when the Skipper realizes that whoever finds the stone next gets three

wishes, the Professor follows the other castaways to search for the stone.

COMMENTS:
- The Skipper foolishly allows Gilligan to save his last wish for the castaways' rescue.

TROPICAL INVENTIONS:
- The castaways' bait trap

CASTAWAY QUIZ #29:
According to the Skipper, which idol does the cat's-eye Gilligan finds belong to?
(For answer, see page 359)

30: FORGET ME NOT ⊗

Writer: Herbert Margolis
Director: Jack Arnold

While building a platform to signal the navy, which will shortly be holding maneuvers off the island, Gilligan accidentally pulls down a beam, hitting the Skipper in the head, giving him amnesia. When the Skipper and Gilligan return to camp, the Professor sends the Skipper back to his hut while he checks his medical book. After Gilligan tries to provoke his memory, the Skipper finds Ginger hanging the  wash and makes advances toward her, until the Professor stops him and explains the situation to Ginger.

The Professor explains the Skipper's condition to the others, adding that sometimes a second blow on the head will return the victim's memory. That night after the Skipper switches hammocks with Gilligan, Howell sneaks into the crew's hut and hits Gilligan in the head. After the Skipper asks to switch hammocks again, Lovey enters and hits Gilligan in the head.

The next day the Professor hypnotizes the Skipper, bringing him back to his childhood, where he sees the other castaways as children. That night the Professor hypnotizes him again, bringing him to an island in the South Pacific, and when woken, the Skipper, seeing the other castaways as Japanese soldiers, runs into the jungle.

After searching the island, the Howells inform the Professor and Gilligan that, according to the radio, the navy will be offshore that afternoon. The Howells practice semaphore with the signal flags, and when the Skipper, watching from the edge of the jungle, sees who he thinks are Japanese soldiers leave, he takes the radio, rifle, and ammunition.

While the girls build the signal tower, the Skipper, seeing them as

Japanese soldiers, captures and imprisons them. When the Howells return to practice semaphore on the signal tower, the Skipper captures them. When Gilligan and the Professor realize the Howells, girls, gun, ammunition, and radio are missing, the Professor deduces that the Skipper must have taken everyone prisoner.

The Professor and Gilligan find the others unguarded in a cage and try to free them, but the Skipper appears and imprisons them as well.

173

When Gilligan, looking through his telescope, spots the naval ships passing the island, the Professor desperately tries to hypnotize the Skipper but winds up convincing Gilligan and Howell that they're the Skipper, resulting in a huge argument between them. When the Skipper tries to quiet them, Gilligan hits him in the head with his telescope, curing him. The Skipper knocks Howell's and Gilligan's heads together, curing them as well. The castaways run to the signal tower, but Gilligan, unable to spot any boats offshore, falls from the tower, giving himself amnesia.

COMMENTS:

- The castaways have a rifle and ammunition whose presence on the island remains unexplained.

TROPICAL INVENTIONS:

- Semaphore flags

CASTAWAY QUIZ #30:

What do the Howells use to hit the Skipper in the head?
(For answer, see page 359)

31: DIOGENES, WON'T YOU PLEASE GO HOME?

Writer: David P. Harmon
Director: Christian Nyby
Guest Star: Vito Scotti

When Gilligan tries to hide something from the Skipper, the other castaways start spying on him. When Gilligan tells the Professor that he's merely been hiding his diary, the Professor informs the Skipper, Ginger, and Howell, who immediately suspect that Gilligan has written nasty observations about them.

After the Skipper, Ginger, and Howell each try to coerce Gilligan into letting them see his diary, Gilligan, tired of being pestered, throws his diary into the lagoon, upsetting the others. Lovey finds Gilligan holding the bayonet he confiscated from the Japanese sailor who previously visited the island [Episode 15], pleads with him not to kill himself, and explains that the others are angry with him because of his ability to tell the truth.

When Gilligan discovers the Skipper writing his own diary, Gilligan explains how he rescued the castaways from the Japanese soldier as it actually happened [see Episode 15]. According to the Skipper's version, the muscular Skipper protected the girls from a live grenade by allowing it to explode in his hands and freed Gilligan (who was strung up and being subjected to water torture by the Japanese sailor) by crushing the sailor's machine gun with his bare hands. After hearing this tale, Gilligan finds Howell writing his own journal and learns that Howell allowed himself to be captured by the Japanese sailor as a ruse, retrieved a shovel from his shoe, tunneled the others free, and then using a whip, freed Gilligan by flinging the Japanese sailor into the lagoon. According to Ginger (who's keeping her own diary), she found Gilligan tied to a tree, donned a judo jacket, beat up the Japanese sailor, and ran off to free the others.

When Mary Ann runs back to camp with Gilligan's diary, which washed back on shore, she reads a passage to the others that praises them all. Gilligan returns, and the other castaways, deeply humbled, treat him with dignity and respect. That night, after Howell, Ginger, and the Skipper each burn their diaries, they stop Gilligan from burning what they consider to be the only true record of the shipwreck. Gilligan reveals that he was about to burn *A Boy Scout's Guide Through New Jersey.*

COMMENTS:

- The excessive amount of paper and writing utensils on the island remains unexplained.

CASTAWAY QUIZ #31:

What are Ginger's measurements?
(For answer, see page 359)

32: PHYSICAL FATNESS ⊗

Writers: Herbert Finn & Alan Dinehart
Director: Gene Nelson

After Gilligan discovers the Professor in his hut concocting a phosphorescent yellow dye marker, he runs to tell the Skipper, who's split his pants. When Gilligan asks the Skipper what he'll do after being rescued, the Skipper, realizing the shipwreck put him out of business, decides to reenlist in the navy, and Gilligan agrees to accompany him. After Mary Ann mends the Skipper's pants, the Skipper bends over to pick up a banana and splits his pants again.

When the Skipper discovers that navy regulations put his maximum weight requirement at 199 pounds, he weighs himself on the Professor's scale, which—only going to 200 pounds—breaks. Gilligan, weighing the Skipper in the castaways' fish scale, measures him at 221 pounds. When the Professor tells the Skipper that he'll have the dye marker within a week and needs a specially designed raft built to release the dye marker in the sea, the Skipper realizes he only has one week to lose twenty-two pounds if he wants to join the navy.

At dinner Gilligan passes the Skipper a lone piece of lettuce on a plate. That night the Skipper, unable to sleep, tries to sneak out of his hut, but a vine tied to his leg pulls Gilligan out of his hammock. Later in the night the Skipper sneaks into the Professor's hut and opens the food locker—to discover Gilligan.

The next day while Gilligan builds the raft, the Skipper runs ten laps around the island, followed by exercises with Ginger. When Mary Ann calls everyone for lunch, the Howells forbid the Skipper to attend, and Lovey hands him a bottle of reducing pills.

When Gilligan weighs the Skipper in at 201 pounds, he casually sits in the scale, and the Skipper realizes his little buddy is five pounds underweight. After Gilligan finishes eating a bunch of bananas, Mary Ann and Ginger bring him bowls of crab and pineapple. The Professor, ready to launch the raft that night, asks Ginger to help him with the dye. Before Mary Ann leaves, she asks the Skipper to feed Gilligan, and shortly after, Howell brings Gilligan a bowl of bouillabaisse, and Mary Ann returns with a coconut cream pie. When the Skipper calls Gilligan to examine the raft, Gilligan accidentally throws the pie in his face. When the Professor sets the bowl of dye on the table and helps the Skipper bring the raft to the lagoon, Gilligan starts eating the dye.

When the Skipper calls for Gilligan to bring the phosphorescent dye to the raft, a glowing Gilligan shows up carrying an empty bowl.

That night the Skipper forces Gilligan to stand atop the signal tower, rotating in place as a signal light.

COMMENTS:
- The Skipper doesn't have to join the navy upon his return to civilization; his insurance company will cover the value of the *Minnow*. Otherwise, Howell would undoubtedly buy him another yacht.
- Gilligan cannot drink this particular phosphorescent dye marker without experiencing serious, if not fatal, side effects.

TROPICAL INVENTIONS:
- The Professor's phosphorescent dye marker
- The Professor's scale
- The castaways' fish scale
- A signal raft

CASTAWAY QUIZ #32:
From what does the Professor synthesize the phosphorescent yellow dye marker?
(For answer, see page 359)

178

33: IT'S MAGIC ⊗

Writers: Al Schwartz & Bruce Howard
Director: Jack Arnold

When Gilligan fishes out a crate of magician's props from the lagoon, the Professor suggests they use the magic tricks to frighten off savages who visit the island, and Ginger, having once worked with a magician, agrees to teach each of the castaways a trick. Later Howell, wearing the magician's outfit, changes his wand into silks. Lovey tears up a five-dollar bill and re-turns it to a whole bill again. Gilligan handcuffs himself to Howell, and the next morning, after having slept handcuffed to Howell, frees them from the handcuffs.

At breakfast when the Howells show up handcuffed, Ginger explains how the trick works. When Gilligan pulls the cloth from the table, pulling everything else off with it, the Skipper orders him to put all the magic tricks in the supply hut. Gilligan returns to overhear the others complaining about him.

Ginger, displaying the disappearing box trick for the others, instructs Gilligan to exit through the back door on her signal. After Ginger makes Gilligan "vanish," he fails to reappear. The Professor, explaining that Gilligan obviously overheard their derogatory discussion earlier and ran away, suggests they form search parties. After finding Gilligan hiding in a cave, each of the castaways calls on him and apologizes, but he refuses to return to camp.

That night the Skipper delivers a plate of food to Gilligan; the Howells deliver a plate of food, a blanket, and Howell's teddy bear; and the Professor and the girls bring him another blanket and plate of food. Back at camp, Ginger suggests they throw a party for Gilligan, and to get Gilligan there, the Skipper suggests they scare him out of the cave using the monster masks from the magician's crate.

Dressed as monsters, the Skipper, the Professor, and Howell frighten Gilligan back to camp, where he fills a scooper with the magician's flash powder. After resting the scooper on the table while he gets a torch from the fire, Gilligan accidentally picks up the wrong scooper, leaving Mary Ann with the flash powder, which she mixes into the cake batter. Gilligan runs back into the jungle where the men reveal themselves, apologize, and bring him back to camp for the party. While Gilligan makes a speech, the candles burn so low that the cake explodes, showering the castaways and sending Gilligan through the hut's ceiling.

COMMENTS:

- The Professor could use the magician's flash powder to improvise signal flares, but he fails to recognize the opportunity.

CASTAWAY QUIZ #33:

To whom did the crate of magician's props originally belong?
(For answer, see page 359)

34: GOOD-BYE, OLD PAINT ☺☺

Writer: David P. Harmon
Director: Jack Arnold
Guest Star: Harold J. Stone

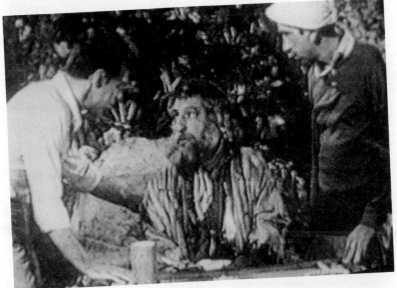

After Gilligan discovers an abstract painting that each castaway denies having painted, the artist emerges from the jungle, introduces himself as famous painter Alexandri Gregov Dubov, and explains that having fled civilization, he's been on the island for over ten years.

After making a number of unreasonable demands, Dubov offers to tell the castaways how to get off the island if Mary Ann feeds him. After eating several courses, Dubov tells the Professor and Gilligan he has a transmitter, but refuses to reveal its whereabouts. Dubov declares the crew's hut as his own, and when the Skipper objects, the Professor and Gilligan inform him about the transmitter.

That night Howell wakes the crew (who are sleeping in the clearing) and explains his underhanded scheme: They'll have Dubov paint a portrait of Ginger, rave over it, and convince Dubov he's regained his mastery, so he'll radio for help.

The next day Dubov, convinced that Picasso and Chagall have painted Ginger, "persuades her" to pose for him. When Lovey looks in on Dubov, he chases her away, and later when Gilligan finds a pot cooking over a fire, he unwittingly tastes a spoonful of Mary Ann's paint thinner. When Dubov finishes the picture, the castaways rave over it, and Dubov, flattered by their praise, announces that he'll radio for a boat. When Gilligan reveals Howell's plan, Dubov takes his painting and angrily walks into the jungle.

The next morning Gilligan, having found the painting of Ginger in the jungle, inspires Howell, who, after consulting the others, decides to set up Gilligan as Dubov's rival genius. Howell tells Gilligan to paint an abstract that they'll laud, compelling Dubov to radio for art critics to decide which of them is the master painter.

Mary Ann fans a pot of turtle soup, attracting Dubov back to camp. After Gilligan paints the Skipper, Howell brings the painting to Dubov and asks him to name his price as Lovey showers the artist with praise. When Gilligan claims the painting, the Howells follow him into the jungle. After Dubov sets up all his paintings with a For Sale sign, he beckons Howell, who offers to buy the For Sale sign. When Gilligan shows up with another painting, Mary Ann and Lovey insist on posing for him.

That night Dubov wakes Gilligan and asks him for painting lessons in return for the transmitter. The next morning as the Skipper tries to transmit an SOS, the corroded transmitter falls apart. Gilligan finds a note inside from Dubov explaining that since the island isn't big enough for two geniuses, he left on a raft made from his paintings.

COMMENTS:

- Curiously, the castaways take almost a year to discover Dubov, who's been on the island for ten years.
- If Dubov can get off the island by building a raft made from his paintings, the castaways could surely do the same— unless Dubov used all the stretch canvas.

TROPICAL INVENTIONS:

- Mary Ann's paint thinner
- Stretched canvas
- Paints and brushes

CASTAWAY QUIZ #34:

What does Ginger pose as for Dubov?
(For answer, see page 359)

35: MY FAIR GILLIGAN ⊗

Writer: Joanna Lee
Director: Tony Leader

When Gilligan pushes Lovey out of the path of a falling boulder, saving her life, Howell adopts him. Gilligan moves in with the Howells, who spend a week teaching Gilligan etiquette, gin rummy, proper dress, and finance. Now Mary Ann refuses to let Gilligan hunt butterflies with her, and the Professor and the Skipper refuse to let him help them tar a hut. When Gilligan spills tar all over the Skipper, the Skipper doesn't yell at him. Gilligan finds Ginger hanging the wash, and eager to help her hang the clothes so they can go butterfly hunting together, Gilligan accidentally tears one of Ginger's gowns.

After the Howells tell Gilligan they're going to throw a party for him, Gilligan watches enviously as the other castaways entertain themselves around the communal table. As the others sing around the campfire, Gilligan reads the financial papers with the Howells, as Lovey tailors a blazer for him.

That night Gilligan dreams he's a king sitting next to his parents (the Howells), who refuse to let him go butterfly hunting until he sees his subjects. Mary Ann asks him to grant her a farm, the Professor

requests equipment to discover frozen food, Ginger asks for a dance from him, and the Skipper asks for a fleet of ships to sail for the Orient; but Gilligan turns them all away. When they all refuse to play with him, he yells, "Off with their heads!" Suddenly a cage drops over them, and a guillotine falls from the ceiling. Gilligan crushes his crown and wakes up screaming.

Gilligan tells the Skipper that he doesn't want to be a Howell but doesn't know how to tell them. The Skipper suggests they ask the Professor, who suggests they ask the girls. Finally, Ginger concocts a scheme. The next night at Gilligan's debut, Gilligan asks Howell for a $10,000 monthly allowance, reveals that he promised Ginger $50,000 for a new play, and explains that he lost a new *Minnow* to the Skipper in a card game. When the Professor claims the martini Gilligan mixed for him is too dry, Gilligan refills the cup and pours it over the Professor's head. When the girls return with a coconut cream pie, Gilligan throws it at Ginger but hits Howell. Howell brings Gilligan inside, criticizes his behavior, and refuses to be his father. When Gilligan leaves, Howell confides to Lovey that he knew Gilligan was acting.

The next day when Howell learns that the Skipper saved Lovey's life by placing a net over the quicksand pit, he adopts him.

TROPICAL INVENTIONS:
- Gilligan's butterfly net

CASTAWAY QUIZ #35:
When Howell adopts Gilligan, what does Gilligan's name become?

(For answer, see page 359)

36: A NOSE BY ANY OTHER NAME ⊗

Writer: Elroy Schwartz
Director: Hal Cooper

While picking coconuts, Gilligan falls from a palm tree, getting a swollen nose. Realizing this is the first accident they've had on the island, the Professor decides to teach all the castaways first aid. After Mary Ann and Lovey bandage Howell, they accidentally toss him off the table, spraining his arm, then do the same to the Skipper and the Professor.

When the Skipper and the Professor find Gilligan applying a cold compress to his nose, Gilligan pleads with the Professor to operate on his nose. Lovey decides to cheer up Gilligan by convincing him that his new nose makes him more attractive. Ginger flatters Gilligan, and Mary Ann, finding him admiring his nose in his hut, invites him for a stroll that evening. But later after overhearing the women discussing their scheme, Gilligan pleads with the Professor to operate on his nose, which the Professor agrees to do the next morning.

That afternoon Gilligan inhales the anesthetic the Professor cooks up from plants and passes out. Later the Skipper and Howell, explaining that Gilligan can have his choice of any nose, cover Gilligan's head with clay to make a mold for a mask of Gilligan's face so he can try various clay noses. When the clay dries on Gilligan's head, he searches for the Skipper, frightening Ginger and Mary Ann (who are modeling clay noses), Lovey, and when he looks in the mirror, himself. After finding Gilligan, the Skipper, having forgotten to put a divider down the middle of the mask, chisels the clay mold from Gilligan's head. After the castaways make a clay model of Gilligan's face, Gilligan tries various clay noses.

The next morning while preparing for surgery, the Howells pass out from the anesthetic, and finally the Skipper puts Gilligan under. Five days later when the Professor finally removes the bandage over Gilligan's nose, the castaways marvel over Gilligan's nose, but Gilligan, looking in a mirror, can't understand why he's got his own nose—until the Skipper explains that they faked the operation to allay Gilligan's anxieties while his nose healed naturally. Later while trying to teach the Skipper how to swing a golf club, Howell hits the Professor, giving him a swollen nose.

COMMENTS:

- The presence of six surgical outfits on the island remains unexplained.

TROPICAL INVENTIONS:

- A coconut carrier
- The Professor's anesthetic
- The Professor's operating room
- A clay mask of Gilligan's face

CASTAWAY QUIZ #36:

Whose nose does Gilligan select for himself?
(For answer, see page 359)

THE SECOND SEASON

37: GILLIGAN'S MOTHER-IN-LAW ☺☺

Writer: Budd Grossman
Director: Jack Arnold
Guest Stars: Russ Grieve, Henny Backus, Mary Foran,
    Eddie Little Sky

A native family arrive on the island to find a husband for their fat daughter, who chooses Gilligan. While building a pedal-powered fan for Mr. Howell, the Skipper sends Gilligan to get more palm fronds. Searching the jungle, Gilligan encounters the native family and runs back to the Skipper and Howell, who attempt to communicate with the natives. Convinced the natives want the Skipper to marry their daughter and realizing a marriage affords them the opportunity to get off the island, Howell insists that the Skipper betroth her. The Skipper flees, and while he's barricading himself behind his hut door, Gilligan climbs in through the window and tries to convince the Skipper to marry the girl. When the Professor climbs inside and explains that the chief wants Gilligan to marry his daughter, Gilligan leaps out the window and runs into the jungle.

While the Howells search the jungle for Gilligan, Ginger, searching with the Professor, notices a moving reed in the lagoon, but when the Professor reluctantly walks into the lagoon, an alligator chases him back out. When Gilligan, hiding in one of the caves, hears a loud roar, he runs into the jungle, where the natives catch him and return him to the other castaways.

As the Professor acts as an interpreter, the chief explains that Gilligan must first pass the marriage test. After Gilligan carries the bride around in circles, the native women hold Gilligan to a tree as the chief throws knives at him. The chief explains that the groom's family must throw a party for the bride's family.

That evening after the Skipper dresses Gilligan in a grass skirt, the castaways throw a festive party by torchlight for the native family. As the native women dance with Gilligan, he stumbles into another native, Haruki, who challenges Gilligan to a contest for the girl's hand—a duel with spears to be held first thing in the morning.

The Skipper and Howell help Gilligan practice by throwing spears, but Gilligan almost skewers them. Later when Ginger tries seductively

to convince Haruki to cancel the duel, he screams, and when the Professor races to her aid, Haruki explains that she's not exactly the kind of girl he'd bring home to his mother.

The next morning the Skipper tosses a two-headed coin to decide who throws first, urging Gilligan to choose heads, but Gilligan chooses tails. Haruki allows Gilligan the courtesy of the first throw, and at the sound of a drum Gilligan and Haruki take five paces and turn to throw their spears. Gilligan hits coconuts in a palm tree above Haruki, but as Haruki takes aim with his spear, the coconuts fall, knocking him unconscious. The fat girl runs to Haruki's aid and insists on marrying him. When the castaways, eager to go to Haruki's island, are told they're not invited to the wedding, Gilligan angrily yells gibberish, incensing the chief, who chases him into the jungle.

When Haruki, starting back to his island in his canoe with Gilligan to be his best man, explains that Gilligan must first pass the best-man test, Gilligan jumps overboard and swims back to the island.

COMMENTS:

- The Professor had previously invented a pedal-powered bamboo fan [Episode 19], which the Skipper now takes credit for inventing.
- The castaways could build their own canoes and paddle to the natives' island.
- The Professor, able to communicate with the natives, could simply ask them how to get off the island.

TROPICAL INVENTIONS:

- The Skipper's pedal-powered fan
- The Professor's moonshine

CASTAWAY QUIZ #37:

What is the best-man test?
What language do the natives speak?
(For answers, see page 359)

38: BEAUTY IS AND BEAUTY DOES ⊗⊗

Writer: Joanna Lee
Director: Jack Arnold

During lunch, when the radio reports the winner of the Miss America contest, Ginger gets bitterly upset. The Skipper toasts Ginger as the most beautiful woman on the island; Howell toasts Lovey as the most gracious; and Professor toasts Mary Ann as the sweetest. An argument ensues, so Gilligan proposes a beauty contest on the island for Miss Castaway.

With the Skipper as her coach, Ginger, dressed in her leopard-skin bathing suit, practices reciting from a play for the talent competition. Meanwhile the Professor coaches Mary Ann in isometric exercises, attaching the hook from the fishing rod to her swimsuit so he can hold her in place while she swims in the lagoon. Gilligan wanders by, and thinking the Professor has caught a fish, pulls in the line, pulling off Mary Ann's bathing suit.

Realizing that the deciding vote will rest with Gilligan, each group of castaways decides to play up to him. After Gilligan talks with a gorilla in the jungle, he shows up at camp for lunch, where the Skipper and Ginger give him a plate of lobster. The Professor and Mary Ann take the lobster away and give Gilligan a plate of herbs and fruits. Howell offers him a plate of hors d'oeuvres and a glass of liquor from his private stock.

When Gilligan realizes that the others are trying to sway his deciding vote and refuses to be the judge, the others take back their food. When Gilligan peels a banana for himself, the gorilla comes along and takes it from him.

While Gilligan walks through the jungle discussing his dilemma with the gorilla, the Skipper finds him and convinces him that Ginger, brokenhearted for not being on Broadway, deserves to win. While Gilligan continues walking alone, the Professor trips him, appeals to his sense of reason, and convinces him that Mary Ann deserves to win to reward her unfulfilled desires. While Gilligan talks things over with the gorilla, Howell comes along and after making an unsuccessful bribe attempt, convinces him that Lovey needs to win the contest to renew her pride as the eldest of the three women.

That evening the Professor emcees the beauty pageant and after the swimsuit competition, asks the women to give a short speech on what they want out of life. Mary Ann wants a world of peace and harmony; Ginger thanks everyone for allowing her to be in the contest; Lovey thanks the judge for being the son of an American mother. Gilligan busily scrawls notes.

After announcing the talent competition, the Professor encounters difficulty starting the record player, and when the Skipper gets up to help him, nearly stepping into a bucket of glue, he unintentionally inspires Howell, who pours the glue on the stage. When Mary Ann, performing a soft-shoe dance, steps in the glue, the Professor accuses Howell of foul play. As Lovey recites "The Midnight Ride of Paul Revere," the Professor surreptitiously blows sneezing powder at her, disrupting her performance. Howell accuses the Professor of foul play, and when the Skipper introduces Ginger, who sings a slinky version of "Let Me Entertain You," Howell and the Professor fire peashooters to distract her performance and Gilligan continues scribbling down notes.

When Gilligan steps to the stage to announce his decision, he says each woman deserves to win, but with all due respect he chooses the gorilla. Later that night when the men demand to see Gilligan's notes to learn who really won the contest, they discover that he'd been playing tic-tac-toe during the pageant.

TROPICAL INVENTIONS:

- The Professor's seaweed shampoo
- The Professor's crushed-blackberry rouge
- The Professor's powdered-hibiscus skin powder

CASTAWAY QUIZ #38:

What's Miss Castaway's name?
(For answer, see page 359)

39: THE LITTLE DICTATOR ⊗

Writers: Bob Rodgers & Sid Mandel
Director: Jack Arnold
Guest Star: Nehemiah Persoff

A motorboat pulls up to the lagoon, and two soldiers exile a Latin American dictator, tossing him a suitcase. While picking berries, Gilligan backs into the dictator, who introduces himself as Pancho Hernando Gonzales Enrico Rodriguez, former president of the Republic of Equarico. After eating the berries, Rodriguez marches Gilligan back to camp, where the other castaways learn that there are five bullets left in his gun.

After searching the island, Rodriguez names it Equarico West, declares himself President, and fires his second bullet. Later the men meet secretly and agree to get Rodriguez to fire off his four remaining bullets. They get him to shoot off a third bullet to impress them, but when Howell bets Rodriguez that he can't hit a distant tree stump, Rodriguez realizes he's being manipulated. At Howell's urging, Ginger entices Rodriguez to teach her how to shoot, and after she fires off a shot, Rodriguez grabs the gun back.

Howell later positions Gilligan in the shrubs to signal the Skipper, who, standing in a distant tree holding a rope, will hoist the net lying in front of Rodriguez's hut. Gilligan, shooing a fly with his hat, unintentionally signals the Skipper, who leaps from the tree holding the rope, stringing Howell in the net. As Rodriguez steps from the hut, the Skipper hands Gilligan the rope, and Howell lands on the dictator as Gilligan's pulled up into a tree, dangling from the rope.

Angered, Rodriguez ties Gilligan to a tree, aims his pistol, and fires—only to discover his gun's empty. Later, while Rodriguez paces in the crew's hut, Lovey tells him he's free to live as a member of their small democratic community.

That night after Rodriguez tries to convince Gilligan to become leader of the island, Gilligan falls asleep and dreams that he's President of a Latin American nation. Speaking on the balcony of his palace, Gilligan, advised by Rodriguez, promises the people "this, that, and the other thing." Inside the palace, after his cabinet sings salutatory praises, Gilligan notices bullet holes in the national flag. Mary Ann tells Gilligan there's growing dissatisfaction in the country, bringing him to the window where he sees people running in the street—a

problem Rodriguez advises him to dismiss. Over Rodriguez's objections, Howell, the minister of finance, informs Gilligan of the country's economic crisis, bringing him to the window where he sees depression shacks. The Skipper, Gilligan's secretary of the navy, brings him to the window to see a sinking mast ship that Rodriguez calls "propaganda." Ginger, Secret Agent 0036, brings Gilligan to the window to show him the state of the nation—an Indian attack. When Gilligan turns around to discover that Rodriguez has shot all his ministers, he runs down the stairs, but Rodriguez, yelling after him, insists that Gilligan's nothing but a puppet ruler, suddenly holding marionette strings above him, making him dance like a puppet, and finally dropping him to the floor.

Gilligan suddenly wakes up and runs to the lagoon to find Rodriguez boarding a motorboat to return to Equarico, where the loyalists have returned to power. As he departs, Rodriguez promises to send a rescue ship.

Several days later, while the Professor teaches the castaways Spanish, a sudden radio broadcast reveals that Rodriguez, unseated again by a counter-counterrevolution after he insisted he was dictator over an island inhabited by seven people, was parachuted into exile over the Andes mountains.

COMMENTS:

- The castaways have plenty of opportunities to take the gun from Rodriguez.
- While teaching the castaways Spanish, the Professor uses a blackboard that's never been on the island before.

TROPICAL INVENTIONS:

- Howell's rope trap

CASTAWAY QUIZ #39:

What name does Howell claim has been suggested for the island?

(For answer, see page 359)

40: SMILE, YOU'RE ON MARS CAMERA ☺☺☺☺

Writers: Al Schwartz & Bruce Howard
Director: Jack Arnold
Guest Stars: Booth Colman, Larry Thor, Arthur Peterson

While searching for a bird, Gilligan wanders past the supply hut, where Howell calls him inside to see how many feathers Gilligan's collected for a pillow he wants to make for Lovey. Only desiring feathers from exotic birds, Howell tosses Gilligan's batch of sparrow and pigeon feathers onto a tall reject pile, insisting that Gilligan collect more, swearing him to secrecy.

At Cape Canaveral two scientists, unable to activate an unmanned Mars space probe's television camera in time to see the space probe land outside the castaways' supply hut, briefly regain visual transmission, seeing a hut and palm trees. Gilligan, searching for feathers, knocks over the spacecraft and frightened, runs back to camp. The Professor recognizes the space probe and sends Gilligan back to camp to follow radio reports while he and the Skipper examine the craft.

When Gilligan returns to announce that a radio report revealed a spacecraft has sent back pictures of Mars, the Professor explains that this spacecraft transmitted those pictures. After dismantling the space probe, the Professor explains that they've lost the camera lens, and the Skipper suggests an immediate search.

When Ginger, searching the island with Mary Ann, reaches through a small opening between two tall rocks, she grabs what she thinks is the lens—Lovey's diamond engagement ring, being worn by Lovey. When Gilligan sees the Professor and the Skipper heading toward the supply hut, he runs to block the door, but the Professor orders Gilligan to monitor the radio.

When the Professor and the Skipper, unable to find the lens, return

195

to the crew's hut, Gilligan reveals a magnifying glass he found. The Professor immediately recognizes the lens, exciting Gilligan, who claps his hands, smashing it. When the Professor suggests they make glue from tree sap, Gilligan, demonstrating how to get sap from a tree, thrusts a knife through the wall of his hut, accidentally stabbing Howell, who's standing outside. While watching Gilligan collect sap, the Skipper steps into several sticky puddles. After Gilligan cooks the glue in a black kettle, inadvertently gluing his lips together, the Professor glues the lens back together and replaces it on the spacecraft.

While the castaways gather before the camera with SOS placards, Gilligan covers the pot of glue still heating over the fire and joins the others. When the Professor suggests that the castaways relax until the camera's reactivated, Gilligan places the signs behind the camera. When they hear a noise and take their positions, Mary Ann realizes the noise is coming from the kettle, and the covered boiling pot of glue suddenly explodes, covering the castaways with glue. They chase Gilligan into the supply hut, jumping into the pile of feathers. When the scientists reactivate the camera, they see feather-covered chicken-people running from the hut. As the castaways wave at the camera, Gilligan runs to get the signs, tripping over the bamboo leg supporting the spacecraft, breaking the camera and destroying the transmission. Angered, the castaways chase Gilligan into the jungle.

COMMENTS:

- We never learn if Mrs. Howell ever gets her pillow.
- The Professor could replace the space probe's camera lens with a lens from one of the Howells' many cameras.
- The Professor can't seem to recall that he invented glue several times prior to this incident, and the Skipper seems unable to recall that Gilligan's always collecting tree sap.
- NASA scientists seeing pictures of the island would not mistake it for Mars.

TROPICAL INVENTIONS:

- Gilligan's glue

CASTAWAY QUIZ #40:

What are the names of the two scientists monitoring the Mars probe at Cape Canaveral?
(For answer, see page 359)

41: THE SWEEPSTAKES ⊗

Writer: Walter Black
Director: Jack Arnold

After Gilligan, dressed as a waiter, delivers drinks to the Howells at their private country club, he turns on the radio, learning that the winning million-dollar Argentinian sweepstakes number matches the number on the sweepstakes ticket he just happens to have in his pocket. Learning that the winner can collect the money anytime, Gilligan runs to tell the others.

When Gilligan returns with the Howells' drinks, they admit him to their club. Howell administers the oath, and Lovey gives him his own club blazer. Lovey tries to teach Gilligan etiquette, and Howell explains how to dream like the idle rich. Gilligan offers each of the other castaways his personal IOU for $50,000 so they can join the Howells' club. That evening the Skipper, Mary Ann, Ginger, and the Professor present their IOUs to the Howells and enter the club. Howell, realizing he's never actually seen Gilligan's sweepstakes ticket, demands to see it as collateral for the four IOUs. When Gilligan can't produce the ticket, Howell throws them all out of his private club, taking back his blazer. The next day the five outcasts search unsuccessfully for Gilligan's sweepstakes ticket.

That night Howell dreams he's a prospector in the old West, coming into town with his donkey, Sea Biscuit, to have his gold assayed. The Professor brings him into his office and makes out a deed for one million dollars, advising Howell not to lose it. Howell gives him a $50,000 IOU for his services, and the Professor suggests he hire Marshal Gilligan for protection. Howell gives Marshal Gilligan an IOU for $50,000 for his services, and they enter the saloon, where the saloon-hall girl (Ginger) pours him two complimentary drinks. After Howell orders another round, drinking from the bottle, Ginger charges him $50,000 for the swig, accepting his $50,000 IOU. The school-marm (Mary Ann) enters the saloon, crying because she needs $50,000 to save her ranch, and Howell gives her his personal IOU. When Howell sits down to play three-card monte with a cardsharp (the Skipper), he bets $50,000, giving him a $50,000 IOU. When the cardsharp pulls out a gun and demands to see Howell's deed, Howell can't find it. Gilligan arrests him, the Professor suggests they string him up, putting a noose around his neck, and Howell wakes up screaming.

Howell and Lovey immediately race to Gilligan's hut, wake him, and find the Argentinian sweepstakes ticket pinned above his hammock. When Howell tells Gilligan to tell everyone they're back in the club, Lovey notices that the sweepstakes ticket is two years old, but Howell swears her to secrecy.

The next day while Howell golfs with Gilligan, the radio announces the name of the actual sweepstakes winner. Gilligan, realizing Howell knew all along, calls him a nice guy, infuriating him.

COMMENTS:

- The Howells previously taught Gilligan etiquette and behavior of the wealthy when they adopted him. [Episode 35]

TROPICAL INVENTIONS:

- The Howells' private country club (furnished with lounge chairs)

CASTAWAY QUIZ #41:

Who actually won the Argentinian sweepstakes?
(For answer, see page 359)

42: QUICK BEFORE IT SINKS ⊗

Writers: Stan Burns & Mike Marmer
Director: George M. Cahan

After Gilligan empties lobster traps at the lagoon one morning, the Professor, noticing that the measuring stick he's been using to mark the tide is almost completely submerged, concludes that the island is sinking. The men agree not to panic the women, and when Gilligan walks by on stilts, the Professor suggests that they find the highest ground on the island and secretly build a new hut. Lovey asks the men to help landscape the camp, and the Professor soon finds himself moving a huge boulder at Ginger's instructions for a rock garden.

That night the men, determined to hide news of the impending disaster from the women, stay up all night building a hut. When they return to their huts at dawn, the women wake them to continue landscaping the camp. That night as the Skipper and Gilligan continue building the hut after forty-eight hours without sleep, Howell shows up wearing Lovey's bathrobe, and the Professor informs them that according to his tide marker, the island should be underwater within a week.

The next day the men send Gilligan to tell the women. When Gilligan tells Ginger they have only a few days left on the island, she assumes they're being rescued. After Gilligan tells the Professor and the Skipper about the misunderstanding, Ginger excitedly kisses the Skipper, who explains that the Professor has fixed the transmitter, and Ginger runs to tell the others.

Later that afternoon, the Professor, having rigged a phony transmitter, puts Gilligan under the table, instructing him to disguise his voice as a radio announcer. When the women arrive, the Professor speaks into the transmitter, the Skipper pedals the generator, and Gilligan, assuming a French accent, speaks to the women from under the table. When Gilligan tells Lovey to wear her blue dress to the rescue, Mary Ann steps on Gilligan's foot, exposing him, and the men reveal that the island is sinking. Lovey takes charge; Ginger suggests they build an ark; and Mary Ann suggests they put a hut on top of the raft they built several months ago.

The Professor suggests they test the completed ark while Gilligan stands inside. As the Skipper and the Professor rock the ark, the

furniture slides inside, and Gilligan flies out the ark door. After securing the furniture to the ark floor, the Skipper and Gilligan sit at the table inside while the Professor rocks the ark. As the crew tries to eat from plates that slide back and forth over the table, Gilligan stabs the Skipper with his fork and pours coconut milk over him. When the Skipper and Gilligan lie in their hammocks as the Professor continues rocking the ark, the entire hut collapses.

Gilligan later brings lobsters up from the lagoon, carrying the Professor's measuring stick. When Gilligan explains he's been using the stick to keep his lobster traps from floating away, setting it out farther each day to catch more lobsters, the Skipper and the Professor order him to clean up the collapsed ark.

COMMENTS:

- When the Professor suggests that the men build a hut on the highest point on the island, he overlooks the possibility of building a hut on stilts or in a treetop.
- The Professor, relying solely on a measuring stick (while ignoring the unchanging shoreline) to conclude that the island is sinking, displays astoundingly poor deductive skills and a questionable knowledge of geology.

TROPICAL INVENTIONS:

- Lobster traps
- Gilligan's stilts
- Gilligan's ark

CASTAWAY QUIZ #42:

When the castaways build an ark, what do they name it?

(For answer, see page 359)

43: CASTAWAYS PICTURES PRESENTS ⊗⊗⊗⊗

Writers: Herbert Finn & Alan Dinehart
Director: Jack Arnold

While floating out on a raft in the lagoon, Gilligan tells the Professor and the Skipper he saw a sunken ship about fifteen feet underwater. The Professor suggests that they raise it and sail it back to Hawaii. When the Skipper dives with a mask, he discovers that the boat has no starboard side but sees a couple of crates. The Professor suggests that they start salvaging operations the next morning.

The next day, unable to fit the Skipper into a wet suit, the Professor insists that Gilligan wear it. The women pedal the air pump, feeding air through a vine to Gilligan, who dives alongside the Skipper in his long underwear. While the other men supervise from a raft, Howell falls into the lagoon. When Gilligan later surfaces with his wet suit inflated like a balloon, Howell pops it, sending Gilligan flying across the lagoon.

After raising the crates, the castaways open them, finding silent-movie equipment and theatrical costumes from South Sea Film Productions. The Professor suggests they use the equipment to make a move chronicling the shipwreck and then send it out on a raft where somebody will hopefully find it and send help.

Howell directs the film as Gilligan works the camera. They film a scene in which the Skipper carries each of the castaways out from the lagoon; a scene in which Ginger passionately kisses the Professor for proposing the idea of the movie; a scene depicting the dangers the castaways face every day (Mary Ann encountering a native [Gilligan] who ties her to a stake and dances his dance of death); and a scene in which the Skipper shows the location of the island (in which each of the castaways jumps into the frame to insist upon his own point of reference).

After the Professor prints the film, the castaways project it on a bed sheet by having Gilligan pedal the generator to power the projector. The film is a collection of incoherent scenes printed upside down, in reverse, and double-exposed.

Several days later, while sitting around the communal table listening to the radio, the castaways learn that the film washed ashore, won first prize at the Cannes Film Festival, and anonymously submitted, is guessed to be the work of Ingmar Bergman or Vittorio De Sica, or both.

COMMENTS:

- The Professor could combine the parts from the movie projector and the NASA spacecraft [Episode 40] to build a transmitter.
- The castaways could easily send a note along with the film.

TROPICAL INVENTIONS:

- Pedal-powered air pump
- Pedal-powered movie projector
- The Professor's darkroom

CASTAWAY QUIZ #43:

Who owned South Sea Film Productions?
(For answer, see page 359)

44: AGONIZED LABOR ⊗

Writer: Roland MacLane
Director: Jack Arnold

One night Gilligan and the Skipper learn from the radio that Howell Industry's holdings have collapsed, wiping out the company's entire assets. The next morning the Skipper orders Gilligan to tell the Howells the news, and together they find the Howells on the lagoon, planning the facilities of Howell Oil company. The others try to tell the Howells the news, and finally Gilligan spills the beans.

Later, back in his hut, Howell, determined to pyramid the cash he brought along, learns from the radio that a government lien has been put on all assets of Howell Industries, including any cash Howell happens to have in his possession.

When Mary Ann brings Howell flowers, a bee stings the millionaire. When the Skipper helps Howell fill a pitcher with water from the falls, he accidentally spills the water all over him. When the Professor, who's built Howell a bamboo practice polo-pony, has Howell saddle up, it breaks, and Howell falls off. Later, while reeling in a fish from the lagoon, Ginger and Gilligan unwittingly whack Howell in the face with the fish.

When Lovey finds a suicide note from Howell, the Skipper suggests the castaways search the island. Meanwhile Howell, trying to choose a palatable method of suicide, eliminates the noose, the Wasubi berry, and jumping off a cliff. When Gilligan suddenly sees Howell standing over the cliff, he runs for him, falls over the cliff, and catches hold of a branch. After the Skipper rescues Gilligan, they return to camp with Howell.

When Gilligan tells Howell he'll simply have to get a job upon returning to civilization, the Professor proposes that the other castaways teach the Howells how to earn a living. The Skipper tries to teach Howell how to stoke a furnace, Mary Ann tries to teach Lovey how to sew, and Gilligan tries to teach her how to act. Later the men suggest that the Howells become domestic servants, since the job centers on a familiar lifestyle. That night the Howells host dinner, and as the waiter, Howell showers the castaways with seaweed soup and tossed salad. When Lovey says dinner will be ready shortly, the coconuts she's cooking in their shells explode.

The next day when Mary Ann finds a suicide note from the Howells,

the other castaways run to the cliff with the radio, which broadcasts a vital news correction: Powell Industries, not Howell Industries, went bankrupt.

COMMENTS:

- Lovey previously demonstrated an ability to cook and sew. [Episodes 13 and 25]

TROPICAL INVENTIONS:

- Howell's bamboo practice polo-pony

CASTAWAY QUIZ #44:

What facilities does Howell plan to build on the lagoon after their rescue?
(For answer, see page 359)

45: NYET, NYET—NOT YET ☻☻☻

Writers: Adele T. Strassfield & Bob Riordan
Director: Jack Arnold
Guest Stars: Vincent Beck, Danny Lega

When the Skipper and Gilligan discover a Soviet space capsule on the lagoon, the Soviet cosmonauts paddle to shore and introduce themselves as Ivan and Igor, explain that they've landed on the island by accident, and promise the castaways that the Soviet navy will bring them all to Moscow.

After being fed by the girls and greeted by the Howells, Igor and Ivan recruit the Skipper and Gilligan to help pull their capsule onto shore. That night the Professor, eager to radio for help from the Soviets' capsule, shares his suspicions with the other men that the Soviets (who secretly suspect that the castaways are secret agents from a covert American space program) landed on the island to establish a base. Howell summons Ginger, who goes down to the lagoon, finds Igor alone guarding the capsule, and invites him to join her for a midnight swim on the other side of the island. When Igor follows Ginger, Gilligan and the Professor board the capsule. While the Professor searches for the radio, Gilligan shorts out the capsule's electrical system—in time for the cosmonauts' return.

The next day after the Professor repairs the capsule's console, the cosmonauts contact a Soviet submarine offshore, arranging to be picked up the following morning at eleven o'clock. While the girls pack, Lovey asks them to pack three minks for her, requiring the girls to sit on a suitcase to force it shut. When the suitcase springs open, the mink coats fly across the room.

While wandering through the jungle, Gilligan overhears the cosmonauts plotting to abandon the castaways so their accidental landing will go undiscovered by the West. Igor and Ivan decide to invite the castaways to a celebration, where, using the two bottles of vodka Igor smuggled aboard the ship, they'll drink them under the table and then tie them up.

When Gilligan tells the other men, they send him to fill one of the Soviets' vodka bottles with water. Gilligan swims up behind the capsule, tosses rocks into the jungle to divert the cosmonauts, boards the capsule, empties out a bottle of vodka, fills it with water, and marks it with an X. When the cosmonauts suddenly return, Gilligan distracts

them by throwing another rock into the jungle and then swims away.

That night when the Soviets present two bottles of vodka, the men insist on checking the bottles to make sure they get the marked one. After they all fill their glasses, Igor insists upon the Russian tradition of changing glasses, and after they all do so, the Professor interrupts, insisting upon the American tradition of changing glasses. Sometime later, the men drag the cosmonauts out into the jungle, dismissing Gilligan's suggestion that someone stand guard over the cosmonauts.

When the men show up at the lagoon at eleven o'clock the next morning to find the capsule gone, Gilligan reveals that he set his watch to a Manila radio station (three hours behind). That night while lying in their hammocks and listening to the radio, the Skipper and Gilligan learn that according to Tass, the two Russian cosmonauts were picked up in the Black Sea, eighteen inches from their target area.

COMMENTS:

- Howell never attempts to bribe the Soviets with his millions.
- Oddly, the Professor, who speaks an incredible array of languages, can't understand Russian.
- The castaways could offer the Soviets the NASA spacecraft they found [Episode 40] in return for a trip home.
- The tea urn and a framed photograph of Lenin standing on a table inside the capsule could not endure a space voyage.
- There is no Russian tradition of switching glasses before drinking a toast.

CASTAWAY QUIZ #45:

What's the Soviet space capsule named?

(For answer, see page 359)

46: HI-FI GILLIGAN ☺☺

Writer: Mary C. McCall
Director: Jack Arnold

While Gilligan helps him bring provisions and supplies into a cave in preparation for an approaching typhoon, the Skipper accidentally hits Gilligan in the mouth, causing his jaw to become a radio receiver.

The Professor explains that atmospheric conditions, the shape of Gilligan's skull, and the molar jolted up against a tooth with a silver filling have turned Gilligan into a radio receiver, allowing him to tune in different stations by turning his head. While the Professor listens to the radio for an update on the typhoon, the Skipper brings Gilligan, who's interfering with the reception, to the girls, where he broadcasts their exercise program. When the Professor refuses to allow Lovey to listen to the radio, Howell finds Gilligan for her.

That night the Skipper, unable to fall asleep with Gilligan broadcasting, sends his little buddy outside, where he continues broadcasting, waking the Howells and the girls.

The next day after the Professor learns that the typhoon has passed the tropic of Cancer and is headed to an uninhabited island southwest of Hawaii, Gilligan trips, breaking the castaways' radio and returning his tooth to its normal position.

When the Professor can't fix the radio, Howell suggests they turn Gilligan back into a radio by hitting him in the mouth. Gilligan volunteers, asking the Skipper to hit him in the mouth again, trying to provoke him, but as Gilligan moves his head, the Skipper punches a tree. After Howell sets up a rope trap that will cause a sack of corn to fall, he calls Gilligan but growing impatient, looks out the door, hitting himself in the mouth.

When Gilligan accidentally stumbles, turning himself back into a radio, the Professor learns that the typhoon is headed straight for the island. The castaways move to the cave but can't fit inside with all the supplies. The Professor has the men draw straws to determine which of them will stand outside. Gilligan shortens his straw, and while he stands outside, holding onto a palm tree during the storm, the Skipper, discovering that Gilligan broke his straw in half, joins him. The Professor, claiming to have claustrophobia, joins the Skipper and Gilligan, and one by one the others join Gilligan. While they hold onto the palm tree, lightning strikes the cave, destroying it.

The next day the Professor explains that the electrical storm broke up the typhoon and fixed Gilligan's tooth.

COMMENTS:

- While a punch in the mouth can actually transform a man's head into a radio receiver, an electrical storm cannot break up a typhoon.

CASTAWAY QUIZ #46:

When the men draw straws, who actually gets the shortest straw?
(For answer, see page 359)

47: THE CHAIN OF COMMAND ⊗

Writers: Arnold and Lois Peyser
Director: Leslie Goodwins

Having found a Papuan headdress on the island, Gilligan, the Professor, and the Skipper gather bamboo poles and coconuts (to make
coconut bombs) to prepare against the possible headhunter attack.
When a tree falls next to the Skipper, barely missing him, the Skipper
decides to choose his replacement.

Overlooking Gilligan, the Skipper finds the Professor, who reveals
his plan to build a fort against the headhunters and insists upon
examining all possibilities. Dismayed by the Professor's indecisiveness,
the Skipper meets up with Gilligan, who, demonstrating a long bow he
built, almost shoots him. When the Skipper finds the Howells discussing
what to wear to a capture and learns of Howell's plan to offer the
headhunters ransom money, he disheartenedly leaves, finding Gilligan,
who demonstrates his newly built slingshot. The Skipper finds the girls
using the rolled bandages as curlers in Ginger's hair.

When the Skipper finally chooses Gilligan as his replacement, he
trains him how to act tough, exhibit leadership qualities, and march
his army. The Skipper, explaining that each weapon will be called by
number and each castaway by letter, demonstrates how to call the

castaways to gather weapons. When the Skipper asks Gilligan to take over, Gilligan calls out letters and numbers haphazardly, wreaking havoc. When Gilligan insists that he'd be a more effective leader if the Skipper wasn't observing, the Skipper agrees to go down to the lagoon while Gilligan marches his troops.

When Gilligan searches for the Skipper, he discovers a note from the Skipper, who claims to have been abducted by savages. When Gilligan runs back to camp, the Professor insists on detecting the tides, and Howell declares the note phony. As the Professor and Howell argue, Mary Ann encourages Gilligan to take charge. Gilligan assembles the castaways and orders them to follow his command and search for the Skipper. After marching the castaways through the jungle, Gilligan sets up a trap from a sheet of canvas, orders the Professor to keep lookout from a tree, the Howells to get first aid supplies, and the girls to return to their huts. Gilligan suddenly realizes they've trapped the Skipper. Having discovered that the native headdress was made in Paris and belonged to Lovey, the Skipper disappeared to test Gilligan's leadership qualities.

COMMENTS:

- The Professor once again displays questionable scientific expertise, identifying one of Lovey's hats (clearly labeled "Made in Paris") as a native Papuan headdress.

TROPICAL INVENTIONS:

- Coconut bombs, war clubs, and spears
- A catapult
- Shields and helmets

CASTAWAY QUIZ #47:

What grade did Skinny Mulligan flunk?
(For answer, see page 359)

48: DON'T BUG THE MOSQUITOES ⊗⊗⊗⊗

Writer: Brad Radnitz
Director: Steve Binder
Guest Stars: Les Brown, Jr. & The Wellingtons
(Ed Wade, George Patterson, Kirby Johnson)

When the Skipper and Howell force Gilligan, listening to America's number one rock 'n' roll group, the Mosquitoes, to turn off the radio, they discover the Mosquitoes, who've been dropped off by helicopter, playing their instruments by the lagoon.

The Mosquitoes explain that they've come to the island for rest, and Gilligan introduces them as Bingo, Bango, Bongo, and Irving. Bingo agrees to rescue the castaways—if they'll cooperate. Later while the Mosquitoes practice in the supply hut, Mary Ann and Ginger fawn over the boys, and Lovey, carrying a pair of scissors, chases them into the jungle to cut their hair.

That night after the Mosquitoes give the castaways a concert, Bingo announces that they'll be spending a month on the island. When the dismayed castaways can't understand why Howell's smiling, Lovey explains that he's wearing earplugs.

While trying to fall asleep as the Mosquitoes continue practice, Gilligan tells the Skipper that they'll have to be very quiet if they want the Mosquitoes to stay on the island, inspiring the Skipper, who runs to share his plan with the others. Later the girls raid the Mosquitoes hut and accidentally break Bongo's guitar; the Professor asks to trace Bongo's brain waves while he plays; Gilligan enters with coconuts; Lovey bursts in with a pair of scissors; and finally Howell proclaims himself their new manager. When Bingo announces that they're leaving the next day, the castaways dance from the hut.

The next morning the Skipper and Gilligan, unable to find the Mosquitoes, run to tell the Howells, causing Lovey to faint. When they finally find the Mosquitoes rehearsing, Bingo explains that after last night's tense scene, the Mosquitoes need to stay on the island for at least two months to unwind. That night while the Mosquitoes practice and Howell discusses the Mosquitoes' temperaments with the crew, Gilligan says entertainers like entertainers, inspiring the millionaire.

The next day when Ginger confirms that all groups want an opening act, the men decide to form their own band. Ginger outfits Gilligan in drainpipe pants with an alligator-skin vest, Lovey brings him a wig, and the Professor brings him drums. The costumed men, playing an indiscernible song on the castaways' stage, alienate the Mosquitoes. When Gilligan tells Ginger to "never criticize anybody else unless you can do better yourself," he inadvertently inspires her. Later at the stage when the three women sing "You Need Us" as the Honeybees, the Mosquitoes happen by and enjoy their performance.

The next day while the castaways pack, the Professor reads a note from the Mosquitoes, who, threatened by the Honeybees' talent, left that morning when their helicopter came by with provisions. So they'll be no hard feelings, the Mosquitoes left behind one of their albums.

"YOU NEED US"

As sung by the Honeybees

(Ginger Grant, Lovey Howell, and Mary Ann Summers)

ALL THREE: You need us, you need us.
Like a clam needs a shell.
Like a prisoner needs a cell.
Like a dingdong needs a bell.
You need us.

GINGER: You need me, you need me.
Like a picture needs a star.
Like a golfer needs a par.
Like a teenager needs a car.
You need me.

MARY ANN: You need me, you need me.
Like a baby needs a toy.
Like wire needs a buoy.
Like a girl needs a boy.
You need me.

LOVEY: You need me, you need me.
Like a diamond needs a ring.
Like a harp needs a string.
Like a queen needs a king.
You need me.

ALL THREE: You need us, you need us.
Like a bee needs a buzz.
Like a peach needs its fuzz.
So that's why you need us.
Buzzzzz.

COMMENTS:

- The Mosquitoes play their electric guitars at astoundingly high volumes considering they don't have amplifiers or electricity.
- Howell could offer the Mosquitoes large sums of money, their own record company, or a variety of lucrative rewards in exchange for an immediate rescue.

TROPICAL INVENTIONS:

- The Professor's coconut headphones
- Bamboo drums and guitars
- Four Beatle wigs

CASTAWAY QUIZ #48:

What album do the Mosquitoes leave behind for the castaways?

(For answer, see page 359)

49: GILLIGAN GETS BUGGED ⊗

Writers: Jack Gross, Jr. & Michael R. Stein
Director: Gary Nelson

When the Skipper finds Gilligan building a bathtub from bamboo, a strange bug lands on the back of Gilligan's neck, and after the Skipper swats it with a palm frond, Gilligan can't say whether it bit him.

From the Skipper's description the Professor identifies the bug as the deadly Mantis Carni, explaining that if bitten, Gilligan only has twenty-four hours to live. He suggests they watch Gilligan to see if he exhibits the symptoms: aches and pains in the joints, loss of appetite, and severe itching. After the Skipper finds Gilligan (who's been kneeling and has hit himself in the hand with the hammer) holding his thumb and complaining of aches in his knees, he sends Mary Ann and Ginger with a coconut cream pie to see if Gilligan has an appetite. When the girls find Gilligan (who, unbeknownst to them, just finished eating a bunch of bananas), he insists he's not hungry and accidentally drops the pie on the ground. Ants, attracted to the pie, crawl up Gilligan's legs, and the Howells, sent to observe Gilligan by the Skipper, find him scratching.

At Lovey's suggestion the castaways decide to throw a party for Gilligan. That night at the party as Gilligan lights the candles on his cake, the castaways, rising to sing, start crying and leave the table. The next day the Professor explains that although he doesn't have the proper ingredients, he can synthesize an antidote using chemicals found on the island: calcium carbonate (from clam shells), cellulose sulfide (mustard plants), and ferric nitrate (papaya roots).

While the Professor works in his hut, Gilligan volunteers to help, accidentally breaking a bowl and knocking over a table. The Professor reveals that someone on the island is sick and refusing to reveal whom, asks Gilligan to help the Skipper with the clam shells. Gilligan finds the Skipper wearing gloves, facial netting, and grinding up clam shells. A bug suddenly bites the Skipper, and when Gilligan confirms its identity, the Skipper tells him they both have less than twenty-four hours to live, and they both run back to camp. Meanwhile Ginger and Mary Ann, wearing netting and searching for papaya roots, get stung and run back to the Professor. Then the Howells, wearing protective netting and searching for mustard plants, both get bitten by the bug and run back to camp.

The castaways all beg the Professor for the serum he hasn't yet synthesized (since they've yet to bring him the ingredients). While the castaways sit mournfully around the communal table, the Professor comes out of his hut with a bug on his arm and asks if it's the bug that bit them. The Professor, who's attracted the bug with sugar, explains that he's been bitten a number of times because this particular branch of the Mantis family is not poisonous.

When the Skipper finds Gilligan taking a bath in his finished tub, the bug lands on Gilligan's neck, flies off, and dies in mid-flight—exactly twenty-four hours after first biting Gilligan.

COMMENTS:

- You can obtain calcium carbonate from clam shells, ferric nitrate from papaya root, and cellulose sulfide from mustard plants, but since a poisonous insect called the Mantis Carni does not exist, a serum made from these ingredients wouldn't serve any purpose.
- The Professor, claiming to be taking the scientific approach, attracts the Mantis Carni to bite his arm several times to "prove" it's not the poisonous species.

TROPICAL INVENTIONS:

- Gilligan's bathtub
- The Professor's laboratory

CASTAWAY QUIZ #49:

What does the Mantis Carni look like?
According to the Professor, how many species are in the Mantis family?
(For answers, see page 359)

50: MINE HERO ⊗⊗

Writers: David Braverman & Bob Marcus
Director: Wilbur D'Arcy

While the Skipper builds a raft, Gilligan, fishing on the lagoon, reels in a World War II mine. When he sets down his fishing rod and runs to get the Skipper, the fishing pole falls over and activates the mine. Unable to arouse the Skipper's interest, Gilligan finds the Howells playing badminton and tells them about the mine. Thinking Gilligan's discovered a valuable mine, Howell swears him to secrecy and draws up partnership papers.

Meanwhile the Professor, planning to melt down the castaways' metals to make an anchor for the raft he and the Skipper plan to launch, sends the girls off to gather their metals and jewelry. After Gilligan refuses to give Mary Ann his metal four-leaf clover charm, Ginger fails to seduce it from him.

When the Professor informs the men that there's not enough metal to forge an anchor, Gilligan brings them to his iron mine, which the Skipper immediately recognizes as a World War II mine. When the Professor realizes it's ticking, they all panic and run back to camp, trampling Gilligan, who then runs through the girls' hut and out their back wall.

Claiming that the mine's explosion could trigger a chain reaction with the natural gases on the island, the Professor volunteers to deactivate it. After the Skipper sends the women to the other side of the island, the Professor demagnetizes himself before approaching the mine, which he explains may be magnetized and equipped with a delayed-timing device.

When Gilligan runs to help the Professor, his lucky charm is suddenly attracted to the mine. When Howell runs to help Gilligan, his watch is pulled toward the mine. Suddenly they're both drawn to the mine, unable to pull themselves free. The Professor, deciding to

219

"neutralize the magnetic field by crossing the mine's electromagnetic waves with ultra-high-frequency waves," runs to get the radio.

The Professor returns and tries to locate the right radio frequency while Howell and Gilligan try to pry themselves free—which they succeed in doing when the Skipper grabs the radio and shakes it. Placing his lucky charm aside, Gilligan crawls under the mine with a brass wrench to loosen the fitting, tunnels under the mine, and crawls out from the other side. After the Professor admits that he can't make a lubricant to dissolve the rust surrounding the fitting, Gilligan suggests they hurl the mine away with a giant slingshot, inspiring the Professor, who suggests they use the raft to tow the mine out to sea. As the Professor and the Skipper are about to decide which of them will tow the mine out to sea, Howell tells them he saw Gilligan running to the lagoon. When the Skipper and the Professor find Gilligan paddling the raft, they urge him to cut the line, since the raft's attracting the mine, and Gilligan sends the mine out to sea as he paddles back up on the beach.

As the castaways cheer for Gilligan, the mine floats back into the lagoon, where it suddenly explodes, sending a shower of fish up on the beach.

COMMENTS:

- The castaways have more than enough metal to forge an anchor: they have a trunkful of cannonballs [Episode 16], the remaining parts of a Mars spacecraft [Episode 40], and a silent-movie projector [Episode 43].
- A World War II mine does not have enough magnetic force to attract Gilligan and Howell by their jewelry against the pull of their weight.
- Magnetic waves cannot be neutralized with ultra-high-frequency waves from a transistor radio.

TROPICAL INVENTIONS:

- The Professor's clamshell bellows
- The Professor's sand timer
- The Howell's badminton net, rackets, and shuttlecock

CASTAWAY QUIZ #50:

Who is Ginger's favorite movie star?
(For answer, see page 359)

51: ERIKA TIFFANY SMITH TO THE RESCUE ☺☺

Writer: David P. Harmon
Director: Jack Arnold
Guest Stars: Zsa Zsa Gabor, Michael Whitney

After her private boat drops her off at the lagoon, wealthy socialite Erika Tiffany Smith bumps into the Skipper, who explains how the castaways were marooned. When Gilligan introduces himself, Erika explains that she's looking for a desert island on which to build a luxury hotel. Gilligan runs to tell the others, and as the Howells recall making Erika's acquaintance, the Skipper escorts her over. While the Skipper runs to get Erika a fan, Howell discusses Erika's plan to buy the island to build a resort hotel. When the Professor and Mary Ann introduce themselves, Erika takes an interest in the Professor.

After Gilligan tells Ginger the news, Ginger, seeking Erika, finds the lovelorn Skipper, who asks her advice on how to win Erika's affections.

When Ginger suggests poetry, the Skipper practices reciting his naval poems. Meanwhile the Professor and Erika stroll around the island exchanging compliments. When she asks him what his plans are upon returning to the United States, he tells her he wants someone by his side to do research—which Erika misinterprets as romantic interest.

When Gilligan later finds the Professor reflecting, the Professor confides that Erika has been hinting that she'll finance his research lab so he can study the mating cycle of the angleworm. When Gilligan suggests that he simply ask her directly, the Professor finds Erika with Howell (agreeing to buy the island at whatever price he asks). When the Professor announces that he has a question to ask Erika, she accepts what she tells Howell is the Professor's marriage proposal.

Erika asks the Skipper to captain her private yacht, and he agrees if Gilligan can be his first mate. Later while strolling together, Erika talks romantically while the Professor waxes scientific. When the Professor later asks Ginger for advice, she tries to teach him how to kiss.

Meanwhile Erika agrees to buy the island if Howell tells the Professor that she can't marry him. While Erika returns to her yacht, promising to send a ship to pick up the castaways in two hours, Howell explains the situation to the Professor, relieving him. As the castaways pack, an electrical storm flares up, and the Skipper sends Gilligan to the lagoon to look for Erika's ship, which doesn't show.

Three days later, after the storm's passed, the castaways wait at the lagoon. Later the radio broadcasts an interview with Erika Tiffany Smith, who tells all about the castaways. The navy, however, can't decode her logbook, which, written in English translated from Hungarian, fails to detail the island's longitude and latitude.

COMMENTS:

- The sailor who brought Erika to the island should know its whereabouts. "Actually, that particular sailor had a coronary and died, if you want to know the underlying truth," explains creator Sherwood Schwartz.

CASTAWAY QUIZ #51:

How many hours a day does the Professor spend cataloging the flora and fauna on the island?

(For answer, see page 359)

52: NOT GUILTY ⊗⊗

Writer: Roland MacLane
Director: Stanley Z. Cherry

After Gilligan, fishing on the lagoon, reels in a crate containing coconuts wrapped in pages of a Honolulu newspaper, the Skipper finds a story claiming that one of the castaways murdered Randolph Blake immediately before setting sail on the *Minnow.*

Suspecting the Professor, Gilligan and the Skipper find him in his hut having just invented a guillotine to chop coconuts, and frightened, the Skipper and Gilligan quickly excuse themselves. When Gilligan suggests they warn Ginger and Mary Ann, they find the girls brewing poison to get rid of the mice around their hut. "And if it works," adds Mary Ann, "we're going to try to get rid of some other horrible creatures around here too." That night as the Skipper combs the newspaper story for another clue, he learns that the killer used a spear gun. At Gilligan's prompting, they search the Howells' hut, where the Skipper finds a gun. Gilligan wakes the Howells, and as the crew leaves, the Skipper accidentally drops the news clipping.

As the Skipper and Gilligan try to fall asleep, each convinces himself that the other is the murderer, and they wake up the next morning sitting in chairs on opposite sides of the hut, holding huge clubs. Meanwhile the Howells find the newspaper clipping, run to the Professor, discover his guillotine, and leave. When Ginger and Mary Ann find the newspaper article, they run to the Professor's hut and hand him the newspaper article before noticing his guillotine. After reading the clipping, the Professor asks the girls to pledge not to be suspicious, and when they agree, the remaining castaways, hiding in the Professor's hut, agree as well.

That night around the communal table, the Professor admits that he knew Randolph Blake and prior to the cruise, confronted him for claiming authorship of his Marine Biology paper. Howell admits that prior to the cruise he had a heated argument with Blake, who, managing the only store in the Howell chain losing money, was embezzling. Ginger admits that she had a date with Blake the night before they sailed, and when he told her he was engaged to be married, she angrily slapped his face. Mary Ann admits that Blake was from her hometown, where he forced her father into bankruptcy, and she told him off before the cruise.

At Gilligan's suggestion, the Professor insists they reenact the crime. After setting up their hut as Randolph Blake's Boating Equipment Store, complete with a bamboo cash register and spear gun, the Skipper orders Gilligan to act the part of Blake.

As Gilligan stands behind the counter and the Skipper hides beneath, the Howells enter, accuse Blake of theft, and return to use the phone in their car. The Professor enters, accuses Blake of literary theft, threatens to cancel Blake's subscription to Scientific Quarterly, and exits. Ginger walks in, kisses Blake, and when he shuns her, she adamantly refuses to ever date him again. Finally Mary Ann enters, confronts him, cries, and runs out. When the Skipper insists they repeat the reenactment, Gilligan slams the door, causing the spear gun to fire itself, pinning his coat to a bamboo post. The Skipper realizes Blake was killed by accident.

Later while lying in their hammocks and listening to the radio, Gilligan and the Skipper learn that the authorities determined that Blake's murder was an accident. When the Skipper has Gilligan close the door, the spear gun falls, firing a spear that snaps one of his hammock's supporting ropes.

SURVIVORS OF THE *MINNOW* SOUGHT IN BLAKE MURDER CASE

HONOLULU—Survivors of the *S.S. Minnow*, which left Honolulu immediately after the murder, are being sought for questioning. All other suspects have been cleared, and it is believed that one of the seven missing persons aboard the *Minnow* is the killer.

COMMENTS:

- The odds of four people who don't know each other having a common enemy who they each confront the night before sailing on a charter boat are even more remote than the chances of fishing a crate from the ocean that contains a copy of the newspaper article reporting that individual's murder.

TROPICAL INVENTIONS:

- The Professor's guillotine
- Ginger and Mary Ann's mouse poison
- The Professor's spear gun

CASTAWAY QUIZ #52:

What do Ginger and Mary Ann make poison from?
(For answer, see page 359)

53: YOU'VE BEEN DISCONNECTED ☺☺☺

Writer: Elroy Schwartz
Director: Jack Arnold

While looking for turtle eggs after a storm, Gilligan finds a long cable washed to shore and calls for the Skipper and the Professor, who recognize it as a telephone line, explaining that they can telephone for help.

After digging up the cable, the Skipper orders Gilligan to tell the others. Meanwhile while listening to the radio in her hut, Ginger learns that Hollywood producers are currently casting for a movie tentatively titled *The Ginger Grant Story*.

After the Skipper suggests that they break the line to force the phone company to send a repair crew, the Professor insists they tap into the line and build a telephone receiver with parts from the radio. After the Skipper breaks the hacksaw's last blade trying to cut into the cable, the Professor sends Gilligan to get Lovey's diamond necklace. Meanwhile Ginger is writing down her recollections of everything that's happened on the island since the shipwreck for the movie.

Back at the lagoon the Professor has Gilligan pedal a chain saw he's made from the diamond necklace to cut through the cable's casing, but without a motor they're unable to build up enough friction. At Gilligan's suggestion the Professor decides to burn through the cable by building a blowtorch. The Skipper digs for natural gas, hits a main, and fills a bottle with gas. When Gilligan uncorks the bottle, takes a whiff, and falls to the ground, the Skipper absentmindedly breathes from the bottle, falling to the ground. While the Professor burns through the cable, Gilligan inadvertently leans against the torch, scorches his behind, and jumps into the lagoon.

Explaining that the cable carries two thousand calls, the Professor hooks two wires to a conch-shell speaker, tapping into a Portuguese conversation. While the Professor boils down sap from a rubber tree to make a dialing mechanism, Gilligan sticks his hands in the glue, making gloves. After the Professor connects his receiver and dialing mechanism to the cable wires, Mary Ann dials a random number, interrupting a call between a couple, causing the female party to think her boyfriend is seeing another woman and to hang up. After dialing random numbers for three hours, Gilligan and Mary Ann are finally answered by a couple, who, busy kissing, simply take the receiver off the hook and hang it up again.

While the Skipper helps the Professor separate various wires, using colored vines to determine which wires will reach the United States, Gilligan runs from the jungle into the wires. After Gilligan telephones the St. Louis Bijou movie theater, learns what's playing, and gets disconnected, he reaches the San Diego operator and explains their situation, but the disbelieving operator disconnects him. A storm suddenly breaks, and the castaways run for shelter.

The next day, discovering that the telephone cable has been pulled back out to sea, the Skipper and the Professor explain that the bare telephone wires, exposed to the salt water, will eventually corrode, requiring the telephone company to send out a repair crew in a few months. When Gilligan admits that he covered the wires with the Professor's rubber glue, the other castaways force Gilligan to dive repeatedly into the lagoon, searching for the cable.

COMMENTS:

- We never learn anything more about Hollywood's plans for *The Ginger Grant Story.*
- The Professor should have had the foresight to secure the cable to the island.

TROPICAL INVENTIONS:

- The Professor's pedal-powered chain saw (using the bicycle pump and Lovey's diamond necklace)
- The Professor's blowtorch
- The Professor's telephone receiver and dial

CASTAWAY QUIZ #53:

What foreign languages does Lovey speak?
What foreign languages does Howell speak?
(For answers, see page 359)

54: THE POSTMAN COMETH ⊗

Writers: Herbert Finn & Alan Dinehart
Director: Leslie Goodwins

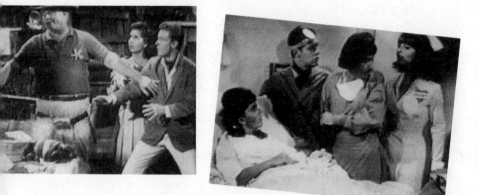

After Gilligan tosses a bottle into the lagoon containing a note from Mary Ann to her boyfriend (which she writes every week), Gilligan wanders back to camp, where he finds the Skipper pedaling the generator to recharge the radio's batteries. When Gilligan turns on the radio, he learns that Mary Ann's boyfriend, Horace Higgenbothem, a native of Horner's Corners, Kansas, got married.

The men send Gilligan to tell Mary Ann, who, busy cooking, turns on the radio to listen to a soap opera, *Old Doctor Young.* When Gilligan approaches, he listens to the soap opera from the edge of the jungle, gets absorbed in the story, and returns to the other men. The Professor decides to tell Mary Ann but ends up informing her that the mushrooms she's cooking may be poisonous, advising her to get rid of them.

Ginger advises the men not to tell Mary Ann, explaining that she needs another man to take her mind off Horace, volunteering to show them how to romance Mary Ann. Lovey shows Gilligan how to woo a woman; Howell tries to teach the Skipper to recite poetry; and Ginger practices the art of romance with the Professor.

Gilligan, dressed and acting like Charles Boyer, brings Mary Ann flowers in her hut; the Skipper, dressed and acting like Matt Dillon, follows with more flowers; and the Professor, dressed and acting like Cary Grant, follows with more flowers, provoking a fight with the other men. Mary Ann runs to the Howells, who tell her to return to her hut to calm them, and as she's about to go back inside, she overhears the Professor, the Skipper, and Gilligan talking and thinks she's dying from the mushrooms she ate. When Mary Ann tells the Skipper and Gilligan that she overheard their conversation, they tell the Howells, and reveling in the news, the Howells suggest they throw a party, upsetting Mary Ann.

That night Mary Ann dreams she's in a hospital bed where a nurse (Lovey) tells her she has a fatal disease. Dr. Zorba Gillespie (Howell) enters, and when Mary Ann asks for old Doctor Young (or young Doctor Young), he tells her they're flying in three surgeons. Dr. Boyer (Gilligan) enters and diagnoses Mary Ann as dead; Doc Dillon (the Skipper) enters, followed by Dr. Cary Grant (the Professor), who diagnoses her as suffering from Roomus Degloomus, which, he claims, translates to "mushrooms." A nurse (Ginger) enters, leads the men to the sinks to scrub up before surgery, and reveals a tray of surgical instruments.

As Ginger tries to calm her, Mary Ann wakes up, finding Ginger shaking her and the men standing by her side. When Mary Ann tells them she's dying from the mushrooms, the Professor admits that the mushrooms weren't poisonous, and Gilligan explains that they were trying to romance her to take her mind off Horace Higgenbothem, who, he reveals, married someone else. Mary Ann admits that she never actually had a boyfriend. Envious of Ginger, she was merely sending letters to make everyone think she had someone back home. At noon when Mary Ann asks Gilligan and the Skipper what they're preparing for lunch, the Skipper jokingly says mushrooms.

COMMENTS:

- The Skipper's holster, gun, cowboy hat, and sheriff's badge could have come from the crate of costumes that the castaways found. [Episode 43]

TROPICAL INVENTIONS:

- Pedal-powered battery recharger

CASTAWAY QUIZ #54:

Whom did Horace Higgenbothem marry?
(For answer, see page 359)

55: SEER GILLIGAN ⊗⊗⊗

Writer: Elroy Schwartz
Director: Leslie Goodwins

When the Skipper finds Gilligan building a birdhouse, Gilligan begins answering the Skipper's questions before he can ask, reading his mind. Convinced that Gilligan can read his mind, the Skipper brings him to the other castaways, where Gilligan reads the Professor's, Mary Ann's, and Ginger's minds. Howell tries to figure out Gilligan's secret (to help him make more money), and when Lovey suggests Gilligan ate something that disagrees with him, Howell eats with Gilligan, giving himself a stomachache.

While Ginger tries to psychoanalyze him, Gilligan offers her some sunflower seeds. After eating the seeds, Ginger reads Gilligan's mind,  and realizing these are no ordinary sunflower seeds, they find the Skipper and the Professor arguing whether Gilligan can actually read minds. When Ginger reveals that the Skipper and the Professor are both thinking about her figure, she displays the sunflower seeds, which, according to the Professor's book on rare tropical plants, are from a plant that became extinct three centuries ago. According to legend, these seeds were used by prehistoric tribes to induce mental telepathy.

That night Gilligan, woken by the Skipper, sleepily agrees to bring him to the bush in the morning. Independently, Howell and Ginger later wake Gilligan to secure the same agreement.

The next morning, Gilligan brings each castaway a bag of seeds, which they immediately consume. While Gilligan later helps the Skipper, he accidentally pushes him through a hut wall, and reading each other's mind, the Skipper and Gilligan learn each other's sinister thoughts. Ginger and Mary Ann, able to read each other's mind, wind up insulting each other, and Howell ends up walking out on Lovey. The Professor tells Gilligan that he thought the seeds would be a good idea but reading Gilligan's mind, learns that Gilligan disagrees; Mary Ann thinks Ginger doesn't do her share of the work; the Professor and Howell blame the shipwreck on the Skipper. Overhearing the castaways fighting among themselves, Gilligan sets the bush on fire.

That night after the Skipper lists Gilligan's chores for the next day, Gilligan tells the Skipper it's a good thing he can't read his mind.

COMMENTS:

• Plants with seeds that induce mental telepathy do not exist.

CASTAWAY QUIZ #55:

What plant do these mind-reading seeds come from?
(For answer, see page 359)

56: LOVE ME, LOVE MY SKIPPER ⊗

Writers: Herbert Finn & Alan Dinehart
Director: Tony Leader

While delivering invitations to the annual Howell Cotillion, Howell bumps into a tree, dropping one of the invitations. After Gilligan finds his invitation under the door of his hut, the Skipper, unable to find his invitation, discovers that the Professor's been invited and later finds Ginger trying to choose a dress to wear to the Howells' party. When the Skipper can't figure out why he wasn't invited, Gilligan refuses to attend the party. The Professor, Ginger, and Mary Ann suddenly enter, announcing they too refuse to attend the party without the Skipper. The Professor suggests they throw a costume party in honor of the Skipper.

Lovey finds the RSVP notes and learns that the others have been invited to another party—to which the Howells haven't been invited. The Howells console each other, and when Lovey wonders what Howell did to offend the other castaways, she insults him, and he refuses to attend her cotillion.

Meanwhile the Skipper prepares his pirate costume for his party. When Gilligan walks through the jungle to the supply hut to look for a costume, he trips and falls, accidentally finding the Skipper's lost invitation. When the Skipper relays his apologies to Lovey, she thanks him for allowing her to see Howell in his true light. Meanwhile Gilligan apologizes to Howell, who, using the supply hut as a Harvard Club annex, stubbornly refuses to return to his wife.

The Professor suggests that the other castaways try to reunite the Howells, and Ginger outlines a plan. She invites Lovey to the Skipper's party, coaxing her by offering to let her wear her Oriental-dancing-girl costume. Meanwhile Mary Ann invites Howell, who refuses to attend. Later while Howell mixes a martini, Ginger seductively entices him to agree to attend the party to dance with her, telling him that she'll be dressed as Marie Antoinette. Ginger returns to her hut and tells Mary Ann to raise the hem on the dancing-girl costume. Later when Lovey tells Ginger that the Oriental-dancing-girl costume is too short, Ginger suggests they switch costumes.

That night at the party, Gilligan, dressed as Tarzan, swings from a vine, crashing into the table and through the wall of his hut. While the castaways attend to Gilligan, Howell comes through the clearing dressed as the Blue Boy, sees who he thinks is Ginger dressed as Marie Antoinette, and starts dancing with her. Howell keeps stepping on her feet, and when he explains that he can't dance with anyone but his wife, Lovey reveals herself and forgives him. When the Skipper and Ginger try to cut in, the Howells insist that all their dances are taken.

The next morning Gilligan tells the Skipper how much he loves parties, but when the Skipper orders him to clean up the mess, Gilligan expresses his hatred for parties.

COMMENTS:

- The castaways could have salvaged the costumes from the trunk of silent-movie camera equipment that once washed ashore. [Episode 43]

TROPICAL INVENTIONS:

- The Professor's food preservative (made from sodium nitrate and calcium carbonate)
- Costumes

CASTAWAY QUIZ #56:

What costume does the Professor wear to the party?
(For answer, see page 359)

57: GILLIGAN'S LIVING DOLL ☺☺☺

Writer: Bob Stevens
Director: Leslie Goodwins
Guest Star: Bob D'Arcy

When Gilligan stops doing the laundry to look for his rabbit's foot, he and the Skipper see someone parachuting to the island. While searching the island for the parachutist, Gilligan wanders into a robot, which mimics everything he says. The Professor speculates that the air force, putting the robot through a survival test, will eventually come looking for it.

Quizzing the robot, the Professor discovers that it was launched from Hickam Field, Hawaii, on a radiation-detection flight destined for Vandenberg Air Force Base. He soon decodes the robot's schematic and programs it to perform all the unpleasant tasks on the island. When the Skipper orders the robot to do the laundry, Gilligan wanders by, looking for his rabbit's foot. When Mr. Howell leads the robot away to caddy for Lovey and himself, Gilligan searches through the washing machine. When the Skipper orders the robot to finish the laundry, the robot shoves Gilligan into the washing machine and starts pedaling— until the Skipper and Howell stop him.

While the Howells golf, the robot mathematically calculates how Lovey should putt. Later the castaways learn from the radio that since the robot was accidentally ejected from a plane by remote control, the authorities have decided to call off the search. At Gilligan's suggestion the Professor reprograms the robot and orders it to build the boat it says it's programmed to build in seventeen hours four minutes eleven seconds. The next day when the men arrive at the lagoon with their suitcases, they discover that the robot's built a small model of a three-masted schooner.

Howell orders the robot to build a carrier from steel. Lovey orders the robot to build a bridge to Hawaii, which the robot replies will require eighty-nine years four months. Howell orders the robot to build a searchlight, which the robot responds is not possible without electricity. Later that night when Ginger seductively promises to introduce the robot to women robots, he starts steaming. The next day Gilligan suggests they have the robot build a radio station.

After the Skipper realizes they could teach the robot to swim to Hawaii, Gilligan tries to teach the robot how to maneuver its arms to

236

237

swim—without any success—until he decides to teach the robot the dog paddle. The next morning at dawn, the Professor, the Skipper, and Gilligan bring the robot to the lagoon to secretly test its ability to swim. When the Professor orders the robot to swim out twenty yards and return, it walks into the lagoon, sinks to the bottom, and then walks back out, still able to recite the castaways' prerecorded SOS. When Gilligan suggests the robot walk to Hawaii, the Skipper calls the plan preposterous—until the Professor concurs with Gilligan. After the Professor programs the robot to walk to Hawaii, he explains that the journey should take one-hundred-eleven hours. The robot will stay on course because it has sonar to avoid undersea obstacles, and an automatic pilot to get back on course. Still, the Professor admits that the robot could hit an underwater mine or get tangled in a fishing net. The castaways sing farewell as the robot walks into the lagoon.

A few days later, while listening to the radio, the castaways learn that the robot made it to Hawaii, but when scientists checked the robot's voice, the castaways' message was scrambled. Gilligan's rabbit's foot, found inside the robot, demagnetized the receptor spools.

COMMENTS:

- Oddly, the robot was programmed to build small model boats and aircraft carriers, but nothing in between.
- While the robot spends seventeen hours building a boat, none of the castaways look in on it.
- Since the castaways possess the *Minnow*'s generator, a Mars spaceprobe [Episode 40], and a silent-movie camera and projector [Episode 43], the robot could build a radio transmitter from the assorted parts. Failing that, the Professor could build a radio transmitter from these devices and parts from the robot.

CASTAWAY QUIZ #57:

What's the robot's model number?
(For answer, see page 359)

58: FORWARD MARCH ⊗

Writer: Jack Raymond
Director: Jerry Hopper
Guest Star: Janos Prohaska

When Gilligan offers the Skipper an avocado that just landed in the bushes, the Skipper recognizes it as a grenade, and they run before it explodes. While the men try to decide on a course of action, Howell suggests they surrender with a white flag. While the men debate the merits of Howell's suggestion, Gilligan asks Lovey for a white flag—not realizing that the men have dismissed the idea. When Ginger volunteers to capture the enemy by seducing him, the Professor insists that her capture will only create more problems. As Lovey sends off Gilligan with one of Howell's white shirts, the Skipper tells him they've changed the plan.

After another grenade suddenly explodes nearby, the men concentrate on defense. When the Professor, pointing to a map of the island drawn on a blackboard, suggests they scout the island, Howell, insisting that he's commanding general of the armed forces, appoints the Professor chief of intelligence and the Skipper secretary of the navy. When they leave to scout the island, Howell marches Private Gilligan. After Mary Ann and Lovey, dressed as nurses, make the beds of the base hospital (the Howells' hut), Howell sends for Ginger, who, as head of the USO, enters, and takes off her spy coat to reveal a tight bodysuit.

When the Skipper and the Professor return empty-handed, they find Howell commanding Gilligan, who fires a peashooter, missing the target and hitting the Skipper. Suddenly gunfire blazes through, and the men all hit the ground. Unscathed and still not seeing anyone, the Professor and the Skipper decide to continue their search. Howell,

noticing that Gilligan has been wounded by his tiepin, orders him to report to the hospital, where Lovey and Mary Ann examine him. While they run off to prepare the bandages, Ginger sings "It Had to Be You" to Gilligan.

The Professor and the Skipper return with a fully loaded machine gun they found lying in the brush. While the men theorize over their unseen enemy's motives, Gilligan spots a gorilla who pulls the pin from a grenade and throws it at them. Howell instinctively fires the machine gun into the sky, scaring off the gorilla. Gilligan runs to see if the gorilla is all right and returns with several wounded coconuts.

After finding the gorilla in a cave, the Professor explains that the gorilla is probably imitating soldiers he saw using the weapons. The men find a small entrance at the back of the cave, dig the opening wide, and send Gilligan inside, where he finds two boxes of grenades. Given a vine and instructed to tug on it when he's tied it around the boxes, Gilligan, suddenly encountering the gorilla, impulsively tugs the vine, causing the Professor and the Skipper to pull out the gorilla.

After the Professor explains that the gorilla is a rare breed that can be stared into immobility, Gilligan voluntarily stands before the gorilla, mesmerizing him. While the Professor and the Skipper sneak behind the gorilla toward the cave, Gilligan swats at a fly buzzing in his face, breaking the trance. The Professor and the Skipper return to the jungle, but the gorilla captures Gilligan, carrying him off.

The Professor and the Skipper, following the sound of explosions, find Gilligan and the ape throwing grenades over the lagoon. After exhausting the grenades, Gilligan hands the gorilla a remaining red disk, which the gorilla throws over the lagoon, creating an enormous mushroom cloud on the horizon.

Later as Howell awards Gilligan with the Order of the Diamond Cufflink, the gorilla throws a coconut cream pie (that Mary Ann had left behind a rock as a surprise) at Gilligan.

COMMENTS:

- We never learn how the explosives got on the island.
- The Professor's claim that the gorilla is a rare breed that can be stared into immobility is unfounded.

TROPICAL INVENTIONS:

- A chalkboard (stone slate on a bamboo easel) and chalk
- A hospital base
- A bamboo bunk bed

CASTAWAY QUIZ #58:

How does the Skipper like his steak?
(For answer, see page 359)

59: SHIP AHOAX ☺☺☺

Writers: Charles Tannen & George O'Hanlon
Director: Leslie Goodwins

Fearing that the castaways are being driven closer to island madness, the Professor overhears the Skipper and Gilligan, who've painted a line down the middle of their hut, fighting. Ordered to rid their hut of the other castaways' suitcases, Gilligan returns suitcases to the Howells and the girls, who are fighting in their respective huts. When Gilligan

sits down with Ginger, who's fortune-reading with a deck of cards, Ginger holds up a card and noticing a pot of flowers beginning to rattle on her shelf, predicts a terrible earthquake, which suddenly occurs. As Gilligan runs to tell the others, Ginger laughs knowingly. When Ginger later explains the trick to the Professor, he persuades her to convince the others that a ship is coming, to prevent island madness.

Later when the castaways, sulking around the communal table, discover that the radio is broken, the Professor, promising to repair it in time for the six o'clock news, returns to his hut with Ginger. He reconnects the one wire he disconnected so Ginger can listen to the news to "predict" the six o'clock news. When Ginger returns to the others and predicts the evening news, they refuse to believe she has psychic powers—until they hear the six o'clock news.

That night Ginger, reading a crystal ball at the castaways' stage, sees seven people on an island and several large ships with the words "Rescue Mission" written on their sides. When a radio broadcast suddenly announces that one hundred ships will search for the *U.S.S. York* in the same area that claimed the *S.S. Minnow*, the castaways congratulate Ginger, who faints.

The next morning after Gilligan hands him a flyer announcing Ginger's fortune-telling business, the Professor finds Ginger alone in her hut and chastises her for falling for her own act. But before he can stop her, Gilligan comes in and asks to have his fortune told, chasing out the Professor.

Later that afternoon the Howells, having invited Ginger to their hut for tea, tell her how close they've grown to her and present her with two of Lovey's furs—in return for the prices one hour before the stock market opens when they return to civilization. After Gilligan beckons them to listen to the radio news, the castaways learn that the rescue ships, having found the *York,* are returning home. The Professor explains that Ginger told him earlier about the *York's* rescue and promises to give the exact time and day of their rescue that night.

While the Professor tries to convince Ginger to continue her act, Gilligan, eager to have his fortune told, accidentally breaks the crystal ball; the Professor, however, insists that Ginger can predict the future with a séance.

That night when Ginger, seated with the others at a table on the stage, summons the spirits to make the table rise, the Professor, sitting underneath, raises and lowers the table at Ginger's command. When Ginger asks the spirits if they're ready to speak, the Professor blows a conch shell. When Ginger passes out pieces of paper for each of the castaways to write out his questions, Gilligan, eager to speak with Uncle John, who can't read, pockets his slip of paper—never to discover the note from Ginger reading: "Please, don't tell anyone I'm a fake." Each of the castaways keeps his questions to himself—except for Gilligan, who asks when the rescue ship will arrive. "When the moon is blue," says Ginger.

Several nights later when Gilligan, spotting a blue moon, runs to light the signal fire, the Skipper shows him the note Ginger gave him. Gilligan, removing his paper from his pocket, discovers the same message. Thinking they're the only people Ginger trusts, they return to their hut as a ship passes by the island.

COMMENTS:

- Ginger's crystal ball and large deck of cards, whose presence on the island go unexplained, could have been contained in the previously discovered crate of magician's props. [Episode 33]

CASTAWAY QUIZ #59:

With whom did Ginger break into show business?
(For answer, see page 359)

60: FEED THE KITTY ⊚

Writers: J.E. Selby & Dick Sanville
Director: Leslie Goodwins
Guest Star: Janos Prohaska

After Gilligan hears a lion roar, the Skipper, sawing a piece of wood from a crate that washed ashore, discovers the printed words "Felis Leo," which the Professor recognizes as the zoological classification for lion. As the men search the jungle for the lion, Lovey, waiting with the girls behind a large rock, starts sneezing, explaining that she's allergic to cats, and notices the lion sitting above them. The women  race back to camp, and after the lion follows Lovey into her hut, the women barricade it inside and run off.

Gilligan, unable to find the women, climbs inside the Howells' hut and hearing the lion roar, barricades himself inside. After realizing he's barricaded himself in with the lion, he pulls a thorn from the lion's paw. The other castaways, having set up a rope trap outside the Howells' hut, catch Gilligan, who returns to the hut and leads out the lion on a leash. When the lion sees the Skipper as a bull, Howell as a boar, Lovey as a goat, the two girls as deer, and the Professor as an owl, the Skipper orders Gilligan to take the lion away, but Gilligan, unwilling to see the lion caged, decides to move to the other side of the island.

Gilligan trains the lion with a can of corned beef. When Howell brings him lunch, Gilligan, demonstrating the tricks he's taught the lion, asks Howelll to finance a circus upon their return to the mainland. While Howell pictures himself as the ringmaster, the lion roams off and finds Ginger, whom Gilligan convinces to be queen of the high wire. Lovey finds Howell dressed as a ringmaster and Ginger as a high-wire queen and asks to be in the horse show.

When Gilligan realizes he's running out of corned beef, the lion pictures him as a can of corned beef. When the Skipper demands that Gilligan return the washtub and planks he's using for his circus act, Gilligan asks the Skipper to be a clown in his circus. Mary Ann finds the Skipper dressed in a clown's outfit, trying to learn how to juggle coconuts, and he suggests she join the circus as his assistant in a hatchet-throwing act.

When Gilligan learns there's no more corned beef, the Skipper and the Professor demand that the lion be caged. As the Skipper starts to clean up the tub and planks of wood, the lion returns, and the frightened Skipper hides himself under the washtub. When Gilligan returns to find the lion sitting on top of the washtub, the Skipper starts talking from underneath, and Gilligan mistakenly believes the lion has eaten the Skipper. Gilligan calls for help, the lion walks off, and while Gilligan's explaining the situation to Howell, the Skipper crawls out from under the tub, and Gilligan, turning around to see him, passes out.

That night Gilligan sits out on the beach with the caged lion until the Skipper brings him back to camp. The next morning the Skipper and Gilligan return to find the lion, only to find him floating out on the lagoon in his cage, swept out by the tide. That night the radio reports that a U.S. destroyer found a full-grown Nubian lion drifting at sea in a bamboo cage, in good shape despite having consumed thirty-six pounds of corned beef.

COMMENTS:

- Since the castaways experienced a blight [Episode 7] where they didn't have any canned rations, the case of canned corned beef must have washed to shore.

TROPICAL INVENTIONS:

- Gilligan's circus
- Lion's cage

CASTAWAY QUIZ #60:

What was the lion's original destination?

(For answer, see page 359)

61: OPERATION: STEAM HEAT ☺☺☺

Writer: Terence and Joan Maples
Director: Stanley Z. Cherry

When the Skipper finds Gilligan carrying buckets of hot water to the other castaways, Gilligan brings him to a hot-water geyser he's discovered—which, the Professor realizes, indicates underground volcanic activity.

After reading up on volcanic patterns, the Professor leaves for the other side of the island to examine the volcano. While Gilligan begins constructing a bamboo pipeline from the geyser, the Howells empty a trunk they intend to fill with hot water, the girls anticipate having hot water to wash the dishes, and the Skipper prepares the shower stall for a hot-water line. When Howell, the Skipper, and Ginger each ask Gilligan to lead the pipeline for their purposes, Gilligan insists on giving everyone hot water and begins building a three-way pipeline.

Meanwhile on the other side of the island, the Professor measures a noticeable rise in the earth's temperature, listens to the earth through a bamboo stethoscope, witnesses a flash of white light when the temperature rises eight degrees, and measures the earth tremors with a Richter scale.

Meanwhile when Gilligan, annoyed at the others for pestering him for hot water, wishes the earth would swallow them up, the earth suddenly trembles. When Gilligan notices snow falling from the sky, the Professor, returning to camp, says it's volcanic ash and points to the active volcano.

Claiming that he can neutralize the volcano by countering its energy force with an equal energy force, the Professor explains that he's making a crude form of nitroglycerine—from sulfuric acid (from the crystalized copper in the caves), glycerol (from papaya seeds), and

potassium nitrate (from the rocks at the lagoon)—which will extinguish the volcano when exploded in a tunnel near its base. The Professor asks Gilligan to collect vines and the Skipper to bring him a timing device.

When Ginger tells Gilligan that she was once in a movie in which two natives threw themselves in a volcano to appease it, Gilligan, convinced she's going to throw herself in the volcano, chases after her. After the Skipper brings the Professor a clock he bought from the Howells, he runs to find Gilligan. Frustrated, the Professor leaves to find a vine for himself.

The Skipper returns to the Professor's hut just in time to see Gilligan drinking from one of the Professor's beakers. Convinced that Gilligan drank the nitroglycerine, the Skipper sits him outside and runs for the Professor. Gilligan warns Lovey and Mary Ann not to touch him, since he may explode.

When the Professor returns with the Skipper, he reveals Gilligan only drank water, and prepared to bomb the volcano, he instructs Gilligan to bring the others to the lagoon. When Gilligan finds Ginger, they both fall into a pit. Unable to climb back out, they walk through a cavernous steam tunnel, until Gilligan realizes this is where the Professor's going to throw the bomb.

When the Professor and the Skipper toss the bomb into a pit, Gilligan catches it. After Gilligan and Ginger toss it between themselves, Gilligan tosses the bomb back up to the Skipper, who falls into the pit. The Professor lowers a vine, and they each climb out. Realizing the bomb's tied to Gilligan's foot, the Professor quickly unties it and tosses it back in the pit. As the four castaways run, the bomb explodes, extinguishing the volcano.

COMMENTS:

- Since the castaways already have a shower [Episode 6] and a bathtub [Episode 49], the Skipper has no reason to bathe in the lagoon.
- Since there's a waterfall on the island, the castaways could always run water pipes through an improvised hot-water heater.
- Exploding a bomb at the base of an active volcano will not prevent an eruption.

TROPICAL INVENTIONS:

- The Professor's jumbo thermometer
- The Professor's stethoscope
- The Professor's Richter scale
- The Professor's nitroglycerine

CASTAWAY QUIZ #61:

With what does Howell try to bribe Gilligan?
(For answer, see page 359)

62: WILL THE REAL MR. HOWELL PLEASE STAND UP? ☺☺

Writer: Budd Grossman
Director: Jack Arnold

While listening to the radio, Gilligan learns that Mr. Howell has been rescued. Gilligan brings the radio to the Howells, who, upon hearing the broadcast, realize a double has taken Howell's place. After claiming that Lovey drowned in the shipwreck, the impostor reveals his plans to return to the helm of Howell Industries and to liquidate Howell's Amalgamated stock. When Howell runs to the lagoon to swim back to the mainland, Gilligan and the Skipper drag him back out.

Howell gathers the castaways, announces his urgent need to return to civilization, and offers one million dollars to the person who gets him off the island. When Howell learns that his impostor is selling his Apex International stock, he runs into the lagoon, and once again the crew drags him back out. When Howell learns from the radio that his impostor is merging Howell Industries with Consolidated Export, he runs into the lagoon, where the crew drags him back out again.

After the Professor suggests that the castaways pool their resources, he reviews their ideas and claims that the only practical one is his: constructing a pontoon boat using the bicycle pump to build a paddle wheel. But Gilligan, standing on the roof of a hut wearing a pair of wings, suggests that Howell fly back to Hawaii. He jumps from the roof and flys in place—until the Skipper tells him he can't fly.

After building the pontoon, the girls give Howell provisions and the social register; Lovey takes pictures of him without film; and the Professor gives him a flare pistol for an emergency. But when Howell launches the pontoon, it sinks in the lagoon.

While listening to the radio, Howell learns that his impostor has flown to Hawaii to set off on a yacht with forty-nine girls. After the Professor tries to psychoanalyze Howell, he asks the Skipper and Gilligan to sneak into the Howell's hut that night to steal the radio. When they accidentally wake the Howells, Gilligan turns on the radio, and a special news bulletin reveals that the impostor fell overboard from the yacht.

The next morning the impostor swims to the shore of the island and finding the real Howell lying in a lounge chair, sneaks up behind him, knocks him in the head with a coconut, and drags him into the bushes. The impostor emerges wearing Howell's clothes and sits in the chair, where Lovey brings him another drink. Gilligan returns to find the real Howell waking up in the jungle in different clothes and then passes by the impostor, unable to figure out how Howell changed his clothes again so quickly. When the real Howell finds the impostor sitting in his chair, the impostor claims that Howell is the impostor, and they ask Lovey to decide. Both men have a mole on their left elbow, Lovey recognizes the clothes on the impostor, and when Howell

quizzes the impostor, he answers all the questions correctly. The Professor happens by with the radio, which reports that the man thought to be Howell was a phony; his signature was the proof. When the impostor runs into the lagoon and swims away with Howell's pants and wallet, Howell runs after him, but the crew drags him back out again.

When the castaways learn from the radio that an unidentified survivor was rescued from the Pacific, they realize the impostor will never reveal their whereabouts.

COMMENTS:

- The Professor gives Howell a flare pistol for an emergency, despite the fact that Gilligan shot off the castaways' last signal flare. [Episode 53]
- The odds of Howell's look-alike assuming Howell's identity are better than the chances of that same look-alike falling overboard from a yacht and swimming to shore of the uncharted island where the real Howell has been shipwrecked.

TROPICAL INVENTIONS:

- Howell's pedal-powered pontoon

CASTAWAY QUIZ #62:

What is Howell's favorite reading material?
What is Howell's favorite exclusive club?
Which would Howell rather keep: his money or his wife?
(For answers, see page 359)

63: GHOST A GO-GO ⊗

Writer: Roland MacLane
Director: Leslie Goodwins
Guest Stars: Richard Kiel, Charles Maxwell

When Gilligan hears howling in the middle of the night, he lifts the window shade, seeing a ghost. The next morning after convincing Gilligan to stop hiding in the closet, the Skipper trips over Gilligan, who's on the ground, looking for the ghost's footprints. Mary Ann tells Gilligan she heard strange sounds; Ginger claims a table and a magazine are missing; and Howell accuses Gilligan of putting his practice polo-pony up in a tree and dancing outside their hut in a white nightshirt. The Professor, trying to determine who made the mournful cries everyone heard, makes the sound, and Gilligan, passing by, runs into the hut and jumps into the Skipper's arms.

That night when Gilligan refuses to go to bed, the Skipper forces him to go outside and count to ten. While Gilligan's outside, the Skipper covers himself with a sheet, but when Gilligan returns, he notices the words *S.S. Minnow* stamped on the sheet. While insisting ghosts don't exist, the Skipper sees a ghost outside and faints. After Gilligan pours a bucket of water over the Skipper's head, Mary Ann, Ginger, and the Howells run in and demand the crew's hammocks, insisting that the island is haunted. When they all climb into the Skipper's hammock, it breaks.

The next day, the Professor gathers the castaways to determine a logical explanation. When the girls recall a missing sheet, the Professor suggests a search. While searching for the sheet, Gilligan hears howling, and after a voice tells him to get off the island, he walks into the ghost. Pertrified, Gilligan runs to the lagoon, where he finds the Skipper with a boat, provisions, and a note from the ghost. The Skipper orders Gilligan to tell everyone to come down to the boat with their bare essentials. Lovey arrives wearing her furs. Howell carries a trunk of money, and the girls each carry a bag of makeup.

The Professor, suspecting foul play, suggests that they first send the boat out with seven dummies aboard to make sure it's safe. That night the Skipper and Gilligan set the boat into the lagoon with the seven dummies aboard, and as the castaways watch from the edge of the jungle, the boat explodes. The ghost, also watching from the edge of the jungle, removes his sheet, and using a walkie-talkie, reports to

his contact that the castaways are dead and the coast is clear to assume offshore oil rights. The Professor suggests that the castaways round up seven sheets and give the ghost a dose of his own medicine. When the spy sees the castaways roaming around in their sheets howling, he takes off his sheet, calls for help on his walkie-talkie, jumps into the lagoon, and swims away.

The next day after Gilligan finds the castaways' clothes on the lagoon, the Skipper, having fixed his hammock, sees his shirt walking on the table and picks it up to find Gilligan's turtle.

COMMENTS:

- The "ghost" looks like a man wearing a sheet over his head and would not fool anyone.
- Oddly, the explosion that destroys the dummies and the boat doesn't damage the castaways' clothing.

TROPICAL INVENTIONS:

- The castaways' dummies

CASTAWAY QUIZ #63:

Where is the spy from?
(For answer, see page 359)

254

64: ALLERGY TIME ⊗

Writer: Budd Grossman
Director: Jack Arnold

When the Skipper can't stop sneezing one night, the Professor insists on watching him closely. The next morning, while building a Ping-Pong table, the Skipper is no longer sneezing—until Gilligan comes along.

After the Professor determines that the Skipper's not allergic to any objects gathered by the castaways, Gilligan brings the Professor a duck egg, causing the Skipper to start sneezing. When the Professor, holding the duck egg, sends Gilligan to the other side of the clearing, the Skipper stops sneezing; when Gilligan returns, so does the Skipper's sneezing.

After the Professor has Gilligan bathe with a special nonallergenic soap, the Skipper, finding Gilligan combing his hair, starts sneezing violently again. The Professor blindfolds the Skipper and brings in the

castaways one at a time on the theory that the allergy is psychosomatic, but when Gilligan walks in, the Skipper begins sneezing.

That night as Gilligan packs to move in with the Professor, the Skipper continually sneezes, blowing out the candle, which Gilligan keeps relighting. When Gilligan, trying to fall asleep in the Professor's hut, wakes the Professor, the Professor starts sneezing. When Gilligan moves in with the Howells, they start sneezing and ask him to leave. When he moves in with the girls and they start sneezing, Gilligan wanders off into the jungle with his blanket and pillow.

The next morning while the Skipper searches for Gilligan, Mary Ann finds a note from Gilligan pinned to the supply hut, explaining that he's moved to the other side of the island. At the Skipper's urging, the castaways search for Gilligan. The Skipper sneezes his way through the jungle, convinced he's on the right trail. When the girls start sneezing near a cave, Mary Ann runs to get the others. Ginger tries seductively to entice Gilligan to return to camp, but sneezing violently, has to excuse herself. The others gather, start sneezing violently, and have to leave.

When the Professor tells Howell and the Skipper that he's developed a vaccine to the Gilligan allergy, they bring Gilligan back to camp. When the Professor reveals a large bamboo syringe, the castaways try to convince Gilligan to take the vaccine. When the Professor explains that the castaways, not Gilligan, will require two to three shots a week as long as they're on the island, Gilligan voluntarily returns to the cave.

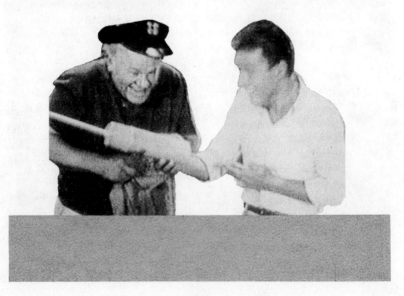

That night the Skipper, lonely for Gilligan, wakes up the Professor and requests the vaccine. When he passes out at the sight of the syringe, the Professor administers the vaccine. The next day after the other castaways, having admired the Skipper's loyalty to Gilligan, take the vaccine, Gilligan runs out from the jungle and explains what's making everyone sneeze: the oil from the papaya nuts that he's been using for hair tonic.

Later the Skipper and the Professor tell Gilligan that he needs a vaccination to guard against the excessive amount of papaya oil absorbed into his scalp, revealing an enormous bamboo syringe, terrifying Gilligan, who accidentally backs up into a smaller syringe, inoculating himself.

COMMENTS:

- The Professor accomplishes a scientific miracle: he develops a vaccine to the Gilligan allergy without knowing its cause.
- While each of his fellow castaways experience reactions, Gilligan fails to show an allergic reaction to the papaya nut oil despite the fact that he wears it in his hair.
- The odds against finding seven random people with an allergy to papaya nut oil shipwrecked together on an uncharted island are at least five billion to one.
- We never see the castaways use the Ping-Pong table the Skipper and Gilligan start building.

TROPICAL INVENTIONS:

- The Professor's nonallergenic soap
- The Professor's "Gilligan allergy vaccine"
- The Professor's bamboo syringes
- Gilligan's papaya-oil hair tonic

CASTAWAY QUIZ #64:

How does Gilligan realize the castaways are allergic to the papaya nut oil in his hair tonic?

(For answer, see page 359)

65: THE FRIENDLY PHYSICIAN ⊗⊗⊗⊗

Writer: Elroy Schwartz
Director: Jack Arnold
Guest Stars: Vito Scotti, Mike Mazurki

A mad scientist, Boris Balinkoff, arrives on the island by boat, finding Gilligan asleep by the signal fire. After Gilligan brings Balinkoff to meet the others, the men decide to send Gilligan and the Skipper back with Balinkoff to his island so they can sail his yacht back for the rest of them.

When he gets the Skipper and Gilligan back to his castle on his island, Balinkoff, claiming that two of his men took his yacht, returns to the island for the other castaways. After Balinkoff's assistant, Igor, brings the Skipper and Gilligan steak dinners, a dog walks in and meows like a cat. After the Skipper and Gilligan find several torture devices in the castle's dungeon, they return to the dining room to find Balinkoff carrying a parrot on his shoulder. When the parrot roars like a lion, Balinkoff explains that through his research he's discovered a way to electronically switch the minds and bodies of animals, ordering Igor to bring the Skipper and Gilligan to the dungeon.

While Igor chains Gilligan and the Skipper to the wall, the other castaways walk through the castle. While the women wait in the dining room, Howell and the Professor search the castle for Gilligan and the Skipper. When Howell sits down in a chair, the wall behind him rotates him into an office where Balinkoff explains his plans, proposing that they transfer their minds into the bodies of the world's leaders and take over the world. When Balinkoff shrugs off Howell's twenty-million-dollar offer, the millionaire sits back down, rotates back to the other room, and runs to tell the others about Balinkoff's plan. The castaways soon find themselves chained up in the dungeon—except for Howell and Gilligan, who soon return in each other's body. When Igor comes down the stairs, Gilligan (in Howell's body) jumps him, but Igor triumphs and manacles them both.

After Igor brings the Skipper and Lovey to the laboratory and locks them in separate glass booths, Balinkoff throws a lever, sending electrical impulses through both chambers. Once the Skipper's and

Lovey's minds are switched, the Professor and Mary Ann are transposed, and finally, Ginger's mind winds up in Igor's body. At the Professor's suggestion Ginger (in Igor's body) frees the other castaways from the dungeon, using her new body's physical strength.

The Professor (in Mary Ann's body) leads the others back to the laboratory, puts Howell and Gilligan in separate booths, pulls the lever, and switches their minds back into their proper bodies. After switching Lovey and the Skipper back, the Professor has the Skipper operate the lever to return him and Mary Ann to their appropriate bodies. When Balinkoff enters, followed by Igor (in Ginger's body), the Professor has Ginger (in Igor's body) get inside a booth, and the castaways push Igor into the other booth as the Professor activates the machine. The castaways then shove Balinkoff into the booth with Igor, and when a cat and dog run into the empty booth, the castaways lock them inside and pull the lever, transferring the minds of the animals into the bodies of Balinkoff and Igor. As the castaways flee, Balinkoff and Igor (in the bodies of the cat and dog) and the cat and dog (in the bodies of Balinkoff and Igor) chase each other through the castle.

After returning to their island in Balinkoff's boat, the Professor suggests they return to Hawaii in the boat. As the castaways run to pack their clothes and provisions, the boat suddenly sinks in the lagoon.

COMMENTS:

- Switching minds and bodies is scientifically impossible.
- Rather than returning to their island, the castaways should gather provisions and leave directly from Balinkoff's castle.
- The castaways could stay in the castle, imprison Balinkoff, Igor, the cat, and the dog, dismantle Balinkoff's invention, and build a transmitter to radio for help.
- The castaways could raise the sunken boat from the lagoon, patch it with rubber from a rubber tree, fortify it with additional planks of wood, and send out Gilligan and the Skipper for help.

CASTAWAY QUIZ #65:

What's Boris Balinkoff's parrot's name?
(For answer, see page 359)

66: "V" FOR VITAMINS ⊗

Writer: Barney Slater
Director: Jack Arnold

After examining the fatigued Skipper, the Professor claims that he's suffering from a vitamin C deficiency, an ailment that will soon affect each of them in turn according to size. That night Gilligan reveals an orange but when the Skipper calls the other castaways, Gilligan claims it's the last.

The next day Howell picks a tennis ball from Gilligan's back pocket, and when he asks to buy the orange, Gilligan refuses to sell. While walking through the jungle, Gilligan stumbles upon Ginger, who tries seductively to persuade him to surrender the orange. That afternoon when Gilligan sets the orange down before the other castaways and announces that he's decided to give everyone a slice, the Professor explains that one slice won't do anybody any good. While the castaways argue over the orange, the fruit shrivels up under the hot sun. Gilligan humorously suggests giving the orange a burial, inspiring the Professor, who suggests they plant the seeds.

That night when Gilligan takes over sentry duty, the Professor tells him to make sure the tiki torches stay lit to warm the seeds. As the torches flicker, Gilligan falls asleep and dreams that his mother (Lovey) asks him to take her jewel box to the market to trade for a half dozen oranges. On the road he meets up with a hustler, Lester J. Frothingham III (Howell), who trades him the box of jewels for magic beans. When Gilligan returns home, Lovey shows him a cupboard filled with canned beans, throws his magic beans out the window, and leaves. When Gilligan climbs the beanstalk growing outside the window, he finds a castle in the cloud. A French maid (Mary Ann) answers the door and tells him the castle is home to a cruel giant who hoards oranges. The giant approaches, and the maid tells Gilligan to hide behind the crates. The giant (Skipper) chases Gilligan around the crates and runs off to slay a dragon. Gilligan grabs the goose that lays the golden orange, but before fleeing with the maid, he insists upon rescuing the prisoners in the dungeon: an ugly old man (the Professor) and an ugly old woman (Ginger). The giant returns and grabs Gilligan, who wakes up screaming.

As Gilligan laments falling asleep and letting the torches go out, the Professor runs up with grapefruits and lemons, which Gilligan, fully aware of, didn't realize were citrus fruits.

COMMENTS:

- The Professor does not have the chemicals or equipment necessary to detect a vitamin C deficiency with a blood test. Furthermore, a vitamin C deficiency would not affect people according to their weight.
- Gilligan has a tennis ball whose presence on the island remains unexplained.
- According to his dream, Gilligan sees Lovey as his mother; Howell as a hustler; and the Skipper as an overbearing ogre. What's more, in his dream Gilligan denies the existence of the brother he previously claimed to have [Episode 40], revealing a deeply buried subconscious conflict.
- When the giant chases Gilligan, the unconvincing effect was achieved by using a stand-in: Bob Denver's son, Patrick.

TROPICAL INVENTIONS:

- The Professor's blood pressure gauge

CASTAWAY QUIZ #66:

What's Mary Ann's formula for growing oranges?

(For answer, see page 359)

67: MR. AND MRS. ??? ☺

Writer: Jack Gross, Jr. & Michael Stein
Director: Gary Nelson

While Gilligan waits on them, the Howells learn from the radio that the reverend who married them, Buckley Norris of Boston, is a fraud, invalidating their marriage. When Howell suggests they remarry as soon as they're rescued, Lovey demands that Howell move out after they divide up their personal effects. Ginger suggests that the Skipper marry the Howells, but when the Professor insists that the Skipper only has authority at sea, Gilligan suggests they build a raft so the Skipper can perform the ceremony on the lagoon.

When Gilligan tells the Howells, Lovey asks him to hold her wedding band while she and Howell plan the details. After building the raft, the Skipper practices the wedding ceremony with Mary Ann and Gilligan. When Mary Ann asks Gilligan to kiss the bride, he falls into the lagoon.

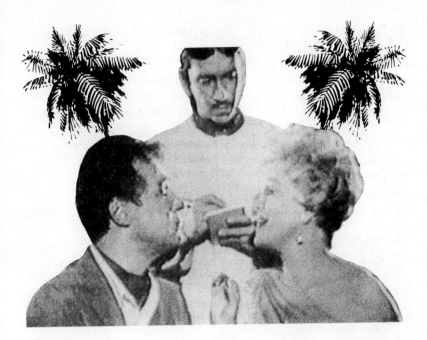

That evening the Professor helps the bride, groom, bridesmaid (Ginger), and the best man (Gilligan) aboard the raft. When the Skipper, conducting the ceremony, asks for the ring, Howell, unable to remove the ring from Gilligan's finger, hands the Skipper a cigarband, upsetting Lovey, who refuses to be wed with anything but her wedding band. Incensed, Howell refuses to remarry her, walking off the raft and into the lagoon.

Later Howell moves into the crew's hut with all his luggage, demanding a long list of amenities, and forcing the Skipper and Gilligan to move out. After Lovey moves in with the girls, Ginger conspires with Mary Ann to reunite the Howells. Ginger finds Howell counting his money and explains that Lovey would come back to him if he makes her jealous. Meanwhile the Skipper and Gilligan convince Lovey that Howell would come back to her if she makes him jealous by feigning romantic interest in the Professor.

That night at dinner Howell dines with Ginger, the Professor dines with Lovey, and Gilligan, serving as the waiter, provides Mary Ann and the Skipper with continual status reports. When Lovey says she'll be the Professor's patron, Howell reacts by promising Ginger jewels and travel. While the two couples dance to a record player, the Skipper, dressed as a headhunter, runs into the clearing. When Howell hits the "headhunter" with a coconut, knocking him unconscious, the Howells reconcile their differences.

The next day listening to the radio, the Howells learn that the previous day's report mispronounced the fradulent minister's name; all marriages performed by Boris Nuckley, not Buckley Norris, are invalid. When the Skipper and Gilligan later overhear the Howells arguing again, they return to their hut and barricade the door, but Howell manages to get inside with his suitcases, insisting they provide him with a number of amenities.

COMMENTS:
- Since they're shipwrecked castaways, the Skipper is legally permitted to marry the Howells.
- If the Skipper were only allowed to perform marriages at sea, they would have to be at least five miles from land.
- If the minister who married the Howells was a fraud, the Howells, living together as a married couple for over twenty years, would be married according to common law.
- The odds against having a mispronounced news report pertain to the Howells are the square root of the odds against the mishap's occurring twice.

TROPICAL INVENTIONS:
- A raft

CASTAWAY QUIZ #67:
From whom did Lovey get her wedding ring?
(For answer, see page 359)

68: MEET THE METEOR ⊛⊛⊛

Writer: Elroy Schwartz
Director: Jack Arnold

When Gilligan and the Skipper find a large glowing meteorite that's hit the island, the Professor warns them not to go near it, explaining that meteorites pick up "all sorts of strange rays," frightening Gilligan away.

The Professor builds a Geiger counter in the supply hut to determine if there's cause for alarm, swearing the crew to secrecy. While standing guard outside the supply hut, Gilligan creates havoc by inadvertently giving Ginger, Mary Ann, and the Howells conflicting information and continually disturbing the Skipper and the Professor.

After measuring the meteorite with the Geiger counter, the Professor explains that "there was no radiation near the meteor at all. However, there were cosmic rays, which aren't as deadly as interstellar radiation, however, they can kill you." Gilligan digs for lead, which the Professor intends to use to build a reflective screen to focus the

267

cosmic rays up into the sky where a weather plane or radiation detection center will spot them, investigate, and send rescue. To protect themselves from the radiation the Professor intends to impregnate their clothes with molten lead to fashion protective suits, and while trying on a pair of lead-coated pants, Gilligan falls over.

After the Professor, the Skipper, and Gilligan (wearing lead suits, hats, glasses, and makeup) set up the reflective screen around the meteorite, the Professor's Geiger counter registers minimal radiation levels. Returning to check on the meteorite, they discover the bamboo screen missing and an enormous tree standing where Gilligan had tripped over a small tree. The Professor explains that the cosmic rays sped up the tree's aging process, reducing the bamboo screen to dust. Within a week, he says, they'll all die of old age, and he swears the crew to secrecy.

When the Professor learns from the radio that an electrical storm is headed toward the island, he suggests that they attach a lightning rod to the meteorite. Gilligan runs to tell the others the good news, having previously revealed the secret bad news.

After coating bamboo poles with lead to create a lightning rod, Gilligan falls asleep and dreams that the castaways are celebrating their fiftieth anniversary on the island. Gilligan, bearded and gray, helps the Skipper to the party; an aged Howell helps a feeble Lovey choose her jewelry; the doddering Professor escorts a faded Ginger and elderly Mary Ann to the party. At the party Howell proposes a toast, the girls suggest a dance, and while Gilligan listens to the radio, the aged announcer says a storm will hit the island, and while the others run inside, Gilligan stays at the table and wakes up to find himself in the midst of the storm.

While running to the meteorite with the lightning rod, Gilligan is struck by lightning, trips, and tosses the lightning rod into the meteorite, disintegrating it. The next morning the Professor informs the Skipper and Gilligan that he can't find any trace of cosmic rays.

COMMENTS:

- The Professor erroneously tells the Skipper and Gilligan that meteorites glow from "picking up all sorts of strange rays"; meteorites glow from intense friction heat.
- Despite the Professor's contradictory claim, cosmic rays are a form of radiation.
- The Professor's plan to build a reflective screen to focus the meteorite's cosmic rays up into the sky to be spotted by weather planes or a radiation detection center is clearly his most farfetched rescue scheme.
- Disintegrating a radioactive meteorite will not eliminate the radiation.

TROPICAL INVENTIONS:

- The Professor's Geiger counter
- Lead reflection shield
- Lead radiation suits and makeup
- Lightning rod

CASTAWAY QUIZ #68:

What's Howell's polo pony named?

(For answer, see page 359)

69: UP AT BAT ⊗

Writer: Ron Friedman
Director: Jerry Hopper

While inside an unexplored cave, Gilligan's bitten in the neck by a bat the Skipper recognizes as a vampire bat. The Professor advises them to seal up the cave's entrance, have the girls bandage the wound, and refrain from worrying the others with their superstitious belief that Gilligan's going to turn into a vampire. While the girls leave to get bandages, Gilligan picks up Ginger's mirror, which has lost its backing, and unable to see his reflection, convinces himself he's turning into a vampire and runs off.

That night the Skipper wraps a scarf around his neck and ties a string from Gilligan's foot to his own. Sleepwalking in the middle of

the night, Gilligan unties the string from his foot, wraps his blanket around his shoulders, walks into the Howells' hut, and goes for Lovey's neck. When Lovey screams, waking Gilligan, he convinces himself he's turning into a vampire. After explaining that Gilligan's obsession has allowed his subconscious to take over, the Professor concocts a placebo antivampire potion to "cure" Gilligan. The Skipper wakes up the next morning to find a bat in Gilligan's hammock.

Convinced that Gilligan's turned into a bat, the Skipper warns the girls, who disbelievingly suggest that Gilligan fly to the mainland with a note. While the Skipper searches for the Professor, the bat flies into the girls' hut. The Professor catches it and assures the girls it's nothing but a common red fruit bat. Meanwhile Gilligan locks himself in a caged cave with his blanket and alarm clock. When the Skipper finds a note from Gilligan, he calls the Professor, who suggests a search.

That night Gilligan dreams that the Howells, seeking lodging in Belfrey Hall in 1895 Transylvania, are greeted by an old hag (Mary Ann). Her mistress (Ginger) wakes her vampire husband (Gilligan) from his coffin, informing him that they have guests. After leaping out the window and falling to the ground, Gilligan (having forgotten to turn into a bat) climbs back in the window. Ginger pulls out a folding bed to hide the coffin, asks Gilligan to hide, and escorts the Howells inside. Meanwhile Inspector Sherlock (the Professor) and his assistant Watney (the Skipper) are greeted at the door by the old hag (Mary Ann), who wrote to them five years earlier to investigate the castle. When Watney hears a scream, he and Inspector Sherlock go up to the room to find Gilligan biting Lovey's neck. A fight ensues, and the Professor knocks out Gilligan with a punch.

Then the Skipper wakes Gilligan and explains he was bitten by a mere fruit bat.

TROPICAL INVENTIONS:

• The Professor's antivampire potion

CASTAWAY QUIZ #69:

What is the Professor's antivampire potion made from?
(For answer, see page 359)

70: GILLIGAN VS. GILLIGAN ⊗⊗⊗

Writer: Joanna Lee
Director: Jerry Hopper

When Mary Ann reports a missing coconut-pineapple pie to the Professor and the Skipper, Gilligan wanders by, licking an empty pie plate. Denying responsibility, Gilligan searches for the pie and following a trail of pie crust, finds his look-alike eating the pie.

Gilligan's double (a Russian spy given Gilligan's looks through plastic surgery and sent to the island for forty-eight hours to spy on the marooned Americans—who, the Russians think, are really engaged in some top secret work) communicates with his Russian commander stationed offshore by talking into an open Swiss army knife, informing him that he's been seen by Gilligan.

After the spy cuts the laundry line with the laser beam in his pocketknife, Ginger accuses Gilligan of breaking the clothesline—a charge Gilligan denies. After the spy asks Lovey if he sounds and looks like Gilligan, his commander orders him to take Gilligan's place.

The spy eavesdrops on the men, who decide to search the jungle for the look-alike Gilligan insists he saw holding a shiny gold pocketknife. The Professor, the Skipper, and Gilligan split up to search through the jungle, and when Gilligan finds a knapsack and yells for the others, the spy knocks him out with a coconut, drags him behind the bushes, and ties him up. When the spy tells the Professor and the Skipper he yelled because he fell into a pineapple patch, the Professor suggests that Gilligan merely saw his reflection in the lagoon and the sunlight reflecting off a leaf. When the spy mentions the knapsack, he arouses the suspicions of the Professor, who decides Gilligan's suffering from a mental breakdown. The spy reports to his commander, who orders him to question all the castaways to discover their purpose on the island.

The spy asks the Skipper why they're on the island, inadvertently blaming him for the shipwreck, and is tossed from the hut. The girls discuss Gilligan's strange behavior, and when Mary Ann shows concern, Ginger says he's merely experiencing growing pains. The next morning the spy makes a move on Ginger, who fights him and flees. The spy goes to Howell's hut, accuses him of cheating at chess, and is thrown out.

At a secret meeting in the supply hut, the Professor advises the castaways that Gilligan, suffering from delusions, should be humored until he frees himself from whatever has gripped him. The real Gilligan frees himself, runs back to camp, and tells the others that he was kidnapped—only to be humored.

Gilligan spots the spy entering the Howells' hut and chases after him. The spy, hiding in Lovey's mirrored closet, opens the closet door and mirrors Gilligan's movements. When Gilligan feigns a sneeze, the real spy sneezes, and Gilligan chases him into the jungle. The spy, ordered to return to his ship, starts up the motorboat and leaps back on shore to kill Gilligan with the death ray on his 200-function pocketknife. When Gilligan points out that the spy's boat took off without him, the spy leaps into the lagoon and swims after it. Unable to fathom this experience, Gilligan decides against telling the others

That night after Gilligan denies his previous stories and the Skipper reassures him that he's cured, the Professor enters with the rusted 200-function pocketknife.

COMMENTS:

- The chances of winning the Iowa State Lottery are better than the odds against a Gilligan look-alike visiting the island in the wake of a previous visit by Mr. Howell's look-alike.

CASTAWAY QUIZ #70:

What's Gilligan's Soviet double's secret agent number?

(For answer, see page 359)

71: PASS THE VEGETABLES PLEASE ☺☺☺☺

Writer: Elroy Schwartz
Director: Leslie Goodwins

While fishing on the lagoon Gilligan reels in a crate of vegetable seeds, discards the top, which reads "Warning: Experimental Radioactive Seeds," and runs to get the Skipper. The castaways, marveling over the seeds, make plans for a vegetable garden. Later Gilligan pulls the Skipper's plow, and after Mary Ann explains that the soil is too heavy for plants, the Skipper sends Gilligan for some sand to help the drainage.

Three days later when Gilligan notices the plants growing before his eyes, he calls the castaways, who pick gargantuan carrots and cucumbers, looped corn, and pretzel-shaped green beans. The Professor speculates that salt water caused the extraordinary growth. After eating their favorite vegetables (Gilligan has spinach; Mary Ann has carrots; Lovey has beets), the castaways learn from the radio that a box containing radioactive seeds is missing. Gilligan reveals the warning label on the bench he made from the crate's cover.

When the Professor, unable to find any information in his books, speculates that the vegetables could be fatal, the castaways faint. The Professor urges the castaways to keep moving, and while the Skipper walks Mary Ann, she suddenly spots a boat offshore that the Skipper can't see. When the Skipper calls the Professor, who can't see the boat

either, Mary Ann explains that she can see the Professor's book sitting on a tree stump on the hill, a half mile away, turned to page 117. While setting up a signal fire, the Professor realizes that the radioactive treatment of the carrots magnified the carotene, strengthening Mary Ann's eyesight.

When Gilligan returns with a huge log that the Skipper can't lift, the Professor attributes Gilligan's strength to the radioactive spinach. While Gilligan breaks off branches, Mary Ann reports the ship's disappearance. Meanwhile Lovey, who ate the sugar beets, races around her hut, runs through the clearing, dances on the communal table, and disappears into the jungle.

After Gilligan lifts the Skipper in his lounge chair, the Skipper sends him for some coconuts, which Gilligan, not realizing his strength, breaks. When Gilligan tosses a coconut to the Skipper, he throws it through the wall of their hut. The Professor explains that to cure their radioactive reactions the castaways must eat soap prepared from a tree. As the castaways all eat the soap and start blowing bubbles, the Professor explains that the soap's hydrocarbons are absorbing the radioactivity. That night after the Professor says they're all cured, Gilligan, still eating the soap, blows an enormous bubble that explodes.

COMMENTS:

- The Professor, guessing that the peculiarly shaped vegetables resulted from watering the seeds with salt water, reveals his questionable botany expertise.
- Radioactive poisoning cannot be absorbed by eating soap; the Professor, having previously invented a Geiger counter [Episode 68], could detect the vegetables' radiation levels.

TROPICAL INVENTIONS:

- A bamboo watering can
- A plow
- The Professor's soap

CASTAWAY QUIZ #71:

What is the castaways' soap made from?
(For answer, see page 359)

72: THE PRODUCER ☺☺☺☺

Writers: Gerald Gardner & Dee Caruso
Directors: Ida Lupino & George M. Cahan
Special Guest Star: Phil Silvers

As a plane circles the island, the Skipper orders Gilligan to drive the castaways' pedal-powered bamboo car back to camp to get the radio. But Ginger, who's just learned that Hollywood producer Harold Hecuba is circling the world to find talent for his new movie, refuses to give Gilligan the radio. Gilligan returns to the lagoon, where Harold Hecuba, whose plane has crashed, rides up to shore in a motorized rubber raft towing a second raft filled with supplies. After introducing himself, Hecuba demands amenities the castaways don't have and insists upon giving the orders if the castaways wish to return to civilization with him (his flunkies are following him).

After Gilligan and the Skipper drive Hecuba back to camp, Hecuba demands the Howells' hut for himself. When Lovey offers him flowers, Hecuba, claiming to be allergic, throws them away and insists that the Howells work as his servants.

When Mary Ann, fixing dinner, objects to Hecuba's behavior, Ginger explains that all Hollywood producers are that way. While serving Hecuba dinner, Ginger acts like an Italian peasant and Marilyn Monroe, but when she reveals that she was trying to impress him with her acting ability, Hecuba insults her. Humiliated, Ginger runs crying to Gilligan and the Skipper, refusing to return to the mainland as an unknown has-been.

The next day after the Skipper tells the Professor that Ginger refuses to go back to the mainland, Gilligan suggests they stage a musical starring Ginger to impress Hecuba and boost Ginger's spirit. Suggesting they rehearse at night, Gilligan finds a copy of *Hamlet* which they can make into a musical using the Howells' records.

Several nights later at the castaways' stage, the Professor, operating the record player, introduces the castaways' production of *Hamlet*, waking Hecuba, who wanders over to the stage to watch the performance. Gilligan plays Hamlet, the Howells play Claudius and Gertrude, Ginger plays Ophelia, the Skipper plays Polonius, and Mary Ann plays Laertes. Hecuba interrupts, takes charge of the production, and forces the castaways to rehearse. Dismayed with their performance, Hecuba decides to show the castaways how to act by repeatedly running backstage to change costumes—until he passes out onstage.

The next day after Gilligan alerts the Skipper that Hecuba's gone, the Professor discovers a note from Hecuba explaining that he didn't want to disturb their sleep when a rescue boat came in the middle of the night. The castaways later learn from the radio that Hecuba, returning to civilization, is preparing to produce a musical version of *Hamlet*.

COMMENTS:

- Hecuba arrives on the island with two inflatable rafts that the castaways could use to leave the island.

TROPICAL INVENTIONS:

- The castaways' pedal-powered bamboo car

CASTAWAY QUIZ #72:

What movie did Hecuba intend to produce before *Hamlet*? (For answer, see page 359)

HAMLET

A Musical
by
the Castaways
of Gilligan's Island

Act I

[*The curtain rises. Hamlet stands stage center.*]

HAMLET:
(*Sings*)

I ask to be or not to be,
A rogue or peasant slave is what you see;
A boy who loved his mother's knee,
And so I ask to be or not to be.
So here's my plea, I beg of you,
And say you see a little hope for me.
To fight or flee, to fight to flee,
I ask myself to be or not to be.

[*Enter King Claudius and Queen Gertrude.*]

CLAUDIUS AND GERTRUDE:
(*Sing*)

He asks to be or not to be,
A rogue or peasant slave is what you see;

GERTRUDE:
(*Sings*)

My son who loved his mother's knee,

CLAUDIUS AND GERTRUDE:
(*Sing*)

And so he asks to be or not to be.
So here's his plea, we beg of thee,
And say we see a little hope for he.

HAMLET:
(*Sings*)

To fight or flee, to fight to flee,
I ask myself to be or not to be.

[*Exeunt Claudius and Gertrude.*]

HAMLET:
Hark! I do believe I hear the fair Ophelia.

[*Enter Ophelia.*]

279

OPHELIA:

My Lord Hamlet is troubled.

HAMLET:

Yea, verily, my heart is heavy. I cannot marry thee,
Ophelia. There is nothing left for you, but to get thee to
a notary.

OPHELIA:

Ah, my poor Hamlet. Ah, my poor Hamlet.

(*Sings*)

Hamlet, dear, your problem is clear,
Avenging thy father's death;
You seek to harm your uncle and mom,
But you're scaring me to death.
While I die and sigh and cry,
That love is everything;
You're content to try to touch,
The conscience of a king.
Since the day when your dad met his fate,
You just brood and you don't touch your food;
You hate your ma, mad at my pa,
You'll kill the king or some silly thing.
So Hamlet, Hamlet, do be a man, let
Rotten enough alone.
From Ophelia no one can steal ya,
You'll always be my own,
Leave the gravedigger's scene,
If you know what I mean.
Danish pastry for two,
For me, for you.

HAMLET:

In truth Ophelia, you have said a mouthful.

OPHELIA:

Hamlet, I have so much more to offer. But hark! Me
thinks me hear the heavy footsteps of my father, Polonius.

HAMLET:

And the laughter of your brother and my friend, Laertes.

OPHELIA:

Oh, they must not find us here. But where to hide?

HAMLET:

Hide anyplace. But don't go near the water.

[*Exeunt Hamlet and Ophelia.*]

LAERTES:
Father, my ship sails at the tide.

POLONIUS:
A moment, my son, for I have something to tell you.

LAERTES:
But I ask only for my allowance.

POLONIUS:
Ah, but I shall give you something far more available: advice.

LAERTES:
Do you know how much wine you can buy in Paris with advice?

POLONIUS:
Paris is a wild and wicked town. And you are but a young and innocent boy.

LAERTES:
(*To audience*)
Oh, could I tell him a few stories.

POLONIUS:
Heed my words, Laertes, and you'll be safe.

LAERTES:
Unless I listen, I won't get my spending money. So I'll listen, I'll listen.

POLONIUS:
(*Sings*)
Neither a borrower nor a lender be,
Do not forget: Stay out of debt;
Think twice, and take this good advice from me,
Guard that old solvency.
There's just one other thing you ought to do,
To thine own self be true.

[*Enter entire cast.*]

ALL:
(*Sing*)
Neither a borrower nor a lender be,
Do not forget: Stay out of debt;
Think twice, and take this good advice from me,
Guard that old solvency.
There's just one other thing you ought to do,
To thine own self be true.

[*Finis.*]

C U R T A I N

73: VOODOO ☺☺☺

Writers: Herbert Finn & Alan Dinehart
Directors: George M. Cahan

When the Skipper finds Gilligan in a cave, searching for his lucky rabbit's foot and digging up primitive artifacts, a native witch doctor, hiding nearby with Gilligan's rabbit's foot, stabs a voodoo doll of Gilligan in the neck with a long needle. When Gilligan feels the pain, he and the Skipper flee the cave.

The Professor claims the vases are invaluable Mayan artifacts, but the Skipper, convinced that they're cursed, refuses to look at the handiwork. The Professor insists the pain in Gilligan's neck was a muscle spasm, but the Skipper explains that witch doctors make lifelike voodoo dolls of people using one of the individual's personal effects.

While Ginger and Mary Ann try on beaded necklaces, the witch doctor, standing outside their window, holds voodoo dolls of the two girls back to back. While the girls are stuck together, the witch doctor takes two of their personal effects and then frees them by pulling the dolls apart.

After Lovey discovers that her lipstick and Howell's wallet are missing, the Professor claims that the relic Howell's wearing as a brooch is worth a fortune. While Gilligan gives the Skipper a haircut, Howell offers them twenty dollars to excavate more valuables from the cave. While the castaways go to the cave, the witch doctor takes a lock of the Skipper's hair. While the castaways admire the relics, the witch doctor, on the other side of the island, dangles Gilligan's voodoo doll from a string, causing Gilligan to dance uncontrollably—behavior that, the Professor claims, results from the power of suggestion. When the witch doctor puts a flame under the dolls' feet, the castaways suddenly get hot feet and run from the cave to cool their feet in the lagoon. Still, the Professor insists volcanic activity centered under the cave merely warmed their feet.

Meanwhile the witch doctor, cursing the Professor, stiffens his doll, turning the Professor into a frozen zombie. After Ginger fails to snap him out of the trance by kissing him passionately, the Skipper and Gilligan return all the relics to the cave to make peace with the evil spirits. But the witch doctor tickles the feet of the crew's dolls with a feather, causing them to laugh hysterically. Unable to break through to the Professor, the Howells try to appease the evil spirits by leaving a roll of money in the case. The witch doctor takes the rubber band, tossing away the money.

The next day while Gilligan tries to feed the Professor, Ginger volunteers to perform a native dance to cure the Professor. That evening while Ginger dances in a grass skirt, rain suddenly breaks, and the castaways run inside, leaving the Professor standing in the downpour. The next day the Skipper notices that Mary Ann still has a relic and has Gilligan return it to the cave. Discovering the voodoo dolls and the castaways' belongings, Gilligan brings them back to camp, where the Skipper breaks the Professor's trance by showing him his pocketknife. The Professor, denying the existence of zombies, asks how he got wet.

After Gilligan makes a voodoo doll of the witch doctor and stabs it with a knife, the witch doctor suddenly yells, runs from the jungle, leaps into the lagoon, and swims from the island.

COMMENTS:

- The Professor recognizes the artifacts as works of the Mayans, a tribe of Central American Indians, whose work would not be found in the caves of an uninhabited South Pacific island.
- The witch doctor possesses the rabbit's foot Gilligan previously sent back to Hawaii inside a robot. [Episode 57]
- The Skipper and Gilligan willingly return to what they consider to be a cursed cave to dig up more artifacts for Howell for a mere twenty dollars—without bargaining for more money.
- Mr. Howell's look-alike previously left the island with Howell's wallet. [Episode 62]

TROPICAL INVENTIONS:

- Gilligan's voodoo doll of a witch doctor

CASTAWAY QUIZ #73:

What personal effects does the witch doctor take from Ginger and Mary Ann?

(For answer, see page 359)

74: WHERE THERE'S A WILL

Writers: Sid Mandel & Roy Kammerman
Director: Charles Norton

When the castaways visit Howell, who's sick in bed with a stomachache, the millionaire decides to show his gratitude by rewriting his will to include the castaways. After dictating his new will to Lovey, Howell gathers the castaways at the communal table and hands them copies. That night the castaways revel in their wealth. Gilligan plans to buy a skateboard, licorice, pickles, and a tree house; the Skipper plans to buy a boat with a swimming pool; Ginger intends to back her own Broadway play; Mary Ann plans to live in London and spend summers on the French Riviera; the Professor plans to build a research laboratory with his own nuclear reactor.

The next day while walking through the jungle, Howell sees the Skipper talking to Gilligan, and an arrow strikes a nearby tree, just missing him. Convinced that someone is trying to kill him, Howell shares his suspicions with Lovey and then seeking the girls, falls into a hole they've just covered with palm fronds. After sharing his suspicions with Lovey again, Howell searches for the Professor, who accidentally pushes a boulder off a cliff, almost killing the millionaire.

Later while the castaways secretly plan a surprise party for Howell, the Professor explains that he was searching for mushrooms under the boulder, and the girls explain that they were building a pit to catch a wild boar for barbecue ribs.

Meanwhile Howell, barricading his hut with suitcases, decides to confront the others. Wandering past the supply hut, he overhears the castaways trying to decide who will slaughter the boar, and convinced they're talking about him, he runs back to his hut. Howell packs and moves to the other side of the island, leaving Lovey behind.

When Lovey discovers that the others were merely planning a surprise party, the castaways agree to search for Howell. While Howell stops to rest, his suitcases sink into quicksand. Hearing the castaways calling for him, he sets his pith helmet in the quicksand and hides behind a rock. When the other men discover Howell's hat floating in the quicksand, they mistake him for dead and decide to give him a funeral.

Back at camp the Skipper eulogizes Howell, who, sitting up in a nearby tree, watches his own funeral. After the castaways each praise Howell, they rip up their copies of his will. Realizing the castaways didn't care about his money, Howell falls from the tree. That night at a party for Howell, Lovey bursts out of a cake.

TROPICAL INVENTIONS:

- Ginger and Mary Ann's wild boar trap

CASTAWAY QUIZ #74

What does Howell will the Skipper?
(For answer, see page 359)

75: MAN WITH A NET ☺☺

Writer: Budd Grossman
Director: Leslie Goodwins
Guest Star: John McGiver

While Gilligan is fishing on the lagoon, a butterfly collector throws a net over a butterfly on his sailor's cap. While following the butterfly collector, the Skipper and Gilligan learn that Lord Beasley Waterford, searching for the pussycat swallowtail, the rarest butterfly in the world, will rescue the castaways once he catches the butterfly, which he suddenly spots. When Gilligan shouts for joy, Lord Beasley misses the butterfly.

The Professor explains that a butterfly collector could take years to catch the right specimen and suggests the castaways make nets and help. Accompanied by the Howells, Lord Beasley sinks into a quicksand pit. Accompanied by the girls, he leaps off a cliff while trying to catch the butterfly. While the castaways all soak their feet after searching the entire island, Lord Beasley walks past wearing a deepsea diving suit, and at Gilligan's suggestion Lord Beasley leads the Skipper and Gilligan mountain climbing.

That night Howell finds Beasley sticking pins in a map of the island and offers him $300,000 to rescue them, but Beasley, preoccupied with his map, sticks Howell with a pushpin.

When Mary Ann finds the Professor in the jungle, trying to memorize facts about butterflies so he can convince Lord Beasley to leave the island, she suggests he use crib notes. When Lord Beasley discovers that the Professor's been using notes to identify various caterpillars they've encountered while searching the jungle, he decries him.

When Gilligan fires Beasley's flare gun, Beasley announces that he

has the flare and refuses to leave the island until he catches the pussycat swallowtail. The next morning Beasley marches the castaways through the jungle, and when he allows them to rest for a half hour, he suddenly spots the butterfly, and as they all run after it, Gilligan shoos it away.

That evening after the Skipper paints a caged moth to look like the pussycat swallowtail, he calls Lord Beasley, who, stepping out into the rain with the cage, returns with a caged white moth.

The next day the Professor distills alcohol to get Lord Besley drunk so they can convince him to fire the flare gun. Gilligan brings Lord Beasley to the communal table, where the castaways, gathered for a celebratory tea, propose several toasts. When Beasley drinks them under the table, he suddenly notices the butterfly on a rock, captures it, puts it in a jar, and fires his flare gun. Unable to wake the castaways, Beasley leaves the island without them.

When the castaways wake up two days later with hangovers, Gilligan discovers that Beasley's things are gone, and they learn from the radio that Beasley, having returned to the United Kingdom, is departing for Antarctica, preoccupied with butterflies, and hasn't told anyone about the castaways.

COMMENTS:
- The pussycat swallowtail doesn't exist.
- The castaways happen to have a palette, paints, and brushes from a famous painter's previous visit. [Episode 34]

TROPICAL INVENTIONS:
- Butterfly nets

CASTAWAY QUIZ #75:
What's the title of the sequel Lord Beasley's writing to his first book, *The Butterfly and I*?
(For answer, see page 359)

76: HAIR TODAY, GONE TOMORROW ⊗

Writer: Brad Radnitz
Director: Tony Leader

When Gilligan wakes up one morning to discover that his hair has turned white, the Professor, unable to offer an explanation, suggests that Gilligan go on as if nothing has happened, assuring him that the girls won't be shocked by his white hair. When the girls discover Gilligan's hair, they pass out. When the Professor, confiding in the Skipper, speculates that Gilligan could be suffering from a rare tropical disease causing the deterioration of his entire system, Gilligan, over-hearing this and convinced that he's turning into an old man, returns to his hut, sits in a rocking chair, and acts like an old man. The Skipper, unable to convince him otherwise, brings the other castaways to his hut, where Gilligan, wearing bifocals and talking like an old man, wills his possessions to them.

That night Ginger and Mary Ann try to seduce Gilligan to awaken his youthful vigor, but fail to arouse him. At Lovey's suggestion

the Professor makes hair dye from vegetable coloring and secretly dyes Gilligan's hair while he's asleep. The next morning the Skipper wakes Gilligan, discovering he's completely bald. After the Skipper convinces Gilligan to wear his hat as if nothing has happened, the girls find Gilligan doing the laundry, remove his hat, and faint. The Professor asks Lovey to refrain from laughing when she sees Gilligan, but when Gilligan approaches, they can't contain themselves.

The Skipper and the Professor later find a note from Gilligan, who's gone to live in a cave to avoid any further embarrassment. When Ginger brings Gilligan a wig made from her own hair, Gilligan refuses to wear it. When Mary Ann brings him a wig made from coconuts, a woodpecker attacks it.

That night the Skipper, unable to sleep, discovers that he's gone bald and moves into the cave with Gilligan. The next day the Professor brings the crew two wigs the Howells once wore to a costume party as George and Martha Washington. At dinner the Skipper's wig falls in his soup, and when Gilligan laughs, the Skipper pulls the wig from his head and throws it in his soup. When Howell bends over to pick up his napkin, Lovey notices a hole in his pants. When Howell blames the hole on Gilligan's laundering, the Professor realizes that the crude bleach that burned a hole in Howell's pants caused Gilligan's and the Skipper's hair loss. Gilligan runs into a hut and returns with a blanket that he quickly wraps around Ginger; her heavily bleached dress suddenly falls apart under the blanket.

291

A few weeks later the Professor explains that the strong vapor of the sodium hypochloride in the bleach saturated the crew's scalp follicles, hastening Gilligan's and the Skipper's hair growth.

COMMENTS:

- While crude bleach might cause baldness (and severe skin rash), sodium hypochloride vapor would not hasten hair growth.

TROPICAL INVENTIONS:

- The castaways' bleach
- The Professor's hair dye
- Ginger's and Mary Ann's homemade wigs

CASTAWAY QUIZ #76:

What does Gilligan will to the Howells?
(For answer, see page 359)

77: RING AROUND GILLIGAN ⊗⊗⊗

Writer: John Fenton Murray
Director: George Cahan
Guest Star: Vito Scotti

Mad scientist Boris Balinkoff inconspicuously returns to the island by boat with a small monkey. While helping the Skipper build a raft for the Professor (who claims that a change in the currents will carry a raft out into the shipping lanes), Gilligan, searching the jungle for more vines, finds a ring Balinkoff tossed at him and slips it on his finger.

That night Balinkoff, speaking into a transmitter, turns Gilligan into a human robot, orders him to the cave, shows him the large computer that keeps him under Balinkoff's control as long as he wears the ring, and explains that the castaways will help him commit the greatest crime of all time.

The next morning when Gilligan checks to see how the women are progressing with the raft's sail, Lovey borrows his ring. That night when Balinkoff, speaking into his transmitter, issues his commands, Lovey packs a suitcase with money, knocks out Thurston, and returns to the cave where Balinkoff sends her back to her hut.

The next morning when Lovey asks the Skipper to return Gilligan's ring, he slips it on his finger. At Balinkoff's command, the Skipper destroys the raft with an ax and snapping out of the trance, orders a confused Gilligan to rebuild the raft. When Gilligan asks Ginger to

hold his ring, she slips it on her finger and at Balinkoff's command destroys the raft with the ax and returns to the cave. When Howell stops by to see how Gilligan's progressing with the raft, Gilligan destroys it with the ax. When Ginger returns the ring, Gilligan, who's rebuilt the raft, hands her the ax, confusing her.

As Balinkoff sleeps in the cave, the monkey activates the computer and squawks into the transmitter, and while the Professor and Howell watch from the supply hut, Gilligan starts leaping around like a monkey. Balinkoff wakes up, stops the monkey, and Gilligan, who's been swinging from a tree, wakes from the trance.

That night while the castaways sleep, the monkey brings Gilligan a bag full of rings, and at Balinkoff's command Gilligan slips a ring on each castaways' finger without waking them. Balinkoff, planning to rob Fort Knox, orders the castaways to collect coconuts to stage a dress rehearsal.

The next morning when the Skipper wakes Gilligan and demands an explanation for the coconuts piled in the corner of their hut, Gilligan notices a ring on the Skipper's finger. The other castaways, gathered outside, have discovered their rings, and as the Professor notices a sign reading "Fort Knox" over the crew's hut, Balinkoff, sitting in his boat on the lagoon, orders the castaways to steal the gold bullion from the crew's hut. The castaways stand guard with rakes and shovels, the Professor ignites an explosive charge, and Gilligan drives the pedal-powered bamboo car to the hut, where the others load it with coconuts. Balinkoff orders them to go faster, and after they've filled the car with coconuts and driven to the lagoon, he demands the

294

coconuts. The castaways throw coconuts at Balinkoff, smash his transmitter, and snap out of their trances in time to see Balinkoff leaving the island in his boat. As the castaways call after Balinkoff, Gilligan impulsively drives the bamboo car into the lagoon. While under Balinkoff's spell, the castaways missed the opportunity to send a raft out into the changed currents.

COMMENTS:
- We never learn how Boris Balinkoff, changed into animal form [Episode 65], returned to human form.
- Controlling humans with magic rings is scientifically unfeasible.
- We never learn if the castaways ever find the computer Balinkoff leaves behind in the cave.

TROPICAL INVENTIONS:
- Another raft

CASTAWAY QUIZ #77:
What's Boris Balinkoff's pet monkey's name?
(For answer, see page 359)

78: TOPSY-TURVY ☺☺

Writer: Elroy Schwartz
Director: Gary Nelson
Guest Stars: Eddie Little Sky, Allen Jaffe, Roman Gabriel

While headhunters' drums beat in the distance, Gilligan bumps his head and coming to, sees everything upside down. While Gilligan sits at the communal table, the Professor runs off to find a cure, the Skipper leaves to make some spears, and Ginger comes by looking for Mary Ann. Meanwhile as Howell practices his fencing in his hut, Lovey suggests they appease the headhunters with her rhinestone jewelry.

When the Professor tells Gilligan and Mary Ann that the captivora berry may cure Gilligan's optical disorders, Mary Ann refuses to pick berries while the headhunters' drums are beating—until Gilligan no-

tices that the drums are no longer beating. Meanwhile on the other side of the island, three headhunters commiserate over their broken drum.

Growing hungry, Gilligan bumps into a papaya tree, and as a headhunter tries to attack him, Gilligan inadvertently ducks out of the way, allowing the headhunter to half his papaya. The Howells' approach scares the headhunter off.

After synthesizing medicine in his hut, the Professor finds the Skipper standing on his head talking to Gilligan and has Gilligan sip the medicine. When Gilligan opens his eyes, he sees double. Explaining that Gilligan is merely experiencing a temporary reaction to the captivora berries, the Professor sends the Howells and the Skipper out to collect more berries so he can prepare another extract to offset the side effects, warning Gilligan that until then he may experience hallucinations.

Alone, Gilligan walks from his hut to bananas on a table as headhunters watch from the edge of the jungle. As the headhunters prepare to chop off his head, Gilligan ignores the "hallucination," which disappears when the girls bring him more berries. When they return to the jungle, the headhunters capture them.

As Gilligan sits eating a banana with a headhunter about to chop off his head, the Howells bring him more berries, unknowingly scaring the headhunter back into the jungle. As the Howells return to their hut to nap, the headhunters capture them and bring them to a bamboo cage where Ginger and Mary Ann are being held.

After the Professor and the Skipper feed Gilligan a new batch of captivora berry extract, Gilligan sees multiple images. "The extract must have reacted in some weird geometric progression," laments the Professor, who decides to reverse the process by having Gilligan drink water to dilute the extract. Gilligan's vision returns to normal, but when he says he still sees the natives, the headhunters capture the Professor and the Skipper, and Gilligan runs into the jungle.

After watching the headhunters guard the castaways from the edge of the jungle, Gilligan returns to camp to get the bowl of captivora berry extract. Pretending to drink from the bowl, Gilligan attracts the natives' curiosity. While the headhunters drink from the bowl, Gilligan frees the other castaways, and the natives, frightened by the multiple images they see, flee the island.

When Mary Ann rewards Gilligan with a coconut cream pie, he drinks the captivora extract to see five pies, but unable to grab a pie on the table, he punches the table, sending the pie into the Skipper's face.

COMMENTS:

- A bump on the head will not cause an individual to perceive images upside down.
- Since captivora berry doesn't exist, its extract could not possibly induce double or multiple vision.
- The establishing shot of the castaways in the natives' cage reveals that the cage is missing two walls.

TROPICAL INVENTIONS:

- The Professor's captivora berry extract

CASTAWAY QUIZ #78:

What do the captivora berries the Professor needs look like?
(For answer, see page 359)

79: THE INVASION ☺☺☺

Writers: Sam Locke & Joel Rapp
Director: Leslie Goodwins

While fishing on the lagoon, the Skipper catches a government briefcase labeled "Do Not Open." The Professor tells the castaways that the briefcase, once handcuffed to a secret agent, obviously contains vital state department secrets that the government will spare no expense to track down and asks the castaways to pledge not to open it.

That night the Skipper and Gilligan, unable to sleep, sneak into the Professor's hut and discover the briefcase beneath a cage of birds. Gilligan stands on a stool, stumbles, and wakes the Professor, who finds him wearing the bird cage on his head. Later Mary Ann stands in the clearing with a fishing rod, while Ginger distracts the Professor long enough to attach the fishing lure to the briefcase. After the Professor sends Ginger back to her hut, Lovey distracts him while Howell, dressed like a cat burglar, climbs in through the window of his hut. When Mary Ann reels in the briefcase, Howell follows after it, only to be discovered by the Professor, who grabs the suitcase, exposing the girls.

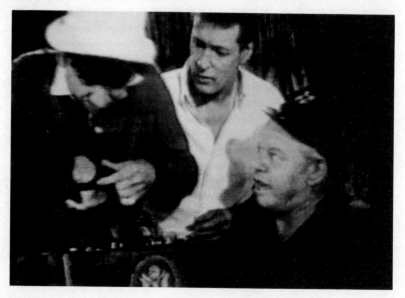

298

The next morning at breakfast the Professor announces that the briefcase is missing and accuses each of the castaways. Howell admits that he took it; the girls admit taking it from him; the Skipper admits taking it from them; and Gilligan admits having it at the table. Angered, the Professor accidentally springs open the briefcase. He slams it shut again, but not before seeing a secret file labeled "United States Defense Plans Against Secret Attack." While the Professor speculates that an enemy agent (having killed a U.S. agent to get this briefcase) could be on the island, Gilligan handcuffs himself to the briefcase. After the Professor tries to pick the lock, the Howells show up with a suitcase filled with keys. But the Professor says handcuff keys are specially shaped.

That night Gilligan, still handcuffed to the briefcase, dreams he's secret agent 014. The chief (the Professor) asks him to bring a briefcase, equipped with a self-destruct button, to the secretary of defense. Gilligan shows him his comb that is a radio-telephone/radar unit, a razor that doubles as a pistol, and a nail file that doubles as a magnetic antibullet shield. Meanwhile outside the office, Mary Ann, EVIL agent 10, speaking into her compact, tells a bald Howell that she will dispose of Gilligan as he comes through the door. As Mary Ann's about to kill Gilligan with a .45-caliber chrysanthemum, he shoots her with his bow tie.

Later, EVIL agent 5 (Ginger), speaking to Howell through a soup ladle, plans to kill Gilligan with a poison kiss, but Gilligan, wearing lip guard, kills her. Gilligan then goes home to his mother (the Skipper), who brings him a bowl of homemade soup. But when his mother tries to take the briefcase off his arm, Gilligan pulls her wig off to reveal EVIL agent 1 and forces him to eat the soup.

At EVIL headquarters, Howell tells Lovey that since all his agents have failed, he's eliminated the secretary of defense himself and plans to pose in his place. When Gilligan arrives, Howell takes the briefcase, pulls out a gun, and shoots Gilligan, who turns out to be a robot. The real Gilligan enters, but Howell distracts him, grabbing the gun and the briefcase.

As Gilligan's woken by the Professor and the Skipper, the briefcase pops open. Gilligan finds a key to open the handcuffs, and the Professor learns that the documents are from World War I. When the Howells enter, Gilligan, still disoriented from his dreams, runs into the jungle.

Later at the lagoon Gilligan tells his dream to the Skipper and the Professor, who laugh at the idea of a booby-trapped attaché case, but when the Skipper tosses the briefcase into the lagoon, it explodes.

COMMENTS:

- The Professor, refusing to allow the castaways to open the government briefcase, merits either reward or psychological analysis.

CASTAWAY QUIZ #79:

In his dream, what spy organization does Gilligan work for?

(For answer, see page 359)

80: THE KIDNAPPER ☺☺

Writer: Ray Singer
Director: Jerry Hopper
Guest Star: Don Rickles

The Skipper and Gilligan find a ransom note for Lovey, demanding that Gilligan and the Professor deliver $10,000 in tens and twenties in a bag to the hollow log seven paces from a rock on the north side of the island in exactly one hour. After the girls help Howell with his money, the Professor and Gilligan deliver it to the predetermined spot, where Gilligan gets stuck inside the hollow log, lifts the log into the air, trips, and lands on a rock, flying up into the air.

After the castaways find Lovey bound, blindfolded, and unable to describe the kidnapper, Ginger finds a ransom note demanding that the Howells place $20,000 in the mouth of the statue of the old native god on the south side of the island in return for Mary Ann. When Mary Ann returns to the Howells' hut, Gilligan finds a ransom note demanding that he and Mary Ann deliver $30,000 in return for Ginger.

After Ginger's released, she tells the others the kidnapper intends to continue kidnapping everyone. That night the Professor, the Skipper, and Gilligan set up a rope trap by torchlight. Gilligan sits on a rock as bait while the Skipper and the Professor hide nearby. When the kidnapper puts out the torch, Gilligan yells for help. The Professor relights the torch, finding Gilligan hanging from the rope in a tree, and the Skipper escorts the kidnapper from the jungle.

The next day an imprisoned Norbert Wiley admits that he left civilization because he's a compulsive kidnapper and got caught in a storm that beached his boat on the other side of the island. Gilligan runs back to tell the others while the Skipper and the Professor run to find the boat. After unintentionally offending Lovey (by telling her he ransomed her friend, Mildred Vandemere, for $50,000), Wiley showers the Howells with flattery. Wiley later tells his problem to Gilligan and the Skipper, flattering them both.

While the Professor repairs the boat's engine, the castaways try to convince the Professor to free Wiley. When he refuses, Ginger psycho-analyzes Wiley, and after telling the Professor that Wiley's merely a victim of his environment, she asks him to help Wiley help himself by freeing him. At Ginger and Mary Ann's insistence, the Professor reluctantly agrees. That moment the Skipper finishes fixing the motor,

and when Gilligan starts it up, the motor takes off into the jungle, taking Gilligan with it. The Skipper chases after him, and the motor emerges from the jungle carrying them both through the wall of a hut.

After the Professor and Ginger free Wiley from the jail, the castaways throw a party for him. At the party Wiley thanks the castaways for having faith in him. After dancing with Mary Ann, Wiley cuts in on the Howells, lifting Lovey's necklace from her neck. He later dances with Ginger, stealing her earrings, and while helping Howell to his seat, he pickpockets his wallet. Before dinner Wiley thanks the castaways for giving him a break and excuses himself from the table to think of his good fortune.

While the Professor admits his error, Lovey suddenly realizes her necklace is missing, and as the others notice that they're all missing something, a boat engine roars and they run to the lagoon to find Wiley leaving in his boat. In a note he left behind, Wiley explains that the strain of going straight was making him a nervous wreck. The Professor turns to Ginger, reiterating his initial position that they couldn't reform a criminal.

COMMENTS:

- Ginger's obsessive desire to free a compulsive criminal from imprisonment—jeopardizing the castaways' rescue hopes—indicates that she, not Wiley, requires psychological attention.

TROPICAL INVENTIONS:

- A bamboo prison

CASTAWAY QUIZ #80:

What does Wiley steal from Gilligan?
(For answer, see page 359)

81: AND THEN THERE WERE NONE ⊗

Writer: Ron Friedman
Director: Jerry Hopper

While Gilligan helps Mary Ann hang up a fallen clothesline, Mary Ann suddenly disappears. The Professor, deducing that Mary Ann has been abducted by natives, suggests a search, resulting in Ginger's disappearance. Speculating that perhaps headhunters came to the island searching for brides, the Professor suggests dressing Gilligan as Lovey for bait. After standing in the jungle dressed as Lovey, Gilligan calls for the Skipper and the Professor, who, disguised as trees, frighten him. After Howell, disguised as a tree, follows without Lovey, the Skipper finds Lovey's abandoned tree trunk in the jungle. The men run to the lagoon to stop the headhunters from leaving the island with the women, but the Professor, realizing there never were any headhunters, claims that one of the men has cracked under the strain of island life—becoming a Dr. Jekyll and Mr. Hyde.

That night Gilligan, realizing he was alone with Mary Ann, Ginger, and Lovey, convinces himself he's become a Mr. Hyde. Meanwhile the Professor brings Howell to the spot where the three disappearances took place, and they both fall into a booby-trapped pit. The next morning when the Skipper and Gilligan discover the Professor and Howell are missing, the Skipper sends Gilligan searching and falls into the pit. Gilligan, searching through the jungle, hears the other castaways' voices and convinced that he's being haunted by those he killed as Mr. Hyde, backs up into a tree and knocks himself unconscious.

Gilligan dreams that a court trial is being held in London to determine whether he's Mr. Hyde. The bailiff (Skipper) announces the court hearing, Dr. Gilligan enters, and a poor cockney flower girl (Mary Ann), believing him innocent, introduces his defense attorney: Mary Poppins (Lovey). The bailiff calls the court to session, and Judge Lord Anthony Armstrong Hanging (Howell) takes the bench, and the prosecuting barrister (Professor) calls forth a witness, the Lady Red (Ginger), who claims that Dr. Gilligan turns into Mr. Hyde at the mere mention of food. As she names several foods, Dr. Gilligan turns into Mr. Hyde, and the others grab him.

Gilligan wakes up tangled in the clothesline and hearing the castaways yelling for him, falls through the trapdoor with the clothesline, enabling the others to climb back out.

COMMENTS:

- Gilligan has a monster mask from the crate of magician's props that the castaways once fished from the lagoon. [Episode 33]

TROPICAL INVENTIONS:

- The castaways' tree disguises

CASTAWAY QUIZ #81:

What, according to the Professor, was the purpose of the booby-trapped pit?

(For answer, see page 359)

82: ALL ABOUT EVA ⊗

Writer: Joanna Lee
Director: Jerry Hopper

After a homely, bespectacled woman with a suitcase anchors her motorboat on the lagoon, Gilligan and Ginger, searching for seashells, find the boat. When the Professor and the Skipper fail to find a radio aboard the boat, Gilligan discovers footsteps in the sand and a high heel shoe.

While the castaways search the island, Gilligan and the Skipper catch Eva Grubb, a librarian who, having been shunned by men, spent all her money to buy a boat to get to a deserted island. Eva hands the Skipper the keys to the boat in exchange for his promise to take the castaways off the island.

After the Skipper introduces Eva to the other castaways, the Professor, having observed her disturbed behavior, refuses to leave Eva behind—until the Skipper suggests they send a boat back for Eva upon their return to civilization. After Gilligan accidentally tells Eva the castaways' plans, the Skipper and the Professor, attempting to start up the boat, discover that Eva took the spark plugs from the engine to prevent them from carrying out their plans.

The Skipper and the Professor inform the Howells, who invite Eva to tea and fail in their attempt to bribe her. Later that night Ginger suggests that they make Eva beautiful to raise her self-esteem so she'll want to go home. The next day after the women dress Eva, fix her hair, and help her with makeup, they discover that she looks exactly like Ginger. Convinced that she's beautiful, Eva returns the spark plugs to the Professor, who has been trying to fashion spark plugs from seashells.

After Eva overhears Ginger expressing her doubts to Mary Ann that Eva will survive back home as a Ginger look-alike, Lovey invites Eva to

306

a bon voyage party that evening, insisting that no one would be able to tell her from Ginger. Inspired, Eva knocks out Ginger, ties her up, and reveals her plan to take Ginger's place, return to civilization with the others, and masquerade as Ginger in Hollywood.

Eva shows up at the party dressed as Ginger. When Howell seeks Eva, Eva runs back to Ginger's hut, changes to another dress, dons her eyeglasses, and returns to the party. When Howell seeks Ginger, Eva runs back to Ginger's hut, changes back into the first dress, removes her glasses, returns to the party as Ginger, and unable to see, drops a glass of champagne. When Lovey announces that she wants to give Eva a gift, Eva runs back to Ginger's hut, quickly changes her dress, dons her glasses, returns to the party, and receives a beautiful necklace. When Gilligan seeks Ginger for a dance, Eva immediately runs back to Ginger's hut, changes back into her dress, returns to the party, and hides her glasses down the front of her dress. While dancing with Eva, Gilligan accidentally crushes her, breaking her glasses. Eva mistakenly starts dancing with Lovey, sits and misses her chair, and causes Howell to spill champagne all over her dress. When Ginger suddenly appears at the party and explains Eva's scheme, Eva offers her deepest apologies—which the castaways accept.

The next morning when the girls can't find Eva, the castaways run to the lagoon, where they find a note from Eva in place of the boat explaining that her apology was merely an act and she's returned to civilization to take over Ginger's career.

COMMENTS:

- The odds of a Ginger look-alike landing on the island in the wake of a visit from a Howell look-alike [Episode 62] and a Gilligan look-alike [Episode 70] are at least forty-seven billion to one.
- We never learn whether Eva Grubb makes it back to the States and effectively takes over Ginger Grant's career.

TROPICAL INVENTIONS:

- The Professor's henna shampoo

CASTAWAY QUIZ #82

When did Eva Grubb have her first date?
(For answer, see page 359)

83: GULLIGAN GOES GUNG HO ⊗⊗

Writer: Bruce Howard
Director: Robert Scheerer

While walking past the girls' hut, Gilligan, overhearing a confrontation, sees Ginger shoot the Professor with a gun. Gilligan finds the Skipper, who's found phosphorescent rocks that the castaways can use for an SOS signal, and returning to the girls' hut, they find the Professor lying on the bed, Mary Ann washing out a bloody hankerchief, and Ginger holding a gun. Ginger explains they were practicing a scene from a play with a blank gun, and when the Professor fell, he hit the table.

After the Howells ask the Professor about the excitement earlier and discuss the need for better protection, the Professor gathers the men and suggests electing the Skipper sheriff to uphold the law. The Skipper appoints Gilligan deputy and orders him to learn the criminal code.

The next day while Gilligan, holding a nightstick, directs pedestrian traffic, the Professor and the Skipper collect phosphorescent rocks. Meanwhile a two-man aircraft combs the Pacific in search of castaways reportedly seen on an uncharted island. Gilligan catches Howell borrowing the Skipper's binoculars without his permission and arrests him. When Howell offers him a bribe, Gilligan whistles for the Skipper and the Professor, who ask Howell to accept the penalty, locking him in the cave cage serving as their jail.

As the search plane flies toward the island, Gilligan guards Howell. While the girls prepare lunch, the Skipper, returning to collect phosphorescent rocks, leaves Gilligan in charge. Gilligan stamps out the girls' fire and burns his feet. Ginger laughs at him, and when Gilligan arrests her, Mary Ann tries to stop him, resulting in her arrest. Lovey brings the girls and Howell a file baked inside a chocolate cake, and when she allows Gilligan to have a piece, Gilligan bites into the file.

and throws her in jail. When the Professor returns to camp with two buckets of rock and a stick of dynamite, Gilligan throws him in jail for possession of a concealed weapon.

When the Skipper returns to camp and discovers everyone's in jail, he demands the key to free the others. When the Skipper lets himself in the cage, leaving the key in the lock, Gilligan locks them all inside. Deciding to break out of the jail, the men try to crash through the bamboo bars. Ginger, having starred in a few prison films, stages a fight between the Skipper and the Professor—a scene from a movie Gilligan's seen. Meanwhile the men aboard the search plane complete their mission, but decide to search one last island.

Ginger suggests that the castaways make noise so Gilligan will open the door, but Gilligan, having see that film, demonstrates what happens: He opens the door, locks himself inside, and throws the key outside. Suddenly the Professor hears a plane flying over the island. The pilots see nothing since Gilligan imprisoned the Skipper and the Professor before they could set up the SOS signal. As the other

castaways prepare to kill him, Gilligan bursts through the cage door and runs into the jungle.

COMMENTS:
- A blank gun's presence on the island remains unexplained.
- Pilots flying over the island would spot the castaways' huts.

TROPICAL INVENTIONS:
- The Professor's dynamite
- Gilligan's whistle

CASTAWAY QUIZ #83:
What law does Ginger break, resulting in her arrest?
(For answer, see page 359)

84: TAKE A DARE ☺☺☺

Writer: Roland MacLane
Director: Stanley Z. Cherry
Guest Star: Strother Martin

While the Skipper's fishing on the lagoon, Gilligan, listening to a radio game show, *Take a Dare*, learns that if a contestant, George Barkley, dropped off on a desert island with a shortwave radio, can survive alone for a week, he'll win $10,000. While Gilligan and the Skipper collect bananas, a well-dressed man emerges from the jungle and steals their fish.

When the crew returns to camp, they accuse the others of taking the fish; the girls accuse Gilligan of stealing the plates and frying pan; the Professor accuses Mary Ann of taking his hammock; and the Howells accuse the others of stealing their silverware. While searching the jungle for the missing objects, the Skipper and Gilligan discover a man lying on a hammock talking into a transmitter, and the Skipper, realizing they've found *Take a Dare* contestant George Barkley, grabs the microphone and begins calling for help. When the Skipper can't get a response, he brings the transmitter to the Professor, who realizes that Barkley removed an essential part. The Professor explains that if the game show discovers the castaways presence on the island, Barkley must forfeit the $10,000 prize.

Howell invites Barkley to his hut, opens his safe, and offers Barkley $30,000 to fix the transmitter, but Barkley refuses, convinced that the Howells' money is phony and their jewelry imitation. That evening Ginger, taking matters into her own hands, seductively arranges to meet Barkley at nine o'clock, but when he refuses to bring the missing part of the transmitter, she spurns him.

The next day when the Professor and the Skipper discover that the transmitter's missing, they hear Barkley on the radio on *Take a Dare*. When Gilligan and the Skipper spot Barkley broadcasting from the top of a hill, the Skipper grabs the microphone and starts calling for help, but not before Barkley signs off and disconnects the microphone. When the Skipper and Gilligan return to camp, Howell, listening to the radio, insists that he heard only Barkley on *Take a Dare*.

Later while broadcasting, Barkley arranges to be picked up the next day, and attacked by the Skipper and Gilligan, he throws the transmitter off a cliff, where it smashes on the rocks below. The next morning the castaways take lookout positions, planning to yell when they sight a boat and run to where it lands. When the Skipper asks Gilligan why he's looking up in the sky, Gilligan explains that he's watching a helicopter take off. He was told to yell if he saw a boat, he reminds the Skipper, not a helicopter.

While listening to *Take a Dare* on the radio, the castaways learn that Barkley's $10,000 prize was hidden in the bottom of his transmitter. After the Skipper and Gilligan search unsuccessfully for the $10,000, Howell finds it.

COMMENTS:

- The castaways could easily convince George Barkley that Howell is the millionaire he claims to be.

TROPICAL INVENTIONS:

- Howell's wall safe

CASTAWAY QUIZ #84:

What does the game show contestant take of the Skipper's?
(For answer, see page 359)

85: COURT-MARTIAL ⊛

Writer: Roland MacLane
Director: Gary Nelson

While napping on the beach, the Skipper and Gilligan learn that the Maritime Board decided that the *Minnow*'s disappearance was the Skipper's fault, relieving the Skipper of his command. While the castaways search for the despondent Skipper, Gilligan finds him tying a noose from a vine, and after returning him to his hut, Ginger suggests they reenact the shipwreck.

The Professor brings the Skipper to a clearing where Gilligan stands at the wheel of a mock *Minnow*. Mary Ann, sitting at pedal-powered fan, will create wind and thunder, and Ginger, holding a bucket of water and working an electrical generator, will make lightning and waves. As the Skipper reenacts the shipwreck, the Professor tugs on ropes, rocking the mock *Minnow*, Mary Ann pedals the fan, and

Ginger throws buckets of water at the ship. The Skipper orders Gilligan to throw the anchor overboard, which Gilligan does—without first securing it to the ship.

When the Skipper later finds Gilligan in the jungle, tying a noose from a vine, he suggests that they both move to the other side of the island. That night Gilligan dreams that he's Lord Admiral Gilligan, the youngest admiral in the fleet, aboard a masted ship carrying the Queen Mother (Lovey) and her two daughters (Ginger and Mary Ann). Suddenly three pirates (the Skipper, Howell, and the Professor) climb aboard the ship, capture Gilligan, and lock the women below. Meanwhile Gilligan, on deck in a cage, uses his belt to reach the keys, freeing himself and the women. When he returns to the deck to find the pirates stealing the treasure, he tosses them each a sword, including his own. He then swings from a rope, finds another sword, and fences with them. Finally they cut his sword, and as they're about to push him off the plank, Gilligan's awoken by the Skipper.

The Professor runs up with the radio, which is broadcasting a bulletin announcing that on the day the *Minnow* set sail the radio operator issued the weather information from the previous day, failing to mention the approaching storm, freeing the Skipper from blame.

COMMENTS:

- The castaways, capable of building an elaborate mock *Minnow*, should be able to build a suitable raft to leave the island.

TROPICAL INVENTIONS:

- A mock *Minnow*
- A pedal-powered fan and thunder panel
- A lightning generator

CASTAWAY QUIZ #85:

In Gilligan's dream, what are the Skipper's, Howell's, and the Professor's pirate names?
(For answer, see page 359)

86: THE HUNTER ☺☺

Writers: Bill Greshman & William Freedman
Director: Leslie Goodwins
Guest Stars: Rory Calhoun, Harold "Oddjob" Sakata

A helicopter lands on the lagoon while Gilligan sits nearby listening to the radio. Gilligan greets Jonathan Kincaid, a big game hunter, and his assistant, Ramoo. As Gilligan runs off to tell the others, Kincaid decides that seven stranded castaways on an uncharted island afford him the perfect opportunity to hunt the most difficult game of all—a human. Kincaid tells the gathered castaways that he has radioed the proper authorities, who will be sending a boat the next morning at ten o'clock. As the castaways pack, Kincaid interviews them to see which one will make the best quarry.

That night as the castaways throw a farewell party, Kincaid announces that he's going to hunt one of the castaways—adding that if the one he's hunting can elude him for twenty-four hours, he'll see to it that the castaways are returned to civilization. After Kincaid narrows his choice down to Gilligan, Ramoo takes Gilligan away. The Professor decides to make a break for the helicopter and radio for help, but Kincaid advises the castaways that he's removed the tubes.

While Ramoo gives Gilligan a rubdown and feeds him dinner, Howell offers Kincaid a half million dollars in cash to call off the hunt, which he refuses to do. Later Ginger tries to seduce Kincaid, suggesting that they have a drink first. She inconspicuously empties a vial of clear liquid into one of the bamboo glasses of pineapple juice. But Kincaid sets his glass on the table—where Gilligan drinks it and passes out, ruining Ginger's playact.

The next day at noon Kincaid sets the alarm on his watch and gives Gilligan a fifteen-minute head start. Meanwhile Ramoo, armed with a

315

spear, holds the remaining castaways prisoner in a cave. While the other castaways argue, Lovey leaves the cave, confronts Ramoo about his conduct, and walks past him. As Ramoo is about to throw his spear at her, the Skipper wrestles him to the ground. Meanwhile on the other side of the island, an exhausted Gilligan runs from Kincaid. As the Skipper and the Professor watch from the shrubs, Kincaid fires and Gilligan falls into the castaways' freshwater trough. When Kincaid reaches into the trough, Gilligan pulls him in and leaps out, waterlogging Kincaid's gun.

While Kincaid goes off to find Ramoo to clean his gun, the Professor and the Skipper disguise Gilligan as a tree, sweeping away Gilligan's tracks in the sand with a palm frond. Kincaid and Ramoo appear and noticing that Gilligan's trail disappears at that spot, deduce that he must be nearby. Kincaid decides to test his rifle first and instructs Ramoo to draw a target, which Ramoo naturally chalks onto Gilligan's tree, but when Kincaid takes aim through his sight, the tree begins to move. "Must be my malaria acting up," he says, and by the time he realizes it's Gilligan and aims his rifle, his watch alarm sounds, and Kincaid sticks to his word about calling off the hunt—although not to his word about rescuing the castaways. If the authorities ever learn that he was hunting a human, he says, they'll lock him away.

A month later while the men are listening to the sports report on the radio, they learn that Kincaid broke down after a shooting match and was taken to a hospital in a straitjacket while repeatedly muttering the mysterious word "Gilligan."

COMMENTS:
- The Professor could easily hotwire Kincaid's helicopter and take off, but he fails to recognize the opportunity.

TROPICAL INVENTIONS:
- Professor's clear knockout solution

CASTAWAY QUIZ #86:
What movie is this episode based on?
(For answer, see page 359)

87: LOVEY'S SECRET ADMIRER ⊗

Writers: Herbert Finn & Alan Dinehart
Directors: David McDearmon
Guest Star: Billy Curtis

When Lovey wakes Thurston in the middle of the night, he finds a note tucked under her pillow from a secret admirer. The next morning Howell, accompanied by Lovey, accuses both the Skipper and the Professor of having written the note, which they both deny, leaving only Gilligan suspect. When the Professor builds a lie detector (by wiring the ship's horn to the batteries from the radio) that indicates that the Skipper, Gilligan, and he are all innocent, the Professor deduces that there must be someone else on the island.

That night as a dark figure creeps into the Howells' hut and leaves another note, the Professor and Ginger turn on a flashlight, revealing Howell. The Skipper and Mary Ann show up with a bamboo lantern, and Gilligan pops up from under the bed.

The next day Thurston explains to Lovey that he thought it might be amusing for a woman her age to receive anonymous love letters. Misinterpreting her husband's intentions, Lovey tears up the letters, refusing to see him again. That night after the girls console Lovey, she turns on the radio and falls asleep listening to Uncle Artie tell the story of Cinderella.

317

She dreams that she is Cinderella, doing the chores for her wicked stepmother (the Skipper). A knight arrives with invitations to the prince's ball, and the stepmother tells him that her two beautiful daughters, Gizelle (Mary Ann) and Fredrica (Ginger), will be there. When the two girls go off to the ball, Lovey's fairy godfather (Gilligan) appears and temporarily changes her into a donkey before giving her a beautiful gown. He warns her to return by midnight, explaining that as a new fairy godfather he can only work eight hours by union rules.

At the palace two knaves (the Skipper and the Professor) dance with the two sisters—until the prince (Thurston Howell) enters and dances with the two girls. Fairy godfather Gilligan pops in to observe Lovey's arrival. The prince falls in love with her instantly, and after Gilligan gets rid of the two sisters, they dance together. When the clock strikes midnight, Lovey runs, and Thurston finds an old boot—which Gilligan quickly changes into a glass slipper—that she's left behind.

Lovey wakes to find Thurston, who just happened to be passing the hut, sitting by her side and forgives him. The next day as Gilligan sits in the lie detector amusing himself, Mary Ann asks him whether he ate one of her pies. When Gilligan says no, the lie detector sounds.

COMMENTS:

- According to Lovey's dream, she sees Gilligan as a well-meaning though slightly offbeat and incompetent guardian angel; Thurston as a prince; Ginger and Mary Ann as ugly; and the Skipper and the Professor as ordinary simpletons.
- While the love notes are handwritten on pink stationery, both clues go unexamined. Oddly, Lovey can't recognize her husband's handwriting.
- The Professor can build a complex lie detector, but he still can't build a simple radio transmitter.

TROPICAL INVENTIONS:

- The Professor's lie detector (the ship's horn wired to the radio's batteries)
- A bamboo lantern

CASTAWAY QUIZ #87:

What was the name of Gilligan's pet turtle back home?
(For answer, see page 359)

88: OUR VINES HAVE TENDER APES ☺☺

Writers: Sid Mandel & Roy Kammerman
Director: David McDearmon
Guest Star: Billy Curtis

When Gilligan finds an ape-man sleeping in his hammock, he races to tell the Skipper and the Professor, and while trying to explain what he saw, he suddenly notices the ape-man in a nearby tree. The ape-man beats his chest and swings from a vine into the Professor and the Skipper, landing on top of Gilligan. After the Skipper and the Professor scare him into the jungle, the ape-man jumps over the Howells, who are having drinks in front of their hut, and frightens Mary Ann and Ginger, who are collecting fruit with a giant bamboo shopping cart.

Later the men search through the jungle to capture the ape-man. After Mr. Howell displays that his umbrella doubles as a sword, he accidentally leaves the umbrella half behind. When Gilligan goes back to get it, he finds the ape-man, who climbs to the top of a coconut tree and starts pelting them with coconuts, destroying Howell's umbrella. When the ape-man finds Howell in his hut and snaps his golf club in two, Lovey chases him away. After Mary Ann makes up herself to look unattractive, the girls barricade their hut door, but the ape-man climbs in the window and carries Ginger off to a cave.

319

That night when the ape-man brings Ginger a coconut, she learns that his name is Tongo. As Tongo's momentarily distracted by the sound of the men combing the jungle, Ginger hits him in the head with the coconut and runs.

The next day the Skipper and the Professor convince Mary Ann to lure the ape-man into chasing her through the jungle and into a bamboo cage disguised as a hut. Captured, Tongo leaps around the cage, and at the Professor's suggestion the castaways leave Tongo to allow him time to calm down. Alone, Tongo takes out a tape recorder and dictates his diary, revealing that he's an actor practicing to get the lead role in a jungle movie.

Later while Gilligan tries to communicate with Tongo, the Professor and Ginger, who've been watching from a distance, realize the ape-man wants to be friendly and let him out of the cage. After a real gorilla comes out from the jungle and carries off Tongo, the Professor, the Skipper, and Gilligan discover that Tongo dropped a tape recorder. After playing Tongo's recording to the other castaways, the Professor insists that they rescue Tongo, who in turn can rescue them from the island. At the women's suggestion the castaways decide to lure the gorilla away from Tongo with another gorilla—a costumed Gilligan.

After the girls sew Mrs. Howell's furs into a gorilla outfit, Gilligan lures the gorilla into chasing after him through the jungle. While the men chase after Gilligan, the girls tell Tongo they're on to him. When Gilligan returns and reveals himself to Tongo, the gorilla chases him back into the jungle. As the other castaways chase after Gilligan, Tongo walks off into the jungle dejected.

Later after the castaways have searched unsuccessfully for Tongo, he appears in a helicopter above them. He throws down a note explaining that he can't take the castaways with him, because if the story ever got out about him with the gorilla, it would forever ruin his career as the ape-man.

COMMENTS:
- Howell could promise to buy Tongo his own movie studio if he'll help to rescue them.
- The castaways never search the island for Tongo's boat, helicopter, or plane.

TROPICAL INVENTIONS:
- A bamboo cage
- A bamboo shopping cart
- A gorilla outfit (sewn together from Mrs. Howell's furs)

CASTAWAY QUIZ #88:
In what movie is Tongo trying to land a role?
(For answer, see page 359)

89: GILLIGAN'S PERSONAL MAGNETISM ☻☻☻

Writer: Bruce Howard
Director: Hal Cooper

While Gilligan and the Skipper bowl one afternoon with wooden pins and a rock bowling ball, an electrical storm flares up, and Gilligan, struck by lightning, gets the bowling ball stuck on his hand.

The Professor claims that somehow Gilligan's body absorbed enough electricity from the lightning to have crystalized certain metallic elements in his body, which created a magnetic field, molecularly attracting the rock, which has a high content of iron ore. Disbelievingly, the Skipper grabs Gilligan, receiving an electrical shock, and Gilligan drops the bowling ball, breaking the Professor's table.

When the Skipper helps Gilligan into his hammock, he receives a series of electrical shocks. That night the Skipper has difficulty sleeping since Gilligan keeps hitting him with the bowling ball.

The next day Ginger feeds Gilligan while the Professor connects the pedal-powered electrical generator (from the *Minnow*'s engine) to an electrode that will enable him to zap the stone to break it apart. Mary

Ann runs to get Gilligan, who's wheeling a handcart to carry the bowling ball. But an electrical storm flares up again, and as the Professor tries to zap the bowling ball, lightning strikes Gilligan a second time, knocking apart the palm-frond-covered shelter, freeing the rock from Gilligan's hand and turning him invisible.

Later in the Professor's hut, the Professor admits that he doesn't know what to do. Mary Ann brings Gilligan his favorite drink, and Ginger, wearing a nurse's uniform, examines him. Finally the Professor develops a cure. He wraps Gilligan in strips of cloth impregnated with lead ore, claiming that they'll absorb any charges Gilligan's emitting, making him visible again. When Gilligan, wrapped as a mummy, returns to his hut to lie down, he walks past the girls' hut, scaring them. As Ginger runs, her comb catches one of Gilligan's bandages, unwrapping him.

That night at dinner as the Professor declares the need to rewrap Gilligan, the Skipper reads a note from Gilligan that says he's moving to the other side of the island. "Why would he do a foolish thing like that?" asks the Professor. Howell offers a reward for any information, hoping Gilligan will return to collect the reward himself. "I wonder if Gilligan knows how much we love him," ponders Ginger. Mary Ann cries, excusing herself from the table. When the castaways suddenly see fruit rising from the table and landing on Gilligan's plate, they realize he's been listening to them the entire time. Infuriated, the Skipper chases Gilligan, who, while insulting him, reappears. The strips of cloth must have worked, observes the Skipper, chasing Gilligan into the jungle.

COMMENTS:
- A person struck by lightning will not become magnetized.
- If being struck twice by lightning actually turns a person invisible, invisibility wouldn't include his clothes.
- Since the castaways previously built a bowling alley [Episode 16], building a second alley and carving a stone ball seems slightly pointless.

TROPICAL INVENTIONS:

- A bowling alley (wooden pins and stone bowling ball)
- A pedal-powered generator linked to an electrode
- A bamboo handcart
- Iron-ore-soaked cloth

CASTAWAY QUIZ #89:

When Gilligan turns invisible and leaves a note telling the others that he's moved to the other side of the island, how much reward money does Howell offer for any information leading to his return?

(For answer, see page 359)

90: SPLASHDOWN ⊚⊚⊚⊚

Writer: John Fenton Murray
Director: Jerry Hooper
Guest Stars: Jim Spencer, Scott Graham,
    George Neise, Chick Hern

The United States launches a rocket, Scorpio 6, manned by astronauts Tobias and Ryan, who will rendezvous with an unmanned capsule launched two weeks earlier. The Professor, following the radio reports, informs the Skipper and Gilligan that Scorpio 6 will pass 155 miles directly over the island on its ninth, sixteenth, and twenty-third orbits. By utilizing the spare transistor and diodes from the radio, he hopes to communicate with the capsule.

Overly excited, Gilligan runs to tell the Howells and the girls, who, misunderstanding him, run to greet the astronauts at the lagoon. After the Professor explains the situation, the castaways build a four-man, pedal-powered carousel to power the generator from the *Minnow*'s engine to send a signal from a bamboo telegraph. As the castaways pedal and the Professor wires an SOS, the radio reports a mysterious static. The Professor encourages the others to keep pedaling, explaining that the authorities will trace the interference back to the island, but the capsule travels out of their range.

Later when the radio reports that Scorpio 6 is over Mexico, where the astronauts can see the lights of Mexico City, the men decide to spell out SOS using tree trunks and setting them on fire to signal the astronauts. When the Professor realizes that the tree trunks should be soaked with something flammable, the men give up—until Howell announces that he's going to drown his sorrows in a bottle of brandy. That night as the men ignite the tree trunks soaked in brandy, Gilligan accidentally sets fire to his pants and trips over the logs as he runs to soak his bottom in the water trough. The astronauts spot three letters that spell out S-O-L and interpret it as a greeting to astronaut Sol Tobias.

The next day after the radio reports that the astronauts have lost contact with the unmanned capsule, the Skipper and Gilligan see the space capsule land on the lagoon. The Professor insists that the Skipper and Gilligan ride the capsule out to sea, where they'll be spotted by search teams, offending the other castaways. Near daybreak the Howells sneak aboard the capsule and hide beneath a blanket.

Back at mission control the authorities, unable to locate the capsule and fearing that top secret instruments will fall into the wrong hands, plan to destroy it by remote control at nine o'clock. At five to nine the Professor has Gilligan and the Skipper board the capsule, but when the Skipper tries to shove off, the capsule won't budge. When the Professor instructs them to toss all excess weight overboard, Gilligan eventually pulls the blanket off the Howells. Howell hands Gilligan a wad of bills, which Gilligan hands to the Skipper, who throws it overboard. Discovered, the Howells rat on the girls. While the Professor admonishes them on the beach, Gilligan informs them that the capsule is floating away. When the Professor tells the Skipper and Gilligan to board the capsule again, it explodes.

COMMENTS:

- If not for the Howells' and the girls' greed, the Skipper and Gilligan would have been killed.
- Since the Great Wall of China is the earth's only manmade structure visible from outer space, astronauts orbiting the earth couldn't possible see six-foot-long letters from space— even if they are flaming.
- When the astronauts radioed that they'd spotted an island's greeting to Sol, journalists would have tried to figure out from what island the message came.

TROPICAL INVENTIONS:

- A bamboo telegraph powered by a four-man, pedal-powered carousel
- Signal logs soaked in brandy

CASTAWAY QUIZ #90:

What unmanned capsule lands on the lagoon?
(For answer, see page 359)

91: HIGH MAN ON THE TOTEM POLE ☺☺

Writer: Brad Radnitz
Director: Herbert Coleman
Guest Stars: Jim Lefebra, Al Ferrar, Pete Sotoge

Gilligan, the Professor, and the Skipper find a totem pole carved by the Kapuki, the most ferocious cannibals in the area. The head atop the totem pole bares a striking resemblance to Gilligan, who convinces himself that he's a descendant of a long line of headhunters.

The Howells, convinced that a relaxing drive will assuage Gilligan's fear, have him chauffeur them in the castaways' pedal-powered bamboo car, but whatever the Howells say reminds Gilligan of headhunters. When the Skipper later finds Gilligan chopping the head off the totem pole, he superstitiously points out that Gilligan has chopped off the head. When Gilligan, concerned for the others' safety, packs to move to the other side of the island, the Professor, hoping to cure him psychologically, hands him an ax and volunteers to be the first head in Gilligan's collection. When Gilligan throws the ax out the window, he realizes he's not a headhunter after all.

Meanwhile three Kapuki natives land on the island, discover the headless totem pole, and declare that the perpetrator must die. The

Professor and the Skipper, who've decided to put the head back on the totem pole, spot the natives. When Gilligan discovers the head back on top of the totem pole, he runs into the jungle—until he finds the Skipper and the Professor, who explain the situation. While the Skipper and the Professor inform the Howells, Gilligan finds the girls taking a mud bath in a mud bog and seeing only their heads, mistakenly thinks they've fallen victim to the headhunters.

Meanwhile the natives capture the Howells and prepare a boiling caldron. The Professor, watching from the bush with the Skipper, realizes that Gilligan can free the Howells if he can convince the Kapuki that he's their great king resurrected. Mary Ann makes up Gilligan in a tribal costume, and the Professor teaches him Kapuki. Realizing the Kapuki are about to kill the Howells, the Skipper, who has been keeping an eye on the situation, jumps out from the bush and orders them to stop, resulting in his capture. While Gilligan takes a last look at himself in the mirror, the Kapuki capture the girls and the Professor.

Gilligan races to the clearing to find the others tied to trees and the Kapuki sharpening their knives. Gilligan accidentally knocks the head off the totem pole and climbs up behind it to replace it with his own. Before the Kapuki knife the castaways, they bow to pray to the head atop the totem pole, and Gilligan loses his balance and falls down from behind the totem pole. When the Kapuki chase him, Gilligan stumbles, tossing the head back into the sand, frightening them away.

The next day Gilligan brings the men to show them the new head he carved for the totem pole's top—in Howell's likeness.

COMMENTS:

- The Professor displays leadership, coming up with all sorts of psychological games to cure Gilligan and to save the castaways from the Kapuki.

CASTAWAY QUIZ #91:

What name do the Kapuki natives call the head atop the totem pole, that looks like Gilligan?

(For answer, see page 359)

92: THE SECOND GINGER GRANT ☻☻☻

Writer: Ron Friedman
Director: Steve Binder

After watching Ginger sing "I Wanna Be Loved by You" to entertain the castaways, Mary Ann, wishing she could be like Ginger Grant, falls and hits her head, causing her to believe she is Ginger. After examining Mary Ann, the Professor suggests the castaways go along with her fantasy until he can come up with a cure, advising Ginger to dress like Mary Ann.

Mary Ann, dressed like Ginger, asks Gilligan to practice a scene with her, kissing him passionately, while the other men dress Ginger like Mary Ann, using one of Lovey's wigs. That night Ginger serves the castaways an unappetizing dinner and later finds Mary Ann shortening all her gowns.

The next day when Mary Ann sees Ginger hanging up laundry without her wig, she faints. Explaining that Mary Ann is experiencing traumatic shock, the Professor decides to try hypnosis. Gilligan peeks through the window to watch the Professor hypnotize Mary Ann, falling into a trance as the Professor tells her she'll become Mary Ann when she hears the name Mary Ann. The Skipper pulls Gilligan away from the window, and when the

Professor wakes Mary Ann and says her name, she remains convinced that she's Ginger.

When the Skipper finds Gilligan taking a bath in his hut and mentions Mary Ann, Gilligan screams, splashes the Skipper, and chases him from the hut. Gilligan, thinking he's Mary Ann, wraps himself in a towel and runs to the girls' hut, where he finds Ginger wearing what he thinks are his clothes. After pulling Gilligan out from under Ginger's bed, the Professor hypnotizes him back to his normal self.

The Professor suggests that they ask Mary Ann to put on a show for them that night; the real world of Mary Ann, he explains, will push out the dream world of Mary Ann. After Howell introduces Mary Ann as Ginger Grant, she sings "I Wanna Be Loved by You," forgets the words, and while dancing, falls. When Gilligan helps "Ginger," she insists she's Mary Ann, unable to understand why Ginger is wearing her clothes.

COMMENTS:

- "They dubbed my voice in all the *Gilligan's Island* episodes when we had to sing, in all the group stuff," recalls Dawn Wells. "Even in 'For He's a Jolly Good Fellow,' it wasn't me singing. I got everybody off key....Jackie DeShannon used to do my stuff originally. When I played Ginger, I did sing, because she was supposed to be off-key, and I did that real well."
- Since the Professor previously used improvised pendulums to hypnotize the castaways, the presence of a gold hypnosis pendulum on the island remains unexplained.

TROPICAL INVENTIONS:

- The Professor's retinoscope

CASTAWAY QUIZ #92:

What does Ginger serve the castaways for dinner?
(For answer, see page 359)

93: THE SECRET OF GILLIGAN'S ISLAND ⊛⊛⊛

Writers: Bruce Howard & Arne Sultan
Director: Gary Nelson

The Skipper and the Professor find Gilligan in a cave where he's discovered a prehistoric stone tablet of hieroglyphics, which, according to the Professor, may indicate the way off the island. They carry the stone tablet out of the cave, and after the Professor explains that it's just a section of a much larger tablet, he sends the other castaways to search the other caves for the remaining pieces.

When Mary Ann and Ginger leave the pot of acid the Professor needs to clean the tablets simmering over a fire, Gilligan happens by and thinking that the kettle contains soup, tries to taste it, but the girls return in time to stop him. Meanwhile the Howells, searching through one of the caves, discover one of the tablets. Using a bamboo paintbrush, the Professor cleans the tablet with his acid, and the castaways assemble the three pieces only to learn that they're still missing a piece.

While Mary Ann and Ginger search through a cave, a bat appears, chasing them into a corner where they accidentally discover another piece of the tablet. To keep Gilligan from breaking the tablet, the Skipper sends him off to get some fruit. After the Professor explains that they're still missing a pivotal piece of the tablet with the map's legend, Gilligan returns carrying two plates of fruit on a stone tray that the other castaways recognize as the missing piece—exciting Gilligan, who drops it, smashing it into small pieces.

That night after the Professor finishes gluing together the remaining piece, he explains that according to the stone it will take a half day for a boat to get to the spot where the ocean currents will carry it to Hawaii. The Professor suggests that Gilligan and the Skipper make the trip the next morning on a raft and send a ship back for the rest of them.

The Skipper brings Gilligan back to their hut and puts him to bed. Afraid to go out in the raft, Gilligan dreams he is a caveman carving a stone tablet depicting a picture of the other side of the hill. The Howells claim Gilligan's picture depicts an evil place and threaten to kill him. The Skipper, initially afraid to journey to the other side of the

hill, agrees to go when Gilligan explains that the Professor has invented a device so they can carry food. The Skipper, eager for the women to come along, runs off to convince the girls that it will be easier for them to catch husbands on the other side of the hill.

Meanwhile Gilligan finds the Professor, whose unsuccessful invention, the wheel, falls flat on its side. That night when Gilligan and the Skipper meet to discuss their plans, the Howells capture them and lock them in a cave where Howell stands guard. Meanwhile the Professor and the girls, unable to decipher Gilligan's picture, decide to help free Gilligan and the Skipper. Ginger tries seductively to convince Howell to set them free, but Lovey happens by, knocks out Howell, chases Ginger away, and drags Thurston off. Gilligan and the Skipper free themselves and lead the others to the other side of the hill, where they encounter a Tyrannosaurus rex.

Gilligan wakes up screaming, and as the Skipper calms him, the Professor walks in and explains that he made a mistake: "You see, cuneiform, which is the oldest form of writing, was originated by the Sumerians and is read dimodically. However, I read the tablet as though it were bustrophedon." In other words, the Professor read the tablet from left to right when all ancient forms of writing are read from right to left. The tablet actually diagrams how to get on the island.

Later that day the Professor and the Skipper find Gilligan carving a tablet that reads "Home Sweet Home" for anyone who lands on the island in the next million years.

COMMENTS:

- According to his dream, Gilligan is happy on the island and never really wants to leave. He sees the Skipper as woman hungry, Ginger as sex starved, and the Professor as a bumbling inventor.
- The Skipper finds it incomprehensible that the Professor could make a mistake.

TROPICAL INVENTIONS:

- The Professor's acid

CASTAWAY QUIZ #93:

When Gilligan falls on his head, what does he see instead of stars?

(For answer, see page 359)

94: SLAVE GIRL ☺☺

Writer: Michael Fessier
Director: Wilbur D'Arcy
Guest Stars: Michael Forest, Midori, Mike Reece, Bill Hart

When Gilligan saves Kalani, a native girl, from drowning in the lagoon, she promises to be his slave forever. When the Skipper and the Professor show up at the lagoon, the Professor, recognizing the medallion around Kalani's neck as Matoban, speaks with her in her native tongue, explaining that unless Gilligan abides by this custom, Kalani will return to her tribe, who, insulted, will come and kill them.

The Howells and the girls, eager to have a servant of their own, bid to hire Kalani. However, Kalani only wishes to serve Gilligan, and she follows him, doing all his chores: raking and pedaling the washing machine. The Professor advises Gilligan that the only way to free himself of Kalani is for someone else to win her from him in mortal combat. Howell, eager to have a servant, suggests that they stage a duel in which he pretends to kill Gilligan. The two fence in full regalia, but after Howell "kills" Gilligan, three Matoba natives appear, and the leader, Magundi, challenges Howell to a fight to death for Kalani's hand. Howell exposes Gilligan, and Magundi challenges him, promising to return that night.

Later when Gilligan humorously suggests that he commit suicide to avoid being killed by the natives, the Professor extracts strychnine from a strychnos plant, which when swallowed will paralyze the muscles to make Gilligan appear dead.

That night when Magundi returns to find the Professor and the

Skipper standing over Gilligan, who lies on the communal bamboo table, he believes Gilligan is dead and decides to honor him with a Matoba funeral—burning the body over a fire. Gilligan is placed in a bamboo box on stilts over a fire pit. As Magundi is about to light the fire, the Professor interrupts, explaining that the castaways have a tribal custom of their own: a sacred funeral dance. He claps his hands twice, and while the castaways play instruments, Ginger dances an erotic striptease with veils.

Many veils later, Magundi impatiently interrupts the dance and lights the fire. Awoken, Gilligan sits up, and as the flames leap up, Gilligan jumps down. Kalani calls Gilligan a great fire god, and the Professor, reiterating her claim, tells them to go before Gilligan curses them. Gilligan suddenly screams because his pants have caught fire, scaring off the natives.

COMMENTS:
- Since the Professor previously went to the trouble to invent syringes [Episode 64], the presence of a plastic syringe on the island remains unexplained.

TROPICAL INVENTIONS:
- The Professor's strychnine

CASTAWAY QUIZ #94:
What musical instrument does Mrs. Howell play?
(For answer, see page 359)

(For answer, see page 359)

336

95: IT'S A BIRD, IT'S A PLANE, IT'S GILLIGAN! ☺☺☺

Writers: Sam Locke & Joel Rapp
Director: Gary Nelson

While the United States air force starts a search for a lost jet pack, the XJB, which washed over the side of a ship during tests, the jet pack washes up on the shore of the island, where Gilligan finds it. The Professor realizes that there's enough fuel in the jet pack to fly one of them to Hawaii. They run off to begin testing, but Gilligan, the only castaway agile and light enough to pilot the jet pack, refuses to be a human guinea pig.

Deciding to trick Gilligan into piloting the jet pack, Howell straps himself into the jet pack, threatening to take off, while Lovey tries to convince Gilligan to go in his place. Later Ginger gives Gilligan a long, passionate kiss while Mary Ann straps the jet back onto his back. When the Skipper and the Professor happen by and explain that they've decided to strap a dummy to the jet pack and fly it to Hawaii, Gilligan unstraps the jet pack and runs into the jungle.

After Mary Ann and Ginger build the dummy according to the Professor's specifications, the Professor, convinced that a dummy of the proper height and weight, launched at the proper angle, will fly directly to Hawaii, prepares the launching. When everything's ready, Gilligan slaps the dummy on the back for good luck, accidentally knocking it to the ground, falling on top of it, and igniting the jet pack. Gilligan rides on the dummy along the ground through the jungle and into the lagoon. He falls off, and the dummy and jet pack circle around the lagoon and finally land back on the shore—where the Professor determines that trip through the jungle with all the extra weight depleted most of the fuel supply, impeding a trip to Hawaii. When Howell learns from the radio that a fleet of ships will be searching the area for the jet pack, the Professor, realizing that there's enough fuel left in the jet pack for a fifteen-minute flight, suggests that they send someone up while the ships are in the area to improve their chances of being rescued.

The Professor runs a series of tests to determine which of the other three men is best suited for the task. When the three men are rotated inside a pedal-powered bamboo cylinder, only Gilligan emerges with his equilibrium intact. For Gilligan's astronaut training, the Skipper

swings him back and forth from a vine, exhausting his little buddy, who falls asleep.

Gilligan awakes to find himself strapped into the jet pack and tied to a bamboo launch tower. With the radio strung around his neck, Gilligan blasts off. When he reaches the right altitude for a ship to spot him, Gilligan turns on the radio to learn that the air force has just spotted a UFO. Frightened, Gilligan maneuvers into a cloud where the exhaust from the jet pack causes the cloud to rain, and the air force cancels the search. Later while the castaways dry from the rain, the Skipper chases Gilligan into the jungle.

The next day, after the Professor synthesizes enough fuel for two trips to Hawaii, Gilligan, deciding to make the trip to Hawaii, launches the jet pack, forgetting to strap it to his back.

COMMENTS:

- Rather than trying to trick Gilligan into piloting the jet pack, Howell could offer him money.
- The jet pack, aimed straight up, would fall back to the island or wash up on shore again.

TROPICAL INVENTIONS:

- A pedal-powered rotating bamboo cylinder
- A dummy
- A bamboo launch tower
- The Professor's jet pack fuel

CASTAWAY QUIZ #95:

What does the Professor synthesize new jet fuel from?
(For answer, see page 359)

96: THE PIGEON ☺☺☺

Writers: Jack Raymond, Joel Hammil & Brad Radnitz
Director: Michael J. Kane
Guest Stars: Sterling Holloway, Harry Swoger

When Gilligan discovers a homing pigeon blown off course by a storm, the Professor suggests that after they allow time for the pigeon to regain its strength, they can tie a note to its leg and send it back to the mainland.

That night each castaway sneaks into the Professor's hut to feed the pigeon. The next morning the Professor shows the others the bloated pigeon, explaining that with a strict program of diet and exercise, the pigeon may be ready to make the trip in three weeks. Gilligan names the pigeon Walter and exercises it on a hand-cranked treadmill.

When the Professor finally ties a note to the pigeon's leg and sends him off, the bird flies back to his keeper, Birdy, who reads the castaways' note and convinced that it's a practical joke, replies with a comical note. When the pigeon returns to the island and the Professor reads Birdy's response, Howell writes the reply, offering Birdy a million-dollar cash reward to arrange for their rescue, enclosing a thousand-dollar bill.

Birdy replies with a note expressing his continued amusement, proclaiming Howell dead, and dismissing the bill as phony. The Professor suggests that they send Birdy a picture of themselves standing in front of the *Minnow* wreckage and prints a photograph in his hut. When Gilligan goes to get the pigeon from the cave, he encounters a six-foot spider and runs for help.

The Professor recognizes the spider as the deadly black morning spider and with the Skipper's help, distills spider cider to knock the spider off its feet long enough to grab the pigeon. When the spider drinks the cider from a siphoned turtle egg and staggers away from the cave, Gilligan runs in to get the bird, but the spider returns and blocks the entrance. Unable to scare the spider away from the cave with branches, the Professor lures the spider with a trail of cider to Howell's rope trap, which fails to spring. When Gilligan runs from the cave and gets caught in the trap, the men run inside to grab the bird cage and get trapped by the spider.

After hearing the men calling from the cave, the women attach Lovey's mirror to a bamboo pushcart and wheel it up to the cave's entrance so the spider will be attracted to its own image. As the women turn the cart around to back the spider out of the cave, Gilligan pushes the mirror over, breaking it. After trapping all the castaways, Gilligan frees the pigeon, which flies into the spider, scaring it away.

The castaways send off the pigeon with the photograph, but as Birdy's about to take the note off the pigeon's leg, a prison warden informs Birdy that his parole came through, and Birdy sets all his birds free. When the pigeon returns to the island, the castaways discover the undelivered photograph.

COMMENTS:

- The Professor could have assembled a darkroom from the previously discovered silent-movie equipment [Episode 43]. While he might have the necessary chemicals, he would still have to build his own enlarger and provide his own photographic paper.
- Six-foot black morning spiders do not exist.
- The castaways can always send the pigeon off again.

TROPICAL INVENTIONS:

- Bamboo bird cage
- Hand-cranked bamboo and bark treadmill
- The Professor's darkroom (complete with photography paper, an enlarger, and chemicals)
- The Professor's pedal-powered still
- The Professor's spider cider
- Howell's rope trap

CASTAWAY QUIZ #96:

After whom does Gilligan name the pigeon?
(For answer, see page 359)

97: BANG! BANG! BANG! ☺☺

Writer: Leonard Goldstein
Director: Charles Norton
Guest Stars: Rudy Larusso, Bartlett Robinson, Kurt Duncan

In CIA headquarters, agent Michaels learns that a twenty-five-pound container of a newly developed explosive thermoplastic (a modeling plastic that when hardened will explode at the slightest impact) was lost at sea while being shipped across the Pacific.

Meanwhile Gilligan, roaming around the lagoon with a small pet monkey, finds a crate labeled "Secret Material" that's washed ashore. The Professor recognizes the contents as a synthetic resin, thenaformaldehyde, a molding plastic that will enable the castaways to make combs, buttons, test tubes, even vacuum tubes for storing food. At lunch the castaways discuss the find and decide to mold dishes, costume jewelry, nails, and golf balls.

Later that afternoon the Howells take to the golf links with their new plastic golf ball so Howell can teach Lovey how to drive. But Gilligan's monkey steals the golf ball from Mrs. Howell and tosses it into the jungle, where it explodes. The Howells mistake the explosion for thunder. Meanwhile the Professor uses a pedal-powered dentist's drill to replace Gilligan's lost fillings with the plastic. The girls make dishes and jewelry for themselves, golf balls for the Howells, and nails for the Skipper. At dinner that evening when Gilligan's pet monkey throws a dish into the jungle, it explodes, and the castaways realize the true nature of the modeling plastic. The castaways quickly discard all their plastics, although the Professor reluctantly admits that he can't possibly remove Gilligan's new fillings.

The castaways hide their plastic pieces, which Gilligan's monkey begins to secretly hoard. While Mary Ann feeds Gilligan with a spoon attached to a ten-foot pole, the Professor uses the juice of the triginilla berry as a anesthetic so he can extract Gilligan's plastic-filled teeth with a pair of pliers. When Gilligan sits in the Professor's chair, Ginger starts the anesthetic running through a vine, but the vine leaks, knocking out the three of them.

That night before going to sleep, the Skipper gives Gilligan a teeth brace that the Professor made from tree gum to keep Gilligan's teeth from chattering. That night as Gilligan snores, he blows a huge bubble from the gum. When the bubble pops, Gilligan wakes up screaming, convinced that he's blown himself up. But his hysterics are interrupted by an actual explosion outside where his monkey is throwing the explosives from the roof of his hut. All the castaways come running, hiding behind a rock with the Howells, until the Professor calls them over behind a tree that the monkey defoliates with the explosives.

Gilligan impulsively runs over to the hut and climbs up a ladder to get the monkey off the roof, but while he's climbing the ladder, he sneezes, sending the plastic fillings flying from his mouth, blowing the hut to smithereens. The monkey falls into the Skipper's arms and Gilligan stands on the ladder in tattered clothes. The next day the Professor melts down a couple of pennies and fills Gilligan's cavities with the copper.

COMMENTS:

- While the Professor recognizes the plastic as thenaformaldehyde, he neglects to explore the possibility of its explosive qualities before filling Gilligan's cavities.
- Filling cavities with copper is medically unsafe.

TROPICAL INVENTIONS:

- A pedal-powered bamboo dentist's drill
- A potter's wheel
- Triginilla berry juice anesthetic
- The Professor's tree gum teeth brace

CASTAWAY QUIZ #97:

By what code name does the CIA refer to its plastic-explosive project?

(For answer, see page 359)

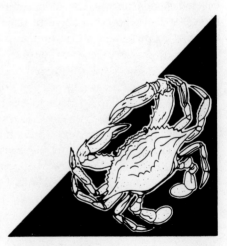

98: GILLIGAN, THE GODDESS ◎◎

Writers: Jack Paritz & Bob Rodgers
Director: Gary Nelson
Guest Stars: Stanley Adams, Mickey Morton,
Robert Swimmer

Three natives canoe to the island, and as Gilligan erects an SOS sign, Mary Ann and Ginger run by, and as Gilligan realizes that they're being chased by three natives, he runs into the sign, which falls on top of him, and the natives trample over him.

When the girls run into Howell's hut, the lounging millionaire wakes up to find the three natives. The king introduces himself as the peaceful Killiwanni and agrees to rescue the castaways in return for a white goddess. While Lovey introduces herself to the king, Gilligan, on the roof of the Howells' hut, throws a net over the natives.

Meanwhile on the lagoon the Professor and the Skipper find a canoe, which the Professor recognizes as the handiwork of the Papuan tribe, and the Skipper finds a cigarette lighter that Killiwanni later explains was given to him by the captain of a passing ship. Killiwanni starts a fire and forces Gilligan to dance while all three women express their eagerness to be the white goddess.

When the natives finish dancing, Howell brings them Lovey dressed as a white goddess, the Skipper introduces Mary Ann as a white goddess, and the Professor announces Ginger as the white goddess. After randomly chosing Lovey, Killiwanni reveals his plans to throw her into a volcano. Discovering that Lovey is married, Killiwanni decides to choose from Ginger and Mary Ann. When the Skipper refuses to allow the king to choose from the girls, the natives return with poisonous blowguns.

Later the men decide to dress as women so the natives will take one of them in their boat where they can possibly spot a ship. Ginger dresses the Skipper in one of her dresses, a wig, and makeup; Mary Ann dresses the Professor; and Lovey finds Howell dressing in one of her wigs and negligees. Finally they decide to dress Gilligan as a woman.

After Howell brings "Gillianna" to the king, Killiwanna performs an officiating ceremony that night, hanging several necklaces made from heavy shells around Gilligan's neck, causing him to fall to the ground. Later while Killiwanni's alone with Gilligan in the girls' hut, the Skipper, standing outside, overhears the king's plan to throw a dummy in the volcano and keep Gilligan for his wife. The Skipper sends Lovey with a bowl of fruit to distract the king.

After Killiwanni chases her from the hut, he presents Gilligan with a ring for his nose. The girls suddenly enter, wearing outfits from one of Ginger's USO tours, tap dance and sing "Bill Bailey, Won't You Please Come Home," and then introduce Howell, who performs a few magic tricks. After kicking Howell out, Killiwanni orders his assistant to guard the door and chases Gilligan around the hut. Promising to kiss him if they play hide and seek, Gilligan takes off his costume and leaves the hut. Killiwanni finds the abandoned wig and convinced that his white goddess vanished before his eyes, decides to leave the cursed island.

COMMENTS:

- Ginger didn't bring any clothes with her on the cruise other than the gown she was wearing; she can't possibly have two dancing outfits on the island from a USO tour.

CASTAWAY QUIZ #98:

What's the name of the white goddess King Killiwanni seeks?
(For answer, see page 359)

THE MOVIES

RESCUE FROM GILLIGAN'S ISLAND ⊗

Writers: Sherwood, Elroy, and Al Schwartz
& David Harmon
Director: Leslie H. Martinson
Guest Stars: Judith Baldwin, Vincent Schiavelli,
Art LaFleur

When Soviet scientists destroy an out-of-control spy satellite to prevent its information storage disk from falling into enemy hands, the disk lands in the lagoon on the island, where Gilligan finds it. Using the disk, the Professor fixes the castaways' barometer and learns that an approaching storm will create an enormous tidal wave that could

347

wash a boat into the shipping lanes. The Professor swears Gilligan to secrecy until he can come up with a solution, but Gilligan inadvertently arouses the other castaways' curiosity, compelling the Professor to explain the situation to the others. Since the impending storm will create a tsunami, the Professor suggests they lash their huts together so they can ride out the tidal wave that will hit in three or four days. While the Howells pack, the other men reinforce the huts. Using the Professor's hand-cranked crane, the Skipper raises a hut off the ground, and after the others reposition it, Gilligan, taking control of the crank, drops the hut on their feet.

As the storm hits the island, Gilligan finishes tying a vine around the joined huts, and the Professor instructs the castaways to bind themselves to the hut. When Lovey calls hysterically for her dog, Fifi, Gilligan runs outside looking for the dog she left home fifteen years ago and grabs hold of a palm tree as the tidal wave swallows the island.

When Howell wakes up, unties himself from the joined huts, and walks out to see the damage to the island, he falls into the ocean. After the Professor rescues Howell, the castaways, unable to find Gilligan, mourn his death. Gilligan, sleeping on a floating palm tree tied to the hut, falls into the ocean. When the castaways hear him call for help, they pull in the rope, lose their footing, and fall out the backside of the hut. Later, as Gilligan, reenacting how he survived the tidal wave, ties the rope around his waist, a shark suddenly grabs the rope and pulls Gilligan into the ocean. When the shark passes the hut, the Skipper and the Professor jump in after Gilligan, holding on to each other as the shark pulls them around in circles. Finally the shark lets go of the rope, departing with another shark.

After the castaways paddle the floating hut for two days, the Howells donate their clothes to build a sail. As the castaways discuss what they're going to do when they get back to civilization, Gilligan, using a magnifying glass, starts a fire to cook some snapper. While the castaways try to put out the fire, the smoke attracts a Coast Guard helicopter.

When the castaways arrive at Honolulu Yacht Harbor, towed by a Coast Guard cutter, they're greeted by cheering crowds, tall ships, and marching bands. The Governor's aide welcomes them back to civilization, presenting them with the key to the city and reading them a telegram from President Jimmy Carter. In Los Angeles the castaways receive a ticker tape parade, and two Soviet spies, watching the proceedings on television at the Soviet consulate recognize the disk that Gilligan intends to wear forever around his neck and plan to

capture it. The castaways, planning a Christmas reunion, go their separate ways, but not before hugging each other affectionately.

While preparing the *Minnow II*, the Skipper sends Gilligan for the mail. Gilligan encounters the two Soviet spies, who, dressed as sailors, offer him a necklace for his pendant, which he refuses. When Gilligan returns with the mail, the Skipper learns that the insurance company won't pay him until he can prove that the shipwreck wasn't his fault by having each of the former castaways sign an affidavit. Gilligan signs the form, and as the crew leaves to visit the other former castaways, the two Soviet spies roll an oil drum at Gilligan, which rolls back at them, knocking them into the water.

Ginger, filming a movie scene, refuses to do a nude scene for her unsavory producer and runs to her dressing room. When the director tries to talk her into returning to the set, she hits him with a chair. The

Skipper and Gilligan arrive, and Ginger, happy to see them, explains her dilemma, insisting that there are plenty of successful movies without nude scenes. The producer, eavesdropping from behind the door, comes around to Ginger's way of thinking and after he tells her so, Ginger signs the Skipper's insurance papers. As the Skipper and Gilligan leave the studio, the two Soviet spies, dressed as cowboys, lasso Gilligan, who manages to slip out from the ropes.

When the Skipper and Gilligan find the Professor working in his university laboratory, Gilligan knocks over a table of scientific apparatus the Professor set up just for him. The Professor, having difficulty readjusting to academic life, is pursued by women, continually inventing things that were invented while he was a castaway on the island, and pressured by the dean to do more public relations work for the university. Outside, the two Soviet spies, posing as exchange students, offer Gilligan money for his pendant, which he turns down. After the Professor signs the Skipper's insurance form, the Soviet spies chase after the departing crew; one Russian runs into a javelin, the second is hit in the head with a shotput.

The Skipper and Gilligan arrive unannounced at the Howells' mansion, where the millionaire and his wife are dining with two couples. The Howells greet the crew and introduce them to their guests, the Devensheers and the Fellows. While the Howells step into the library with the crew to sign the forms, they overhear their guests over the intercom, bad-mouthing the crew. Insulted, Howell throws his guests out and finding the Soviet spies standing at his door dressed in tuxedos, turns them away.

In Kansas, Mary Ann, about to marry Herbert Ruckers, who's waited fifteen years for her, confides in her best friend, Cindy, that she no longer wants to marry Herbert. The Skipper and Gilligan arrive, and Mary Ann, determined to go through with the wedding, shares her secret with them, asking them to stay for the ceremony. Outside, before the two Soviet spies, dressed as farmhands, can talk Gilligan into giving his pendant as a present, the Skipper, telling him that Cindy and Herbert are in love with each other, brings Gilligan to a tractor and cart, which they drive past the altar where Gilligan pulls Mary Ann aboard. The Soviet spies lead the other farmers after them through a field, but Gilligan bowls them over with a watermelon. The Skipper stops the tractor and helps pummel the farmers with watermelons while Cindy marries Herbert.

At the former castaways' Christmas reunion party aboard the docked *Minnow II*, Gilligan suggests a reunion cruise. The Skipper says they'll leave at eight o'clock the next morning, which the Soviet spies, circling the boat in scuba gear, overhear. The next morning as Gilligan prepares to cast off, the Soviet spies pull out a gun, hold up the former castaways, and take Gilligan's pendant. But FBI agents suddenly show up and confiscate the disk, promising to explain in good time.

At sea the *Minnow II* hits another storm, and the Skipper, trying to return to port, learns that Gilligan removed the magnet from the compass. After twelve days at sea the castaways swim to the shore of an island. When Gilligan recognizes the island and claims, "We're home," the others chase him into the jungle.

COMMENTS:

- Fireboats, bands, tall ships, and local people turned up at Marina del Rey for the filming of the castaways' rescue sequence. "That was so real I thought we *were* being rescued," recalls Russell Johnson.
- The Skipper doesn't need his fellow castaways to sign an affidavit for his insurance company since the Maritime Board already determined that the shipwreck wasn't his fault [Episode 85]. Furthermore, a year after the shipwreck, the insurance company would have considered the boat a loss and paid the insured value to the Skipper's estate. If the claim was never filed, the insurance company would hold the money, and upon returning to civilization, the Skipper could file the claim, which would be paid.
- The former castaways demonstrate incredible stupidity by going on a reunion cruise piloted by the Skipper and Gilligan.

TROPICAL INVENTIONS:

- The Professor's barometer
- The hand-cranked crane

CASTAWAY QUIZ:

What will Howell do when he first gets home?
What helicopter finds the castaways?
What's the Skipper's insurance company?
What are the Russian spies' names?
(For answers, see page 359)

351

THE CASTAWAYS ON GILLIGAN'S ISLAND ⊗

Writers: Sherwood, Al, and Elroy Schwartz
Director: Earl Belamy
Guest Stars: Tom Bosley, Marcia Wallace, Ronnie Scribner

Twelve days after being shipwrecked on the island again, the Professor repairs the radio just in time for the castaways to learn from a news broadcast that the Coast Guard has abandoned its search for them. Gilligan wanders dejectedly into the jungle and discovers two disabled military aircraft, a hangar, tools, and drums of gasoline. The Professor deduces that the island must have been used as an emergency landing strip during World War II. At Gilligan's suggestion, the Professor decides to piece the two planes together as one. Gilligan hops in a cockpit, discovers a mounted automatic machine gun, and fires off a full magazine, chasing the other men into the jungle, snapping Mary Ann's clothes line, puncturing the shower's water barrel, and exploding a drum of gasoline.

As the castaways construct the plane according to the Professor's plan, Gilligan pulls a rope, accidentally hoisting the Skipper upside-down in the air. After the castaways complete the plane, the Professor volunteers to fly back to the mainland alone, but, at the Skipper's insistence, the other castaways decide to accompany him. While the Professor takes a seat in the cockpit, the castaways man a four-man pedal-powered bamboo generator to turn the plane's propeller to ignite the engine. The engine starts, and everyone boards the plane except for Gilligan who is pulled aboard just as it's about to take off. After the Professor confides in Gilligan that he's fighting to keep the plane aloft, Gilligan passes out parachutes to the others. The Professor suddenly loses an engine and instructs the Skipper to toss out all extra weight. As Gilligan throws out the last piece of luggage, he accidentally falls from the plane and parachutes back to the island. The castaways agree to forfeit their only hope of rescue to find Gilligan.

When the plane lands, the remaining engine falls off, and the castaways realize that returning for Gilligan actually saved their lives. After searching the island and finding Gilligan hanging from a tree by his parachute, the castaways are rescued by two Coast Guards who spotted the plane on radar. Overjoyed, Howell decides to build a living tribute on the island—a tropical resort hotel.

A year later finds a hotel complex sprawling across the island with private bungalows collectively called "The Castaways." Howell has made each castaway a partner, and the island hotel offers guests the complete escape: no phones, no lights, no motorcars. Gilligan and the Skipper, piloting a small motorboat, bring two couples and a young boy to the lagoon from a luxury liner anchored off-shore. While the Skipper and Gilligan help the new guests register at the hotel lobby, the boy runs off into the jungle. After the Howells introduce themselves to their new guests, Myra & Henry Eliot (a wife trying to teach her husband how to relax from his real estate business) and Dr. & Mrs. Larson (a dentist and his wife), the Professor enters with Polynesian masks to decorate the Shipwreck Room (where Ginger performs nightly) for the evening luau.

When the Skipper brings the Larsons and Eliots to their respective bungalows, he learns that the boy is neither couple's son. While the Eliots unpack, Myra realizes that her husband brought his business suits and briefcase. At the beach, the Eliots join the Larsons who try to help Henry relax.

Meanwhile at the Snack Shack, the boy sneaks out from the jungle, inconspicuously steals the Skipper's hamburger, and runs back into the jungle unseen, baffling the Skipper.

At the beach, Henry Eliot sneaks away from his sunbathing companions and asks Gilligan where he can find a telephone. Gilligan inadvertently reveals that there's a phone for emergencies hidden in the hotel lobby. Eliot searches the lobby, discovers the phone inside a hollow tree, and tries to call his office. After finding her husband, Myra Eliot secretly asks the Howells to help Henry learn how to relax. When Ginger and Mary Ann give Eliot a backrub and massage, they only succeed in inspiring him with a business idea. When the Skipper and Gilligan take Eliot fishing, Gilligan tips the boat, waterlogging the executive's briefcase. After snorkling with the Professor for oysters, Eliot returns to the beach to overhear his wife tell the Larsons that she won't let him leave the island until he learns to relax.

When this typical and highly predictable *Fantasy Island/ Love Boat* plot is finally resolved at the evening luau, the castaways are prepared to play hosts to a parade of even more uninteresting guests with even less interesting problems. Henry Eliot learns to relax, of course, and the Larsons claim the boy as their own.

COMMENTS:

- By adapting *Gilligan's Island* to revolve around the castaways' hotel, the feeble pilot robbed the show of its most alluring premise: seven stranded castaways' attempts to find a way off an uncharted island. Originally filmed and broadcast as a 90-minute pilot film, *The Castaways on Gilligan's Island* has since been re-edited as a one-hour film.
- Having combed every inch of the island for fourteen years, the castaways should have long before discovered the two war planes.
- If the island was an abandoned air strip as the Professor claims, it wouldn't be uncharted.
- When Wrongway Feldman visited the island on two occasions [Episodes 5 & 24], the Professor could not fly an airplane. If the Professor took flying lessons, as Mary Ann now claims, he only did so after being rescued from the island—and in a remarkably short time.

TROPICAL INVENTIONS:

- The Professor's coconut abacus
- A communal shower
- A two-prop plane
- A four-man pedal-powered generator

CASTAWAY QUIZ:

What do the castaways name their plane?
What law firm do the Howells use?
(For answers, see page 359)

THE HARLEM GLOBETROTTERS ON GILLIGAN'S ISLAND ☺☺☺

Writers: Sherwood and Al Schwartz, David Harmon,
    & Gordon Mitchell
Director: Peter Baldwin
Guest Stars: David Ruprecht, Constance Forslund,
    Martin Landau, Barbara Bain, Stu Nahon,
    Chuck Hearn, Rosalind Chao, Dreama Denver,
    Scatman Crothers

The Harlem Globetrotters, flying aboard a chartered plane on a round-the-world tour, crash in the Pacific near a small island. Meanwhile power-mad millionaire J.J. Pierson, secretly aboard his yacht off the far side of the island with his robot George and world-famous scientist Olga Smetna, plots to take over the world. While a guest at the former castaways' new hotel, Pierson discovered a cave filled with a previously undiscovered element, supremium, which Olga explains is "energy in its purest form—molecules of light."

As one of the only living souls who know of supremium (except for Gilligan, who uses a glowing supremium boulder as a bedside lamp), Pierson sends his robot George to scare the castaways off the island. George lowers a tarantula onto the sleeping Gilligan's chest. Gilligan wakes up and convinced he's dreaming, tosses the spider down onto the Skipper. When the Skipper yells, the Professor helps them catch what he identifies as a deadly lycosis centralia. When Ginger and Mary Ann enter with a jarred spider of their own, the Professor wonders how these nonindigenous spiders got on the island.

Meanwhile the Harlem Globetrotters, adrift in a life raft, are attacked by a shark, which they feed basketballs. They soon strike land and start looking for food and shelter.

Meanwhile the Skipper barges in on Mrs. Howell and her son, Thurston Howell IV, lounging in their office, to watch the weather report on their television. Together they learn that the Globetrotters have been declared missing.

At that moment Gilligan stumbles upon the Globetrotters, who are practicing with coconuts. The Globetrotters, mistaking Gilligan for a wild beast, drive him away with coconuts. When Gilligan rushes back to the Howells' office, where he finds everyone watching the television news eulogizing the departed Globetrotters, he finally gets his message across, and the former castaways bring the Globetrotters back to the hotel to give the stranded team a hero's welcome and—much to Howell IV's dismay—free room and board.

Meanwhile on Pierson's yacht Olga demonstrates supremium's power on a battery-operated toy car and then turns the robot George into a powerhouse. Pierson sends George back to the island. Having finished teaching an aerobics class in the exercise hut, Ginger teaches Mary Ann a new dance step, and as they gyrate, George sabotages the bamboo wall of the hut. It falls, but the girls escape injury because they're standing where the open windows fall. George then hands the preoccupied Professor, experimenting in his hut, a test tube of liquid that, when the Professor adds it to his ferns, causes them to keel over. While the girls describe their brush with death to the Professor, George reports his failure to Pierson by radio, and Gilligan and the Skipper fix the wall of the exercise hut.

At the hotel bar Thurston Howell IV learns that Pierson, his father's worst enemy, has arrived on the island. Pierson enters, kisses Lovey's hand, and introduces Olga Smetna to the Professor. After Olga and the Professor praise each other's research and leave for the Professor's laboratory, Pierson wagers Howell IV $10,000 that day will turn to night within sixty seconds, and when Howell IV eagerly accepts the bet, a solar eclipse hits the island. Meanwhile Gilligan, waiting at the dock for Pierson's luggage, meets George paddling a rowboat at superspeed.

While the Globetrotters practice, their trainer announces that Gilligan has challenged them to a game for the championship of the island. The castaways, wearing T-shirts emblazoned with their own personal emblems, lose to the Globetrotters. Pierson and Olga, watching from the sidelines, plan to use the Globetrotters to trick the castaways into signing over their shares of the island.

After Ginger sings "I Wanna Be Loved by You" in the hotel's Shipwreck room, Pierson tells her she would make a perfect star for his movie musical, Gone With the Wind, to be filmed on a tropical island. Ginger eagerly signs what she thinks is a movie contract. The Professor, growing suspicious, informs the Howells that a boulder rolled off a cliff and smashed their empty lounge chairs and advises them to draw up a list of their enemies.

Meanwhile George forces Gilligan to sign over his share in the island and ties him up in the cave. Later on his yacht Pierson romances Mary Ann, gets her drunk on champagne, and telling her he wants to analyze her handwriting, tricks her into signing away her deed to the island.

The next morning when Olga informs the Skipper that Pierson needs an experienced seaman to captain his new nuclear-powered ocean liner, the Skipper takes the entrance exam, and after signing the test paper, the Skipper realizes that he's signed over the deed to his share of the island.

When the Skipper winds up in the cave bound to Gilligan, the two struggle in their bonds until Gilligan crushes a mango in his pocket, lubricating the ropes enough for them to escape. The crew try to move the gigantic boulder blocking the cave's entrance, and after the Skipper discovers that Gilligan, pulling the boulder from outside the cave, slipped out a side opening, the two rush off to warn the Professor and the Howells.

While strolling romantically with the Professor by the quicksand pit, Olga, surprised that the Professor never got the recognition he deserves, decides to nominate him for the Pierson Prize for Achievements in Island Research. Before Gilligan can stop him, the Professor signs what he thinks is an entry form, unwittingly signing away his share of the island.

All the castaways gather in Howell's office, but to receptionist Lucinda's dismay—none of them have appointments. Pierson does, and when Howell IV offers to buy back all the shares Pierson swindled from the former castaways, Pierson declines. Instead he wagers his shares against Howell's share, challenging the Harlem Globetrotters against his own team, the New Invincibles, who have never played professionally. Howell IV agrees to the bet. The next day Howell IV discovers Pierson and Olga setting up a control panel and watches the New Invincibles, a team of robots, practice on the court.

While the Globetrotters and the New Invincibles warm up, the women (Lovey, Mary Ann, Lucinda, and Ginger) cheerlead, and Gilligan finds the Professor in his hut, studying robot schematics to determine their weaknesses. After the television announcer introduces the Globetrotters and the New Invincibles, the game begins, and by halftime the Invincibles lead 95 to 3. When Gilligan tells the Professor that the Globetrotters have tried everything but their crazy plays, the Professor, realizing the robots can only play what they're programmed to do, urges the Globetrotters to strut their stuff. During the second half the Globetrotters pull out all the stops, confusing the robots, and scoring basket after basket. After catching up, two Globetrotters are called out of the game, but Gilligan insists that he and the Skipper take their places. In the final seconds of the game Gilligan freezes with the ball, and finally two Globetrotters toss Gilligan with the ball into the basket, winning the game 101 to 100.

When Pierson informs Howell IV and the Professor that some of his robots removed the supremium from the caves during the game, the Professor reminds Olga that supremium is unstable when stored in large quantities above seventy-six degrees, and Pierson's ship suddenly explodes offshore. Thurston Howell III addresses the crowd, thanking the Globetrotters and inviting them to stay on the island for free—off-season.

COMMENTS:

- Since the Howells previously claimed that they didn't have any children [Episode 35], Thurston Howell IV's existence remains a mystery.

CASTAWAY QUIZ:

What does the winner of the Pierson Prize for Island Research receive?

(For answer, see page 359)

CASTAWAY QUIZ ANSWERS

1. Mrs. Van Hampton's party 2. Powdered eggs 3. 150 4. Alice McNeil 5. *The Spirit of the Bronx* 6. Lovey, Mary Ann, and Gilligan 7. His grandfather 8. Gold Dust #5 9. One pound 10. *The History of Tree Surgery* 11. *Pyramid for Two* 12. Four 13. The Tahatchapooku Oil & Mining Corporation 14. Mad Desire mixed with Flaming Passion 15. UCLA 16. A coconut tied to a bamboo stick 17. The Monarch Bank 18. The First, Second, and Third National Banks 19. They don't 20. The Skipper 21. Irving 22. It's insured by a company Howell owns 23. An inferiority complex 24. Debbie Dawson 25. The Tour Dejeun 26. Five million dollars 27. The *Chronicle* 28. Rex 29. Metuzar 30. Coconuts 31. 37-25-36 32. Potassium chromate, ferric chloride, and calcium phosphate 33. The Great Raftini 34. A Bali dancer 35. G. Thurston Howell IV 36. Richard Burton's 37. (a) Poison darts at six paces; (b) A combination of Polynesian and Papuan 38. Gladys 39. Howell Hills 40. George Bancroft and John 41. Hugo Abernathy of Pealing, Vermont 42. The *S.S. Minnow II* 43. Fifi LaFrance and her husband, Ricardo Laughingwell 44. Howell Oil Company, Howell University, and the Howell Hotel 45. HO¶O CBTA II 46. Howell 47. Eighth 48. *The Mosquitoes at Carnegie Hall* 49. (a) A long green bug with long yellow wings; (b) Seven 50. Ginger Grant 51. Three 52. Wild oleander 53. (a) French and Italian; (b) The international language: money 54. Shipping heiress Sybil Wentworth 55. Never revealed 56.

Julius Caesar 57. XR-1000 58. Rare with onions and fried potatoes 59. Merlin the Mind Reader 60. The Singapore Zoo 61. A pile of one-thousand-dollar bills 62. (a) The social register; (b) The New York Stock Exchange; (c) His money 63. Never revealed 64. His latest batch makes even him sneeze 65. Timothy 66. One part sunshine, two parts water, and three parts prayer 67. Her great-great-great-great-grandmother 68. Sea Biscuit 69. A mild tranquilizer brewed from plants 70. Agent 222 71. Plant fats 72. *Musical Extravaganza* 73. Ginger's scarf and Mary Ann's comb 74. Forty acres of property in downtown Denver 75. *Things With Wings* 76. His comic books 77. Igor 78. Red berries with green dots 79. The Good Guy Spy Outfit 80. His pocketknife 81. A Japanese munitions pit 82. Ten days before landing on the lagoon 83. Ordinance 33 of the municipal code 84. His detective magazine 85. Captain Kidd (Skipper), Captain Hook (Howell), and Long John Silver (Professor) 86. *The Name of the Game* 87. Herman 88. *Tongo the Ape-man* 89. $10,000 90. Scorpio E-X-1 91. Mashuka 92. Fish pie 93. Hot dogs 94. The dinner bell 95. Never revealed 96. His best friend in grammar school, pigeon-toed Walter Stuckmeyer 97. Operation Orchid 98. Wanomi **MOVIE 1.** (a) Kiss Wall Street; (b) Falcon 14445; (c) Pacific & Western; (d) Ivan and Dimitri **MOVIE 2.** (a) *Minnow III*; (b) Mack & Rubin **MOVIE 3.** $500,000, a private laboratory, and a lifetime subscription to *Scientific American*

CHAPTER 7
AN UPHILL CLIMB

after *Gilligan's Island*, most of the castaways encountered great difficulty breaking their typecast image. Some returned to the stage, others pursued television and film, but for the most part, they remained seven very stranded castaways.

BOB DENVER

After *Gilligan's Island*, Bob Denver, born in New Rochelle, New York, on January 9, 1935, starred for two years in television's *The Good Guys* as bumbling, big-hearted cabdriver Rufus Butterworth, who was forever proposing money-making schemes to his best friend, cafe owner Bert Gramus (Herb Edelman). Following its cancellation in 1970, Denver starred with Forrest Tucker and Jeannine Riley in the syndicated *Dusty's Trail*, a *Gilligan's Island* spin-off created by Sherwood Schwartz about a Western wagon train crossing the plains.

363

Denver's film credits include *A Private Affair, Take Her She's Mine, For Those Who Think Young, Who's Minding the Mint?, The Sweet Ride*, and *Do You Know the One About the Traveling Saleslady?* Among his television appearances are roles in "Scamps," "The Invisible Woman," and "High School U.S.A." His many stage successes include *Play It Again, Sam, A Thousand Clowns, The Button*, and *The Owl and the Pussycat*, which he has played in many situations opposite his wife Dreama Peery.

The Denvers make their home in Las Vegas, Nevada.

ALAN HALE, JR.

Born in Los Angeles in 1918, Alan Hale, Jr., son of actor Alan Hale, appeared in dozens of westerns, war films, and guest starred in just as many television shows. Among his many films are *Johnny Dangerously, There Was a Crooked Man, Young at Heart, Sweetheart of Sigma Chi, The Music Man, The Fifth Musketeer*, and *It Happened on Fifth Avenue*.

After *Gilligan's Island*, Hale made guest appearances on *Bonanza, The Wild Wild West, The Lucille Ball Show, The Good Guys*, and *Land of the Giants* to name but a few. His recent television guest appearances include *Murder, She Wrote, Black's Magic, Crazy Like a Fox, Magnum, P.I., Simon & Simon, Love Boat, Matt Houston*, and *Fantasy Island*.

Hale co-owned the Skipper's Lobster Barrel, a seafood restaurant on La Cienega Boulevard in Los Angeles. He is currently preparing to help distribute Nulon, a Teflon-based engine lubricant from Australia.

JIM BACKUS

Born in Cleveland, Ohio, on February 25, 1913, Jim Backus began his career in stock and vaudeville and later played the voice of the Oscar-winning cartoon "Mr. Magoo." His films include *The Great Lover, Hollywood Story, His Kind of Woman, Pat and Mike, Rebel Without a Cause, The Great Man, Ice Palace, Boys' Night Out, It's a Mad Mad Mad Mad World, Advance to the Rear, Where Were You When the Lights Went Out?, Now You See Him Now You Don't, Good Guys Wear Black, C.H.O.M.P.S., There Goes the Bride, Slapstick of Another Kind,* and *Prince Jack.*

His television work includes *I Married Joan, Hot Off the Wire, The Jim Backus Show, The Gift of the Magi, The Rebels,* and *The Gossip Columnist.* On Broadway, he starred in *Our Town.*

Backus has also authored several books, including *Backus Strikes Back,* chronicling his battle with Parkinson's disease. He has just finished writing another book with his wife, Henny.

NATALIE SCHAFER

Born in Rumson, New Jersey, on an undisclosed November 5, Natalie Schafer, widow of Louis Calhern, played Broadway for twenty-five years, where her roles included *Lady in the Dark, Doughgirls, A Joy Forever, Susan and God, Romanoff & Juliet*, and *The Highest Tree*.

Schafer made her film debut as Lana Turner's mother in *Marriage Is a Private Affair* in 1944. Among her many films are *Keep Your Powder Dry, Dishonored Lady, Secret Beyond the Door, Time of Your Life, The Snake Pit, Oh Men! Oh Women!, Anastasia, Bernadine, Back Street, Susan Slade, 40 Carats*, and *Day of the Locust*.

When *Gilligan's Island* ended, Schafer played Lana Turner's mother again in television's *The Survivors*, which only lasted four episodes. She then toured for six months as a sadistic lesbian in *The Killing of Sister George*. She has made guest appearances on *Matt Houston, Chips, Simon & Simon, Trapper John, M.D., Love Boat*, and *Three's Company*.

TINA LOUISE

Born in New York, Tina Louise has appeared in several films including *God's Little Acre, Day of the Outlaw, Armored Command, The Wrecking Crew, The Good Guys and the Bad Guys, How to Commit Marriage, The Stepford Wives,* and *Canicule (Dog Day).* On television, Louise starred in the movies "Friendships, Secrets and Lies," "The Day the Women Got Even," "Advice to the Lovelorn," "The Women Who Cried Murder," "SST Death Flight," "Look What's Happened to Rosemary's Babies," and "Nightmare in Badham County."

Louise starred in "Rituals" and has made dramatic guest appearances on *Black's Magic, Fantasy Island, Dallas, Love Boat, Kojak, Police Story, Marcus Welby, M.D., Cannon, Matt Houston, Knightrider, Chips,* and *Simon & Simon.* She is currently shooting *The Pool,* a feature film written and directed by Luis Aira, and can be seen in *After All These Years,* a romantic comedy written and directed by Don Cato, shown at the 1987 Milan Film Festival.

RUSSELL JOHNSON

Russell Johnson, trained in the theater on the GI bill, has starred in over thirty-five stage productions, including *Delirious, The Management, Peer Gynt, Romeo and Juliet, Bell, Book and Candle, Hamlet,* and *Paradise Lost.* He has appeared in over twenty-five motion pictures, including *MacArthur, The Greatest Story Ever Told, For Men Only, Black Tuesday,* and the cult classic *It Came From Outer Space.*

Since *Gilligan's Island,* Johnson has made guest television appearances on *Fame, Dallas, Dynasty, MacGyver, Lou Grant, Bosom Buddies, Wonder Woman, Rich Man, Poor Man, Marcus Welby, M.D., Cannon, Police Story, McMillan, The FBI, Gunsmoke, Mannix, Ironside,* and *That Girl* to name only a few. He also starred in classic episodes of *The Outer Limits* and *The Twilight Zone* and was the corporate spokesman in television commercials for Texaco.

DAWN WELLS

Dawn Wells has done five feature films and has guest starred on more than one hundred television shows, including *Matt Houston, Vegas, Love Boat, Hotel, Fantasy Island, Simon & Simon, Growing Pains, Down to Earth, Matlock,* and *Alf.* She is a cohost and coproducer for the Children's Miracle Network Telethon for mid-Missouri, which she does annually. Her film credits include *Winter Hawk, The New Interns, The Town That Dreaded Sundown,* and the children's film *Return to Boggy Creek.*

Wells won national acclaim for her starring roles in Neil Simon's *Chapter Two* and *They're Playing Our Song* with the national touring companies. A few of her theater credits include *Vanities, Bus Stop, The Owl and the Pussycat, Gaslight,* and *Romantic Comedy.* She originated the role of Blair Griffin in the premiere of Bernard Slade's thriller, *Fatal Attraction,* with Ken Howard at the Center Stage Company in Toronto, Canada. She was also Guest Artist in Residence while teaching an advanced acting class at Stephens College and Purdue University. There she starred in *Private Lives, Night of the Iguana,* and *The Effect of Gamma Rays on Man-in-the-Moon Marigolds.*

Wells, active with her alumnae college, Stephens, was honored by it as one of the "outstanding women in America" and was commencement speaker in 1984. Wells is a Nevada native, which dates back to when her great-great-grandfather drove a stagecoach from Reno to Virginia City during the gold rush. Having lived in Nashville, Tennessee, Wells has recently returned to make her home in Hollywood.

SHERWOOD SCHWARTZ

The creator of *The Brady Bunch, It's About Time, Dusty's Trail,* and *One Big Family* makes his office at home in Beverly Hills and is currently working on a sequel to *Gilligan's Island.* Schwartz is also seeking a publisher for his own book, *Inside Gilligan's Island.*

ACKNOWLEDGMENTS

If not for the courage of the fearless Sherwood Schwartz, the *Minnow* would have never set shore on that uncharted desert isle. I am especially grateful to him and those actors involved with the show who generously opened their hearts and memories: Bob Denver, Alan Hale, Jr., Jim Backus, Henny Backus, Natalie Schafer, Tina Louise, Russell Johnson, and Dawn Wells.

Special thanks to my editor, Bob Miller, for sharing my enthusiasm, dedication, and vision. Jamie Rothstein stayed on top of things and kept the paperwork fresh and exciting. My copyeditor, Steve Boldt, skillfully checked, re-checked, and cross-referenced every fact in this veritable encyclopedia, fine-tuning every semicolon and waxing every hyphen from top to bottom. Giorgetta McRee's exuberant book design makes this thing readable.

No amount of thanks can properly express my appreciation to my dear friend and agent, Stephanie Laidman, who cut through endless streams of red tape to make this book happen. Without her astounding professionalism, patience, and wonderful sense of humor, you would not be reading this book.

After my family, there are many special people who graciously lent me their moral support, memories, and talents: Adam Castro, Kathy McMahon, Susan Stout, Natalie Chapman, Don Cleary, Jane Berkey, Gretchen van Nuys, Jeremy Wolff, Miles Latham, Vangie Hayes, Mindy Zepp, Darlene Schwartz, Kate Segal, Micky Freeman, Sy Marsh, those darn Corcorans (Alan, Theresa, and Karen Rose), Tony Puryear, Susan Mitchell, and Chris Spear.

Bill Dennis, at Turner Entertainment, was invaluable in helping to grant permission to reprint photographs from the show. Thanks too to Kathy Harris at MGM, Pat Murphy at Turner Entertainment, and Nancy Cushing-Jones at MCA Publishing Rights for enthusiastically digging through the Gilligan archives. Lourdes Richter at Columbia Pictures Publications helped me secure the rights to the Gilligan's Island theme song and provided me with jovial correspondence.

All my love to Debbie White for accepting my marriage proposal despite my temporary obsession with *Gilligan's Island*. I'd be shipwrecked without you.

ABOUT THE AUTHOR

Joey Green was a contributing editor to the *National Lampoon* until he wrote an article in *Rolling Stone* on why the *National Lampoon* isn't funny anymore. A native of Miami, Florida, Green was almost expelled from Cornell University for selling fake football programs at the 1979 Cornell-Yale homecoming game. He was editor of the *Cornell Lunatic*, president of the National Association of College Humor Magazines, and published *Hellbent on Insanity*, a collection of the best college humor of the 1970s and 1980s. Green worked at J. Walter Thompson, where he wrote television commericals for Burger King and won a Clio for a print ad he created for Kodak. He recently returned from five months of aimless travel through Europe, Scandinavia, the USSR, the Middle East, and northern Africa. He is presently a contributing editor to *Spy* magazine, has just written a comedy screenplay, and is currently at work on a novel.

For more shipwreck shenanigans
and castaway collectibles,
send a self-addressed stamped envelope
to:

THE GILLIGAN'S ISLAND FAN CLUB
PO Box 4232
Ithaca, NY 14852-4232
USA